Rose Cottingham

ROSE COTTINGHAM

NETTA SYRETT

CASSANDRA EDITIONS
ACADEMY PRESS LIMITED
CHICAGO
1978

Published by Academy Press Limited
360 North Michigan Avenue, Chicago, Ill. 60601
Printed and bound in the United States of America

—

Library of Congress Cataloging in Publication Data

Syrett, Netta.
   Rose Cottingham.

   I. Title.
PZ3.S995Rk 1977 [PR6037.Y6]   823'.9'12   77-16345
ISBN 0-915864-21-5
ISBN 0-915864-20-7 lib. bdg.

CONTENTS

Contents

To

WILLIAM SOMERSET MAUGHAM

Rose Cottingham

I

A BIRTHDAY SPENT IN DISGRACE

SOMEWHERE in the darkened house a clock struck.
Its deep boom startled Rose out of sleep and she
sat up in bed, amazed and disconcerted to find that she
had closed her eyes at all, so firmly had she determined
to keep awake all night. It was reassuring to find the
room still obscure, though the dawn light was beginning to steal between the chinks of the blind, and she
could just discern the outlines of her sister's little
bed and the white rim of the mantelpiece, upon which
stood the clock she must at once consult. "I'm nine
years old to-day!" The reflection, awe-inspiring and
rather troubling on the score of venerability, rose to
her mind and was blent with anxiety as to the exact
hour, for it was only the last echo of the hall clock
that had reached her.

Rose crept out of bed and peered into the white face
of the little timepiece.

Five o'clock! It was not too late, but she must
make haste, for the fishing-boats went out at half-past
five.

For a mere early morning garden-excursion, such
as she had clandestinely more than once enjoyed, a
jacket over her nightgown had always sufficed. This

1

infinitely more daring adventure, however, demanded the full complement of a lady's wardrobe, and it was at least five minutes before she felt justified in leaving the seclusion of her bedroom, unaware that her frock, which fastened behind, presented a ludicrous spectacle of irregular buttoning.

Very stealthily she opened the door at last, casting an apprehensive backward glance at the flaxen head on the pillow in the bed next to her own empty couch. It did not move. Lucie was sleeping the sleep of childish integrity, and the criminal Rose went on her way down the back staircase trembling as it creaked, till at its foot she reached the lobby where garden hats were kept. Snatching hers from its peg, she crossed the hall into the library, the door of which she opened with some trepidation. She dreaded to enter the dim, silent room, so unfamiliar in the grey dawn, and for a moment she stood hesitating on the threshold, half inclined to creep back again to the lawful shelter of her bed. Pride impelled her to go on. At the age of nine, if ever, one should be done with babyish terrors. It was only the library after all, and in a moment she would be out of doors. In spite of reason, however, it was with a beating heart that she groped her way towards the long window whose heavy rep curtains almost shut out the light. To her fancy a horrible malignancy lurked in their red folds, and she was possessed also by an insane fear of the two arm-chairs which on either side of the fireplace loomed through the semi-darkness. It was only when she had slipped the window-bolts and made her escape into the fresh chill air that she drew her breath once more. Standing on the top of the shallow steps which from the library window led down to the lawn, she hastily

surveyed the garden, as mysterious in the half-light
as the room she had just left; but not terrible, only so
fascinatingly strange that she caught her breath in a
sort of ecstasy. The grass was all grey and pearly
with dew, and Rose's flight to the path under the trees
beyond the lawn was marked by a dark zigzag line
where her feet had brushed the moisture aside. Under
the trees it was nearly dark, but out of doors she felt
no fear, and though the first sharp chirp of a waking
bird startled her, she smiled delightedly, and smiled
again with an even intenser joy when a rabbit dashed
out of the grass on one side of the avenue and with a
rustle disappeared into the copse on the right. The
path sloped rapidly downwards and ended at the white
gate which led straight on to the beach. Long before
she reached the gate, the sea, framed in the boughs of
over-arching trees, came into sight, pearl-coloured,
very gently heaving under a veil of mist. Rose ran
along the beach close to the water's edge till she
reached the slope that curved round to the quay.
Here, a little wooden pier, tarred and rickety, put out
a crooked arm to guard the shipping which lay in its
shelter, and the child saw to her great relief that the
fishing boats had not yet gone. They lay huddled
together in the tiny harbour, while men shouted and
walked about on the quay, busy with coils of rope and
great nets, which they flung to their mates, already
standing or lounging in the boats below.

Rose watched them with breathless interest. She
loved the bustle, the stir, the shouting, and the sense
of an adventure—the adventure of putting out on that
vast grey sea. She envied the fishermen who would
soon go sailing through the narrow channel between
the pier and the cliff yonder, and at the same time in

the depths of her heart she knew that if the unthinkable happened and Rob should offer to take her in his dirty brown-sailed craft, she would be terrified and with shame refuse. She scanned the groups of men on the quay for Rob, and started when she heard his gruff voice behind her.

"Marnin', missie! So you'm come along, arter all? I thought you'd oversleep yourself, that I did!"

"Are you going to start now?" Rose asked shyly.

"Just a-goin', missie. We're off, so to speak!" said Rob, beginning to swing himself down a ladder whose rungs clung to the pier wall like the limpets that elsewhere decorated its surface.

"How long will you be out?" demanded the child, hanging on to the top of the ladder and bending down to speak to him.

"All day and all night, missie. 'Ome to-morrer marnin' p'raps."

She watched him as he leaped from one to another of the small boats which lay between the pier and his fishing-smack the *Eliza Jane*. Its brown sails were being hoisted, and all over the harbour, in the different crafts, there was hauling of ropes and of anchors, fresh shouting, rattling of chains, the billowing of great canvas wings as one by one the boats turned towards the harbour mouth. Rose turned too, and ran with all her might to the pier head, which she reached just in time to see the *Eliza Jane* leading out of the harbour into the open sea. Swiftly, one by one, the other boats followed, spreading their sails like brown butterflies as they glided past her on the water, which was like a huge opal now, shot with gleams of pink and green. The sun was rising, and the fishing-fleet floated away upon a track of dazzling light which

stretched to the far horizon. Rose leaned upon the wall
and watched them, and looked at the flushed, gently
heaving sea, and heard the lap of the water against the
piles of the pier, and the cries of the gulls as they rose
and swooped and circled just outside the harbour.
The smell of tar and seaweed was mixed with her
sensations, which were all joy and exultation and
strange excitement, as though this secret and disobedient adventure of rising at five o'clock in the
morning of her birthday to see the boats go out, were
somehow the prelude to a new and glorious life.

She watched the boats till they were specks on the
now blue and dancing sea, and as she watched her
mood gradually changed. It grew flat and depressed.
The walk home seemed, in thought, very long, and she
felt a strange disinclination to move. Yet move she
must, for it was necessary to be in her nightgown
and also in bed before half-past six o'clock, when
the servants might be stirring and Grandmamma
awake. As she dragged herself from the wall and
turned to go back, she came face to face with a tall,
freckled boy. At another moment Rose would have
been glad to see Geoffrey Winter, to whose delightful
mother she had whole-heartedly given her childish
affection. His appearance (though she could not
explain it, since he ought to have been at school),
probably indicated that Mrs. Winter had really and
truly come home again after a long absence, and that
in itself was sufficient reason for welcoming Geoffrey.
As it was, she met his friendly but surprised face with
the blank look of one who is past caring about anything.

"Why, it's Rose!" exclaimed the boy, beginning to
execute a rapid shuffling dance of triumph in front of
her. "I say, Rose, I've caught you at your tricks.

Where's old Ginger? Does Grandma know you're out? I bet she doesn't, and you'll catch it when you go home. Hulloa!"—this after a pause in his monologue—"what's up? Why don't you say anything? You look pretty green!" he added, struck by the pallor of her face. "What's the matter?"

Rose feebly shook her head. "I don't know," she whispered.

"Well, I think you're going to be sick," said Geoffrey, with blunt directness. "Better cut along home."

Rose tried to "cut along," but she dragged herself so slowly that Geoffrey, looking after her, was moved by compassion.

"Here, you hang on to me," he directed, running up to her and offering her the side of his coat, which she grasped for support. "What have you been eating?" he enquired severely.

"Nothing," answered Rose meekly, a truthful reply by which any one but a schoolboy might have guessed the cause of her indisposition.

"I expect it's green apples," he suggested presently, even more sternly. "If so, it serves you right. Green apples are awful things for girls like you."

Rose was silent, not because she had no inclination to refute Geoffrey's horrid imputation of greediness, but because she felt too ill to speak.

Geoffrey was worried. They had reached the main street of the village by now, and he did not know what to do with the child, who was getting whiter and more white.

"Look here!" he cried, fired with a brilliant idea. "There's Crannock on the milk-cart just going up to your place, I expect. I'll ask him to take you."

Two minutes later Rose was bundled into the back

of the milk-cart, and as it bumped and rattled up the village street Geoffrey watched its progress with some concern.

"She'll catch it if Grandma Lester's up before she gets back!" was his unspoken reflection.

Brook Hall, the Winters' place, was some little distance from the Manor House, where Rose lived in the shadow of the stately, unapproachable lady styled by the boy in his irreverence "Grandma." The Winters were Mrs. Lester's nearest neighbours, and Geoffrey, the only child of his parents, though four years Rose's senior, was seldom indisposed to play with and tease her. During the holidays he was often at the Manor House, and a fortunate epidemic of measles at a preparatory school for Rugby, had brought him home again while the year was yet young and favourable to prolonged mischief. He strolled nonchalantly homewards, while Rose, faint and exhausted, continued her uneasy drive towards the Manor House. One draught of the milk by which she was surrounded, would have revived her, but she looked wistfully and in vain at the rattling cans, shy of making a request to a milkman too obtuse to recognize her need. They reached the cliff road to the Manor House at last, and ill as she felt, Rose's horrible apprehension grew. If it was already time for the milk-cart, it must be late, and Grandmamma was an early riser; and even if she hadn't left her room the servants would be up, and if not they, then, Miss Piddock would certainly have discovered her absence!

By the time the man drove into the paved courtyard at the back of the house, however, she was too physically wretched to care what happened, and she scarcely realized that it was cook who lifted her out of the cart and with shrill exclamations, half-supported, half-carried her into the kitchen, where Mrs. Lester herself, tall, gaunt, and majestic, stood at a table counting the eggs that had just been brought in from the fowl house.

' Rose gazed at her grandmother a moment with apathetic eyes before dropping in a little limp heap at her feet.

She spent her ninth birthday in bed, discovering herself there ten minutes later, her governess bending over her with eau-de-Cologne and a shocked expression, and cook standing in the doorway, holding a bowl of bread and milk.

Mrs. Lester entered the room about ten o'clock, when Rose, fully recovered, was yearning to get up and enjoy the holiday usually conceded to birthdays. One glance at her grandmother's face, however, was sufficient to crush the slight hope she had cherished of any such indulgence, and she instantly assumed her most obstinate expression. Rose never pleaded for forgiveness. Even if it had not been useless to do so, pride and stubbornness would in any case have combined to prevent her.

Mrs. Lester regarded her granddaughter a moment in silence.

"How plain she is!" was her predominant and irritated reflection. To Mrs. Lester, who had been a beauty in her youth, a girl without looks had forfeited her right to anything but modest self-effacement, and it was all the more annoying to find this plain child not only asserting her existence with vehemence, but apparently unconscious that there was any reason to do otherwise.

"I was under the impression that I had forbidden you to get up before you were called?" she began at last in the cold sarcastic voice that Rose hated.

She made no reply.

"Did you hear the remark I made?"

"Yes," returned Rose.

"Yes?" repeated her grandmother icily.

"Yes, Grandmamma," was the child's sulky amendment.

"Your manners are deplorable," observed Mrs. Lester dispassionately. "You will remain in bed to-day, and Miss Piddock will presently give you the lessons you are to learn for to-morrow. Last night I accepted an invitation for you to go to Brook Hall, but I shall now be under the necessity of driving over there to tell Mrs. Winter that you have forfeited her kindness."

She turned and went out of the room, and Rose, sitting up in bed when the door closed, snatched her pillow and thumped it till she was exhausted. She was not to see Mrs. Winter, who had been away weeks and *weeks* in London! It would probably be untold ages before she was allowed to go to Brook Hall.

"I hate Grandmamma! I hate her! I *hate* her!" she muttered, her eyes full of angry, impotent tears. "She's like that thing in India that rolls over people in a car!" she went on mentally. "That's what she is— a Jug—something or other. She likes to see people lying down flat on their faces in front of her. And that's just what everybody does—Lucie, and Miss Piddock, and all the servants—and then she's glad, and thinks herself very powerful and all that!"

In the midst of her fury, Rose felt pleased with her symbolism. It had the effect too, of diverting

her thoughts from her grandmother, for insensibly her
mind rushed off at a tangent, and she began to make
pictures for herself. The pictures, though evoked
from books of coloured illustrations, were very vivid
and interesting. She saw a sky of burning blue, and
dark-skinned people with turbans, and a great car
which bore a striking resemblance to one of the chari-
ots in the circus procession that had recently passed
through the village, all blazing with glass and gold.
And on the top of it, Grandmamma in the long green
velvet riding-habit of a circus lady, pale, unmoved,
and inflexible.

The entrance of her governess dissipated these
enthralling visions, and with their flight Rose's anger
and impatience again flared up.

Miss Piddock's meek and scandalized expression
infuriated her. She hated more vehemently than
usual her pale blue eyes, her sandy hair, her fidgeting
cough, and was ready to resent any and every word
that should fall from her lips.

"What a pity, Rose, that you should choose this of
all days for disobedience," she began in her thin, prim
voice. "Poor Lucie is so disappointed at being unable to give you the present she had for you; but your
Grandmamma says——"

"Oh, do be quiet!" interrupted Rose, goaded to
frenzy. "Any one would think I'd murdered some one,
or committed adultery or something, instead of just
going out before breakfast. Now, why are you getting
red?" she added in surprise, as Miss Piddock's face
crimsoned.

"Don't mention the Commandments in that light
way," she returned in hasty confusion, "especially
when you don't know what you're saying."

"Yes, I do. 'Thou shalt not commit ——' "

"That will do!" interrupted Miss Piddock wildly. "I've marked the geography, the history, and the grammar. And the next time you speak to me in that rude and disrespectful manner, I shall go straight to Mrs. Lester," she added, retreating towards the door.

Even before it closed, with a rapid upheaval of her knees under the bedclothes her pupil had tossed the dull little primers on to the floor. She had heard the inoperative threat too many times to be alarmed.

"She's a sandy cat that's too stupid even to catch mice!" thought Rose, in whose heart the devil had firmly taken up his abode.

It was a heavenly day, almost as warm as summer, with a real summer blue sky. While she raged at her captivity and all it implied, the pleasant whirr of a mowing machine fell on her ears. Voices and laughter were mingled with its sound, and Rose sprang out of bed and crouched low beside the window ledge to see Lucie and Miss Piddock crossing the lawn. Lucie carried her spade and pail. She had evidently not been defrauded of the holiday due to her sister's nativity, and she was now on her way to the beach to enjoy it, apparently oblivious of the prisoner within doors.

With bitterness in her heart Rose watched her dancing across the grass, her fair curls bobbing on her shoulders, her blue eyes every now and then upturned to Miss Piddock with whom she seemed on excellent terms.

"Lucie would like a blackbeetle if it could talk and she could make it pet her," was her contemptuous summing up of her sister's attitude towards life. She held herself in readiness to duck down out of sight in case Lucie or Miss Piddock should turn a regretful backward glance towards her window. Obviously no such thought occurred to them, and after they had passed through the wicket gate on to the path to the sea, the trees screened them from her sight.

The day wore on, broken at one o'clock by a dull meal of cold mutton, brought on a tray by cook, and towards the afternoon Rose had fallen into a not unpleasant condition of reflection that was philosophic in tendency. With the aid of Lucie's pillow and bolster in addition to her own, she found she could comfortably see out of the window. She lay looking at the blue line of sea beyond the treetops, and thinking of it as she had seen it early that morning, mysterious and wonderful under its veil of opaline mist.

"Anyhow, I *saw* it, and I saw the fishing-boats go out," she thought exultingly. "Grandmamma can't take that away from me."

Rose's love of the sea was always associated in her mind with a sense of guilt. It had drowned her mother and her father, and it was certainly wicked to love anything so cruel, so pitiless; for its moods of smiling calm and innocence were only a proof of its treachery.

"I suppose I *am* wicked," she reflected complacently. "But then I don't remember my mother and father, and that makes a difference." She began to think of their portraits hanging opposite to one another downstairs in the drawing-room; of her mother's fair, pretty face so startlingly like Lucie's, and of the young man with the curious, eager expression whom people said she resembled, though Rose herself, often as she had looked in the glass after the visits of family friends, could never find the likeness.

Again to-day she tried to imagine what these un-known parents would have been like. "They couldn't have been worse than Grandmamma," she decided, "and they might have been much better." She liked the look of the young man who happened to be her father.

"I expect he laughed a good deal, and was very funny, and had a temper, and made up his mind about things," she thought rather incoherently. "Mother was just like Lucie, pretty and tame, and always wanting people to pet her."

There was more than a flavour of sour grapes in this verdict of contemptuous youth. Rose affected to despise Lucie, but in her secret heart she envied her. It was nice to be pretty, and a great advantage to have coaxing ways, even though you were a silly little thing and awfully "slow."

"But then I've got brains," continued Rose in her unspoken monologue, suddenly recalling Major Hawley's recent remark to that effect and her grand-mother's contemptuous rejoinder, "so much the worse. What good will they do her?"

Even now the silent fury she had experienced at the time, flared up again. "They *shall* do me good!" she insisted. "And it's a shame to let an idiot like Miss Piddock teach me. Teach? Why, she doesn't know anything. If you ask her a single question that isn't in the book, she gets red like a turkeycock and says it's nothing to do with the lesson I'm learning."

The indictment of Miss Piddock was followed by a favourite daydream. Perhaps if she were sufficiently naughty, Grandmamma would send her to school. The threat had recently several times been uttered, and secretly treasured by Rose. Ways and means

were not wanting. Possibly this morning's disobedience was a step in the right direction. Many more
such steps occurred to her fertile imagination, troublesome in themselves, of course, but if they led to the
desired goal . . . Rose smiled dreamily, and was just
sinking into a pleasant doze, when something flung
through the open window startled her into interested
wakefulness.

The missile lay on the floor in the middle of the
room, and was easily recognizable as a square piece of
toffee wrapped in silver paper.

In a flash Rose was out of bed and looking down
from the window at Geoffrey Winter, who returned her
stare with a grin.

"Grandmamma'll see you!" she protested in a stage
whisper.

"No, she won't, because she's calling at our place
with Lucie," returned Geoffrey, "and I met old Sandy
going down to the village shopping, so the coast's
clear. I say, isn't it beastly dull up there? You just
wait a bit and I'll come up."

He eyed critically the thick branches of ivy that
wreathed the window, at no great distance from the
ground, and then, nimbly as a cat, began to climb.

"Don't break it down and make a mess," Rose
implored between terror and delight as he drew nearer.

In a few seconds he was over the window-ledge and
had seated himself on the foot of the bed into which
Rose plunged. Suddenly remembering her nightgown and also certain injunctions of Miss Piddock's
containing the word "modesty," a vague self-consciousness assailed her. She pulled the bed-clothes
up to her chin and fixed her brown, velvety eyes upon
the boy, who began unconcernedly to eat toffee.

"Here's the bit I threw in," he remarked, picking up the tablet and dropping it on the sheet before her, "and here's lots more grub," he added, tumbling out the contents of his pocket, which included several apples and a quantity of chocolate in a damaged condition.

Rose bit an apple meditatively while she stared at Geoffrey. He had grown enormously, and it seemed so long since their last meeting at Christmas that she felt a little shy of him.

"Why are you home?" she asked presently.

"Measles. Not me. The other fellows."

"How nice. Aren't you glad?"

"Rather! Only pater has got a silly old tutor for me. I'm going to Rugby next term, you know," he added importantly.

Rose was not impressed. "How did you know I was sent to bed?" she pursued irrelevantly.

"Grandma came over on purpose to tell mother, silly. We were expecting you, of course."

Rose blushed distressfully. It was humiliating if inevitable that Mrs. Winter should know of her disgrace.

"What did your mother say?" she murmured almost inaudibly.

"Oh, I don't know. The sort of polite rot grown-ups say to one another about being very sorry and all that. . . . I say, what a cuckoo you were to faint or whatever it was. You might have got in all right if it hadn't been for that."

"Cook says it was because I went out on an empty stomach."

"That's a silly thing to do. *I* go out on my feet."

Geoffrey's humour was rewarded by an appreciative giggle from Rose between two bites of her apple.

"Why on earth didn't you grab something from the pantry before you started?" he proceeded. "I always do."

"Then Grandmamma would say I had been stealing," returned Rose bitterly.

The boy gave a low whistle. "Rot!" he ejaculated. "It must be rotten to be a girl," he added with sudden fervour.

"I should think it is. *You* can go out as early as you like, of course."

"Rather! Only I generally don't want to. Too much fag. I happened to wake up this morning, that's all."

"It must be nice to be a boy," said Rose, with a long sigh.

"Oh, it's pretty decent. But boys have to swot more over lessons than girls," he gloomily proceeded. "The whole of this blessed morning I've been doing Latin with Old Maynard. Thank goodness, I'm going to Rugby next term!"

"Well, you'll have just as much Latin to do there—more, I expect."

"Oh yes, but there'll be the other fellows, and no end of larks. And you can always get out of swotting at school, and you bet I shall. It's a different thing when you've got an old ass sitting beside you, with his silly eye on you all the time. That's what pater thought, I expect, when he made me stay at home this term and have a tutor," pursued Geoffrey, laughing easily. "But what's the good of it? Pater went to Rugby too, and he's forgotten every word of Latin and Greek. Couldn't construe a line to save his life.

And when I come into the place what shall I want with it either? I'd much better be learning about the land. Farming, and manures, and all that. I wish they taught a chap that sort of thing at public schools."

"I'd much rather learn Latin," said Rose. "Anyhow, you'll go to Rugby and I shall stay here and have horried dull lessons with old Sandy-cat, and always be in rows with Grandmamma. . . . Oh, I hate it! I *hate* it all!" she broke out with such sudden, unchildlike vehemence that Geoffrey was startled. She sat upright in bed and threw up her thin brown little arms with a movement full of despair. For the moment life seemed to her too bitter to be borne, and she hated the easy, good-tempered-looking boy who sat drumming his heels on the floor in the proud consciousness of his manhood.

"If only *I* could go to school," she added presently in a sullen voice.

"Girls' schools aren't up to much," Geoffrey assured her, striving tactlessly after comfort. "They're pretty horrid, I should think."

"Everything for girls is horrid!" declared the child petulantly. Her eyes suddenly filled with tears. "And it's my birthday," she added, consumed with self-pity and the desire for comfort and notice. Geoffrey's face also changed.

"I say, what a howling shame to send you to bed on your birthday!" he exclaimed with all the indignation Rose could have wished. Her spirits rose as her tears fell, and she made no effort to restrain them, knowing that if she cried Geoffrey would be sorry for her.

"I say, kiddie, don't cry," he urged uneasily. "I

2

wish I'd known. I'd have brought you a present.
How old are you?"

"N-nine," sobbed Rose.

Geoffrey got up and went to the window. He was
disgusted to find that he had a lump in his throat. It
was, as he put it to himself again, a howling shame to
keep the poor kid in on her birthday, and such a
ripping day too.

"There's some one coming!" whispered Rose, startled by a distant footstep. She swept up the
silver paper hurriedly from the bed, and Geoffrey,
cramming that and several apple cores into his pocket,
pulled Rose's hair affectionately and dropped over
the window-ledge at lightning speed. Rose heard
him scrambling down the ivy, and when some one,
probably one of the maids, passed her door without
entering, she regretted his flight. Geoffrey was nice
sometimes, and his visit had made an agreeable interlude in her captivity. Geoffrey meanwhile strolled
homewards through the golden sunset, stirred by a
regret of which he was profoundly ashamed even
while its presence fascinated him. If it hadn't been
such a rotten thing to do, he would like to have kissed
the poor little kid. She was an ugly little kid really,
but she had jolly eyes. He wished she hadn't cried.
It was sort of beastly to see a kid with jolly eyes
crying.

II

THE early morning escapade of little Rose Cottingham took place more than thirty years ago, when Glencove, now a rising seaside town, was a mere picturesque fishing village on the Devonshire coast.

The house in which she was born—the Manor House —for over a hundred years the dwelling-place of the West-country Lesters of whom Rose's grandfather was the last male survivor, stood high on the cliffs overlooking the sea. It was a fine, dignified Georgian house, shabby within, and fallen from its high estate, but beautiful still with the mellow beauty of time-worn things, and the grace of well-proportioned rooms, wide staircases, and lofty windows.

Neither Rose nor her little sister had known their parents. Their mother, after three years of married life, sailed with her soldier husband to India, leaving her two baby girls in the care of their grandmother at the Manor House, where both children had been born. The husband and wife were to have returned the following year to claim their children and take them to their own home—their first settled home since their marriage. They never returned. In one of those disastrous shipwrecks which for a week move the civilized world to pity and horror, and in a fortnight are forgotten, the young couple went down together; the Manor House became henceforth the home of their children, and Mrs. Lester their sole guardian.

When Rose came into the world, her grandmother, a tall, stately, commanding woman, was approaching her fiftieth year. She had always ruled the life of her daughter, whom she had loved in a condescending fashion, and now wearily, and from a sense of duty rather than from affection, she took up the task of ruling the lives of her grandchildren.

Conscious of what to her was social failure, Mrs. Lester was a somewhat embittered woman whose outlook upon life grew increasingly cynical. She had been beautiful, and though for "gentry" her parents were poor, she could claim long descent. Pride of race was an instinct with her, and ambition her ruling passion. But she who had aspired to a brilliant marriage through which she could have wielded power, exercised influence, and at high altitudes "pulled strings," found herself rather late in life, according to the estimate of her day, married to a no more exalted personage than Hugh Lester. This only when she had discovered that to the achievement of a really satisfactory union, wealth is a surer pathway than either birth, beauty, or both conjoined.

True, the Lesters were "gentlefolk," county people who for centuries had lived on the land they farmed. But they came of a dull, unadventurous, unenterprising stock, Hugh Lester being no exception to the rule, while he possessed other and less worthy characteristics than those which to some extent compensated for the lack of brilliance in his race.

He was exasperatingly weak, rather dissolute, more than a little stupid; and after some efforts to inspire him with her own energy, capability, and resource, Mrs. Lester, with secret disdain, abandoned the enterprise, and practically abandoned him. After the birth of her first and only child, she continued indeed to live under her husband's roof, but almost as a stranger to him. At most he was an acquaintance whom she treated with outward politeness and inward contempt, not only for his clumsy "amours" (as she designated his excursions into the land of romance with farmers' daughters and chambermaids), but also for his occasional outbreaks of drunkenness, and for his general stupidity in the conduct of life. Immorality joined to quickness of intellect, she could have tolerated. It was boorish incompetence that sickened her. Nevertheless, it was characteristic of her era that Mrs. Lester never wished herself unmarried. Spinsterhood as an alternative even to the most wretched union was in her view not so much the greater evil as the supreme catastrophe. In her day no gentlewoman worked. "Professions" for women were still in the womb of time, and even later on, when she heard of their existence, were to her always monstrous births. Marriage, in fact, was the only career open to women, and in her opinion, better a poor career than none at all.

It had at first been a bitter disappointment that her child was a girl, but this was in the early days of her life with Hugh. Later, as she told herself with proud disdain, she knew that he was not worthy to be the father of her sons.

Fortunately girls were not very important, except as pawns in the marriage market. One brought them up properly, which meant that they were well-mannered, well-grown, and superficially accomplished, and at the earliest possible age one married them to men in their own station of life, men able to provide for and to stand no nonsense from them for the rest of their existence. This programme she had more or less successfully carried out in the case of her own daughter. Though Richard Cottingham's financial prospects were not so satisfactory as she could have wished, he was well connected as well as a fine young soldier, likely to rise to honour in his profession, and in the circumstances, as Mrs. Lester reflected, Lucie could scarcely expect to do much better.

By the time the girl was twenty, her father had been dead ten years, leaving an impoverished estate and a heritage of debts to his widow. Mrs. Lester thus found herself in straitened circumstances, and unable when the time came, to give her daughter more than one season in London. It was on the whole fortunate, therefore, that Richard Cottingham, in every other than a pecuniary sense satisfactory, should have fallen in love with the girl almost at first sight, and incidentally that Lucie should have reciprocated his passion. Though it would scarcely have mattered had this not been the case, it was certainly pleasanter to arrange a marriage agreeable to the bride, and Mrs. Lester consoled herself for the lack of present affluence in her daughter's lot by the certainty she felt that Richard would ultimately succeed in his career. Three years later he and his prospects were gone for ever, and only two motherless little girls were left to be brought up on inadequate means, by a world-wearied, disillusioned woman who had thought her task in life over.

If they had been boys Mrs. Lester would have welcomed her duty, however arduous it proved. As it was, it seemed to her thankless work and uninspiring, to begin all over again the training of girls for their one predestined sphere in life. She was prepared for dulness, but not for difficulties. But then she had never encountered a child like her namesake, Rose—a plain, clever, headstrong, rebellious child.

Her own daughter had been easy to manage, and in Lucie, the younger little girl, history repeated itself. Like her mother, she was pretty, gentle, rather timid—everything, in fact, that a girl might reasonably be expected to be. It was Rose who upset all her grandmother's calculations by the possession of characteristics which, but for a curious blindness, she would have recognized in herself.

The truth that in more ways than one Rose resembled her, would have been fiercely and indignantly denied by Mrs. Lester, who no more frequently than other dominating personalities escaped the irony of the gods.

It was possibly just because of this undiscerned fact that her grandmother resented Rose, that she found it difficult to be just to her. Two generations divided them, and qualities common to each, found forms of expression as different as the ages to which they belonged. The result was conflict, and naturally unequal conflict, between the ageing woman of the world who had learned to conceal her emotions beneath a veil of sarcasm, and the unrestrained, passionate child who frankly displayed them.

Long before her granddaughter was nine years old, Mrs. Lester had fully recognized that she must struggle with her to preserve that dominance and authority which hitherto had been ceded to her as a right by almost every individual with whom she had come into relationship. Hence it was that the child, who might have been led but whom it was impossible to drive, was more and more constantly in disgrace, a very thorn in the flesh of a rigid disciplinarian.

III

THE ENCHANTED WOOD

BEFORE her birthday week was over, Rose was again in trouble.

Sent out as usual with Lucie and the governess, she had escaped Miss Piddock's vigilance, and by an adroit flank movement reached the Glencove woods, which climbed from the shore to the top of the high cliffs. Her occupation, indeed, was in itself innocent, for it was that of looking for fairies.

In her attitude towards the existence of fairies Rose was a hopeful agnostic. Her reason denied them; her feeling was that they might and could exist, especially in Glencove woods on such an April day as this. The books lent to her by Mrs. Winter no doubt alleged that all fairies left England when the railways came, terrified by the thunder and screaming of engines through the green country side. But Glencove was so far from a railway-station that perhaps a few might still be found in its woods—if fairies had ever been at all. At any rate, it was a good day to look for them, and with more hope than despair, Rose ran along the winding moss paths in the wood, stopping every now and then to lift a fern-frond, or to peer beneath a specially fine tuft of primroses, vaguely expectant of finding some tiny gossamer creature swinging between two grass blades, or curled within the cup of a flower. That instead of fairies there were insects in the flowers and slugs in the grass, did not much discourage her.

Fairies were known to assume diverse shapes, and possibly the red brown slug she had just disturbed was an elf in disguise. Farther on, towards the heart of the wood, where they could expect to be free from human intrusion, she might surprise a fairy before it had time to turn itself into any obnoxious form.

She began to climb up the steep primrose-starred bank on the right of the path, digging her hands deep into the moss to help herself, and clinging to overhanging roots and hazel twigs on her upward way. By the time she reached the level plateau above the bank, her knees were a fine rich brown from the damp soil, and her frock was stained from neck to hem. Disregarding these trifles for the moment, though she was fully aware that later they would prove no trifles but rather monuments and evidences of crime, Rose gave herself up to delight.

The ground was white with anemones, broken here and there by patches of violets. Overhead a canopy of half-opened leaves let in the sunlight, which flickered deliciously over the flowers; and looking up, she saw lakes of blue sky, on which sailed white feather-like clouds. Far below, on the left, through a veil of butterfly leaves, she caught a glimpse of the sea, stretching away, away to the horizon. All around her was a clamour of bird voices. Wood-pigeons called in their soft, thick notes, blackbirds fluted, cuckoos answered one another from neighbouring valleys, thrushes broke into snatches of plaintive melody, and from the mossy earth and from the sheets of flowers scents deliriously sweet arose.

For the moment the child forgot the fairies. The green world without them was beautiful enough, and she was alone in it—alone with the birds and the flowers and the emerald larches and the yellow, unfolding oak-leaves.   A sense of ecstasy took her, and almost afraid to move lest she should break the spell, she leaned against the trunk of a tree and let her eyes wander from the pools of blue sky to the frail anemones, white and purple-veined, at her feet.   Standing there, motionless and happy in the green wood, Rose was at her best, part almost of the sylvan world, a small, erect, slight thing with a colourless skin, thick, dark, untidy hair, and eyes, her one real beauty, like the soft velvet eyes of some little furry forest creature.

For the time, Grandmamma, Lucie, Miss Piddock, lessons, scolding, and punishments—all the irksome, everyday people and things were forgotten.   She was caught up into an enchanted world, and it was well with her.   And yet not wholly well, for somewhere obscurely in the depths of her childish mind she wanted to *do* something with all this beauty.   What this something was she could not tell, but the desire worried her—the artist's desire to put on record in some form, a loveliness whose mere recognition was not enough: was, indeed, unsatisfying, tormenting. . . .

"Rose!   Rose!"   Two insistent calling voices shattered the magic and brought her prosaically to earth again.

Here were Lucie and Miss Piddock, and the enchanted wood was profaned.   Rose angrily shook her shoulders and frowned her resentment.   For a moment she did not answer, and it was only when two heads, a flaxen and a sandy one, appeared at the top of a steep path leading up from the sea that she moved.

"Here! here! here!   Don't shout so!" she called irritably.   "Why didn't you go home without me?   You knew I should come."

"Knew you would come, indeed! You're a very naughty, disobedient, impertinent girl," gasped Miss Piddock, breathless with her climb and incoherent with annoyance and recent fear. "How dare you run away like that? Lucie and I have been looking for you all the morning, and now we shall be late for luncheon, and your Grandmamma will be very angry. And serve you right! *Look* at your frock, and your hands and knees."

From her higher level on the anemone plateau Rose looked down on Miss Piddock with aversion. She despised her, and made no secret of the fact. She also, though in a different fashion, despised her sister Lucie, who, with upturned face, stood meekly by her governess while she regarded Rose with awe and apprehension. Lucie was an exceedingly pretty child, with long fair curls, a delicate pink and while skin, and eyes the colour of forget-me-nots. In her snowy white serge frock and jacket she looked the picture of dainty, well-conducted childhood.

"Come down now at once, and don't waste time," urged Miss Piddock irritably. "We shall be half an hour late for lunch as it is. How *dare* you run away?"

"Why do you keep on asking me that?" returned Rose. And slipping down the bank before Miss Piddock could protest against a method of descent fatal to underclothes, she reached her governess, talking petulantly all the time.

"I ran away, as you call it, because you and Lucie are so *dull*, and I'm tired of you, and I want to be by myself! And then you come calling and shouting and spoil it all," she went on, grumbling incoherently, her little face sullen with anger. The child who ten minutes before had been happily looking for fairies, was gone, and in her place was the discontented, naughty little creature known to Miss Piddock by three years of bitter experience.

"We'd better run," put in Lucie timidly. "Grandmamma——"

"You and Miss Piddock can run. I'm not going to," declared Rose obstinately. "Grandmamma can't kill me, and I don't care if she does," she added inconsequently.

She took a perverse pleasure in her naughtiness, feeling in her own mind that it was justified. The day had been blighted for her, robbed of all its wonderful mystery and romance by the sudden intrusion into her beatific mood of the cares and duties of everyday life embodied in the person of Miss Piddock. The wood was no longer a vision of mystic beauty, the sky was no longer the floor of heaven, and "a primrose by the river's brim" now, had to her much the same appearance as it presented to Wordsworth's yokel.

Rose's ill-temper was often caused by the swift transitions of moods incomprehensible to her elders and very much of a puzzle to herself. But in the days of her childhood, moods were neither allowed for nor allowed, and in nine cases out of ten were rightly discouraged in children. That the tenth child sometimes suffered was unavoidable, and proved nothing. In a world whose individuals were perfectly adapted to their environment, the tenth child would not have existed. As things were when Rose was young, it was inevitable that the tenth child should be often a little crushed against the wall.

Mrs. Lester was half-way through a solitary lunch when Miss Piddock, very red and flustered, pushed open the dining-room door, holding Lucie's hand for moral support.

She went in terror of her employer, who, however, had never given her a harsh word, nor indeed more words of any kind than were compatible with cold politeness.

"I'm exceedingly sorry we're late," she began falteringly. "But Rose has been troublesome again. She ran away from us, and Lucie and I had great difficulty in finding her."

"And where is Rose now? . . . May I trouble you as you pass to ring the bell so that the maid may bring in the luncheon I sent out to be re-heated."

Miss Piddock flew to do her bidding.

"I was obliged to send her to change her frock. She made it very dirty by climbing in the wood. I warned her to be as quick as possible," she said, returning meekly to her seat.

Mrs. Lester was silent, and her silence continued after her elder granddaughter, immaculate now in a white pinafore, had slipped into the room.

She did not even glance at her, and to Rose this ignoring of her existence was the most effective punishment. It filled her with apprehension and a sort of imaginative horror of what Grandmamma might say or do when she *did* speak.

Her sister's disgrace had the effect of frightening Lucie, whose chatter, generally indulgently tolerated by Mrs. Lester, might have covered the awkward situation. But Lucie, too, was speechless to-day, and it was with relief that Rose saw her grandmother at last rise from the table.

"You will have tea alone in the schoolroom this afternoon and go to bed immediately afterwards," she announced, looking at Rose for the first time with cold eyes. "This is the second time this week that I've been obliged to punish you."

Rose spent a considerable part of her childhood in bed. It was a punishment which, unsuspected to Mrs. Lester, varied in efficacy according to the circumstances of her granddaughter's subjective existence.

If she had "something nice to think about" Rose did not at all object to solitude in a comfortable position, untroubled by interference from Miss Piddock; and while she consumed weak tea and "scraped" bread-and-butter in the schoolroom that afternoon, the beginnings of a delightful fantasy occurred to her. In bed later, when the sunset glow filled the room with wonderful amber light, she lay happily enough, planning with all the artist's zest a piece of work atrocious from every artistic standpoint, but to her as inspiring as the idea of a new masterpiece to a Titian or a Velasquez.

Sarah, the parlour-maid, a good-natured girl, beloved by the children, had recently shown them how to make wool flowers. A gem of handicraft called by Sarah a "convolvus," could be evolved from a large cork, several blanket pins, and wools shading from deep purple to the faintest mauve. You stuck the pins round the cork, and then proceeded to twist the wool about this framework, beginning with a violet tone of purple, and ending towards the rim of the flower, with the faint shades of lilac.

An object of incredible hideousness emerged, but to Rose it was a creation of such surpassing beauty and wonder that she would run upstairs twenty times a day to look at the misshapen "convolvus" she herself had made, enshrined in a precious casket, a shell box from Margate, presented by Sarah and admired by both children to the point of ecstasy. Quite recently she and Lucie had been further initiated into the mysteries of moss-making in green wool, and it was of moss in conjunction with fairies, that Rose was now dreaming. She had failed to find the fairies that morning. Very possibly Miss Piddock was right, and they did not exist. No matter, she would make a fairy world of her own, and it would be a wonderful little dell with sloping mossy banks, on which glow-worms sparkled and ethereal beings reclined. A shallow basket would do for the dell; Grandmamma's work-basket, she reflected joyously, would be admirable for the purpose. That it was not at all likely to be given her for that or any other purpose, did not trouble Rose, who, like every other visionary, ignored practical details. Out of Grandmamma's work-basket then, draped with the wool moss so exquisitely manufactured by Sarah (and so clumsily by herself), would arise the magic vale, clear to her mental vision. There were tiny, *tiny* wooden dolls in the village toy-shop. These, clothed in white tarlatan, holding flower-wreathed pins for wands, should be the fairies, and for glow-worms she could sew, here and there amidst the mossy banks, glass amber beads like those which Lucie threaded in rings and necklaces for her own personal adornment.

A tremor of delicious excitement shook her. The "dell," so absurd as her concrete fancy planned it in material terms, became in a spiritualized version of that fancy a magic place, irradiated with mystic light, touched with a glamour and a beauty transcending all mortal experience. It was to her an escape of the soul, a glimpse of the beatific vision.

A circumstance which might, but fortunately did

not bring her little soul to earth, was the fact that she could by no possibility have fashioned the material form she had planned for the enshrining of her idea. To make a green-wool glade, on which beads were to be neatly sewn, to dress dolls, and with infinite skill to manufacture wands out of pins, was a task of which she was incapable. Rose was not clever with her fingers. It was Lucie who, as her grandmother declared, had "quite a good notion of dressmaking," as evinced by neatly made dolls' clothes; Lucie who could make passably regular "convolvuses" and realistic moss; Lucie who was already deft and clever with her hands. As usual with Rose, she had imagined more than she could bring to pass. But the bitter day for the realizing of her limitations was not yet; and meanwhile the "dell" fortunately remained a dream, and its embodiment of such stuff as dreams are made of.

It served its turn, however, in giving her the happy hours occasionally known to the artist.

When Lucie, escorted by Miss Piddock, came to bed, Rose pretended to be asleep, but so intense was her excitement and delight over the evocation of the dell that it was hours later before real sleep began to overtake her, and then from her first drowsiness her sister's voice roused her.

"Rose! Rose!" she wailed, and Rose immediately sat up and reached out towards the little bed next to hers for Lucie's hand.

"Here I am," she whispered soothingly. "You're not frightened again, are you?"

Any one who had ever heard Rose quarrelling with Lucie, would not have recognized her voice, so maternal was it, so protective in its quality.

In the daytime Lucie might be, and in Rose's eyes

very frequently was, "a silly conceited little thing, always being good and showing off." But Lucie in the night, frightened of the dark and calling for protection, was infinitely pathetic. All the mother instinct welled up in Rose's heart in response to the appeal.

"Hold my hand and go to sleep," she said tenderly. "Why are you frightened?"

"There was such a funny light on the wall just now," quavered Lucie. "I woke up and saw it, and now it's gone."

In her turn Rose experienced a thrill of terror. Perhaps more often than Lucie, she too, was frightened in the night, but the idea of waking her sister never occurred to her. To Lucie she always pretended to be immune from fear, preternaturally brave. To her Lucie was "a little thing" to be shielded.

"It was only the moon, and now it's gone under a cloud," she assured her in such a tone of conviction that the child, pacified and credulous, dropped at once to sleep. As soon as her sister's regular breathing satisfied Rose, she gently disengaged her hand and thrust it, trembling, under the bedclothes. It was torture to her to have it exposed, for at any moment she might feel a cold grasp on her wrist from some unseen being who, ghoul-like, hovered about the room.

For what seemed ages to her, she lay still, scarcely daring to breathe. What was the light that Lucie had seen on the wall? The moon theory so hastily evolved did not convince her. That was, of course, only a fiction for her sister's benefit, and quite possibly she herself might presently see some terrible and mysterious illumination on that opposite wall!

The Bible story of Belshazzar's feast occurred to

her. Suppose some awful sentence in letters of fire
were suddenly to appear above the chest of drawers?
Rose shut her eyes in panic, and as hastily opened
them again to make sure that what she dreaded had
not come to pass. Meanwhile Lucie slept peacefully,
and presently in the midst of her terror, merciful
oblivion fell upon Rose also.

IV

AN UNRULY PUPIL

SHE awoke, after the manner of healthy children, with a sense of elation, all her nocturnal and other troubles forgotten.

It was Saturday, she remembered, and therefore a half-holiday, and it was a fine day. Sarah had just drawn up the Venetian blinds, and the sky was blue.

Rose sprang out of bed and looked out of the window. It was a glorious morning, one of those suspiciously brilliant mornings of April from which the wary deduce rain to follow. But Rose was not wary. It was enough for her that the sun was shining, and she immediately planned a long afternoon on the beach. She and Lucie ran down to the breakfast-room together when the bell rang, and dutifully approached Mrs. Lester for the morning kiss, perfunctorily received and bestowed. Miss Piddock entered a moment later with her usual flustered, deprecating manner, and breakfast began. It was nearly always a silent meal, Mrs. Lester engrossed in the newspaper, and Miss Piddock, who at no time was a conversationalist, devoting herself stolidly to the consumption of eggs and bacon. To-day, however, Rose was not bored, as usual, by the lack of human intercourse. She was in a happy mood, and the familiar breakfast-room with the sunshine pouring in at the long windows, and the green garden beyond, seemed suddenly a beautiful place to her. She pos-

sessed the faculty of occasionally seeing well-known
objects and scenes with new eyes, so that they appeared invested with a peculiar glamour, and to-day
she loved the breakfast-room. Her taste was not
despicable. All the Manor House rooms had the
beauty of admirable proportions, of good fireplaces
and well-spaced windows, and though the carpets and
curtains in some of them were faded and growing
threadbare, they had been beautiful in their day, and
were even now not lacking in a certain pleasant mellow
effect of colour.

"Primroses would look nice in this room, wouldn't
they, Grandmamma?" she said suddenly.

Mrs. Lester lowered her newspaper and looked at
her above it.

"Do you think so?" she asked, and raising it again
continued to read.

Rose flushed angrily. She had absolutely forgotten
yesterday's naughtiness, and her grandmother's cold
voice reminded her that she might still be in disgrace.

"I do hate people who keep things up," was her
secret comment.

She began to fidget and to wonder impatiently how
much longer Miss Piddock was going on eating. To
be late over breakfast meant the curtailment of the
run in the garden which on fine days preceded lessons.

She and Lucie looked at one another hopelessly
across the table, and Rose, counting upon the shelter
of Mrs. Lester's *Morning Post* and the absorption of
Miss Piddock in the bread and marmalade stage of her
breakfast, ventured upon a swift grimace of incredible
hideousness directed towards the downbent head of
her governess.

Lucie incontinently began to giggle, and in spite of

her sister's warning pantomime continued to gurgle spasmodically till Mrs. Lester looked up from her paper.

"Why are you laughing in that foolish way, Lucie?" she demanded, and Rose held her breath. It was just possible that out of fear and lack of resource, her sister might reply, "Rose made a face."

Fortunately, without waiting for an answer, Mrs. Lester merely said, "You may both go if you've finished your breakfast," and with a gasp of relief Rose pushed her chair back.

"Now I trust I shall hear no further complaints of your conduct, Rose," pursued her grandmother, coldly, as she generally spoke to the child, who again felt a rush of angry resentment. It lasted till the garden was reached.

Here all her ill-temper dissolved like magic in the sparkling sunshine. The garden stretched from the house to the edge of the cliff, and a winding, sloping path in one place, and in another a staircase, led down to the sea. It was a rather wild, rather neglected, but nevertheless a romantic garden, fringed with little copses, now starred with primroses. There were many twisting paths moss-grown, over-arched by hazel-trees, and flanked by lilac-bushes, which grew in profusion, and in May were wonderful pyramids of white and purple bloom. Beyond a great variety of flowering shrubs the flowers in the garden, upon which Mrs. Lester was forced to economize were few, but in spring, at least, one scarcely missed them. Rose, at least, asked for no more delectable spot than this wild green world with the sea beyond. To-day it rang with the voices of rejoicing birds, sunlight slanted across the paths, filtered through the opening leaves, and poured its full radiance on the lawn, which, unbroken by paths and flower-beds, stretched right up to the walls of the house.

The children raced about like little wild creatures, darting down paths, where startled blackbirds flew chuckling before them, dashing through the copses, till finally, exhausted and breathless, they leaned over the gate which separated the garden from the path to the sea.

"Shall we have time to go down?" suggested Rose eagerly. "Do let's!"

"No," said Lucie, prudent as ever. "She'll call us in a minute, and then there'll be a fuss and you'll be kept in this afternoon or something." She did not include herself in Rose's possible detention. Lucie almost invariably got off punishment. It was Rose as the ringleader who suffered.

Almost before she had finished speaking, Miss Piddock's voice was heard in the distance.

"There!" ejaculated Lucie, preparing to run.

"Don't go yet," urged Rose impatiently. "We can pretend we don't hear for ever so long. Let's wait till she calls six times."

The game thus instituted proved amusing and provided Rose, at least, with the excitement she loved. It was a nice point to decide on the psychological moment to appear with any semblance of innocence, but having decided to obey the sixth summons Rose was determined, in spite of Lucie's perturbation, to wait for it.

"Squeakier and squeakier!" she whispered between her gurgles of suppressed laughter as Miss Piddock hovered about on the edge of the lawn with reiterated cries.

"That's six," declared Lucie, who would have bolted at the second call but for her sister's firm grasp on her pinafore. "Let me go, Rose!" she insisted, full of apprehension. "I shall tell her if you don't!"

"Little sneak!" was Rose's contemptuous rejoinder, lost upon Lucie, who was off like an arrow from the bow.

She followed leisurely, in time to hear Miss Piddock's dubious acceptance of Lucie's excuses.

"Another time you must stay nearer the house where you *can* hear. Now come in at once, both of you. We're five minutes late already."

Rose did not greatly quicken her steps for the injunction. It was a tragedy to have to go in to the lessons her soul abhorred, on a morning like this when all the outside world rejoiced. She was possessed of a passionate envy of the birds singing so madly in the copses, with no knowledge of books and slates.

"But I believe Miss Piddock would like to teach *them* even!" she thought, with the ineradicable conviction of childhood that all teachers pant with eagerness to instruct. The mental vision conjured up by this sudden idea was vastly amusing, and she began to imagine Miss Piddock, spectacled and ringletted, in a nestful of birds who chirped after her the multiplication table. "But the nest would have to be very big, or Miss Piddock very small," she reflected. "Oh, I *wish* I could draw it." An idle wish, for Rose had no more notion of drawing than the birds who occupied her thoughts.

"Now, Rose! Dreaming again!" Miss Piddock admonished her when they reached the lobby outside the schoolroom where garden clothes were kept. "Take off your hat and coat at once, and put on your pinafore."

Rose mechanically obeyed, her head still full of Miss Piddock's supposed scholastic endeavours amongst the thrushes.

Lucie was already seated at the schoolroom table when Rose entered with her pinafore fastened inside out, and after it had been querulously removed and re-buttoned for her by Miss Piddock, lessons began.

They were of the uninspired and uninspiring sort common thirty years ago when every poor woman with any claim to gentility became, *faute de mieux*, a governess.

The books from which Rose and Lucie learned had been their mother's, when as a child she sat in the same schoolroom and was bored to tears by the prototype of Miss Piddock. Mrs. Lester, who knew nothing and cared less about the then modern education, had not troubled to change them, and Miss Piddock, sharing her ignorance, accepted them as part of the dull machinery by which she earned her daily bread.

They lay piled up on the table before her: *Little Arthur's History of England*, Mrs. Markham on the same subject, a manual entitled *The Play Grammar*, a cheerful but inadequate little volume, *The Child's Guide to Useful Knowledge*, and *The Peep of Day*, a small, fat, pious book tolerated by Rose because of a certain poem it contained beginning briskly with the line—

Satan is glad when I am bad,

which irresistibly appealed to her dawning sense of humour.

Miss Piddock opened the proceedings by setting Rose a sum in simple multiplication, and pushing the slate, the horrible object upon which it was written, towards her. Rose's mother had used a slate; and because at the Manor House nothing changed, her daughter suffered tortures from the grinding noise of the pencil on its unsympathetic surface—torture which goaded her to frenzy when inadvertently she or Miss Piddock made it "squeak."

"I don't know nine times," grumbled Rose, looking with aversion at the multiplier.

"You should be ashamed to own it, then. Go on with your sum at once."

"But it will be all wrong if I don't know nine times."

"Go on," repeated Miss Piddock, taking up *The Child's Guide* to hear Lucie repeat the parrot-like phrases she was supposed to have learned the day before.

Rose had been twice through *The Child's Guide*, but Lucie, less advanced, had only just been promoted to its absurdities.

Miss Piddock began at the first page of interrogations.

"My good child, who made you?" she inquired perfunctorily, reading the first of the incessant questions with which the author plied his victims.

"The great and good God," returned Lucie, her limpid eyes fixed upon her governess.

"What is flour made of?" proceeded Miss Piddock, without a pause, taking query number two.

"Wheat," said Lucie nimbly.

"What has wheat got to do with God?" demanded Rose, surreptitiously playing "naughts and crosses" in the corner of her slate.

"Attend to your sum and don't ask silly questions," observed Miss Piddock.

"It's the book that asks silly questions," returned Rose, unabashed and disobedient. "I never knew such a silly book. You wait till you get further on, Lucie, about the planets, and glue, and cotton, all mixed up together. You won't know which is which by the time you've done."

"Rose, *will* you go on with your own work and allow Lucie to attend to hers?" exclaimed Miss Piddock exasperatedly. "If you knew half what this book has to teach you, it would be a very good thing for you."

"That's what it says at the end," put in Rose, chuckling and irrepressible. "You just look at the end, Lucie! It says—

'What is the use of this little book?'

And you have to answer—

'It has made me wiser and better. It has taught me many things I did not know before.'

And it *hasn't* you know, because——"

"Take your slate and go to that table by the window!" said Miss Piddock in desperation. "And if you continue to talk after I have forbidden you to do so, I shall tell Mrs. Lester."

Rose willingly moved to the seat indicated, for the window commanded a closer view of the garden, and as she sat watching the birds on the lawn, she cast about in her mind as usual for "something nice to think about." The "dell" of the previous night's imagining rose again in her thoughts, but somehow the daylight had not only shorn it of its magic, but brought also the realization of her own incompetence.

"I couldn't do it properly," she decided sadly. "And even if I could, perhaps it wouldn't look right. I *wish* I could draw Miss Piddock teaching the birds." Then suddenly in a flash came the notion, "But I can *write* it!" The idea was blinding in its radiance, and turning over her slate, she began in feverish haste to compose the first sentence of what was to be the funniest fairy story ever written. As she struggled for the words, excitement gradually mounted in her brain. She had never tried to write before. How absurd! Why, of course she could write books. Real books about fairies and mermaids and all sorts of things. It was quite easy to write—only it had never before occurred to her to do it. . . .

"Rose, is your sum finished?" The voice of her story's heroine woke her with a start of annoyance from her new dream of art, and she hastily tried to rub out with her pinafore the few sentences she had written on the reverse side of her slate.

"Bring it to me," said Miss Piddock.

"It isn't done," declared Rose impatiently. "I told you I didn't know nine times."

"Then what have you been doing all this while? What is all this scribbling at the back of the slate? You're a very naughty girl! Now come and say your grammar."

Satisfaction at escaping her "arithmetic" was mingled in Rose's mind with contempt for the weakness of Miss Piddock. She had long ago gauged the poor woman's incompetence, and knew to a hair's breadth how far it was safe to go with her. Only when a long course of insubordination goaded her to the courage of despair, or when Rose's guilt led to the infringement of household rules and without her own incrimination became impossible to conceal, would she dare to appeal to Mrs. Lester. Successfully trading on this knowledge, therefore, Rose evaded much hateful instruction, and often fleeted the school hours, carelessly, amusing herself as best she might.

Abandoning the sum, Miss Piddock now took up *The Play Grammar* and "heard" her pupil repeat the prepared task. It concerned the degrees of comparison of adjectives, and was illustrated by woodcuts showing three plum-puddings in various stages of heated activity. From the "positive" pudding a small puff of smoke ascended, the "comparative" one steamed with praiseworthy energy, while the "superlative" delicacy was a veritable Vesuvius. Three clowns beneath the puddings were intended to portray the relative meaning of "funny, funnier, funniest," but the artist's instructive intent to fix attention on the rules of grammar, was frustrated by the human interest evoked by his clowns in the annoying brain of Rose.

She studied their faces attentively, and despite the broader grin on the countenance of the "comparative" comedian, she considered the "positive" entertainer much more amusing, and insisted upon debating the question with Miss Piddock, consulting her also upon his patronymic and private history. Joey, Sambo, and Uncle Tom were the names which her governess found inscribed in smudged red ink under the portraits of these increasingly facetious gentlemen, and the repetition lesson was interrupted for a querulous lecture on the iniquity of spoiling books paid for by Rose's grandmother.

"Well, she paid for them such a long time ago that I expect she's forgotten," was Rose's defence. "Do you think Sambo has sausages in his pocket when he's at home, Miss Piddock? Joey, you know, has ten children, and their names are Sophia, Mabel, Jack——"

Recalled from this exercise in imagination rather than English grammar, Rose stumbled through her repetition of the next page—a dull page unenlivened by pictures, and was bidden to read aloud the chapter that followed. She demurred, declaring in favour of another chapter setting forth the nature and purpose of the Interjection. This was headed by a picture of a little girl with ringlets and long trousers limping into an Early Victorian room, where "Mamma," brimming over with useful knowledge, awaited her daughter.

Miss Piddock as usual gave in after the customary wrangle and in defiance of all sequence Rose began to read the paragraph which interested her solely on account of the trousered little girl known in *The Play Grammar* as "Fanny." Her reading was punctuated with delighted giggles.

"'La! Mamma!' cried Fanny, 'I have twisted my ankle.'

"'There, Fanny!'" returned Mamma, plunging without a word of sympathy into English grammar. "'You have uttered an interjection.'"

Rose, who had been many times through *The Play Grammar*, never ceased to be amused by this conversational opening. She laughed till Lucie, hitherto industriously and without the smallest comprehension insisting in a copybook that "the whale is a mammal," joined in her mirth and began carelessly to smudge the record of the mysterious fact.

"'*La!*'" repeated Rose mockingly. "Nobody says '*la*' now. And nobody wears trousers like Fanny. This book must have been written ages ago. And do you believe Fanny was interested, like they make out here, in adverbs and adjectives and things? *I* don't. She's as bad as Richard and George and Mary in Mrs. Markham.　Horrid little things!"

"I like Mary best," observed Lucie.

"Oh, do you?　I don't.　They're all little idiots, but I think George is the best.　He's not so——"

Miss Piddock rapped wildly on the table.

"Go on with your copy, Lucie, and you, Rose, attend to the lesson!" she adjured.　"Fanny and George have nothing to do with what the books are trying to teach you.　It's the grammar that matters, and the history."

"Well, they don't matter to *me*," protested Rose with truth.　"It's the children that matter, and I should have made them ever so much nicer.　I should have made Fanny cry and howl about her ankle, and then the mamma would have had to get up and put something on it instead of talking about interjections."

Five minutes of argument leading into the bypaths of the personal history of Fanny, George, and Mary followed, before Rose could be induced to return to the subject unsuccessfully treated in *The Play Grammar*.

Miss Piddock then marked two pages to be learned by heart for Monday, and Rose turned to the reading of Mrs. Markham.

That classic was enlivened by "conversations" between "Mamma" and "the little idiots" who, if the author might be believed, were consumed by a perpetual thirst for historical information.　The chapter of the moment opened more or less as follows:

"*Richard*.　Pray, Mamma, continue your interesting account of the Feudal System."

This, the first paragraph of Rose's reading for the day, served so long as a text for explanations as to what she would do if the egregious Richard once fell into her clutches, that Miss Piddock, after trying ineffectually to stem the torrent of her eloquence, glanced at the clock and shut up the book in despair.

"It wants five minutes to the half-hour," she said, with a long sigh. "You may tidy the book cupboard till it's time to go."

A typical morning of "lessons" was over, and with a shout of relief, her echo of Miss Piddock's sigh, Rose sprang up from the table.

Exultation was followed by a groan.

"Why, it's raining!" she cried. The brilliant morning was already overcast, rain was falling steadily, and the sea, lately blue and dancing, was a mere grey blur.

"Oh, how perfectly *disgusting!* Now we can't go on the beach." Black despair for a moment filled her. Rose was always either in hell or heaven, and passed with inconceivable rapidity from one region to the other. But now, before the portals of the former realm closed upon her, the gates of heaven were opened by the memory of the fairy tale she had planned. It was a good thing it was raining! She would manage to creep upstairs to the bedroom after luncheon and write there undisturbed.

"Well, we can play with the dolls' house," said Lucie placidly. "We haven't played with it for ever so long."

"*I'm* not going to," returned her sister brusquely. "I'm going to do something quite different. I'm tired of the dolls' house.   It's only fit for babies like you."

She was not in the least tired of the dolls' house, but an author's dignity must be maintained, even at personal sacrifice.

V

KINSHIP OF THE SPIRIT

THEY played with it after all, but only when Rose had recovered from a fit of ill-temper caused by the frustration of her plan for literary endeavour.

Greatly to her satisfaction it continued to rain steadily. She no longer wanted to go to the beach. Her only desire now was to put on paper the amusing and fantastic scenes which filled her mind and absorbed her attention to such an extent that during the midday meal she scarcely spoke. As a general rule Rose hated silence. It was she who, despite her grandmother's unapproachable demeanour, sometimes lured her into stories about her mother's childhood, or better still, about the convent school in France where "in the olden times," as Rose described the period of her grandmother's youth, Mrs. Lester herself was educated. On the rare occasions when she was loquacious Rose almost loved her grandmother. She always admired her, impressed in her childish way by the *grande dame* air which so terrified Miss Piddock.

"You're like a queen made of ice, Grandmamma," she once remarked when she saw Mrs. Lester dressed for one of the rare dinner-parties of the neighbourhood, and her grandmother had started, and presently kissed her with more tenderness than usual. She was a little perturbed but perhaps more flattered than not by the somewhat invidious compliment.

4   49

To-day, directly she and Lucie had been told they might leave the table, Rose darted off to the school-room to fetch paper and pencil, and then made for the back staircase, whence she hoped to reach her bedroom without her sister's knowledge. No one would think for ever so long of looking for her there, and she might enjoy the artist's peace in freedom from interruption. Unfortunately, at the foot of the stairs she met her grandmother preparing for a surprise visit to the servants' quarters. Mrs. Lester was famed for her household management, and it was an axiom amongst her neighbours that any maid trained at the Manor House must be "worth her salt."

"Where are you going, Rose?" she inquired, glancing at the exercise book and pencil in her grand-daughter's hand.

"Into my bedroom," said Rose, her heart sinking.

"What for?"

"To write something."

"All writing can be done in the schoolroom," said Mrs. Lester, autocratically displaying her ignorance of the author's high calling. "I cannot have the bed-rooms used for scribbling. Go to the schoolroom and sit with Lucie and Miss Piddock."

"Scribbling!" The insult, though as it happened unintentional, was dire, and Rose returned, raging, to the society of her sister and her governess.

Lucie, quietly engaged in painting fashion-plate ladies with a brilliant crudeness of colour forestalling the methods of the modern Cubist, and Miss Piddock, seated by the window sewing tuckers into the children's Sunday frocks, were startled by her whirlwind entrance and bewildered by her flood of invective.

Everything was too disgusting to be endured!

Never, *never* by any chance was she allowed to do anything she wanted to do. Every one was as dull as ditch water. Grandmamma was the most disagreeable woman that ever lived, and in short, if she had only known the definition, Rose would have summed up life as "one damned thing after another,"—as indeed it seemed to her.

"But what did you want to do?" inquired Miss Piddock mildly, continuing to pleat up lace.

"I wanted to write," snapped Rose.

"Whatever for?" asked Lucie, genuinely surprised that any one should wish to lift pen or pencil when they needn't.

"Well, you can write here," suggested Miss Piddock soothingly, and Rose stamped with annoyance.

Write there! With Miss Piddock looking over her shoulder to find herself lampooned?

"You're all so *silly!*" she cried, flinging herself into a chair.

"And you're so rude," returned Miss Piddock, with the truth that exasperates.

"We might just as well play with the dolls' house," Lucie remarked presently after a silence.

"Dolls' house!" repeated Rose contemptuously. Nevertheless, in the secret recesses of her heart she began to consider the suggestion. The black mood was passing, and the glamour which sometimes surrounded the dolls' house was beginning to gather about it once more. Quite suddenly a new and exciting game to be played with its inmates occurred to her, and she jumped up with so much vehemence that the startled Lucie spilt her painting water all over the table-cloth.

"Come along!" she called, and darted out of the room.

"Is she really going to play?" asked Lucie, obediently mopping up the water with the slate-duster fetched from the cupboard. "Why, she said she wouldn't."

Miss Piddock shrugged her shoulders.

"I suppose so. I don't pretend to understand Rose."

It would have been surprising if she had. Fortunately perhaps for her, Sophie Piddock was neither imaginative nor emotional, and in the whole course of her thirty years she had never felt anything like the excitement either of rage or delight which Rose brought daily to what from a grown-up standpoint were the trivialities of life.

Lucie followed her sister to "the doll's house room," a tiny apartment unused except by the children, and containing only a trestle table upon which stood the toy beloved by Rose when certain moods were in the ascendant beyond all other treasures. It had been specially made for the little Cottinghams after a design dictated by their father's aunt, an elderly spinster who had loved him, and till her death, a year previously, sent annual Christmas presents to his children.

In appearance it was like a modern top flat, with the roof taken off, all the rooms side by side in a long line. But here the modern semblance ended, for the residence was frankly mid-Victorian, and its inmates wore the dress fashionable in Miss Grace Cottingham's youth. "Mamma" and all the servants were crinolined, their useless legs dangling somewhere half-way up their skirts, upon the hems of which they could be made to walk with grace and ease, and in safety left standing without other support. "Papa" was a difficulty, because unfortunately destitute of crinoline, he had always to be propped in front of a chair or leaned against the wall, where, with his glazed hat glued on a little crookedly, he presented an abject and slightly drunken appearance. The children, too, were troublesome, owing to their short frocks; but wire ingeniously twisted round their ankles enabled them, though in somewhat unsteady attitudes, to stand alone, and by the same device "Tommy," the only boy, assumed without extraneous aid a more or less upright position, seriously hampered though he was by a wooden hoop permanently attached by a loop of wire to his right hand.

This hoop he bowled incessantly in the garden which led out of the dolls' house drawing-room—an ingenious garden which appealed to all that was romantic in Rose, to all her love of fantasy. In her eyes that "garden" less then eighteen inches square was one of the loveliest things on earth. It ranked with the "dell" of her abortive dreams. An archway cut in the gold-and-white-papered drawing-room, and framed by lace curtains, gave access to this miniature pleasance which was bounded by a rustic fence and turfed with green baize, in whose midst a round pond of glass, with a swan for ever swimming on it, was skilfully inserted. But the wonders did not end here, for at the bottom of the garden was a little white bench in an arbour made of tiny jessamine flowers, and against the surrounding fence, minute realistic bushes and shrubs were trained. For the rest of the dolls' house she did not greatly care, but the garden never failed to give her a thrill of delight.

The moment Lucie opened the door she saw that Rose was completely absorbed in arrangement for some new and unusual game, and, full of pleasurable anticipation she dragged up a chair beside her and prepared to be amused. Lucie did little more than listen on these occasions, while Rose did the talking for the family, accompanied by running explanations of the next move in the drama.

"What are you going to play?" she asked. "Why have you got out the fairy doll? I thought you said it was no good putting her into the dolls' house because she's dressed all wrong for a real person?"

"Yes, but I've thought of a splendid game!" Rose exclaimed, gulping in her excitement. "It's such a pity to waste the fairy just because she's not dressed properly for the dolls' house. And, of course, she's perfectly lovely, isn't she? Sarah always chooses such heavenly things, and it was awfully nice of her to buy her for us. . . . Well, let's pretend that the fairy lost her way and couldn't get back to fairyland before the gates closed. So in the night she came by mistake into this garden. Let's pretend it's night now. Quite dark, you know, and here's the fairy flying over the hedge. You see, she's got wings, so she *can*." The fairy was duly made to perform the aerial feat, and was finally settled on the rustic bench where her tarlatan frock completely filled the arbour. "Now," pursued Rose, her eyes glowing, "it's getting light, and she can see how perfectly beautiful it is in the garden, so she thinks she'll stay and be nice to all the family and perhaps take them to fairyland for a treat. She's thinking that now. You see? You can tell by her face. Then the Papa comes out into the garden before breakfast and catches sight of her. Where's the Papa? Oh, he's got into the kitchen by mistake! Bring him out, Lucie, and make him walk through the arch."

"Does he like her?" inquired Lucie, conscientiously walking the "Papa" through all the rooms before vouchsafing him a sight of the fairy.

"No, he's going to *hate* her! He was always a horrid man, you remember, he's got such ugly trousers. Now make him see her. That's right. Now make him rush across the grass to try to drive her away. Not through the pond, silly!" . . .

Lucie obediently removed "Papa" from the pond, and scuttled him round its edge, to the arbour.

"There isn't room for him," she objected. "The fairy's frock sticks out so."

"Never mind," said Rose. "We'll make her fly out to meet him. So! Now she raises her wand like this."

"She can't," declared Lucie. "It's *stuck* down."

"Well, pretend; it doesn't matter," Rose impatiently urged. "Now the Papa falls flat down. Make him do it. That's right. Now the fairy bends over him like this, and she says——"

The tumultuous opening of the door checked the fairy's speech to the recumbent "Papa," and instead, with more force than politeness, Rose addressed the intruder:

"Oh, Geoffrey, whatever have you come for? We don't want you. We're just playing a lovely game. Do go away!"

The boy on the threshold grinned amiably. He was used to Rose, and in spite of the joys of holidays, time was beginning to hang a little heavily on his hands.

"Let me play too," he suggested, the grin becoming mischievous. "What's that white maggot doing in the garden? Let's throw it out for the birds to eat!" Before Rose could intervene, he had snatched up the fairy and rushed with her to the window.

Rose was after him like a whirlwind.

"Give her to me!" she cried, her face crimson. "You're a horrid, disgusting boy. Always coming and spoiling everything. Give her to me at once! You're creasing her dress. You're squashing her!"

She beat Geoffrey's arm with her clenched fist, while Lucie, twisting round in her chair, watched the proceedings with interest.

"Say *please!*" laughed Geoffrey, holding the doll tantalizingly above Rose's head.

"I won't say please when it's my own fairy doll and you came and took her away!" screamed the child, incoherent with anger, as she continued to fight for her possession.

"Catch, Lucie!" cried Geoffrey, throwing the abominably treated fairy in her direction.

By a fluke Lucie caught the flying object, and Geoffrey pinioned Rose's wrists.

"Now, Miss Fury, I've a good mind not to tell you what I came for," he said, still laughing as Rose struggled. "And you'll be jolly sorry if I don't," he added significantly.

Rose suddenly ceased to wriggle.

"Not to take me back to Brook Hall?" she demanded breathlessly, her eyes all eagerness.

"Mother's sent the carriage for you."

"And may I go? Does Grandmamma say I may go?"

Geoffrey nodded. "I came up to tell you to get ready, only you flew at me like a little turkey-cock. Mother wanted Lucie to come too, but Mrs. Lester says it will be too much trouble for her to have both of you, so you're to come alone."

"Oh, Geoffrey!" Rose's face was all alight with

joy, her temper and its cause forgotten. "You don't mind, do you, Lucie?" she asked, suddenly mindful of her sister's possible disappointment.

Lucie shook her head. She was a placid child, and to her, neither Brook Hall, nor for that matter anything else of all the many things that so unreasonably excited Rose, caused her much perturbation either of joy or pain. Her mind relieved on this score, Rose rushed upstairs in the maddest spirits to find Miss Piddock packing a bag with her night clothes brush and comb, and other toilet necessaries, as well as her best frock and Prayer Book. Ten minutes later she and Geoffrey, snugly enclosed in the Winters' carriage, were driving towards Brook Hall. It rained persistently, but to Rose the landscape seen through the blurred windows, and in fact, the whole visible world was roseate because of this unlooked-for treat. She had been happy and miserable twenty times that day, as she would be happy and miserable during a countless number of days to follow.

Brook Hall was Rose's earthly paradise, and all the more entrancing because the way to it was difficult. Constitutionally reserved and unsociable, Mrs. Lester's relationship with the few neighbours her rigid notions of class distinctions made it possible to "know," was a formal one, and though, by comparison, the Winters were friends of hers, they were friends to be held somewhat at arms' length. She vaguely disapproved of Mrs. Winter as "advanced," and suspected her of cherishing absurd ideas. In this judgment, indeed, she did not stand alone, for the other county ladies also had their suspicions, based on the fact that Mrs. Winter spent two or three months of every year in London, where she saw the plays of Gilbert and Sullivan, bought fashionable hats, and returned with the latest books, which as every one who had not read them knew, were pernicious to the last degree.

That she should have taken a great fancy to Rose was more of an annoyance than a pleasure to Mrs. Lester, since it was calculated to create a closer tie than she desired between herself and any of her neighbours. As often, therefore, as courtesy permitted, she refused Mrs. Winter's frequent invitations to her little granddaughter, and incidentally strengthened the child's attachment to Brook Hall and its mistress. Rose adored Mrs. Winter, who supplied her with all the intellectual interest lacking in her own surroundings, and the rare visits to her friend's house were her chiefest joys.

Her hostess opened the door herself when the carriage drove up, and Rose rushed into the hall and sprang into her arms.

It was delightful to be hugged and kissed as though her presence were really welcome. It was more than delightful, it was the seventh heaven to have tea in the drawing-room later, close to a blazing wood fire. At home there were no fires, and though it was not really cold, Rose appreciated the luxury never indulged in at the Manor House, of something that was for ornament and not primarily for use.

She sat in her little low chair and ate her cake and drank really strong tea and looked about her in utter content. Mrs. Winter was opposite to her, ensconced in one corner of the sofa, while Geoffrey sprawled at the other end, leaning forward to the table occasionally to spread huge slices of bread with the jam that had been brought in for the children's benefit. Mother and son were curiously alike in colouring and features, but here the resemblance ended. The boy, well grown and tall for his age, with a shock of reddish fair hair and eyes blue and fearless, would make, one was assured, the fine, straight type of Englishman, of the unintellectual kind. Good at sports, capable in affairs, holding few opinions, but these doggedly, unambitious, knowing his limitations and untroubled by them, accepting them rather as blessings than grievances since "having brains must be an awful nuisance," Geoffrey was, in short, a nice boy, with nothing about him to discover. Rose liked him well enough, but considered him, in company with most of her world, rather dull. When he was not teasing her his school-boy facetiousness and clowning sometimes made her laugh, and for this she tolerated him.

His mother, on the other hand, stood to her for everything that was beautiful, wonderful, and interesting. Mrs. Winter was often amused and flattered by her obvious admiration. Oddly enough, with Rose, child as she was, she felt a mental kinship greater than any she had experienced since her marriage,—the people she met on her periodical visits to town not excepted. Some of these London men and women as she knew, had read much, and could talk fluently about what they read. Few of them had thought independently; still fewer had ever *felt* as she guessed this baby of nine had felt. In her own mind she predicted a future for Rose.

"One day I shall be proud to have known her," she said once to her husband, who laughed at her infatuation for "the ugly little Cottingham."

"I can't think what you see in her," he remarked.

"She doesn't seem to me to be so wonderfully clever.
She's an ordinary kid enough."

"'Wonderfully clever'? I don't quite know what
you mean by that. If you mean book-learning, you're
right," his wife returned. "She's very backward, as
you might expect with such a foolish governess as
she's got, poor child. But when you say she's ordinary, I *know* you're wrong, though I can't explain
why."

Mrs. Winter knew it would be useless to try. The
elder and the younger Geoffrey had characteristics in
common, and though she loved them both, she was
often as consciously bored with them as Rose was
unconsciously bored by her daily associates. She and
Rose were born talkers, and each in their respective
degrees suffered from the dearth of what in their
sense of the word was "conversation."

She looked across at Rose now and smiled, not as a
woman usually smiles at a child, but with quite a
sense of companionship, and a certain though vague
understanding. And Rose, returning the smile, reflected that certainly Mrs. Winter was the loveliest
creature in the world. Except in her eyes Mrs.
Winter had no claim even to ordinary prettiness,
though there was a certain charm about her which
excused the child's infatuation. She was a singularly
gracious woman, and this quality joined to a rather
pathetic delicacy of appearance, drew to her more
hearts than one. Always beautifully dressed, she had
a dainty, fragile appearance, which was attractive and
served her as well as beauty.

"Come and see my birds' eggs after tea," said
Geoffrey presently. "I've got some jolly new ones.
I meant to go birds'-nesting this afternoon, and then

this beastly rain came on, so I went to fetch you instead."

"I want to look at the books," returned Rose with decision, and Mrs. Winter smiled again in envy of her youthful disregard of masculine wishes which clashed with her own. She had spent much of her life in looking at things that did not amuse her, and in feigning interest in pursuits alien to her temperament, and had long since learned the lesson of compromise with most of the advantages on the other side. As a woman, Rose would learn it too, of course, but in the meantime she was glad of the holiday which in this respect life concedes to the child.

"Oh, you'll sit stewing over silly books all the time, I know!" grumbled Geoffrey.

"No, I shan't. I like birds' eggs too, but I like books best. Oh, Mrs. Winter, I can finish, *At the Back of the North Wind* now, can't I? I've been thinking about it ever since the last time I came. I do *wish* Grandmamma would let me take books home."

"Why won't she?" inquired Geoffrey, his mouth full of bread and jam.

"She says I'm so careless I should spoil them, and Miss Piddock says when I have a book I don't attend to lessons. But that's silly, because I don't, anyway, you know. Who *would* attend to lessons if they could help it?"

"I should jolly well think not," agreed Geoffrey with fervour. "But what rot! Fancy not being able to read a book if you want to. I'm jolly glad *I* don't live with Grandma!"

"I'm sure Mrs. Lester is still more glad. . . . And, in any case, you're not asked to criticize," put in his mother in the dry voice which the boy respected because she seldom employed it, and it meant rebuke.

Rose heard it too, with some surprise. Even Geoffrey, then, was not allowed *all* the privileges of grown-up people! She had always thought he was, and had envied him in consequence. In her experience, children existed on sufferance. When they were good and gave no trouble, they were at best tolerated, and if "treats" were accorded it was always with due reminder of the clemency of the bestower and the unworthiness of the recipient of such favours. But in Geoffrey's case matters were very different. He was an equal in the household, and an equal beloved and cherished, welcomed in his incomings and sped when he departed, tenderly on his way. Nothing at Brook Hall impressed Rose more than the atmosphere of love and comradeship which surrounded Geoffrey, who looked upon his mother and father as friends and knew nothing of scolding or punishment. She supposed it was because he was a boy. Girls, as she had long ago realized, were in Grandmamma's eyes at least (except when they were naughty), negligible quantities, and in spite of Mrs. Winter's assertion, she shrewdly guessed that if Geoffrey *did* live with Grandmamma he would at least be allowed, in virtue of his sex, many of the privileges denied to her.

Nevertheless her instinct told her that Mrs. Winter's rebuke was justified.

It was, of course, rude to "say things" about Grandmamma, and she hastened to change the subject.

"I wrote to Mr. George Macdonald about *The Princess and the Goblin*," she began, addressing her hostess.

"Did you?" asked Mrs. Winter with interest. "Why?"

"Because it says at the end of the book, ' Perhaps I will tell you more about the Princess one day,' or something like that. And I *did* want the book to go on, so I wrote to him and asked him to finish it."

Mrs. Winter laughed. "Well, has he replied?"

"No; Miss Piddock wouldn't let me send the letter. She said the writing was too bad, and she wouldn't tell me how to spell ' tremendously,' and she said he would only think me a rude, forward little girl. Do you think he would?"

"No," said Mrs. Winter. "But if Miss Piddock did, that was enough. People have different opinions, you know, and no doubt Miss Piddock thought she was right."

"I suppose so," agreed Rose, sighing. The conversation had recalled to her memory one more bitter disappointment. The beautiful story of *The Princess and the Goblin* had been her dream and inspiration for months. No tongue could tell of the glamour which it possessed for her, nor how at all hours of the day, but chiefly during Arithmetic, her mind was filled with the thought of that wonderful silver bath into which the Princess sank, dreaming of beauty beyond mortal ken; and of that mystic fire of roses which only the fairy godmother could touch unscathed; the fire which filled the air with fragrance and made all things clean and whole. And Mrs. Winter sighed too, her regret being for the author of the story as well as for the child and her uncompromising circumstances. She knew of nothing which in her own case would have pleased her better than that "bad writing" and "tremendously" spelt with delightful eccentricity.

Tea was over, and as she watched Rose run to the bookcase and seize upon the book she wanted, for the twentieth time she wished that the child were hers. Geoffrey had long ago outgrown the slight taste he ever had for anything which represented the magic, the glamour, the poetry of life, and that low shelf in the drawing-room contained the books he had left behind as "a lot of kids' nonsense." There was so much of "kids' nonsense" left in his mother, and Rose would have shared her ridiculous tastes.

VI

A PROJECT AND A NOTEBOOK

IT was beyond all dreams blissful to wake next morning in a pretty little room close to Mrs. Winter's bedroom, and to find the sun streaming through the flowered curtains, making the cut-glass ornaments on the dressing-table sparkle with the radiance of diamonds, and the hangings to her bed glow like the petals of a pink flower.

Rose fully appreciated the luxury of Brook Hall. The house itself, though no more stately than her own home, and of a similar Georgian design, was the house of wealthy people; and while everything at the Manor showed signs of wear and decay, all the appointments of Brook Hall indicated prosperity as a background to taste on the part of its owners.

Rose loved her gay little bedroom with the beautiful glass on the dressing-table, and the bathroom next to it with the new shining bath in which it was a pleasure to step, and the white shelves holding toilet-bottles and soaps of exquisite fragrance, and white folded towels.

The bathroom at home, though scrupulously clean, was shabby, and there was all the difference between bathing as a tiresome duty, and bathing like a princess.

She played the "princess" game all the time she was performing her toilet, and the crowning touch to the drama came when, according to the instructions of her hostess, she rang the bell for Kate, Mrs. Winter's maid, to do up her frock and tie the ribbon on her hair.

At breakfast-time there was cheerful conversation instead of silence broken only by the rustling of Grand-mamma's paper and Miss Piddock's low-voiced injunctions as to the proper handling of cups and the care required not to "make crumbs."

Geoffrey pleaded his inability to go to church because, though it was Sunday, his animals had to be fed just the same, and it would take longer with Rose "fussing round," and wanting to feed them too.

"How do you know Rose isn't pining to go to church?" demanded Mr. Winter, facetiously, as Rose of course understood. It was naturally incredible that any one should go to church willingly, but she suffered no alarm, for at Brook Hall, as it seemed to her at least, no one did anything that was distasteful.

"But I don't," she said, suffering Mr. Winter's affec-tation of astonishment politely, as part of the bore-dom one had to endure from the average grown-up person.

"Well then, we'll leave them to their godless ways, my dear," he remarked when he had been sufficiently "funny." His wife smiled, and Geoffrey, followed by Rose, rushed out into the garden together.

Here again, the contrast between the Manor House and Brook Hall was marked, and Rose was impressed and delighted by the flowers, of which there were so few at home. Daffodils, wallflowers, and hyacinths, masses of wonderful colour, filled borders, which later would be a riot of summer blossom, in a garden tended and cared for as only money made such care possible. But beautiful as it was, standing farther inland than the Manor House garden, it lacked the stretch of sea beyond, and Rose would not have parted from that sea for all the flowers possessed by the Winters.

Nevertheless, she wanted to look at them and smell them all, and only Geoffrey's impatience dragged her finally into the yard to see the rabbits, the guinea-pigs, the dogs, and the pony. Once there, she was again wild with delight. At home pets were not allowed, and, like most children, she loved animals.

While Geoffrey went to fetch green stuff for the rabbits, in an ecstasy of pleasure she stroked the noses of the babies through the bars of the hutch, and when on his return he took one of them out and gave it to her to hold, she could not contain her rapture.

"Oh, how soft he is! How lovely and soft!" she exclaimed. "Did you buy these little ones, Geoff?"

"No, of course not. I bought the doe."

"What is a doe?"

"Why, the mother of them. That one."

"Then she's married to Toodles? He's the father, isn't he? Who marries rabbits, Geoff?"

"I don't know," mumbled Geoffrey. Well versed himself in natural history, the idea of sharing his knowledge with a girl, would have shocked him, and he dreaded the next awkward question.

"I expect the pony married these," pursued Rose, turning round to regard "Charlie," who was looking over the half-door of the stable opposite to the hutches. "He's got a white front, and that does for the surplice. But who marries the rabbits in the woods?" she continued. "They must always be getting married because they have so many children. I never thought about that before. Who marries them, Geoff?"

"They don't get married," he returned desperately and very red in the face.

"But they *must* if they have children. Miss Piddock says no one who isn't married has children. I expect God marries the wild rabbits—don't you? And the fairies christen the baby ones. I'm sure they do!"

She thought neither of these things, but the idea presenting itself to her as one that might be elaborated into a story, she at once affected belief, to persuade herself into the acceptance of a new creed for the animal world.

"All rot about fairies," declared Geoffrey, relieved to find himself on safer ground.

"Well, why isn't it all rot about God?" retorted Rose. "You've never seen God and you've never seen fairies. But if you said it was all rot about God, you would be very wicked."

"That's different."

"Why?"

"There's the Bible to tell about Him."

"Well, there are fairy-books to tell about fairies."

"Yes, but they're only made up."

"How do you know the Bible isn't made up?"

"Don't be so silly! Of course it isn't."

"No, I suppose it isn't," agreed Rose slowly, conscious that she had been impious. "But I often wonder how people *know* it isn't. I asked Miss Piddock, and she said she was shocked at me. But then, Miss Piddock's shocked at anything."

"Old ginger-cat!" exclaimed Geoffrey easily, as he stuffed cabbage-leaves into the hutches.

"She's more *marmalade* than ginger. I put a slate pencil up one of her curls the other day when she was c'recting my dictation and it got caught, and she was in a frightful temper!" pursued Rose, with a reminiscent giggle of mirth.

"Did she tell Grandma?" In privacy Geoffrey always thus alluded to the stately lady, of whom he stood in awe.

"No. She's frightened of Grandmamma, you know."

"Jolly good thing for you!" declared Geoffrey significantly.

Rose spent a happy morning, trotting about under the boy's directions to fetch hay, straw, bran, greenstuff, and all the necessaries for a thorough spring-cleaning and rearrangement of the animal quarter. She was glad that Geoffrey did all the dirty work, for Rose was a fastidious young woman. It was only the decorative side of life that appealed to her, and though she loved the animals when they were clean and "tidy" the process by which this desirable condition was attained she was more than content to leave to Geoffrey, who seemed thoroughly to enjoy the occupation.

But at the back of her mind, all the time she was happily engaged in helping with the rabbits, there ran the thought of her projected literary effort, and the speculation as to whether there would be time or opportunity to-day for its fulfilment. Life at the Manor House was not suited to an authoress, and here, if ever, she must write her masterpiece. The opportunity came after luncheon, when Mrs. Winter went to her room to rest, and Geoffrey and his father started off on a business visit to the bailiff of another estate.

"Are you sure you can amuse yourself, dear?"

asked Mrs. Winter. "It's too long a walk for you to
Greenways, but you can sit in the garden and read
till tea-time if you think you won't be dull."

"Please may I have some paper and a pencil?"
asked Rose, with trembling eagerness. And Mrs.
Winter had no further doubts about the propriety of
leaving her guest for an hour or so to her own devices.

She asked no questions, but at once provided writing-
paper in the shape of an empty notebook, and with
this undreamed-of treasure and a pencil "that wouldn't
rub out," Rose fled to the summer-house and the
feverish joy of composition. Though for a child she
wrote quickly and with fair legibility, her hand could
not keep pace with the racing of her brain; but even
so, by the end of an hour many pages of the notebook
were filled with the fantastic history of Miss Piddock (flaringly disguised as "Miss Ginger") and of
the thrushes, who fortunately needed no disguise.
Inspiration, coinciding with the tiredness of her hand
gave out in time, but with the instinctive desire to
round off her story, Rose brought it to a conclusion
of a sort, though it was a hasty and careless one.

She threw down her pencil, and leaning back against
the knobbly rustic bench, looked at the spring garden,
with its haze of new green leaves and its flowers,
brilliant under the cloudless sky. The sunlight
poured full into the summer-house with the warmth
she loved, and for a few minutes she basked in it
like a happy little cat, rejoicing in mere physical
sensation.

Then suddenly and irrelevantly the thought of
death slid into her mind. Curiously enough, death
was never very far from Rose's consciousness, and
would come unbidden while she was playing with the

dolls' house, or sulking over her lessons, or running on the seashore, with a shock of premature realization which made her gasp in terror. It came now while the sunshine streamed upon her little brown hands and warmed her through and through, while she gazed at the delicious blue of the sky and let her eyes wander to the wallflowers and daffodils. She thought of a child in the village who was even now lying dead—Mrs. Goodwin's little girl at the toy shop—whom Sarah had known, and who, as Sarah had told her, was just Rose's own age, "Born on the same day, miss, and only ill on the Thursday and took on the Friday."

"Some day *I* shall be dead," she thought, with a horrible certainty of the truth. "And put in a coffin, like Maggie Goodwin, and then put deep down in the earth, where it's all cold and wet. And I shall never see the sun and the sea again. And never run, and never sit by the fire, and never read a book or pick primroses."

At the vivid picture she conjured up of herself, lying for ever in her coffin with the earth above her, a panic seized her, and she began to tremble as though the eternal chill held her already in its grasp. The torment grew. Her heart beat to suffocation, while her hands and feet grew cold. . . . A shadow fell between her and the sunshine which she no longer felt, and Mrs. Winter stepped suddenly into the summer-house, bringing with her a faint wave of the perfume she always used, and a gentle rustle of silk—an infinitely consoling, soothing presence! Even to Mrs. Winter, however, if Rose had been given time to control herself, she would not have divulged her imaginative terrors. There were reticences about her which went deeper than her surface-quick and passionate moods, and like older people, the child often used her volubility to disguise her real thoughts. But Mrs. Winter had surprised her in a moment of panic, and without reflection she grasped her arm convulsively as though for safety.

"Oh, Mrs. Winter, I can't die! Isn't there any way *not* to die?" she whispered, her voice breaking on the last words.

Mrs. Winter looked down in surprise at the child's white face and frightened eyes.

"But my dear Rose, you're not going to die!" she exclaimed, sitting down beside her, and laughing a little, reassuringly.

"But I shall some day. Every one dies, don't they? Oh! isn't there some way of stopping it?"

"My dear child, whatever has made you think of death?" Tenderly she put her arm round her and drew her close, speaking very gently. To her amazement Rose was shaking from head to foot.

"I don't know. I often do. Oh, I couldn't be put in the earth out of the sunshine. I *couldn't!*" Her voice was still panic-stricken and her eyes wide with terror.

Mrs. Winter paused a moment, feeling for words of reassurance.

"Child, *you* wouldn't be there! Nothing of you that knows or feels would be in the grave."

"You mean if I'm good I should be in heaven? My *soul* would be in heaven? But, Mrs. Winter, I don't want to go to heaven! I don't like the sound of it. It would be *awful*. And heaven never stops, does it? Oh, it's awful to think of for ever and for ever and for ever!"

"Don't try."

"But I can't help it. Sometimes I wake up in the
night and think about eternity."

Mrs. Winter suppressed a smile that was not wholly
of amusement, though "eternity" in the mouth of the
tiny creature beside her was incongruous enough to
provoke mirth if it had not been for the child's almost
terrifying seriousness.

"You see, I don't want to be good!" pursued Rose.
"I don't want even to try, because I don't like it.
I hate the *Peep of Day*, except to laugh about Satan.
I know it's wicked to laugh about him, but the *Peep
of Day* makes me. And I hate church, except when
they sing, 'O all ye stars of heaven, bless ye the
Lord.' I like that, but they don't often have it. Oh,
I do wish the Bible wasn't true, Mrs. Winter, because,
you see, you're *caught* anyhow, aren't you? If I don't
love God and if I laugh about Satan, I shall go first
into the grave, and then to hell, and *that* will go on for
ever and ever, just like heaven. And you've got to go
to one place or the other, whatever you do, so it's
awful, anyhow!" She poured out the trembling words
as though what they represented had been long pent up
in her mind. And indeed, as a dark cloud it had rested
there, in the background of her consciousness truly,
but there always, ready at moments to sweep forward
and blot out the sunshine. Not for the first time,
Mrs. Winter felt her mental kinship with the perplexed child. She too, had experienced the horror of an
inexorable creed alien to her nature from which as a
young thing she had seen no escape. But she had
been brought up in an atmosphere of gloomy piety,
which in Rose's case she knew to be non-existent.
"Religion" in Mrs. Lester's household was a more or
less perfunctory affair, not insisted upon with the

fervour born of a conviction that influences the conduct of life, but merely because church-going and Bible instruction formed part of the customary routine of respectable existence. She realized that Rose had grasped for herself the tremendous issues involved even in a colourless presentment of the faith of her fathers; in a way impossible to an unimaginative child, to whom that presentment would have been mere words, leaving but the very slightest impression.

Something must be said in comfort, but she hesitated to shatter too definitely the foundations of orthodox belief in a child who was not her own.

"You like," she began at last, for the moment ignoring Rose's mention of the eternal habitations—"you like the song that begins, 'O all ye works of the Lord, bless ye the Lord.' That's it, isn't it?"

Rose nodded.

"Well, there was a man called St. Francis who liked it too. He lived long ago, but that song of praise was written long, long even before he was born. St. Francis loved this world, and the sunshine and the flowers and the animals quite as much as you do; but he was quite happy about death, because he knew that to live with God who made the sun and the stars and the flowers would be better and more beautiful even than to live on this lovely earth. And he liked that song of praise so much that he put it into a new sort of poetry, in which he called the wind and the clouds his 'sisters.' And at the end he said, 'Praised be Thou, O Lord, by our sister the Death of the body, whom no living creature may avoid.' St. Francis didn't want to avoid it, you see, because he thought of the heaven that was to come, as an *interesting* place. Now, a poet's idea of heaven is more likely to be nearer the truth than the ideas of rather dull people, who can only imagine that it's a place where you sing hymns for ever. Don't you think so?"

"Yes. But it's only what people *think*, not what they *know*, is it?" said Rose. And again her grown-up friend felt a throb of sympathy.

"Then we must think the best and the most beautiful things," she returned. "If we do that, we shall at least be nearer to God who has made so many good and beautiful things. We must never think of graves and ugliness."

"But there's hell," objected Rose. "St. Francis was good, so he didn't have to think of hell."

"My dear child, neither need you," returned Mrs. Winter, suddenly, greatly daring. "There *is* no hell. That's only one of the dreadful ideas set about in the world by people who without knowing it, are insulting God. Put it out of your mind, and think of heaven, not as a *place* where you will stay for ever but as many new lives, where you will learn, and above all, be *interested*. It's dulness you hate, isn't it?"

Rose nodded vehemently, her eyes alight.

"Well, I'm sure you won't be dull in any of your lives," said Mrs. Winter, smiling at her.

The child hugged her passionately.

"Oh! I'm so *glad* you think like that!" she exclaimed. "I've often wondered whether every one believed things like in the *Peep of Day*. Things that always seem so silly to me. Now, *I* won't believe them any more. I never did, really. But I shan't tell Miss Piddock or *any one!*" she added, for which assurance Mrs. Winter offered up a modicum of silent thanks. . . . "Here's Geoff and Mr. Winter!" she exclaimed almost in the same breath, dashing out of the summer-house to meet them.

Mrs. Winter watched her as she rushed across the lawn, her brief skirt above her knees, her hair flying, her whole little body expressing nothing but the joy in mere animal existence; the worrying little mind for the moment at rest. She watched her with a smile that masked a lurking personal uneasiness.

It was strange that Rose should have chosen this day to talk of death, for to-day it had been in her own mind also, not as a horror but as a release, an infinitely blessed release, from something—a possibility—which she dreaded more than death. During her late visit to town, and unknown to her husband, she had consulted a Harley Street physician about symptoms that were troubling her. He had not been altogether reassuring, and she was under promise of returning to him in the course of a few weeks. Mrs. Winter felt herself turning cold and sick at the bare idea of what the second visit might portend, and then, scorning herself for nervous and probably groundless fears, she got up quickly to go into the house and order tea.

The exercise-book on the table arrested her attention as she moved, and, glad of any distraction from her thoughts, she picked it up and turned over the crumpled leaves. Her husband found her laughing, when a few minutes later, he strolled across the lawn to the summer-house.

"What's that?" he asked, knocking out his pipe.

"A literary effusion by Rose—a satire on Miss Piddock apparently. But it's really clever, Geoff!"

"You think everything that kid does is clever," observed Mr. Winter good-humouredly.

"But it *is*! The end's nonsense, because she got tired of it, I suppose, but the beginning is quite good. Just listen to this bit where 'Miss Ginger' is teaching the thrushes!"

"Oh, my dear, I shouldn't know whether it's what you call clever or not. It would just be a lot of rubbish to me. Tea's ready."

He strolled away, unconsciously leaving his wife as patiently impatient as she had been twenty times a day ever since the end of her honeymoon.

"I hope Rose will marry a man with some sort of understanding," was her half-wistful, half-humorous reflection as she regarded the fine manly figure of her retreating husband. It was that figure which as she now realized had induced her to become his wife, and she shrugged her shoulders with the oft-repeated self-assurance that "one can't expect to have everything." Nevertheless, it was just what as a girl she *had* expected, and she smiled at the folly of youth.

At tea-time, as she was glad to remark, Rose was in the wildest spirits, having apparently forgotten "eternity" as completely as her own philippic on Miss Piddock, abandoned with characteristic carelessness in the summer-house. It was Mrs. Winter who, when they were alone, reminded her of the master-piece.

"I think you'd better not take this home, Rose," she said primly, tapping the exercise-book which with an air of well-simulated displeasure she laid on the tea-table.

Rose blushed and hung her head.

"I took the liberty of reading it," continued Mrs. Winter, turning away to hide the amusement in her eyes, "and on the whole I should advise you to leave

the story with me.   It would be strange if Miss
Piddock appreciated it."

"Will you read me the thing you said you would?"
asked Rose meekly, without committing herself to
anything but an oblique reply; and Mrs. Winter
fetched a book from her room and read to her the
"Hymn of St. Francis to the Sun."

VII

ABSENCE AND RETURN

IT was a year and more before Rose went again to Brook Hall.

Mrs. Winter's second visit to the London specialist though inconclusive on the main point, to some extent allayed her worst fears. The doctor, however, spoke vaguely of "extreme delicacy," and advised her husband to take her for an indefinite period away from home. Her state of health, he stated, still vaguely, was such that the English climate could not fail still further to injure, and, in short, he advocated, in general terms, change of scene as well as change of air.

The house was therefore closed, Mrs. Winter and her husband disappeared into a gulf whose name to Rose was "abroad," and at holiday times Geoffrey joined his parents wherever "abroad" might happen to be.

Meanwhile life at the Manor House went on for Rose with its usual outward monotony and its chequered inward experiences, and she continued to be alternately bored, happy, wretched, excited, or mutinous several times a day.

Boredom, however, that malady popularly supposed to be the peculiar property of the adult, in reality known in its most acute stages to children insufficiently supplied with mental interests, was becoming an increasing factor of her existence. With the departure of Mrs. Winter she had lost the only

person who ever troubled to consider her as a creature
with a mind as well as a body, or to realize that this
mind needed interest and stimulation. No one ever
talked to her about anything but the material concerns of every day, Miss Piddock from incapacity and
dearth of ideas, her grandmother from lack of interest
in feminine creatures, as well as from inability, in any
case, to bridge the gulf between her own fine if narrow
intellect and the mind of a child. There were few
books in the house that Rose cared to read. Those
given her by Mrs. Winter she knew almost by heart,
and the rows of dull-covered volumes in the library
were mostly on theological subjects and land-survey-
ing. The Lesters had never been reading folk, and
for the most part the books in the house were those
which no gentleman's library should be without, and
no gentleman ever reads.

The impulse which had led her to write, died down
after one flowering into satire, and for several years
was quiescent. She missed her friend terribly, and
even when the first poignant sense of desolation had
passed, she continued to miss, though unconsciously,
the stimulation of Brook Hall and all the interest
which it put into a life too narrow and monotonous
for a restless, clever child.

Mrs. Winter's departure was the occasion for her
first lesson in that dissimulation of feeling which every
wise woman practises as an exercise in self-control.
Instinctively she knew that her grandmother looked
upon her fondness for the lady at Brook Hall as a
ridiculous "infatuation" to be held in scorn, and a
lover's loyalty made her avoid, by an appearance of
unconcern, occasions for derogatory remarks about
the object of her devotion.

Mrs. Winter occasionally wrote to the child, and Rose lived for these letters, but surpassed herself in ingenuity in waylaying the postman so that she might receive them unknown to her grandmother and be spared the necessity of being asked in a sarcastic voice to "favour the company with Mrs. Winter's news."

One result of the last talk with her friend had been that Rose's former periodical terror of death ceased to trouble her.   Sunday after Sunday as she endured the enforced quietude of "church" she hugged to herself the reflection that she no longer believed what the vicar, Mr. Collins, nor any of the curates, believed and taught, "though they *were* grown up."   "Mrs. Winter doesn't think there's a hell," she told herself, "and I'm sure she's much cleverer than Mr. Collins. And I don't believe in it either, and what they say about heaven is all wrong too.   And yet they think themselves so grand!"   These secret and gleeful reflections would have been more satisfactory if about this time, and particularly in church, Rose had not begun to suffer from a curious phenomenon which even in after-life she was never able either to explain or to account for.   She would be sitting in the family pew between her grandmother and Miss Piddock, glancing wearily about the well-known church, when suddenly it would become unfamiliar to her.   As she expressed it to herself, she saw it "all wrong."   The gallery, the organ, the choir, though she knew they were the objects upon which she gazed every Sunday, took on a strange aspect; the look of the whole church was "different," and her hands would grow damp and hot, and her forehead damp and cold with the panic thought that she was going mad.   Then presently, as suddenly as the new vision had come, it disappeared, and to her infinite relief, as she put it, she "saw right." The same thing occasionally happened with regard to the rooms at home, or even in respect to a well-known road or field, but the experience was more common in church, and Rose dreaded it beyond all the words which she could never utter on the subject. There was no one to whom she could have mentioned so *bizarre* a thing without being ridiculed for talking nonsense, and Rose did not willingly invite ridicule. Whatever was the explanation of an experience which passed away before her childhood was ended, she never forgot it, and, rightly or wrongly, in after-years the memory of it was a proof to her of the slender border-line which may divide the sane and normal, from the abnormal outlook on visible existence.

Her own outlook upon existence generally, then and for some year or two later, was not a satisfactory one from the point of view of healthy development. For a child of Rose's temperament to be bored meant mischief and trouble, and to the discerning, most of her increasing naughtiness was traceable to insufficient material for the needs of her nature. Intellectually and emotionally, she was starved, and her rebellion was the protest of the hungry.

Glimpses of a world outside her ken were afforded sometimes when Major Hawley, from Greenways, drove over to the Manor House for a chat with her grandmother, whom he very much admired as a "deucedly clever woman." He was a burly, red-faced, white-whiskered individual who talked in a loud voice about some mysterious thing called "politics," in which Grandmamma took great interest, though the meaning of what she said was as unintelligible to the child as though it had been uttered in Chinese.

One day when the Winters had been more than a year away from home, the Major drove over to the Manor House, and Rose, who passed the open door of the drawing-room on her way to join Miss Piddock and Lucie for the daily walk, was called in to shake hands with him.

"I hope you'll have as good a headpiece as your grandmother when you're a woman," he said, after the child's shy greeting.

"I hope she won't—though it's not saying much," returned Mrs. Lester dryly.

"Why not, madam? Why not?" pursued the Major, while Rose looked interestedly from one to the other. "Women will be in Parliament one day if we go on like this. They've got their colleges already, and they'll be beating the men all to fits before we know where we are." He laughed jovially.

"*Colleges!*" repeated Mrs. Lester on a note of scorn.

"You don't agree with them?"

"Perfectly ridiculous!"

"Why? Why do you speak so slightingly of your sex? You, for instance, would have made a splendid statesman." He still spoke jokingly, but Rose understood that there was more than a grain of seriousness in his remark.

"I have no ambition to unsex myself," said Mrs. Lester, drawing herself up.

"Ah, that's it! When you women begin to have ambition you'll carry all before you."

"And make the most ludicrous mess of things."

"Why, Grandmamma?" asked Rose unexpectedly. She was generally too shy to speak before visitors, but the conversation, imperfectly understood though it was, roused her curiosity and made her forget herself.

"Yes, '*why, Grandmamma?*' Listen to the younger generation!" exclaimed the Major, still laughing.

"The younger generation should be seen and not heard," said Mrs. Lester, enunciating a cherished principle. "Run away, Rose. Miss Piddock is waiting."

Rose obeyed, though not to the letter, and as she lingeringly closed the door, she heard the Major repeat, "That child's got brains," and her grandmother's reply, accompanied as she guessed by a shrug of the shoulders, "So you've said more than once before, and, as I always tell you, much good may they do her!" Gratification and anger struggled within her, but gratification won. It was as surprising as delightful to know what Major Hawley thought of her, in spite of her grandmother's depreciatory pendant to his remark.

"But then he doesn't know that I can't say my multiplication table!" she thought, by way of a chastening reminder to herself to avoid improper pride. She did not avoid it; the glow of happiness lasted all the morning, and though by the time she reached the beach she had forgotten its immediate cause, never had the secret games she played seemed so intoxicating, never had the sky been so blue, nor the air so soft and warm. It was low tide that day, the rocks were uncovered, and while Rose sprang from one green seaweed covered stone to another, unknown to Lucie, who followed at a distance, she was an enchanted princess with flowing hair, riding on her milk-white palfrey to a castle of romance. The milk-white palfrey's pace was accommodating, since it

did not prevent her from dabbling in the pools between the rocks and fishing out queer little objects
which she called "bird's-nests." They were round and
prickly and green—the abandoned homes of some sea
creature, and they smelt atrociously. Rose had a
collection of them filled with cotton-wool, previously
sprinkled with an execrable perfume bestowed by
Sarah with a view to neutralizing their natural odour.
A row of these treasures stood on the top of her chest
of drawers at home, with little white shells, called
"niggers' teeth" laid on the top of the cotton-wool to
represent eggs.

It was up to a point, a happy morning, for not only
did the enchanted princess in a retired corner of her
mind undergo the strangest adventures, but at one
and the same time she in her own character found
"bird's-nests" in abundance, and, greatest joy of all,
on climbing over some rocks close to the base of the cliff,
she and Lucie came across a heap of broken ginger-
beer bottles of red glass. These instantly became
jewels of inestimable value, a genie's treasure hoard
discovered by the princess, and Lucie was invited to
join in the building of a magic palace to be composed
entirely of rubies. The sunlight sparkled bravely on
the broken edges of the bottles, making them glow
like crimson fire, and to Rose, for ten minutes, the
fragments of glass were really jewels, and she herself
a feminine Aladdin in a magic cave. Miss Piddock,
who had been sitting under the cliff at a little distance
and now came up to give the signal for departure,
shattered the illusion as well as the palace by a well-
directed shove of her strong right foot.

"I won't have you playing with such rubbish,"
she declared. "Horrible ginger-beer bottles thrown

over the cliff from the inn! And dangerous, too, all that broken glass."

A fury of the most violent description on Rose's part followed her interference, and the homeward procession was a characteristic one after another of the many undignified battles between pupil and preceptress, when insolence was met with inept scolding, and disobedience by futile complaint. Miss Piddock, flushed and indignant, walked on with Lucie, while Rose, sulkily raging, followed with lagging steps.

The nearest way home lay by the sea wall, and here, where the blue-jerseyed fishermen lounged, Rose met a friend. He was rather a friend by proxy than a true acquaintance, for the children were not allowed to talk to the fisher-folk. But Geoffrey was on terms of intimacy with Rob,.a curly-haired giant who had once or twice "passed the time of day" with Rose when she happened to be with the boy; and on one blissful occasion, with after results that were less happy, she had watched his smack, the *Eliza Jane*, sail out at dawn from the harbour. He grinned as she passed him, and Rose, flattered by his notice, smiled shyly in return.

"Never bin to zee us go out again of a marnin', little missie!" he observed.

"No," said Rose, too embarrassed to volunteer further information.

"Got the young measter 'ome again, then!" continued Rob.

"Geoffrey?" stammered Rose.

"Aye. Young Measter Geoffrey from the Hall."

"No. He's away. And Mrs. Winter's away, too," she told him.

"Zeed un drive up to the 'All this very marnin'," declared Rob imperturbably.

Rose's eyes began to shine with delight that was half-incredulous.

"Are you *sure?*" she gasped.

"Sartin sure, missie. The Squire 'e stopped the carriage and spoke to me. An' so did th' young measter. Squire says: 'Th' missus *would* come 'ome, Rob. Couldn't satisfy 'er!' An' there she was, lookin' pleased enough, in the carriage."

It was circumstantial evidence, and when Miss Piddock, some way ahead, turned to beckon furiously, Rose rushed like the wind to rejoin her, all her anger concerning the ruby ginger-beer bottles forgotten in her amazing joy.

"Grandmamma doesn't know, I'm sure!" was her rapid thought, "and I mustn't say a word about it, because she'll find out that I've been talking to Rob. I do *hope* Miss Piddock didn't see me stopping to speak to him."

Miss Piddock, providentially blind as a bat, had *not* seen, and was at a loss to account for the miraculous change of temper in her refractory pupil. Sullen rudeness had given place to spirits so wild and gay that the stiff demeanour of Miss Piddock was powerless to withstand them. Rose simply paid no attention to her offended air, and continued to talk and laugh like a mad thing. She had indeed now "something to look forward to." This was always the restless craving of her nature, asserting itself every morning when she woke, and, if unsatisfied, plunging her into the depths of gloomy boredom. There was no boredom now, for not only was there joy in prospect, but the possession of knowledge unshared by her grandmother filled her with excited glee.

She could scarcely prevent herself from laughing

when Mrs. Lester came into the schoolroom towards evening, an open note in her hand.

"The Winters are back again," she announced, speaking to Miss Piddock. "I didn't expect them so soon; but it seems they arrived this morning."

"Really?" ejaculated Miss Piddock, confused at being addressed by her employer upon any but necessary topics, but realizing that even Mrs. Lester was stirred by an event so important in a neighbourhood of few happenings.

Her polite little tribute to the news was swamped in Rose's unrestrained shout of "*Grandmamma !*" The cry was to some extent acting, necessary acting, but a trifle overdone, and Mrs. Lester glanced with displeasure at the child's quivering face. Despite her previous knowledge of the event, Rose's heart was beating fast with the absolute assurance of its truth.

"There's no occasion to behave like an actress," said Mrs. Lester chillingly, filling Rose with apprehension by her choice of term. Her granddaughter's occasional display of emotion was distasteful to her, and any appearance of "gush" roused her scorn.

"Mrs. Winter asks you to tea to-morrow," she went on. "Is there any reason why Rose should not go, Miss Piddock? Have you any complaint to make about her conduct lately?"

Rose drew in her breath, reminiscences of ginger-beer bottles and heated language recurring to her; but Miss Piddock held her peace, and she could almost have hugged her.

This impulse received a check when after Mrs. Lester's departure her governess remarked irritably: "You don't deserve it, you know, and I was in a good mind to tell your Grandmamma of your disgraceful behaviour this morning, and yesterday when you spilled the ink and were so rude about it, and the day before over your arithmetic."

"She'll do something or other naughty before the afternoon, and not be allowed to go, won't she, Miss Piddock?" remarked Lucie, with sinister quiet.

There had been a feud since tea-time between the sisters, Lucie's complaints as to the awful smell of the "bird's-nests" on the chest of drawers having led to their condemnation and ultimate destruction.

"Little sneak!" muttered Rose wrathfully. "You never do anything yourself because you daren't! I wouldn't be such a tame little caterpillar as you for all the world!"

"Caterpillars turn into beautiful butterflies," declared Lucie, with unusual quickness of repartee.

"They often turn into horrible moths—disgusting things with fluff that comes off," retorted Rose, with a shiver of aversion. "And that's what *you'll* turn into, if you turn at all! But I expect you'll just be a crawling caterpillar all your life."

But she was too happy to continue the quarrel with Lucie, and the evening ended in a radiant peace.

VIII

QUAYLE COLLEGE

IT was only for a few months that the Winters were at home. At the approach of autumn they went to the south of France, and later to Egypt, urged to travel not so much by the advice of doctors, who disagreed maddeningly about the nature of Mrs. Winter's illness, as by the terrible restlessness of Mrs. Winter herself—one symptom of the as yet unnamed malady which slowly but surely was sapping her life.

At first her husband shared these pilgrimages in search of health, but later she went alone, joined sometimes in the holidays by Geoffrey. Thus during two following years it was only at rare intervals that Rose went to Brook Hall. But these brief glimpses of her grown-up friend shone like stars in her memory, and when one brief visit was over she lived for the next.

It was Mrs. Winter who, for her, first lifted the names of countries, towns, rivers, and mountains out of the dull "jography" book into the region of romance. From a long pink boot on a map, Italy became a fairyland of fireflies and olive groves, of blue hills with little huddled towns on their summits, of roses and grapes and lovely pictures displayed in photographs by Mrs. Winter, who possessed the gift of picturesque description and knew how to appeal to the child's love of colour and of sunshine.

Egypt, too, became more than a name to her when a vision was evoked of its mighty river, its great shining stars in the night sky, the pyramids, and, above all, the sphinx, that strange monster, half-woman, half-beast which stirred her imagination and raised her insatiable curiosity.

Mrs. Winter often sighed over Rose, with her so tractable, so easy to manage, at home ungovernable, insolent, and disobedient. Miss Piddock, she learned, had several times screwed up her courage to an attempted resignation of duties which included the teaching and supervision of such an incurably naughty child, only to be practically coerced by Mrs. Lester, who hated change, into "trying it again." Mrs. Winter grieved over the mismanagement, the futile methods of Rose's training, and still more over the effects they were producing on the child herself in the ruining of her temper, the deterioration of her manners, and the sullen bitterness they were engendering, effects of which, though never displayed towards herself, she clearly recognized the existence in Rose's demeanour towards home and home influences. The child's only salvation, she felt, lay in her removal from an unfortunate environment, and without daring to suggest the solution, she longed for the moment when Rose's grandmother would be compelled to send her to school.

By the irony of fate it was Mrs. Winter herself who, when that time came, was instrumental in sending Rose to the last place she would have chosen for a child of her temperament, a child, moreover, almost as dear to her as her own.

It was no fault of Rose's, but rather Mrs. Lester's prejudices against boarding schools in general, that deferred the academic episode in her granddaughter's career. Troublesome as she continued to be, it was not till she had passed her twelfth birthday that her grandmother unwillingly recognized the inadequacy of Miss Piddock's instruction, at least for Rose, and then her lack of knowledge with regard to educational matters led her to the hurried selection of a scholastic *milieu.*

One afternoon early in September of that year she called at Brook Hall.

Mrs. Winter, whose health latterly seemed greatly improved, had been two months at home, and was talking of spending the winter there.

She was gardening when her visitor was announced, and she entered the drawing-room at one of the long French windows, pulling off her gardening gloves as she came.

In spite of all the cheerful accounts she had heard, Mrs. Lester was struck by the delicacy of her appearance. She had grown much thinner, there were hollows in her cheeks, and her blue eyes looked rather unnaturally large and brilliant.

"I hope you're taking care of yourself," she remarked, as she shook hands with her hostess. "Are you going away this winter?"

"Oh dear no, I hope not! It's so nice to be home again. I really *couldn't* go away." She laughed deprecatingly. "I'm so much better, you know. All the doctors are encouraging, and I feel a new creature."

Mrs. Lester held her peace and after some preliminary small talk the object of her visit was approached.

"A school for Rose? Oh, I'm glad you're going to send Rose to school!" exclaimed Mrs. Winter, with rather too much conviction in her eager voice.

"Why?" asked her guest disconcertingly, and Mrs. Winter saw she must proceed with caution.

"Well, she is such a clever child that it seems a pity—" she hesitated.

"That she shouldn't get her head stuffed with modern notions?" put in Mrs. Lester with a grim smile, and though more amused than annoyed, her hostess flushed, fully aware of the inflexible old lady's opinion of her, and conscious of the oblique thrust.

With a sort of grudging admiration she regarded her visitor. Mrs. Lester always seemed to her a fine but rather terrible example of the old school. Her stiff erectness of carriage was, one felt, the direct outcome of the age of backboards. Tall, thin, imposing in figure, her face was still beautiful in a severe, haughty fashion, and her hair, white and silky, drawn up from her forehead in Pompadour style, accentuated the stateliness of her appearance while it intensified the hardness of her features. A woman of character, one might not doubt, she thought, but a narrow, immovable woman, of the type capable of great deeds, but chary of the smaller mercies.

"But all notions were modern once," she ventured mildly. "And one can't put the clock back, can one? It might stop the works."

"The works *want* stopping," declared Mrs. Lester, "when women try to step out of their proper sphere and begin to talk the arrant nonsense which I hear some of them are talking now. Not that I concern myself much with their vagaries. But that's not the point," she added briskly. "I'm sending Rose to school because she wants more discipline than governesses seem able to bestow. Miss Piddock is going, and I shall engage a French woman for Lucie. It's time she spoke the language. Meanwhile I want to hear of a suitable establishment for her sister, and I thought as you move more in the world than I do, you might perhaps help me."

The graciousness of her smile was mingled with a certain superciliousness, which in spite of her irritation amused the younger woman. She knew that Mrs. Lester considered her not only a gadabout, but one of those slightly ludicrous females who meddle with matters too high for their understanding. "And the absurdity of it is that the woman has brains herself," was the subcurrent of Mrs. Winter's reflections. "If she were twenty-five now, instead of sixty-five, she'd be leading the Woman's Movement, not trying to retard it."

Aloud she said: "I'm afraid I don't know very much about girls' schools. That comes of having one's only child a boy, you see. Of course there's Miss Quayle's," she added. "But every one knows of Miss Quayle."

"I don't. Who and what is she?"

"Well, I know nothing of her **personally**. My nieces go to the college, but I see them very seldom, so I haven't heard what they or their parents think of it. I only know that the lady has a great reputation in the London scholastic world."

Mrs. Lester made a mental note of the nieces in question. Ignorant of the democratic nature of Quayle College, she assumed that, if Major Kenway's girls were pupils, the establishment must be run on lines satisfactorily select.

"I'll write to my sister-in-law for particulars if you wish," suggested Mrs. Winter after a pause.

"That will be very kind of you. I want to send Rose away almost at once, and I believe the autumn term, or whatever they call it in schools, begins some time this month, doesn't it?"

"Yes." Mrs. Winter hesitated. "Don't think me impertinent if I beg you not to be in too great a hurry about making a choice," she said at last deprecatingly. "Rose is a queer little person, and it does seem to me so important that she shouldn't get into the wrong atmosphere. She's so clever that——"

"You seem to be curiously impressed with the idea of her 'cleverness,'" put in Mrs. Lester with one of her wry smiles. "The notion isn't borne out by her governess's verdict."

Mrs. Lester with difficulty refrained from a comment uncomplimentary to Miss Piddock.

"I wasn't speaking of book-learning exactly," she returned. "I was thinking more of the *quality* of the child's brain. She *thinks*—and do you know she writes quite cleverly?" she added, turning a laughing face to her visitor.

"I only know she's very troublesome, and very plain," answered Mrs. Lester, smiling again grimly, with complete indifference to her granddaughter's claim to literary achievement.

"What a shame!" exclaimed Rose's friend in animated defence. "*I* don't think she's plain at all. She has a beautiful little figure, and really lovely eyes."

"And that's all even such a flatterer as you can say with truth," declared Mrs. Lester, rising.

"Well, it's a good deal. If I thought you believe all you say about women, I—well, I should be quite angry!" she broke off to declare. "But I'm sure you don't," she went on unveraciously. "You are too clever yourself to undervalue brains in our sex."

"My dear Mrs. Winter," her guest interrupted in

her clear, incisive voice. "Such cleverness as I have, or *had*, lies in the right direction for a woman. I could have managed a socially important house. I might in certain ways have helped a clever man. I might—" she broke off abruptly. "I maintain that unless she marries, a woman need not exist. And what do men care for in women except beauty? They may talk a lot of high falutin nonsense at times, but that's what it means, and the rest is all—fiddlesticks! Rose has no beauty, and, therefore, even granting her the brains of which I have seen no evidence, her chances in life are small. It's a pity to decrease them by encouraging 'cleverness.'"

Disregarding her hostess's exclamation of protest, she moved towards the door, her old-fashioned yet dignified silk gown rustling, and the long veil she wore over her bonnet streaming in the wind. Followed by Mrs. Winter, she reached the portico before which the carriage was waiting.

"How is Geoffrey?" she turned to ask with a smile, good breeding triumphing over the note of acrimony upon which she was unwilling to take leave.

"Very well. He's away on a visit to one of his schoolfellows just now, but he'll be home for a fortnight before he goes back to Rugby, and no doubt you'll see much of him. He's very fond of Rose, you know."

"I can't think what they have in common," remarked Mrs. Lester, who admired the good-looking boy.

"Nothing at all, I think. Rose has all the brains." She smiled, insisting on the point. "Poor old Geoffrey will never be brilliant. But he's a dear boy," she added fervently.

"It's a pity they can't change places. Rose is anything but a dear girl. . . . You won't forget to make the inquiries you kindly suggested?"

Mrs. Winter watched her drive away, sitting erect, with queenly dignity, in the shabby carriage.

"Poor woman!" she found herself repeating with real pity for all the bitterness she divined in a lonely, disappointed life. "Poor little Rose!" she added, with a sigh of even deeper feeling.

Two or three days later she wrote to Mrs. Lester, enclosing prospectuses, but again advising caution.

"Wouldn't it be better," she urged, "to wait a little while? I shall be going to town before Christmas, and I will gladly call at Miss Quayle's boarding-house and give you my impressions."

Mrs. Lester ignored the suggestion. She was a woman who acted promptly, and having made up her mind to send Rose to school, she saw no reason for delay. Even though the fees at the boarding-house in connection with the college were higher than she had anticipated, she consoled herself by the reflection that the place was presumably "select." Mrs. Lester's little item of information concerning her nieces carried the day, and a fortnight later Rose became an inmate of Minerva House.

IX

A DEPRESSING RECEPTION

THUS almost fortuitously, Rose was hurried from the sheltered backwater of existence represented by Glencove, into the midst of what thirty years or so ago was the main stream of that intellectual activity practised on the young in the person of Miss Quayle. She was the type of woman in those days characterized as "strong-minded"—a pioneer, a breaker of traditions, a woman of indomitable will, inexhaustible energy, and ungovernable temper. In the educational world she was paramount. Her efforts had revolutionized the whole system of education for girls, and the huge Grammar School she established in the sixties, had become the prototype for other schools of a like nature throughout the kingdom. By the time Rose came under her dominion, Miss Quayle was past sixty, and her nature, originally overbearing and masterful enough, had been strengthened on these lines by forty years of adulation from her colleagues. In the educational world, possibly the narrowest and most limited of all worlds, Miss Quayle was a goddess —and a goddess to be propitiated. Her votaries adored, certainly, but they trembled at her nod.

Rose first beheld the awe-inspiring little woman late on the evening of her arrival at Minerva House. She had travelled to London with Miss Piddock, who had been requested to make it convenient for her own departure to coincide with that of her pupil, and, fur-

thermore, to deposit the child safely at the scholastic
portals.   During the whole of the journey Rose had
scarcely spoken, overwhelmed as she was with excitement, trepidation, and awe.

She was really going to school at last!   The goal
was reached.   Life, in the sense of the word, was
beginning, and for the moment, at least, she had no
regrets for the home she was leaving.   The improvement in Mrs. Winter's health proved to be only a
temporary rally from her usual condition of semi-
invalidism, and she was already making preparations for another winter season in Egypt.   Even from
the point of view of seeing her friend, therefore, as
Rose philosophically reflected, she might just as well
be in London as at Glencove.   Meanwhile there was
the glorious future to anticipate.   While in one
corner of the carriage Miss Piddock dozed, and at
intervals fidgeted with the hand-luggage, Rose, at
the end farthest removed from her, gazed out of the
window, apparently absorbed in the scenery, but in
reality engaged in piecing together every scrap of
information she had been able to glean from her
always uncommunicative grandmother.   She knew
at least, that at Minerva House, her destination, she
would be one of thirty girls who boarded with Miss
Quayle, and every day went to and fro to the college
for "lessons."   Beyond that fact definite information
ceased, and the rest was merely enthralling speculation which engrossed her for hours, making her
almost indifferent to the sandwiches and milk which
Miss Piddock presently unpacked, and blinding her
even to the new scenery through which she was
passing.

She noticed at last, however, that it was getting

uglier and uglier. Brickfields came into sight on the edges of dreary waste-grounds. Dilapidated, dingy houses grew more frequent, till there were rows and rows of them, with washing flapping in back yards, and untidy women carrying pails, and children seated on rickety fences, shouting and waving to the train in the gathering twilight.

"We're getting near London," remarked Miss Piddock, breaking a long silence.

"It's very ugly," said Rose, struggling with depression.

"These are only the suburbs. But it's *all* dirty and ugly," Miss Piddock assured her. "I wouldn't live in London for anything!"

"Well, I'm going to," returned Rose, trying to be gay.

"Yes; and you'll be longing to get back to Glencove before many weeks are past," declared Miss Piddock, darkly prophetic. "Then you'll wish you'd been a better girl, and think how well-off you were at home with Lucie and me and your Grandmamma."

She spoke with some acrimony. Not only did she consider Rose a heartless child, but she was fully aware that had her elder pupil been more amenable, she herself would not now be seeking another situation, with all the attendant anxieties involved in the process. In normal circumstances a spirited if impertinent rejoinder would have been the result of her somewhat tactless reproach. As it was, a cloud of still deeper dejection fell suddenly upon Rose. She made no reply, and the lights which now at a thousand points began to appear in the fast-falling darkness became magnified and starry, seen through the tears which she would not let fall.

Sophie Piddock was also depressed. That night she was going to a Home for Governesses, and on the morrow she would begin a search for work which in a dull, apathetic, weary fashion she hated—the work she must continue till all semblance of youth was past. And then? Fortunately, Miss Piddock's imagination was not vivid, but even without that aid to misery she was sufficiently low-spirited to have roused in Rose—if she had been ten years older—a very passion of sympathy.

Out of the big lighted station the unhappy pair drove at last in a four-wheeler, a strange, interesting vehicle to Rose's untravelled and dazzled eyes. She had stood helplessly bewildered on the platform while Miss Piddock, with injunctions to her to guard the handbags and not to move, ran about collecting luggage, depositing her own in the cloakroom, and afterwards superintending the hoisting of Rose's box on to the top of the cab. For the first time Rose marvelled at Miss Piddock. It seemed to her little short of miraculous that she should know what to do in the midst of all the strange, unaccustomed noises, the bustle and confusion, the jostling and shouting by which she herself was so stunned and bemused.

It was a blessed relief to creep into the darkness of the cab, and with no sense of responsibility to listen to Miss Piddock's directions to the red-faced cabman.

There followed what seemed to her an interminable drive through streets crowded and brilliant at first, gradually growing quieter and darker, till Miss Piddock, leaning forward to look at the name painted on a curving wall under a lamp-post, remarked: "Here's the road."

It was then that Rose's heart began to sink to the

lowest depths, and involuntarily she slipped her hand under her governess's arm.

Miss Piddock glanced down at her in surprise. Rose was consistent in her dislikes, and never before had she received a voluntary caress from her pupil. Looking at the child's white face and trembling lips, she experienced a little stir of compunction and sympathy. Some vague instinct told her that if she had only known how to manage Rose, their relations might have been happier—at least, less difficult. Tears sprang suddenly to her eyes.

As the cab stopped she stooped and gently kissed her.

"Good-bye, dear. I expect you'll be very happy when you get used to it," she said, with a praiseworthy effort to be cheerful. "I won't come in. There! The door's open. Run up. The man will see to the luggage."

Rose returned her kiss, and in her turn felt surprised at her own insane desire to cling to Miss Piddock. She was at any rate, the one link that bound her to the known, the proved, the familiar, and as she went slowly up the flight of steps to the house which loomed dark and mysterious above the square of light from the open door, a terrible sense of loneliness and desertion engulfed her.

For a moment she stood irresolute and miserable on the threshold, ignored by the maid who admitted her, while her luggage was brought in and carried by other servants to some region unknown.

At last, when the red-faced cabman had shuffled down the steps, the housemaid turned to the child and spoke kindly.

"You're the new young lady, I suppose? Isn't

there any one with you?" she asked in surprise, with a glance out into the darkness towards the retreating cab.

"No. I mean yes. Miss Piddock brought me, but she wouldn't come in," stammered Rose.

"Well, Madam's at supper. I'm sure *I* don't know whether to go in?" The appeal was made to another servant who crossed the hall at the moment, and was received by a shrug of the shoulders and a slight grin.

"Chance it," she murmured.

"You'd better come into the drawing-room a minute," observed the first maid, turning again to Rose and opening a door. "All very well to say chance it," she grumbled over her shoulder to the other young woman. You never know what may 'appen!" She turned up the gas as she spoke, and hurried out, leaving Rose puzzled by the dialogue and for a moment rather curious, till the sinking feeling of loneliness submerged every other sensation. This, then, was the longed-for school, so wonderful in anticipation, so awful in reality!

Standing where she had been left, just within the door, she looked drearily about the room. It was well furnished, but had she known the right word to apply to her impression, Rose would have called it "undistinguished." Involuntarily she thought of the drawing-room at home, which, despite its faded chintzes and dim carpet, gave her quite a different sensation— the result, though she was ignorant of its cause, of noble proportions, dignified old furniture, and the mellowness of ancient things. While she waited she became aware of an angry voice, low at first, but gradually gaining in volume and fierceness. Rose caught a word now and again, and gathered that some one was being soundly rated. There were murmured monosyllabic replies, cut short by the peremptory voice, and finally a shuffling of feet as the culprit slunk away. When the door of the drawing-room was at last flung wide open, Rose caught a glimpse of a retreating, depressed-looking little female, later to be identified as Miss Bird, the housekeeper and general factotum of the establishment.

For the moment, however, her attention was fixed upon Miss Quayle, whose tempestuous entrance into the room was characteristic. Miss Quayle never opened a door in ordinary fashion; she always flung it back, appearing on the threshold like a very small goddess of vengeance.

Very short, very stout, she yet carried her head in such regal fashion as to convey an impression of power and dominance quite awe-inspiring. It was a triumph of mind over matter, for Miss Quayle had none of the physical attributes of the amazon. Her round, rather pale face was plump and soft, her eyes, as Nature painted them, were softly blue, her features blunt and indeterminate. Yet fire constantly flashed from those mild-coloured eyes, and the round face, which, if it had worn a different expression, might have belonged to a gentle old lady accustomed to knitting by the fireside, was frequently quite terrible in its wrath.

Rose eyed her curiously, her glance travelling from the becoming cap of real lace covering Miss Quayle's snow-white hair to the ample folds of the handsome grey silk gown, which suggested a crinoline and surrounded rather than enveloped her naturally well-covered, erect little person. Miss Quayle's dress was as distinctive as her personality, and the child vaguely felt that she was in the presence of some one who *counted*—some one who was going to count tremendously.   She noticed the beautiful opal rings on the hand, tapering fingered, short, white, and plump, which her head mistress held out to her, and into which she hesitatingly put her own.   Some instinct of antagonism warned her that between her and this stout, dominating little lady, who reminded her of the postage-stamp likenesses of Queen Victoria, it was to be war to the knife.

"Now, my dear child, you're very late," was Miss Quayle's greeting, delivered in decisive, condemnatory tone.   "Why did your grandmother not choose an earlier train for you?"

"I don't know," returned Rose, resentful of the peremptory voice.   "Perhaps there wasn't one.   It's a long way from Glencove, you know."

"I'm fully aware of the fact," replied Miss Quayle crushingly, drawing herself up to her actually imposing height of five feet.   "And for that reason an earlier train should have been selected."   She measured the child with her eyes, and in her also, rose the obscure instinct of hostility.   She was going to be a "difficult" girl.   Almost unconsciously, Miss Quayle had grown to expect absolute submission, and Rose's voice warned her that she would have to fight for what was usually conceded from fear.

"The girls have almost finished supper," she went on after a moment, "so you'd better sit down with them as you are, and go afterwards to your room."

Rose followed her rustling skirts across the hall towards a door, from behind which rose a confused babel of noise and talk.   It was flung wide, and instantly silence fell upon the thirty girls seated at two long tables, one in each of two adjoining rooms set at right angles to one another, and so arranged as to be separated at need by folding doors. Dazzled by the light from chandeliers above the tables, Rose had a blurred vision of what seemed to her innumerable faces all turned in her direction before Miss Quayle spoke.

"Take your seats," she commanded, for at her entrance the girls had risen, and the company reseated itself with the same noise of chair-scraping which had arisen at their first movement.

"This is Rose Cottingham," she said, going up to the head of one table, where sat the little black-clothed creature of whom Rose had already caught a glimpse. "Where is she sleeping?"

"In the front top room," murmured Miss Bird nervously.

"Now my dear Miss Bird, those rooms are to be known by numbers. I have mentioned this before. Now which of them do you mean?"

"Number four," faltered Miss Bird, while all the girls within earshot listened with demure faces and secret delight.

"Kindly remember then, to give them their proper names. Please see that this child unpacks only what is necessary for to-night, and let her have her supper as quickly as possible. Prayers at nine o'clock."

She swept out of the room, and from the further end, after a prudent interval, the chatter once more arose with renewed vigour. It was subdued a little at Rose's table, by the presence of a newcomer, the preliminary process of staring, and the subsequent comments which were conducted in more or less audible whispers, of which the child was too bewildered to take heed. She was dimly conscious that the rooms, with their walls painted a dark green, and broken here and there by pictures, were neither bare nor uncomfortable, and that the table was carefully laid and looked bright and pleasant in the gaslight. According to the standard of schoolgirl welfare thirty years ago, Minerva House was a well-appointed place, and, as in Rose's case, at least, to children unaccustomed to much luxury at home, no serious physical discomforts were experienced there.

Mechanically she ate first soup, then milk pudding, and, finally, glad to escape the curious eyes surrounding her, followed Miss Bird to her distant bedroom, where her box stood open, ready for unpacking. There were three beds in the room, she noticed with apprehension, while she took off her hat and tried to put a comb through her tangled hair. Miss Bird pounced upon the outdoor things which Rose flung upon the bed.

"These must all be put tidily away," she warned her. "I hope you're not an untidy little girl? Untidiness is not allowed here."

The remark, Rose felt, was a herald of many coming troubles. She was an incurably untidy child.

A descent to the dining-room, where prayers were read beautifully by Miss Quayle in a voice grave, sonorous, stately, and free from the rancour it held in the habitual intercourse of every day, formed a prelude to the ordeal of undressing in a room with two strange girls. Talking in the bedrooms at night was as strictly forbidden at Minerva House as the mandate was light-heartedly disregarded. Rose's companions whispered and giggled to their heart's content, ignor-

ing the "new girl" as completely as only school
children can achieve the feat of the cut direct, and when
Miss Bird had hurried in, put out the gas, and hurried
out again, Rose cried herself to sleep. In fancy she
heard the waves lapping on the shore of Glencove
Bay, and the screaming of the gulls as they wheeled
above the little harbour where the brown-sailed
fishing boats lay, and the buoys bobbed up and down
in the green water.

X

ONE OF THE DRIVEN

AFTER what seemed ten minutes, and, in reality, was nearer ten hours, she was roused from this vision by the clanking of cans and the entrance of a maid who drew up the blinds.

"Quarter to seven!" she announced, and bustled out to take other cans of tepid water to the neighbouring rooms.

There were grunts and groans from the occupants of the two beds on the further side of the room, and finally one of the girls sat up, yawning, and looking in Rose's direction, met her sombre, unhappy eyes.

"I say, you'd better get up," was her brief remark, and a moment later she added, "What's your name?"

Rose murmured it, and slipped meekly out of bed.

"Don't take my washstand. That's yours nearest to the window," said the girl, later familiar as Kitty French. She turned in bed to shake her neighbour whom she addressed as Joan. The girls began to chatter, apparently oblivious of the child who stood shivering by the washstand dabbling in the half-cold water.

From time to time, when she was not blinded by tears, Rose glanced out of the window, standing on tiptoe to look over the half-curtain of muslin. The prospect without seemed to her to touch the depths of dreariness. Through a yellow fog not too thick to conceal it, she saw across the road a railway cutting

with a steep bank on the further side crested by a
row of houses, their narrow strips of garden blackened
and sodden by the autumn rains.   These gardens
sloped to the railway line.   Rose remembered the
noise of the trains in the night, and how every time
they had thundered past, they shook the room and
for a second wakened her.

As she put on her clothes she listened almost unconsciously to the other girls' talk.   They were big
girls of fifteen and sixteen, and to Rose they seemed
quite grown up.

"Perfectly awful coming back," grumbled Joan,
sponging her face in the intervals of her remarks.
"The Dragon seems to have begun the term in a worse
temper than usual, if that's possible.   Did you hear
her raving at the Bird last night?"   Both of them
laughed, and Rose was quick to catch the mythologi-
cal allusions.

"You'll see, it's going to be a term of rows,"
prophesied Kitty.   "I wonder who'll be the special
victim.   There's generally one picked out.   Last
term it was Janie Price, you remember.   She *lived*
in the Dragon's cave, and always came out sobbing
and howling, poor kid."

"It's the bear's hug afterwards that I can't stand,"
declared Joan.

"Oh, well, *you* needn't talk.   I believe you've only
been in about one row since you came.   You generally
manage to escape."

"One's enough," said Joan darkly.

"I say, don't put on your frock," she called to
Rose, who was slipping her blue serge skirt over her
head.   "Dressing-gowns for cally, you know."

Rose stared blankly.

"What's 'cally'?" she murmured.

"Calisthenics. The bell will ring in a minute."

It rang violently before she could finish the sentence, and with flurried exclamations she and Kitty struggled into the flannel gowns and rushed downstairs, leaving Rose to follow in bewilderment. The staircase when she emerged upon it, was filled with blue, scarlet, or brown-robed figures, and moving with the stream, she found herself presently in a big, empty room in the basement of the house, lighted by a half-glass door which led into a strip of garden.

Miss Bird, clad in a dressing-gown of crimson flannel, was waiting to receive the influx of girls who crowded into the room, jostling one another and chattering as they came.

"Silence! Stop talking!" she called, in a thin, hoarse voice. "Take your places."

They fell into line, and by some process which seemed to Rose exceedingly complicated, were presently drawn up in rows, each girl at some little distance from her neighbour.

"Who is that standing by the door?" demanded Miss Bird, screwing up her short-sighted eyes and peering in Rose's direction.

"The new girl," shouted half a dozen voices, after more than a dozen heads had been turned towards the little pink-clad figure.

"Come out here to the front, and imitate me," said Miss Bird, and in an agony of shyness, Rose obeyed.

"*Arms upward—stretch!*" called Miss Bird. A forest of arms were raised heavenwards, and for a quarter of an hour the drill which at Minerva House preceded the day's work, was continued. From the point of view of health, the ostensible reason for the exercises, it was a somewhat ludicrous performance, since most of the elder girls wore tightly laced corsets beneath their dressing-gowns. This fact, combined with exertion in a fasting condition, not infrequently resulted in faintness, a state of things which teachers as well as pupils conspired to keep from the principal. To faint from any cause whatever, was to Miss Quayle, the unpardonable sin, a feminine weakness relegated to the Dark Ages before the new era of Woman's Rights; a contemptible lapse from vigour to be mentioned with scorn and contumely.

While Rose swung her arms and twisted her neck about in imitation of Miss Bird, she regarded the lady with aversion. She was a mean-looking, rat-faced little woman, undersized and ill-proportioned, who as general factotum at the boarding-house, and scape-goat for all that went wrong on the domestic side of the house, led an unenviable existence. In her relationship to the girls, her *rôle* was that of watch-dog, and as a dog of mongrel type she was despised and generally detested. For some reason, possibly from false economy, Miss Quayle nearly always erred in her choice of subordinates, and Miss Bird, ignorant, irritating, and in slavish fear of her employer, was from every point of view a bad mistake. She was destined to be an evil factor in Rose's subsequent school life.

From time to time, tired of looking at the unpleasant leader of the exercises, her glance wandered to the square of garden visible through the glass door, where a poplar-tree dropped its yellow leaves slowly through the murky fog, and out of sheer depression her eyes filled with tears.

"Attend, Rose!" called Miss Bird sharply, just

before the futile fifteen minutes of whirling coloured sleeves, and legs which, hampered by folds of flannel, could not whirl, drew to an end. *"Right turn! March out!"*

A stampede to the bedrooms followed, where dresses were hastily put on before the prayer-bell necessitated a further rush to the dining-room, each girl standing then, behind her own chair at the table till Miss Quayle entered to read prayers.

After this devotional exercise, another ritual of a purely secular nature took its place. Stationed between the folding doors, a big register in her hand, Miss Bird read the roll-call, and on that first morning Rose was at a loss to understand the formula of the reply, which in every case was the same. *"Present. Not spoken,"* were the cryptic words uttered by each clear-eyed schoolgirl. It was only later that Rose understood the last assertion to refer to the rule of silence in the bedrooms, a guarantee, as Miss Quayle fondly imagined, of obedience to the regulation. As a matter of fact, every girl lied cheerfully. Minerva House bristled with vexatious rules, and this particular prohibition was literally honoured in the breach, even the most punctilious, thinking it no shame falsely to declare innocence. The names followed one another in alphabetical order, as Rose, dreading the mention of her own, soon discovered.

"Rose Cottingham!" called Miss Bird, and, crimson at the sound of her own trembling, scarcely audible voice, she replied as the other girls had done, *"Present. Not spoken."* The latter assertion made on that as well as every other subsequent morning for several years, was true. It was the one and only occasion of its veracity.

8

Breakfast over, Miss Bird pounced upon Rose as the sole newcomer that term.

"Your outdoor clothes are always kept downstairs. Come with me and I will show you your peg and boot-locker," she said, and as though moving in a dream amidst all her unfamiliar, bewildering surroundings, Rose followed to the cloakroom, and received hurried instructions to be ready in ten minutes to start for the college.

It was the sense of rush and hurry which for many days was to confuse and bewilder the child. Girls ran hither and thither calling to one another and shouting unintelligible remarks, while unnoticed and alone in her corner of the cloakroom she struggled to button her boots and to wriggle into her coat. Finally, some one addressed as Miss Mortlake rang a bell, called out "All ready, please!" and a two-and-two procession formed miraculously in the strip of garden and wound out of a side gate into the road.

Rose lingered behind, as lost as a stray dog amongst all the chattering girls, each of whom seemed to know by instinct with whom to walk. After seeing all the couples pass, as she herself waited at the cloakroom door for her flock to precede her, Miss Mortlake, the teacher, took her hand.

"You must be my walking partner to-day," she said kindly. "The girls choose their partners for the week. You'll know them all presently. I think you must be our youngest?" she went on, trying to make Rose talk. "How old are you?"

"Twelve," murmured Rose, and relapsed into silence, and in a sort of nightmare-dream she walked beside the tall thin teacher at the tail of the crocodile.

Miss Mortlake, who seemed to her incredibly aged,

was a lady of a possible forty-five, with a kind, worn, plain face lighted by rather beautiful eyes. She was a survival. Too old to have learned what were then modern methods, she filled a subordinate position at the college, taking odd classes and coaching backward children in elementary subjects. At Minerva House she exercised general supervision, sat in the room during the preparation of home-lessons, never had a moment that she could call her own, and was grateful for a roof over her head and enough to eat. Hers was a pathetic figure, in after years recognized by Rose as such, but at the time accepted as "one of the mistresses," and therefore a natural enemy. It was only at the college that "adorations" were rife. At Minerva House it was the fashion to detest every one in authority, and Miss Mortlake, who despite her kind heart, was prim, and from the girls' point of view annoyingly pious, was included in the proscribed list of "old cats." She tried to make conversation with the unhappy-looking little creature beside her, but misery had stricken Rose dumb, and the walk was almost a silent one. It lay for the most part through mean streets which under a murky sky, looked to Rose's country eyes inexpressibly dreary and hideous.

"Here we are," said Miss Mortlake at last, as the procession turned a corner and a large red-bricked building came into sight. A moment later Rose was within its portals, and had caught her first glimpse of surroundings soon to be familiar to her.

Quayle College was at that time the finest and most imposing of the new type of girls' school everywhere arising. The whole of its architectural design, with its large central hall for prayers and general assemblies, its vaulted roof and surrounding gallery upon which classrooms opened, its platform and its organ, has since been repeated in scores of educational institutions.   It was the type of building to be pre-eminently associated with the academic spirit, and from the moment she entered it, Rose never lost her detestation of plain, distempered walls, cold stone staircases, dadoes of pitch pine and of a certain yellow, painful in its crudeness, henceforth always connected in her mind with Swedish desks.   The atmosphere of the college affected her with a quite peculiar sense of depression, and in later years, whenever she entered any bare, crude building devoted to educational pursuits, she could have wept with the revived distaste induced by that first childish impression.   To her, Quayle College summed up all there was of dreariness, and though in time it was overlaid by the feverish interests of marks, examinations, and places in class, the unpleasing impression persisted as a subcurrent throughout her school existence.

Fresh from the uneventful quiet of her country home, Rose was confused and bewildered by the sight of the hundreds of girls who swarmed up and down the staircases, hurrying hither and thither, all engaged upon seemingly mysterious business which must be conducted in the utmost haste.

She was delivered over by Miss Mortlake to one of the preoccupied teachers who happened to be crossing the entrance hall, and by her, handed to some one else with the remark, "New girl. Examination in classroom ten, gallery floor."

Following this new guide through a labyrinth of passages, a sort of warren in which girls instead of rabbits scuttled and popped in and out of doors, she

was conducted to a peg in a cloakroom, told to remove
her hat and coat, and thence hurried back to the big
hall, already filled row after row with girls of all shapes
and sizes.

Miss Quayle, who invariably drove to the college in a
specially chartered four-wheeled cab of great respecta-
bility, presently ascended the platform, and in her
most august manner read prayers.   The organ pealed,
a hymn was sung, and at the word of command the
girls in their respective classes filed out of the hall.
Rose soon learned to appreciate the remark uttered by
a "Minervarite" on the evening of her first school day:
"We poor, wretched boarders, you see, get all the
beastly things twice over.   All the rules and rows of
the college, and all the prayers of both places!"

For the next five years, life was to bristle with rules
for her, and to be punctuated by prayers.

Her next clear impression was of a whitewashed
classroom lighted on the left by bleak windows with
pulleys.   Into this room were herded the new pupils
of the term, big and little, and to each girl was handed
by the teacher in charge a printed paper of questions
considered appropriate to her years.

Seated at one of the shiny wasp-yellow desks,
Rose glanced hopelessly at inquiries as to the mysterious transmutation of pounds into pence, on the rivers
and mountains of England, on the dates of kings,
and the use of the nominative.   She could offer only
a very few replies to the inquisitive sheet before her,
and again in her heart she execrated the teaching of
Miss Piddock.   The morning dragged to an end, and
was followed by the return walk to the boarding-house,
where at two o'clock dinner was served.   An hour's
recreation was allowed after the meal, before the

settling down to preparation of "home work." On
that first afternoon, with no lessons to prepare, Rose
spent the time in unpacking and arranging her
belongings, under the supervision of Miss Bird. At
nine o'clock, after supper and another prayerful
interlude, the first day closed. It was the preface
to a period of unalloyed misery to which every
possible circumstance contributed its measure of
woe. Rose, to whom "school" had seemed the
promised land, found herself despairingly homesick,
and that her yearning was for a place rather than the
people she had left, in no way lessened her suffering.

She was sick for the sight of the sea, for the sound of
it lapping on the stones of the shore, or swirling round
the wooden piles of the little harbour pier. She was
sick for a glimpse of the dark-bricked front of her
home and for the sunshine on the grass of its garden,
and for the voices of the birds in its trees. Night
after night she conjured up well-known scenes till
exhausted with her tears, she fell asleep. Morning
after morning in school hours she heard no word of a
lesson. In spirit she walked the lanes and woods
round Glencove, or stood by the murmuring sea, or
wandered through all the well-known rooms at home.
And through all her misery there ran a curious undercurrent of surprise. She had never guessed that she
would suffer like this. She did not know that a
feeling for the home of her fathers had entered into
her blood, was part of her, would never to her life's
end die.

Apart from the aching home-sickness, there was
worry and humiliation to harass her day by day, and
bitterness of spirit in the realization of Miss Piddock's
inadequate teaching. Rose was considered terribly

backward, but no judgment of her teachers on this score could equal her own despairing knowledge of the fact.   All the girls even of her own age seemed to her miracles of learning and advancement, an illusion to be presently dispelled certainly, but none the less terrifying while it lasted.

Then there were the girls themselves—those at Minerva House—for of the hundreds who swarmed at the college, Rose was too bewildered to regard as anything but a sort of ant-heap—there were these Minervarites, then, so unapproachable, so haughty, as it seemed to her, so engrossed in affairs in which she had no part.

Rose was the only new girl that autumn term, and it seemed to her ages before her very existence became recognized amongst them.   They were not actively unkind.   They simply ignored her.

In reality, hours being to an unhappy child what weeks are to the adult, it was only a few days before Rose knew every one's name, began to like some of her schoolfellows and to detest others, became conversant with all the most fashionable slang, knew and used all the nicknames bestowed on the teachers, and in short, had settled down to the life she was for five years to lead—a life as stormy, as full of periods of unhappiness, less fraught with moments of joy, but as compensation more interesting, than her previous existence.

Her first day at school heralded much that was to leave an ineffaceable mark upon her character, and indirectly to affect the course of her life.

Its importance lay in the fact that she had definitely reached "the modern movement"—that movement which arising in every generation, is escaped by some, though never by the girl of Rose's type. In any event, somehow, and even without propitious happenings, almost instinctively she would have drifted towards it. For good or evil she belonged by nature to the most swiftly moving current of life's stream, and even if she would, she could not have averted her fate.

As ever, good and evil followed; but it was certainly ill-luck that of the two strongest instincts in her nature—the need to rebel, and the need to love—it was the former which throughout her early girlhood was fostered, while the other, comparatively speaking, starved. In Miss Quayle she encountered a personality as potent to drive her to revolt as that she had discovered in her grandmother, though the two women differed as to their methods. Mrs. Lester represented the negative to Rose's positive, and Miss Quayle the driving force in directions alien to the girl's tastes and temperament. In place of Mrs. Lester's cold sarcasm and narrow prejudices, she encountered the furious temper and the insistent tyranny of Miss Quayle, who, liberal and advanced as were her theoretical views on the independence of womanhood, was a born slave-driver. Her effect upon Rose was the production of a curious blend of hatred, grudging admiration, contempt, and fear.

Even in later years, when she had learned to appreciate the indomitable spirit of the little woman, when she realized what it was not possible for a child to realize, the greatness of the fight she had made in the cause of her sex against ignorance, prejudice, apathy, and derision; when she came to appreciate her power for work, her genius for organization, even when she heard of and admitted to her credit, generous deeds unknown to her as a schoolgirl, Rose's memory of her head mistress remained true to her childish verdict. She never learned to love Miss Quayle. And there were some who undoubtedly loved her. She never even learned whole-heartedly to admire a woman who undoubtedly roused admiration.

XI

THE WRATH OF THE DRAGON

BEFORE the end of the first week Rose had received more novel impressions than in the whole of her previous existence had fallen to her lot.

She was leading two new lives, one conditioned by the circumstances and atmosphere of Minerva House, the other concerned only with the college.

One aspect alone of the boarding-house she thought, fully endorsed Geoffrey Winter's view of the puerility of girls' schools. It was an aspect of worry, harassment, and preoccupation with trifles, unknown, she was sure, in the life of schoolboys. An instance of this was afforded her before the close of the first day.

"Rose Cottingham," called Miss Bird, descending into the cloakroom on the return of the boarders from the college, "you left your indoor shoes outside your locker this morning. You must sign your name. Ethel Cummings," she added, turning to a round-faced, rough-haired girl whom Rose thought looked "nice," "*you* will sign your name in the conduct-book."

"What for?" demanded Ethel, while Rose looked from one to the other in bewilderment.

"You spoke most rudely to me this morning when I told you to fold up your nightdress," returned Miss Bird, the colour rising in her swarthy cheeks. "I hadn't time to tell you then to sign your name. Go upstairs now, both of you, and do it." She shuffled out of the room on her heelless slippers, and murmurs of "Old cat!" arose in the cloakroom, where ten or twelve girls were taking off hats and boots.

"Fancy starting conduct-marks the first day of term!" said some one disgustedly.

"Just like her," grumbled Ethel, sulkily swinging out of the room.

"Hi! You'd better take the new girl along," called some one else. "She doesn't know what to do or how to do it."

"She'll learn," returned Ethel, darkly prophetic. "Come on!" and she nodded to Rose, who followed uncomprehendingly.

"What have I got to do?" she asked meekly as they went upstairs together.

"You'll see. We shall find the old cat eagerly waiting for us in the dining-room with both books open. She simply loves it!" said Ethel.

As she foretold, Miss Bird stood ready for them, two enormous ruled registers open before her on the' top of a low cupboard.

"Now, Rose Cottingham," she said, "put the date in this column," indicating a space, "and write beside it, '*I left my shoes about.*' Then sign your name opposite the entry in *this* line."

Laboriously, in her round unformed writing, Rose duly put the crime on record, while in another book, devoted to breaches of good conduct, with all the haste of custom, Ethel scribbled, "*I spoke rudely,*" and affixed her signature.

"I hope this will be the last time either of you will sign this term," remarked Miss Bird unconvincingly, while she applied blotting-paper to both confessions. "Now go and get your books ready for preparation."

"What's the good of it? What's it for?" whispered Rose on the way out, and Ethel shrugged her shoulders.

"You'll be asking what's the good of several things before you've been here a week," she told her in an irritated voice. "It's one worry, worry, worry from morning till night."

The statement was scarcely exaggerated. Humour, never perhaps a strong factor in the equipment of teachers, was at Minerva House conspicuous by its absence.

Miss Quayle herself had none, and even if any of her subordinates had possessed such a thing, a sense of prudence would have led to its disguise. Life was real, life was more than earnest, it was strenuous to the Principal of Quayle College, and to her lack of humour she joined other even more unfortunate negative qualities. She had no sense either of proportion or of imagination, and her influence permeated the atmosphere of the boarding-house. Venial offences, at most deserving of a casual rebuke, were at Minerva House treated with all the portentous solemnity due to crimes of a heinous nature. Was a girl careless or untidy, interminable lectures followed her offence. Did another talk in the hours consecrated to work and silence, she was interviewed apart, the name of God was invoked, she was gravely assured that she was displeasing to the Deity, and recommended to seek help in prayer.

But among the many inventions sought out by Miss Quayle for the perfection of conduct in the boarding-house, it was the "register" system which early stirred Rose to amused contempt. From the first, she was a daily contributor to one or both of the journals in question, and never without an inward grin at the thought of pages of manuscript devoted to such items as "*I left a book about,*" or "*I banged the door,*" signed in full by the culprit, the only result of the exercise so far as Rose was concerned being the encouragement of a rather mordant sense of humour.

"What would happen if I did something *really* wicked?" she asked Miss Mortlake one day when she had been an inmate of the house some weeks. "I don't believe the Lord cares twopence whether I put my workbag in the cupboard, or leave it on the table!"

Miss Mortlake, who had just made Rose's fiftieth "signing" the text for a religious homily, sighed profoundly, and regarded the child with perplexed eyes. She had a secret weakness for Rose, who in some undefined, vague way, interested her.

Over and above a constant minute and worrying surveillance which Rose never ceased to resent, Minerva House was periodically shaken to its foundations by a "row." The laconic and comprehensive word summed up Miss Quayle's outbursts of wrath over trifles. Those who imagined that the work connected with the college itself and its five hundred inmates might be sufficient to satisfy the energy of its principal, were unacquainted with Miss Quayle. Her activities were ceaseless, and little as she was possibly aware of it herself, strife of any sort had become the breath of life to her. She would return from a long day's activity at the college, and eager for a fray, immediately set to work to investigate the result of all the rules she had framed, in theory for the conduct of the perfect life amongst her boarders, in practice for outbreaks of artificially manufactured crimes.

She would, for instance, pay a surprise visit to the boot-lockers to assure herself that every boot was marked by its owner's name on the lining, and placed tidily on the shelf allotted to each pupil. She would dash open every drawer in a particular bedroom, and descending in a fury worthy of a more important cause, summon the whole household, reducing half of it to tears, and spreading general terror by the thunder of her eloquence and the scorching fire of her condemnation.

"And all about boots!" murmured Rose scornfully, when after one of the locker raids, which occurred towards the end of the term, the girls were dismissed at the end of an impassioned harangue. "It would do her good if one of us eloped or something," she added vindictively, without any precise idea of what an elopement implied.

Thus early and by practical demonstration in what to avoid, Rose learned the value of proportion.

Certain compensations there were, however, at Minerva House, in spite of its chronic atmosphere of worry and unrest. Miss Quayle could be interesting, and to Rose, fresh from a home where no one read and no one in the sense of the word talked, a new world opened when sometimes at supper-time the Principal read aloud, or with the elder girls discussed a book of William Morris, or quoted one of Tennyson's poems.

One or two visits to the National Gallery on Saturday afternoons impressed her greatly, and twice during her first term she went with a party of girls to the theatre, once to see Irving play Shylock, and a yet more thrilling and wonderful experience, on another occasion to see Ellen Terry, at the zenith of her charm and beauty, in the character of Beatrice. For weeks afterwards she lived on the memory of that play, and the thought of it always gave her the sensation of warmth and sunshine. To some extent, at least, and apart from actual lessons, life at Minerva House was stimulating, and her neglected little mind began to work on fresh lines.

To the sum of advantages in her new life might be added its democratic nature. Even at Minerva House her associates were not by any means all drawn from the class to which Rose herself belonged, while at the college the fees were low enough to enable the small tradespeople of the neighbourhood to educate their daughters side by side with the children of a higher rank in the social scale. Young as she was, Rose almost immediately realized her grandmother's horror if she had known the social status of girls with whom her granddaughter for many hours of the day associated. She realized it with a certain mischievous amusement, and a determination never to let her know that in class she sat between a pork-butcher's daughter and the child of a publican in the Camden Road, and liked the latter child immensely.

Sybil Smith, of the public-house, was a clever little girl, with a humorous face, a Cockney accent, and a genius for arithmetic. Rose respected her for her ability in dealing with compound fractions, and liked her for her good-nature. The fortuitous proximity of Sybil Smith, made for Rose the first breach in the barrier erected for her between the classes, by generations of her ancestors. For the first time in her life she became aware that others besides "the people one knows,"—not only existed, but were of importance.   At school, she and Sybil met on equal terms, and the honours were with Sybil.

She began on the whole to enjoy her work at the college, where at least one or two of the mistresses taught well, and where the stimulus of a big class was a blessed contrast to the drowsy, deadening effect of Miss Piddock's so-called instruction. At school she met with encouragement and a certain increasing amount of praise, though at the boarding-house long before the end of her first term she was constantly in disgrace, and had definitely taken the place of Janie Price as the "victim" singled out for the unpleasant notice of Miss Quayle. A passionate revolt against injustice was the outcome of her frequent interviews with the Principal, who by some unlucky chance seldom chose the right and lawful occasion for censure, opportunities for which were certainly not lacking where Rose was concerned.

Not intentionally unfair, Miss Quayle's ungovernable temper often betrayed her into unreasonable words, and deeds of gross injustice, and that it was the temper of an overworked, highly nervous woman was little comfort or explanation to girls who should never have been under her charge. One instance of many such injustices loomed large, and left an ineffaceable and unforgivable impression upon Rose's memory. Years afterwards, though conscious of its absurdity, she never recalled the episode without a rush of hot anger and renewed indignation.

The occasion was an excursion to St. Albans Cathedral on a Saturday afternoon towards the end of her first term.

Miss Quayle, in her most gracious mood—and she

could be gracious—had personally conducted a contingent of the Minervarites, in which Rose, though one of the younger pupils, was included.

Already her head mistress spoke of her in private as a "difficult, but exceedingly clever girl," and she was seldom passed over when any excursion of an educative nature was in progress of arrangement. All at first went well. Rose was awed and impressed by the beauty of the great church, then happily unrestored. She kept close to Miss Quayle, who in her best and most interesting vein discoursed upon the architecture and the tombs, and to the child's admiring wonder, translated aloud their Latin inscriptions. These were the moments when she almost liked Miss Quayle; when, at any rate, she felt for her the most ungrudging admiration. It grew dusk, and the lady looked at her watch.

"We are late," she announced. "Come at once, all of you. We shall only just get the train."

Rose was turning obediently to follow with the rest, when she noticed the danger that threatened Janie Price, who had strayed far enough to be out of earshot. With no other thought than to warn the hapless child that marching orders had been given, she darted in her direction.

"Janie! Hurry up! Miss Quayle says—" she began, but never finished the sentence, so manifestly on the side of law, order, and obedience. A hand grasped her arm, and in mid-cathedral she was violently and ignominiously shaken.

"How dare you?" hissed Miss Quayle, her fury all the more intense because in the sacred precincts it was impossible to give it full-voiced expression. "I repeat how dare you flatly disobey my command and

9

deliberately turn your back when I had just ordered everybody to go?"

Amazed, indignant, and breathless from the shaking, Rose began her defence aloud.

"Why, it was only because Janie didn't hear that I——"

"Silence!" whispered Miss Quayle, in a voice of muttered thunder. Keeping a firm grasp on Rose's shoulder, she swept her down the aisle, followed by a troop of bewildered girls, and watched in amazement by a party of tourists who cast glances of amused pity at the child in custody.

Once outside the cathedral Miss Quayle's insensate rage was unrestrained.

"If you imagine, Rose Cottingham, that I am the woman to tolerate defiance, you deceive yourself!" she thundered, her body swaying to and fro with the passion into which she had worked herself. . . . "Edith Carlton! Where is Edith Carlton?"

One of the elder girls came forward quaking.

"Here, Miss Quayle," she murmured meekly.

"Walk with Rose Cottingham to the station, and you understand me, Edith, I emphatically forbid you to exchange one word with her! See that she makes no attempt to speak to you. Disobedience joined to impertinence I will not tolerate. Now, to the station all of you, and kindly waste no time." Like criminals subdued, brow-beaten, and in terror of a further outburst of which at any moment one of their number might be the unwitting cause, the happy band of schoolgirls hastened two and two to catch the train. Rose and the unfortunate Edith, gaoler against her will, formed the tail of the crocodile whose extreme tip was represented by Miss Quayle, white

with passion, and a quaking girl who, constrained to
walk with her, went in fear of her life, and as soon as
the station was reached, modestly effaced herself in the
crowd.   By this time Rose was crying copiously.
They were tears of anger and passionate resentment.
Why was she not allowed to speak, to explain?   What
was it all about after all?   Why was she humiliated
and treated as a prisoner when if she might speak she
could prove that her intentions had been strictly
honourable and in accordance with commands?   By
the time Minerva House was reached, all her pupils
were as uncomfortable and apprehensive as Miss
Quayle apparently desired them to be, and Rose,
her little being torn and rent with anger, her nerves
ajar and quivering, was almost hysterical.

"Now Rose Cottingham, you may go into the
drawing-room and sit there till I send for you!" was
Miss Quayle's injunction as she bent above the child,
swaying and gesticulating in what ought to have been
and, strangely enough, was *not* a ludicrous exhibition
of rage.   It was an odd circumstance that however
trivial, however uncalled for, the occasion responsible
for what in others would have been childish wrath,
Miss Quayle never at the moment seemed absurd.
She was always terrible, always the avenging goddess,
even when, as most frequently happened, there was
nothing to avenge, and in the view of any reasonable
being nothing even to "make a fuss about."   Theo-
retically she was ridiculous, actually she was awe-
inspiring, and however frequently to herself and in
private conversation Rose compared her to "an
infuriated bluebottle banging about on a window,"
neither she nor any of the inmates of Minerva House
ever lost their fear of her, nor forgot to tremble at

her approach.   A story which long before Rose's arrival had become a classic to be gigglingly recited in whispers illustrated the terror she struck into the hearts of all and sundry of her household.

One evening, believing she had sought her couch for the night—one could not picture Miss Quayle simply going to bed—an unlucky servant locked the study door on the outside, and at one o'clock in the morning a furious knocking and beating roused the sleepers.   Teachers hung over the banisters, girls crowded behind them, servants opened their doors, and the terrified whisper spread that the sound proceeded from the study, and its august occupant was locked in.

There was a moment of awestruck indecision before Miss Bird, greatly daring, crept downstairs and turned the key, wisely effacing herself behind the tumultuously opened door as Miss Quayle, raging against Stupidity and Gross Carelessness, sprang forth.

"It was *worse* than a lion!" was the usual termination to the story, and no one ever considered it an exaggerated conclusion.   No one therefore smiled even covertly, at the spectacle of an infuriated lady of sixty brandishing her arms in the vicinity of a small sobbing child of twelve.   And Rose was driven into the drawing-room.

"What's it all about?" whispered the girls as they trooped into the cloakroom to take off outdoor raiment and prepare for supper.

"Nothing at all—as usual," muttered the ex-gaoler, Edith Clayton.   "Rose went to call some kid, Janie Price, I think, who hadn't heard what the Dragon said.   Any one who wasn't raving mad could see what the child meant by running back, and you'd have thought it would be considered quite the right thing to do. But it's turned into a crime, as everything here always is! I thank my stars I'm leaving this term. I've had enough of it. . . ."

Edith went loftily out of the room, carrying her books, and the other girls exchanged glances.

Edith was a "senior," and usually reserved in manner. It was gratifying to have a senior on the side of the younger and more rebellious contingent at Minerva House.

No one was surprised when Miss Quayle dashed the plates about at supper-time. To an observant beholder the impatience with which at all times Miss Quayle touched or handled inanimate objects, spoke of disordered nerves. But there were moments when the symptom became acute, and if she pushed dishes away from her and rattled knives, forks, and spoons at the table with more than usual vehemence, her pupils feared the worst, and those unlucky enough to be placed next to her ate a meal flavoured with apprehension.

Before supper was over that evening Miss Quayle rose with exceeding violence and rapped upon the table. Every awestruck eye was turned in her direction.

"I wish it clearly understood," she announced in a voice still vibrating with anger, "that no one addresses a single word to Rose Cottingham till my permission is given . . . Miss Bird!" The call was unanswered. It was repeated with rising annoyance. "Miss Bird! Now, where is Miss Bird? Miss Mortlake, why is Miss Bird absent from this room?"

"I'll find her," stammered Miss Mortlake, half rising.

"Please keep your seat!" adjured the Principal
irritably. "I cannot imagine why she is not here.
Ah, Miss Bird," as the terrified little housekeeper,
who had been called away by the cook on some
domestic mission, scuttled in. "In future please do
not absent yourself at meal-times. Kindly give
Rose Cottingham her supper in here when the other
girls have gone, and then send her upstairs to bed."

Miss Quayle rustled from the room, and in panic-
stricken silence, the household heard her bang her
study door.

Rose cried herself to sleep, unconsoled by the furtive petting and whispered exclamations of "Shame!"
bestowed by her room-mates. In a hurricane-like
interview with Miss Quayle (if a storm of reproach and
condemnation could be called an interview), she had
been given no chance of drawing breath, much less
of an explanation. Invited to express contrition after
she had once managed to gasp incoherently, "I
didn't do anything," she had remained obstinately
silent. Speech, indeed, would have been an impossi-
bility in face of the fresh twist given by Miss Quayle
to her words in a torrent of invective on the heinous
sin of lying. Now, all she had to anticipate was an indefinite prolongation of the "row," and its wearying,
maddening corollaries. Rose was experienced in
"rows," and everything fell out as she foresaw. She
was conducted to school next day by Miss Bird, who
an abject little sycophant, in terror of Miss Quayle,
addressed no word to her. The morning's instruction,
so far as the girl was concerned, was a farce, for still
smouldering with indignation and a bitter sense of
injustice, she was incapable of paying attention.
The return walk in the same circumstances, with the

hated proximity of Miss Bird, only fanned the flame
of resentment which solitary meals and solitary preparation of "home work" did not tend to allay. After
supper came the dreaded interview in the study, for
by this time she was aware that not only would she
never be given the chance to "explain," but that even
if she were allowed to speak in self-justification it
would profit her nothing, since all that her head
mistress was now "out for" was to wring from her a
confession of guilt.

Fully half an hour was spent by Miss Quayle in
walking up and down the study in the manner of a
caged and infuriated tiger, assuring the tired little
creature who shared her cage that she possessed the
worst character it had ever been her ill-fortune to
encounter.

A headstrong, obstinate, rebellious, disobedient,
and insolent girl was this Rose Cottingham, who, forsooth, had the effrontery to defy her, Miss Quayle,
the herald of the new day for Woman, the founder
of the new learning, the trainer and fosterer of all
great and glorious qualities of womanhood soon to be
displayed to a dazzled world! This trend in her
oratory, as Rose anticipated, led to a change of tactics.

"And you!" she exclaimed with renewed vehemence, wheeling round towards the child, "you who
have brains, you who have character, you who
might be an ornament to this great school, who might
win it fame and honour, you turn those qualities with
which God has endowed you *against* the splendid
institution which nurtures you, troubling and hinder-
ing its work instead of joyfully carrying it forward!
Now, my dear child," she continued in the same
breath, descending without any sense of bathos from

the heights of general principles to the particulars of scholastic expediency, "I should like you to go in for the Junior Cambridge. You ought to do remarkably well. You can take honours if you do not allow your incurable obstinacy in Arithmetic to stand in the way. Now listen to me, Rose Cottingham! I refuse to allow you to override me in the matter of Arithmetic. It is idle to tell me that a girl of your ability cannot bend her mind to any subject she pleases. But you profess not to 'like Arithmetic'"— the inflection of Miss Quayle's voice was superb in its scorn, "and you have the insolence, forsooth, to imagine that I shall accept that as a reason for its neglect! Now, Rose Cottingham, my dear child, give me your attention. I insist that you shall master this subject. . . ."

The tirade which followed scarcely penetrated to the child's tired brain, and when Miss Quayle at length returned to the immediate subject of dispute, the portentous, heaven-shaking occurrence in St. Albans Cathedral, she could only cry weakly out of sheer nervous exhaustion. As it happened those tears were her salvation, for Miss Quayle, also somewhat weary, assumed the words of contrition which, even in her weakness, she would never have uttered.

"Now, my child, that you are sorry for your contempt of authority, we will let the matter rest," she avowed magnanimously. "Come and kiss me, my dear, and in your prayers to-night remember that 'he that ruleth his own spirit is better than he that taketh a city.'"

She enveloped Rose in the embrace known to Minerva House as the "bear's hug" without which no "row" ever terminated, and when at last she

ventured gently to struggle from her arms Rose
was aware from the tenor of her Principal's remarks
that the Junior Cambridge had ousted holy writ.

"You must have special coaching in Arithmetic,"
she heard her murmur, before dazed and still resentful, she at last crept upstairs to bed.

In the night Rose woke with resentment for the
moment in abeyance, and the somewhat bitter sense
of humour which the atmosphere of Minerva House
was strengthening, in the ascendant. "*Better is he
that ruleth his own spirit,*" she quoted to herself
disdainfully. "Why doesn't she rule hers? Every
bit of all this row she's made herself out of nothing
at all but her own vile temper! She's a horrid, unfair
old beast, and all that talk about how clever I am, was
only to try to make me give in and say I was sorry for
what I never did. Her cap wagged like anything
all the while she was raving at me!" . . . Rose giggled
hysterically under the bedclothes at the memory of
what had been at the time a sufficiently terrible
experience, and told herself she now knew how a tiger
would look in a lace cap with a pink velvet rosette
over his ear. This agreeable play of fancy, however,
was but the bubble on a deep sea of indignation and
revolt, not only against her present circumstances
but, in a fashion more or less unconscious, against
fate for the accident of her sex and its resultant
disabilities.

"*Boys'* schools are not like this!" she reflected with
reminiscences in her mind of Geoffrey's talk and all
the happy irresponsibility it reflected. "Boys are let
alone. They're not always being worried and preached
to about God, and told to say they're sorry, and sign
their names in registers because they've left a book

about.   It's beastly to be a girl, because women are so silly!" was her last sleepy reflection.   "They make such a fuss about nothing, and they're so *serious*. When I'm grown up I shall never be serious, and I shall let my children alone, and never talk to them about God and ruling their spirits, because I shall know how sick it makes them.   And I'll never be unfair, and I'll never behave like a bluebottle that's going to have a fit."

With these salutary resolutions, induced by the atmosphere of the school in its effort towards the right training of the young, Rose fell asleep.   Not without profit were her schooldays, since, as she later realized, the art of living consists mainly in the discovery of what to avoid.

XII

DISILLUSION AND GROWTH

THE Christmas holidays, passionately longed for, were not all that fancy painted.

Brook Hall was empty, and Lucie, towards whom absence had made Rose's heart grow fonder, was a distinct disappointment. During the term, especially at night, she had missed her sister, and she had often pitifully wondered if Lucie ever woke in the dark and stretched out her hand in vain for comfort. But Lucie had now all the comfort she desired in the person of her new governess, Mademoiselle La Touche, a lively, chattering Frenchwoman whom she adored; and very meanly—in Rose's opinion, at least—she used her newly acquired French as a means of keeping her idol's attention fixed exclusively upon herself. Her grandmother was as coldly unapproachable as ever, and rather to Rose's relief evinced very little interest in her granddaughter's school life. Searching inquiries might have led to awkward results, for as it was, one of the very few questions she asked, concerned the daughters of Major Kenway, whom Rose did not know even by sight, since they were merely day boarders at the college and in a much higher form than her own. "You must live in a sort of rabbit-warren, I should think!" she remarked with a rather contemptuous sniff, and, remembering her first impressions, Rose was inclined to agree with the substance if not with the manner of her observation. It was fortunate that Grandmamma did not inquire too closely into the breed of the rabbits. She felt lonely and "out of it" at home, and its dulness struck her afresh. Only the well-known and well-loved house itself was any comfort to her—that and the sea and the harbour and the fishing-boats, alone failed to disappoint her.

On the whole, she was glad when the holidays were over.

"I suppose nothing's so nice as you think it's going to be," was her reflection on her way back to school. It was the first time that such an idea had occurred to her; a milestone in her childhood pointing to maturity.

She was glad not to enter Minerva House this time as a stranger, glad to be embraced by old friends and to understand all the jargon of the first night's chatter; to be able to take her part in it as a recognized inmate of the place. Long after the girls in her room had gone to sleep, she lay awake, fired with all sorts of ambitious schemes for the future, planning triumphs, eager for the term's work. The day of the "St. Albans row," as in thought she always referred to it, made a landmark in Rose's school history. Strenuously as she denied it to herself, Miss Quayle's words had flattered and stirred her to the depths of her being.

"*You who have brains, you who have character*"— the angrily expressed opinion rang in her ears with gratifying effect, though at the bottom of her heart she was dubious and fearful; doubtful of its truth. A profound diffidence lurked always in the depths of Rose's consciousness, ready at any moment to rise to the surface and poison her moments of seeming triumph, whether these were social or intellectual. Popular amongst her schoolfellows as, on the whole, she had become, she could not take her popularity complacently, nor as a matter of course. Its evidence was always a surprise to her; she went always in terror of losing it, and a careless word or an unintentional slight plunged her into agonies of wounded susceptibility. The assurance of her plainness which at home, tacitly if not openly, she had always received, had sown seeds of self-mistrust, which lying dormant in her early childhood, sprang into life now that she had reached schoolgirl's estate. At school her success waxed and waned according to her remembrance or forgetfulness of what she considered her terrible ugliness. When, as sometimes happened, for days together she forgot to think of her personal appearance, she was the most popular girl at Minerva House, and for the time she was happy and grateful. Then there would come a morning when the sight of her own face in the looking-glass, while she tied up her hair with brown ribbon, would discourage her for the day. She became gloomy and dull, and reflected bitterly that it would be little wonder if the other girls avoided her, since a face like hers must be repellent even to the charitable.

In the same way and with regard to intellectual success, if coming out top in a History examination filled her for a moment with exultation, she would remember her name at the bottom of the list for Arithmetic or English Grammar, and become abased in spirit at the thought of her colossal stupidity in all the really important branches of human knowledge. This term, however, in spite of herself, fired by Miss Quayle's flattering estimate of her capabilities, she meant to overcome every obstacle to fame and glory. This term she would be a real success!

Of the many passions which inflamed the restless, active brain of Miss Quayle, pride in her college ruled. Her ambition for it knew no bounds. At the time of its founding, examinations, scholarships, prizes, academic honours of all sorts,—new ideas then in the education of girls, had assumed in her mind the gigantic proportions of vital and fundamental necessities, and the obsession never lost its hold. To these outward signs of progress, she sacrificed everything. A clever girl was at once marked down as an asset to the college, one who must and should win honours for it, and if possible pass from its strenuous shepherding to one or other of the universities for women, spreading thus, the glory of Quayledom to those fresh intellectual fields and pastures new.

It was unfortunate for others besides Rose, that recognizing only one type of "cleverness," the despotic little woman tried to force every girl into the sole groove which led to academic success. She damaged many of them in the process.

To any being of discernment, half an hour spent with Rose when she was obviously doing her best to understand an arithmetical problem, would have brought the conviction that it was waste of time to send her in for an examination which, under a system making failure in that, failure in all other subjects, she had not the remotest chance of passing.

Possessing no such discernment however, Miss Quayle chose to believe that the girl's hopeless incapacity on the mathematical side, sprang from obstinacy and lack of endeavour, and the result to her pupil was goading, harassment, overwork, and constant unmerited scolding.

With a few intervals of idleness, which probably

saved her from nervous breakdown, Rose's life for the next year or two was a constant struggle for efficiency on lines unsuited to her capabilities, and its effect on a complex, highly strung nature was just what any one possessing the valuable sense of proportion might have foreseen.

During her preparation for the "Junior" her less excitable friends complained that she was "changeable," that "you never knew how to take Rose Cottingham." By turns, in the wildest, maddest spirits when she was praised for an essay or a history paper, and in the depths of despair when all her sums were wrong, her moods were sudden and fitful—the result of disordered nerves and a worried brain. Doing and feeling nothing by halves, her horizon was bounded by the frowning thunder-cloud of the Junior Cambridge, and nothing in heaven or earth existed for her but columns of weights and measures, lists of dates, and rules of grammar.

It was significant, nevertheless, that though her schoolfellows grumbled that there was no fun to be got out of Rose Cottingham nowadays because she was always "stewing," they never ceased to discuss her amongst themselves.

"She won't pass the Junior, you know," declared Chrissie Field as she walked down the little strip of garden at the back of Minerva House, with her arms about the respective waists of Sylvia Buckhurst and Mary Cartwright. "She's certain to fail in Arithmetic, and then she's done for."

"I can't think why the Dragon says she's clever!" observed Mary. "She never comes out top in her form, and she's *awful* at all sorts of things. A First Form kid could beat her."

"She *is* clever for all that," declared Sylvia Buckhurst decidedly. Sylvia, as the eldest girl at Minerva
House, and leaving at the end of the term, was listened
to with respect. "She may be stupid over Arithmetic,
but there's something about her that none of the rest
of us have got. Somehow or other we all talk about
her, don't we?—though she hasn't been jolly for ages
and there's never a word except lessons to be got out of
her. I don't quite know what it is about her that's
different from most kids, but you'll see when she's
grown up she'll do all sorts of things that none of us
will think of doing."

"What sort of things?" asked Chrissie.

"Oh, *I* don't know," returned Sylvia vaguely.
"She might run away with a chimney-sweep, or write
poetry, or marry a duke."

"She's not pretty enough," objected Chrissie.

"That's got nothing to do with it. If she *wanted*
to marry a duke she'd make him think he wanted it
too."

Leaving the future duke out of the question, the
sapience of Chrissie Field in regard to the nearer
prospect of the Junior Cambridge, was not at fault.

The following term Rose *was* "done for," and by the
agency of the fatal Arithmetic. It was not, however,
quite the affair of simple failure it might have been,
for fate held a special trick of irony in store, bitter not
only for her, but for the ambition of Miss Quayle,
who had looked upon the "Junior" as a stepping-stone
to higher things.

When the result of the examination came, she made
of it the occasion for a public display of indignation
and impressive oratory.

For days beforehand, Rose had lived in suspense,

scarcely daring to breathe lest at any moment the dreaded yet longed-for news might arrive.

At last one morning, the door of her classroom was flung back by a hand impossible to mistake, and Miss Quayle entered like an avalanche, and precipitated herself upon the teaching-platform, which the form-mistress hastily vacated.

"The news of the Junior Cambridge has reached me," she began, and the class noticing the peculiar vibration in her voice heralding a "row," sat breathless. "How many candidates are present here?" Half a dozen hands went up, the trembling hand of Rose amongst them, and Miss Quayle fixed her with an eye stormily blue before beginning to read the names of the victors. At the end of the list she made an impressive pause.

By this time Rose's heart had almost ceased to beat. She had failed, then—failed after months of straining every nerve, after the nights she had kept herself awake for hours, repeating dates of "leading events" and the hated columns of the weights and measures; after all her anxiety, her care, and her trepidation!

"One girl," announced Miss Quayle in her vibrating voice, "has failed in one subject only, and that, the subject which disqualifies her in everything. She has failed in Arithmetic, and but for this she would have taken first-class honours in History and Liter-ature. Need I say that candidate is Rose Cottingham, a girl of great ability but of incurable obstinacy, and filled with the spirit of rebellion. Rose Cottingham, if you had chosen you could have won great distinction amongst the Juniors. But you did *not* choose. You elected to trifle with a subject on which you are weak —a subject which with a little will you could have

tackled and mastered. I am filled with indignation.
I am——"

The rest of the angry harangue was lost upon the
child, crushed by the bitterness of a tantalizing defeat
so near to victory; and when Miss Quayle presently
swung out of the room with the words, "I will see you
later, Rose Cottingham," the ominous remark left her
indifferent.

The impending scene in the study at Minerva
House was as naught in the face of her own overwhelming disappointment, and the whispered condolences of
the girls in her immédiate vicinity fell on deaf ears.

At the luncheon break, when the class swarmed
into the dining-room, Rose was surrounded. But
with a set, sullen face she broke away from her com-
forters, and in defiance of rules, began to wander
about the corridors nursing her misery.

Here Miss Woods, the mistress who had been present
during Miss Quayle's oration, encountered her.

"What are you doing in this passage, Rose?" she
asked gently. "You're breaking rules, you know."
Then, struck by the despair in the child's face, she
stooped and put her arm round her shoulder. "Never
mind, dear!" she whispered. "It was splendid to
have deserved honours in the other subjects. You've
worked very hard and we're quite proud of you."

"Yes, but it's all no g-good!" wailed Rose, struggling with her tears.

Miss Woods looked at her pityingly. She was one
of the younger teachers, and a rebel at heart. She
found many things about Quayle College and its
Principal, to rouse her secret wrath, and she spoke
suddenly with decision.

"When you are older, Rose, you'll find that examin-

ations and marks and prizes and all that sort of thing
are not so important as they seem to you now." Then,
smiling a little: "Still, I know that's rank heresy,
and also poor comfort until you can believe it," she
added. "And I'm awfully sorry, dear child. But
try to remember that it's the *work* that counts. The
exam. doesn't matter twopence! Now here comes
your class. Get into line quickly."

She hurried on, calling with perfunctory sharpness,
"*Left, right! left, right!*" as the Third Form girls in the
approved order, marched in single file out of the dining-
room. Rose fell in at the end of the line, full of gratitude if not of comfort. She liked Miss Woods. It
was so jolly of her to say "awfully," when slang was
strictly prohibited by Miss Quayle. But she wondered
what "rank heresy" meant in that particular connection? Pondering over it, she came to the conclusion
that the phrase was directed against the Principal,
and a glow of satisfaction was followed by an increased
affection for Miss Woods.

It was funny that some grown-up people, at any
rate, didn't think much of examinations! Hitherto,
for months and months, they had seemed to her the
only important things in the world. But perhaps Miss
Woods was right. Her words, at any rate, pierced a
slit for Rose in the walls of her school environment,
through which there came a glimmering light from a
bigger world outside. She determined to pretend she
didn't care a bit about the old exam. and to establish
a reputation for originality, while she avoided the
condolences of her schoolfellows. Nevertheless, in
secret she fretted, and her fretting had a deeper origin
than mere failure in the hated Arithmetic. Rose
had begun to recognize her limitations, to experience

a faint foreknowledge that her ambitions would always outrun her achievements. As she later expressed it, she had a mind that was "illuminated only at intervals." Between the bright spots, there were spaces where all was confused, shadowy, and never brought into efficient working order with the rest.

It would be a year at the earliest before she could enter for the Senior Cambridge, and during that year, Rose deliberately "slacked," as in a big school any boy or girl bringing good will to the task can slack, and the result in many, though not scholastic, ways was favourable. Instead of spending all her recreation time in feverishly committing to memory, dates and lists of irregular verbs, she read everything she could lay hands on, though the books she wanted were not attained without difficulty.

For the younger girls at Minerva House a separate bookcase was kept, from which volumes were doled out to them by Miss Bird, the Senior library being in Miss Mortlake's charge. Here the shelves contained novels by Dickens, Thackeray, George Eliot, and Kingsley, and it was these Rose coveted and was not permitted to borrow. She overcame the difficulty by exchanging *Ministering Children* or *Misunderstood*, acquired from the Junior library, for *Hypatia* or *Adam Bede*, extracted from the Senior shelves by Lucy Manning, a girl of seventeen, who never wanted to open a book. Lucy was perfectly willing to pass on a volume to "the kid" and to return it at the moment when the despised *Ministering Children* was handed back to Miss Bird by Rose, who had just been devouring the novel presumably read by the elder girl.

Due care had nevertheless to be exercised lest Miss Bird should chance to see the titles of books which by such devious paths had come into her possession, and Rose's acquaintance with *David Copperfield, Villette,* and *Vanity Fair* was clandestine, and all the more precious for the circumstance.

No longer preoccupied with school-work, hating it rather in the revulsion of feeling caused by the result of the "Junior," Rose's mind, never idle, turned in various other directions. Her fourteenth birthday was near at hand; she was growing; developing physically, and with the physical change came a mental ferment which by turns perplexed and excited her. Curiosities she had never felt before, beset her. There were mysteries which she longed to solve, over which she brooded for weeks, furtively seeking for their elucidation in books, or from hints let fall by wiser schoolfellows. These were few and far between, and too cryptic for Rose's comprehension. The girls at Minerva House were, on the whole, a "decent set." Amongst the elder ones reticence was looked upon as good form, and if occasionally barriers were broken down and confidences as to knowledge, more or less imperfectly acquired, were exchanged, Rose's childlike appearance which always made her considered even younger than she was, shut her off from the converse of advanced young women. As events worked out, it was a pity, for by ill-luck she was destined to obtain answers to her secret questions in a manner even less to be desired.

The term after her fourteenth birthday, Rose returned to school to find that Kitty French and Joan Milbank, the two girls with whom she shared her room, had been removed; their beds being now occupied respectively by a new girl, and, horror of horrors—Miss Bird!

The news was broken to her ten minutes after her
arrival by Kitty French, who, meeting her on the staircase, embraced her with fervour, and amid many
exclamations of "Shame!" and "Perfectly vile!"
poured out the hateful tidings.

"And you just wait till you've seen the new girl,
darling!" she added, at the end of her voluble addr ss.
"Her name is Millie Cripps, and she's too *awful*—the
commonest creature you ever saw! She oughtn't to
be allowed in the place."

Kitty's stricture as it happened, had more justice on
its side than is usually contained in a schoolgirl's
opinion of a newcomer. Millie Cripps was an uncouth, clumsy girl of fifteen, whose unhealthy-looking
skin and pig-like eyes represented with fair accuracy
the mind within her unattractive body. It was probably with some inkling of the fact that Miss Quayle
placed a teacher in the room, on the assumption that
her presence and the rule of silence in the bedrooms
at night would be an efficient safeguard against an
influence possibly evil. Naturally, the precaution
failed. For at least a couple of hours before Miss Bird
came upstairs, Millie Cripps talked, and in fascinated wonder, Rose listened. Too interested at first to
heed the voice of conscience, it was only when Millie's
conversation began to revolt rather than to fascinate
her, that she protested, merely to find that her companion derived fresh zest from the knowledge that
she was "shocking the kid." Night after night, long
after the girl was snoring, Rose lay awake and full of
shame for her own weak conduct, resolved to smother
her head in the bedclothes, rather than listen. Then
curiosity proving too strong for her, she would fail in
her determination, and, in spite of herself, give ear

next evening to Millie's abominable misinterpretations
of some of the physical facts of life. She grew wretched
with the burden of this secret, shame and shyness
combined forbidding her to speak of it to any one,
and it was an inexpressible relief when at the half
term Millie Cripps disappeared from Minerva House
to return no more. But mischief had been done.
Things simple and natural in themselves had been
defiled, and it was long before Rose was able to shake
off the nightmare horror of Millie's revelations. She
did so at last by forcing herself to the conclusion
that Millie had "made it all up out of her horrid mind,"
and with this partly veracious conjecture she succeeded in driving the matter at least from her surface
thoughts.

It was at this time and as the result of her recent
experience that she began to wish she were "really
religious." Religious girls, she was quite sure, would
never have listened to Millie Cripps, nor suffered
from a curiosity which she now felt to be unholy. She
began to watch some of the Minervarites, and made
the discovery that one or two of the elder ones genuinely liked going to church, and *really* prayed when they
were there, instead of covering their eyes for a moment
as she did, and jumping up with relief as soon as the
rustle of the congregation indicated that she might
move with impunity.

She began also to read her Bible at night. Instead
of passing surreptitious notes under her desk to her
neighbours as had been her wont, she paid attention to
the Scripture lessons, and listened in church to the
sermons of the Rev. Edward Butts, a dull but fluent
preacher unaware of the "chiel" in his congregation "taking notes," and destitute of the humour

to appreciate the fact even if he had been aware
of it.

Rose listened critically to perorations which had a
tendency to recur in slightly varied forms.   There was
one which she knew almost by heart:

*"My friends, I am speaking to true believers.   We
need no justification for our faith beyond that inward
assurance which dwells in the heart of each one of us.
Let us follow that inward light, that it may lead us into
the way of peace and finally into life everlasting."*

"That's all very well!" declared her obstinately
sceptical little mind.   "*You* may have an inward
assurance, but I haven't!   And the heathen are just as
certain as you are, that *they're* right.   So being sure
doesn't count for anything.   And yet *something*
must be true, I suppose?   I wonder what it is!"

At the bottom of her heart, though at present
unconfessed even to herself, she hoped it wasn't
Christianity.   Already she vaguely felt the irksome-
ness of a definite creed.   "It would be so exciting
to wake up after you're dead and find there was something quite new and very nice, and not at all what you
expected," was the way in which she expressed her
desires for a future life.   In her Bible she marked with
several underlinings from a blunt pencil, Pilate's oft-
quoted interrogation.

Gradually she relaxed her habit of attention, and
church once more became a dreaming-place, an
opportunity for conjuring up scenes strange or remembered, as backgrounds to little scraps of dialogue
which somehow floated into her mind, and became so
insistent that when later opportunity arose, she felt
impelled to scribble them down at the end of an
exercise-book, or on any scrap of paper that came to

hand. Till this period of idleness and indifference to school-work set in, she had almost forgotten her childish attempts at writing, and even now, she scarcely realized the reawakening impulse in the many preoccupations which engaged her attention.

Freed from her absorption in "lessons," she was, to some extent at least, affected by all the crazes which schoolgirls develop, and will probably develop till the end of time, in spite of the healthy modern outlet of games, then unknown either at Minerva House, or at the college. Thus, when it became the fashion to read sad books and cry over them, Rose selected a conspicuously retired corner of the sitting-room or the garden, and having earnestly endeavoured to weep over *Eric*, or one of the pathetic tales of Miss Florence Montgomery, was mortified to discover that no tears would come. She envied the superior susceptibility of Chrissie Field and May Cummings, over whose cheeks the salt drops rolled in profusion at the mere indication of a deathbed scene accompanied by gentle piety.

Such exercises in sheep-like following of an ideal, always resulted very speedily for Rose in a revulsion of feeling. Soon after her attempts to rave about *Eric* or *Queechy*, she was leading the movement against "soppiness," and setting the fashion for books of lurid adventure, and what were popularly supposed to be impassioned love tales in the supplement to the *Family Herald*. This contraband literature was supplied by two weekly boarders, May and Lulu Robinson, who every Monday morning returned from home with various magazines and novels concealed in their handbags, which they passed on to Rose as the recognized daring reader and critic of advanced fiction. In this way she devoured the works of "Ouida" and derived infinite gratification from the fact that according to May Robinson, not only were they "frightfully improper," but their discovery meant instant expulsion for her and for every girl who had turned their poisonous pages.

Rose enjoyed the sense of guilt but failed to discover the impropriety. It never occurred to her to apply to them the knowledge gleaned from Millie Cripps, and though the basely presented information was there, waiting in her mind, it was not till years later that this information fell into place as anything related to actual existence.

But the glowing, highly coloured prose of "Ouida" stirred her imagination sentimentally, and even better than the novels, she grew to appreciate the accounts of real love affairs as recited by the Robinson girls, big, buxom creatures who at sixteen and seventeen were already developed women. Never very particular as to the class from which she drew any of her pupils, Miss Quayle's judgment, though not so badly at fault as in the case of Millie Cripps, had again betrayed her with regard to the Robinsons, who were rather loud, more than a little vulgar, and indubitably inclined to "fastness." They were on terms which included kissing as part of the flirtation-game they played with most of their brothers' friends, and a few stray men whose acquaintance they made at subscription dances on Saturday evenings. Assignations with these youths made up the interest of their lives, and by reflection, contributed also much excitement to Rose's own existence. The sisters shared the bedroom next to hers, and the surreptitious return at bedtime of the books they lent her, gave her an opportunity for listening to long rhapsodies on the perfections of the "Frank" or "Charlie" of the moment.

"What is he like?" Rose inquired of Lulu one night, while May kept guard at the head of the stairs in view of a possible surprise visit from Miss Bird.

Lulu heaved a profound sigh, and while she absently buttoned her nightdress, gazed before her as though she had just beheld the beatific vision.

"My dear, he's perfectly *divine!*" she whispered. "Very tall, with beautiful curly hair, and passionate dark eyes. I never saw such eyes. They go *through* you!" She sighed again, and Rose thrilled.

"Look what he gave me last Sunday," continued Lulu. "It hangs round my neck, and I never part with it day or night." She held out for Rose's inspection a silver pencil-case attached to a ribbon, and Rose touched it reverently.

"There's something written on it," she said in an awestruck voice.

"Yes. That's so beautiful. Read it."

"'*Baby, from Frank,*'" whispered Rose, and looked up inquiringly.

"He always calls me 'Baby'," said Lulu with another sigh, and Rose hastily extinguished in her own breast a gleam of amusement unworthy of the occasion. Lulu was such a fine, fat baby! The reflection was gone in a flash, and again she looked with awe and wonder upon Lulu's round, fat countenance.

Is this the face that burnt a thousand ships?

She had by chance come across Marlowe's lines in a grammar-book that day. They had arrested her, and they leaped to her mind with no sense of incongruity or cynicism, if with a certain disappointment inevitable in the comparison of Lulu with Helen of Troy. Yet Lulu, it seemed, had succeeded in rousing what, after her study of "Ouida," Rose now called a "wild passion" in the heart of the divine Frank. She never doubted that it was a wild passion, though what the term precisely signified, was not clear to her. In any case, it must be a very wonderful, awe-inspiring, and beautiful experience to have a man in love with you, and she gazed at Lulu with envious respect.

"Does he kiss you?" she asked shyly.

"Kiss me?" Lulu laughed at the simplicity of the question. "My dear, I should think he does. I'm nearly suffocated."

"Is it nice?" murmured Rose again, still more shyly. It was with difficulty that she could bring herself to ask the question, but curiosity prevailed over embarrassment.

"*Nice?* Why, it's heavenly, of course. Hasn't any man ever kissed *you?* No, I suppose not," she went on, with what Rose thought painfully was a disparaging glance. "You're such a kid."

"I'm only a year younger than you."

"Well, I had lots of boys after me when I was fifteen," said Lulu with conscious pride. "But then, I didn't look such a kid as you when I was only eleven. Don't you know any boys?"

"No," returned Rose humbly. She had forgotten Geoffrey.

"Good Lord! How dull. Not one?"

"Oh, well, there's the boy who lives at Brook Hall, the nearest house to ours. But I've known him all my life."

"How old is he?"

Rose made a rapid calculation. "He's eighteen now," she said, vaguely surprised to find Geoffrey already elderly.

"And he hasn't kissed you?" demanded Lulu incredulously.

Rose laughed. The notion was so utterly ludicrous. "How absurd you are! He's—just Geoffrey. Go on about Frank. When will you see him again?"

"Next Saturday, when I escape out of this vile old hole. We're going to a subscription dance that Pa doesn't know anything about. He'd kill me if he knew, because I'm not supposed to go to dances yet. But of course I do. May and I toddle off to a friend's house to dress, and tell Pa we're staying the night at Mimi's to go to a late Confirmation class. He's so green he believes anything." Lulu giggled aloud, and her sister came rushing in, full of apprehension.

"Do shut up!" she implored. "The old cat's on the next landing. She'll be up in a minute. Clear out, Rose!"

Rose whisked into her room, undressed with lightning speed, and just managed to spring into bed as Miss Bird turned the handle of the door.

"You'll have to sign your name three times before you start for school to-morrow, Rose," she remarked, with a covert note of satisfaction in her voice. "You've left a book, a writing-case, and some needlework about. That makes ninety-five entries this term, and Miss Quayle will see you about it to-morrow."

Rose ostentatiously turned over in bed and shut her eyes as though too sleepy to attend, and Miss Bird, hesitating a moment, continued: "And you'll take a conduct mark as well for rudeness."

"What rudeness?" drawled Rose, opening one eye in affected sleepiness.

"Yes, what has she done, Miss Bird?" demanded the two other girls in the room in indignant concert. "She hasn't said a word. It's a shame!"

Miss Bird scurried out, making no reply.

"She's afraid of us, because she's only known us as seniors," remarked Enid Nicholls, loud enough to be overheard and careless of the result. "She thinks she can bully Rose because she was a kid when she first came. Mean wretch! I expect she's listening at the door."

A shuffling of feet outside confirmed Enid's surmise, and Rose laughed.

"She daren't tell of you. *You're* all right," she said, "but she knows the old Dragon will listen to anything about *me* because I'm a bad character and unworthy of this noble institution."

She laughed again, but bitterly, as she very successfully mimicked Miss Quayle's voice and manner. "Good-night," she added brusquely, "I'm going to sleep," well knowing that sleep was far from her. She was full of irritated annoyance, for she had determined to meditate upon love, and instead, her thoughts had been turned into the old wearisome, exasperating channel of rows and exhortations and "all this everlasting school nonsense," as by this time she designated the whole system represented by Minerva House.

XIII

UNDOUBTEDLY the greatest event in Rose's school life was the coming of Helen Fergurson. Her advent occurred at a moment when existence was becoming flat, stale, and unprofitable. The crushing defeat of the Junior Cambridge had resulted for her in a sort of reckless idleness, a general laxness of mind and body. Work had lost its zest, teachers who had been interested suffered disappointment, and though warfare with Miss Quayle was still active it had taken a different form, and was carried on chiefly through the agency of Miss Bird. Rose had never troubled to conceal her contempt for the little general factotum, and Miss Bird returned the girl's dislike with interest, proving to her own, if not to Rose's, satisfaction, that insignificant as she seemed, she could yet inflict the pinpricks of incessant harrying. Without actually bringing complaints against her to Miss Quayle, of whom she stood in even greater terror than the timid Miss Piddock had ever felt for Mrs. Lester, she contrived with great ingenuity to obtrude the fact of the girl's general carelessness upon her notice. "Rows" with Miss Quayle were now concerned solely with trivialities, and lacked the flattery implied by her former exhortations to win glory for the school. Miss Quayle also was disappointed in Rose's mental capacity, and had begun to look upon her as the mediocre schoolgirl, distinguished

159

from the herd merely by her superior talent for giving trouble.

Helen Fergurson arrived at the half-term just after Rose's fourteenth birthday. She came into the dining-room one evening at supper-time, escorted by Miss Quayle, and even before Rose glanced at her, she was quick to notice that in the Principal's demeanour there was an unusual touch of graciousness, a certain inexplicable air of pride and satisfaction.

"Now Helen, my child, where will you sit?" she began, and her voice sounded soft and purring in the dead silence which always fell upon her entrance into a room. "I will, I think, put you next to Mary Cartwright, who has just won a scholarship for us." She smiled graciously upon Mary (who instantly became crimson with confusion), and at the same time placed her plump white hand upon the shoulder of the newcomer. "I want you two to be great friends," she added, still in her most gracious vein. "Mary, this is Helen Fergurson, the daughter of Professor Fergurson, of whom you must have heard. We should be very proud to have Professor Fergurson's daughter as an inmate of this house, and I'm very sure she will follow in her father's footsteps and we shall soon be proud of her for her own sake."

The faces of the assembled girls wore appropriate expressions of interest, and unaware of the active foot exercises beneath the board, Miss Quayle smiled benignantly upon them, and once more, patting her *protégée* affectionately upon the shoulder, rustled away.

Impatient of the nudges and furtive giggling of Lulu Robinson, Rose irritably drew away from her, and forgetting her manners, continued to stare at the new girl, from whom she could not take her eyes.

There was something distinctive about her; something which she had never before remarked in a school-girl, something which roused her admiration and instinctive sympathy.

"She isn't like a girl," she reflected. "She's like a grown-up lady who looks upon us all as children. And she's very pretty. No, not pretty—beautiful!"

She watched her as her glance travelled slowly, gravely, and without shyness or embarrassment round the table. She was probably between fourteen and fifteen, not tall for her age, but of rather large frame. A perfectly plain tight-fitting black dress cut a little low in the neck, was finished with a tucker from whose frill rose a pretty white throat supporting a curiously arresting face and head. The head was covered with very thick short fluffy hair of such pale gold that in some lights it looked silvery, and the face beneath the thatch of hair, which almost touched dark, level eyebrows, was of a pearly transparency, with scarcely a trace of colour in the cheeks. It was a very refined, clear-cut face; delicately chiselled, and lighted by luminous eyes neither blue nor green, though the green predominated.

These eyes wandered slowly from face to face, and at last met the brown, velvety ones of Rose, who sat exactly opposite. They rested there for what seemed a long minute, and travelled no further. As though suddenly conscious that she was staring as well as being stared at, the new girl calmly withdrew her gaze, and stretching out her hand for a biscuit from the dish in front of her, went on with her supper without again looking up from the plate, whose pattern she seemed to study with minute attention. Meanwhile, the rare colour which came only when she was excited or angry rushed into Rose's face. She was excited now—oddly, curiously excited by the presence of the newcomer. She had the sensation of finding some one for whom she had been looking all her life, and the close proximity of Lulu Robinson annoyed her.

"Oh, *do* be quiet!" she whispered impatiently after the order had been given to stop talking and open hymn-books. "I hate being nudged like that, and I don't know what you're giggling for."

"Rose Cottingham, you're talking," exclaimed Miss Bird, timing the remark to fall upon the ears of Miss Quayle, who was just entering the room to read prayers.

Miss Quayle paused on the threshold, the fury which she could summon at a moment's notice, possessing her.

"Rose Cottingham insubordinate as usual?" she exclaimed. "Get up, Rose. Go into my study and wait for me there. Miss Bird, how many times to-day have you already been obliged to speak to Rose Cottingham?"

Miss Bird, darkly crimson, muttered something which the Principal's angry voice cut short.

"Begone into the study!" she repeated in the shaking voice which her anger always induced. "Begin the hymn at once, please, Miss Mortlake. What are you waiting for?"

Miss Mortlake laid trembling fingers on the keys, and as Rose slowly crossed the hall to the study, the first line of the hymn reached her—

Through the day Thy love has spared us.

"It doesn't last till the evening, though," she thought with gloomy ribaldry, applying the words to her head mistress. "And there was precious little love to start with! I wonder how long she'll keep me up to-night, banging her fat hand on the table and bouncing about the room?"

She shrugged her shoulders, and, safe while she heard the murmur of Miss Quayle's voice invoking a blessing on her household, luxuriously curled herself up in a corner of the sofa by the window. With impatience she dismissed the prospect of the impending "row," her mind full of the new girl. She had caught her glance of cool amazement at Miss Quayle's sudden outburst of wrath, and the memory of it amused and interested her.

"She doesn't look as though she'd fit in here at all," she reflected. "She looks too grown-up for all this nonsense!" Rose sighed impatiently, staring out into the little garden, from which, through the gathering dusk, there floated up the scent of mignonette and musk plants.

"We are all slaves here—just slaves!" she went on, talking to herself. "It's awful not to be grown-up. The new girl's much more grown-up than I am. I like her. Oh, I *do* hope she'll like me!" The desire came with a sudden fervour that was almost a prayer, and so wrapt was she between hope and fear, that she missed the unmistakable sounds of prayer ending, and had only just time to scramble off the sofa and assume a meek attitude in the neighbourhood of the empty fireplace, before Miss Quayle flung back the study door.

Her prayer seemed to some extent recognized when next day Helen Fergurson spoke to her in the cloak-room just before the procession started for school.

"Will you walk with me?" she asked, contrary to all precedent in the unwritten law which decreed that no new girl spoke unless she were first addressed. In the midst of her confused delight, Rose noticed the form of the question. It was not "May I walk with you?" but "Will you walk with *me?*" and she found no fault with words which from any other lips she would have denounced as "cheek."

She was engaged for the week to Lulu Robinson; but Lulu, fortunately offended by the remark of the previous evening, was already going about amongst the girls explaining not only that Rose Cottingham required "taking down a peg," but also her jolly gladness about the ensuing "row," as well as her irrevocable decision that wild horses should not induce her to walk with a kid who evinced such unparalleled effrontery.

Not unnaturally, therefore, Rose considered herself free. She walked with Helen every day that week, and by Saturday she and the "new girl" were inseparable, and for the first time in her life, Rose was in a state of blissful infatuation which made every hour of the day a romance.

Exaggerated devotions for the teachers at the college, as well as for one another, were—as in every school, common amongst the girls. But from these Rose had held stiffly aloof, liking mildly in some cases even if in others she detested with vehemence. Now she knew what it was to give her whole heart to a human being and to be alternately in the seventh heaven and in the depths of misery. In adoring Helen Fergurson she remembered as something comparable, her childish devotion to Mrs. Winter. But strong as that had been, it was a different, a *younger* emotion, the love of a child for its mother, lacking in the exaltation which coloured her feeling for Helen. It was a sentimental feeling certainly, but it was something more and better than that, for mind as well as heart was involved in it. Definitely with Helen, as dimly long ago with Mrs. Winter, she felt a mental kinship, even though with deep humility she realized her own ignorance and childishness in the face of what seemed to her the stupendous "cleverness" of her new friend, for whom she lived, of whom at night she dreamed, whose mere presence in a room filled her with happiness.

It was for Rose one of those friendships for which adolescence, though doubtless the right explanation, does not cover the whole ground. There was something in it more lasting, more valuable than exists in the majority of those schoolgirl infatuations which according to temperament, the adult views with tolerant amusement, or with undue severity of condemnation. Less than justice has been done to certain friendships of youth in which the participants all unconsciously are lovers, but lovers dwelling in the Golden Age, innocent and ignorant as babes in Paradise.

It was such a Paradise that Rose entered with a companion in many ways not unworthy either of her love or her admiration.

Helen Fergurson was the daughter of a well-known *savant*, a man of letters who enjoyed several distinct kinds of celebrity. In the literary world he was acclaimed by some, as a philosopher whose outlook on existence was expressed with a beauty of style which overlaid, if it did not atone for, the nebulousness of its teaching. To another section of the thinking world, he appealed as one of the academic leaders of a then modern movement in socialism, praiseworthy in theory, even if in practice a certain amount of impracticability might also be laid to its charge.

His house was celebrated as the meeting-place of kindred spirits, men and women of undoubted mental distinction, though possibly lacking in sound commonsense. One cannot have everything, and the Fergurson coterie certainly represented, if not the intellectual, at least, as its members themselves avowed, the "spiritual" side of a perfectly sincere attempt at the regeneration of the world.

Helen was motherless, and as the only and much-loved child of her father she had from her babyhood moved freely in an atmosphere calculated to encourage precocity. A child of quick intellect, she had acquired from the men and women who surrounded her, a vocabulary and a power of verbal expression unusual in a girl of her age; impossible to one, however naturally gifted, whose lot had not fallen in such circumstances. Unwillingly perhaps, Professor Fergurson had lately begun to realize his daughter's need of younger companions than those she had hitherto been accustomed to meet, and influenced more than he was aware by the sister who kept house for him, he at length decided to send the girl to school.

For the methods of Miss Quayle he experienced a characteristically theoretical admiration. As an outsider, looking only at the splendid organization of the college, and full of sympathy for its ideals concerning the general improvement and mental elevation of womanhood, he was fully persuaded that Minerva House would in every respect provide his child with a suitable and congenial environment. That she might share to the full the life of girls of her own age, though living in London, he heroically determined to place her for a year at least as a boarder with Miss Quayle, who welcomed her responsibility with gratification and conscious pride. Not every day did it fall to the lot of a schoolmistress to number amongst her flock a girl of such academically distinguished parentage, and Miss Quayle was more than content with the glory which the coming of Helen shed upon her own scholastic path.

Rose was possibly the only one of her pupils to share her gratification. With the rest of her schoolfellows Helen was at once unpopular, and but for Rose she would have stood alone in a hostile crowd. It was Rose alone to whom Helen was anything but a "stuck-up thing!"

Deeply as she was impressed by the "new girl's" intellectuality, it was not that, so much as her character, which struck awe and admiration into her very soul. There was an aloofness about Helen, a certain calm reasonableness which set a great gulf between her and the ordinary gushing schoolgirl, with her sentimentalities, her grumblings, her exaggerated ravings over trifles, her general air of irresponsibility as of a creature under tutelage, governed. Helen, on the contrary, seemed to be a law unto herself, even while she accepted and obeyed the rules of school life.

"Half of them are supremely ridiculous," she said, with a shrug of her shoulders in answer to Rose's vehement criticisms. "But they exist, and it's less trouble and more dignified to accept them. You don't think I would demean myself to a struggle with a woman like Miss Bird, do you?"

Rose felt abashed. She was constantly so "demeaning" herself, and till now she had never considered her dignity. Helen was right, of course, but to a nature like her own, the implied advice was a counsel of perfection. For Miss Quayle Helen soon evinced a dislike, but it was a cold and grave dislike, very different from Rose's stormy hatred.

"She's a very unbalanced woman with a strong commercial instinct," was the verdict she expressed one day on the way to school when Rose had been fulminating against some act or words of the Principal.

"What do you mean exactly?" she asked, hesitating before the phrase which was new to her.

"Well, she wants the school to *pay*, you understand. Not only in money, though I suspect her of that too," declared Helen loftily. "At any rate, to pay by the results of examinations and scholarships, and she drives likely girls to work just for the sake of them."

"She'll drive *you!*" Rose assured her. "You're so awfully clever!" She sighed, remembering the number of classes which divided her at college from Helen, who was in the Upper Fifth.

"No, she won't," returned Helen calmly. "My father doesn't wish me to go in for examinations. I told her so last night."

"Were you in the study last night?" asked Rose breathlessly. "When?"

"After you had gone to bed. She talked for hours." Helen smiled a little, reminiscently.

"What about?" demanded Rose, all eagerness.

"About my wonderful brain, and how it might win honour and glory for the school. You know the kind of thing. You've heard it many times yourself, I'm sure."

"Not lately," said Rose rather gloomily. "She's given me up. She thinks I'm no good. And it's quite true, you know—I'm not."

"What annoys me," pursued Helen, in a detached way, "is that ridiculous embrace which she thinks is necessary to bestow after any conversation. I dislike being embraced."

"Oh, Helen!" murmured Rose, in reproachful misery.

"Don't be silly. I don't mean by you—that's quite different. I mean by a large woman who doesn't interest me—like Miss Quayle."

"Well, didn't she say you were to go in for the Senior?" asked Rose, happy again,

"Yes. I told her my father's views, and she said she disagreed with him emphatically. You know how she says that sort of thing. It was quite amusing to watch her getting so foolishly excited." Again Helen smiled. "She said she should write to him. She may. My father happens to have a mind of his own."

They had reached the college door, and Rose grasped her friend's hand. Their respective classes did not meet at all during the morning, and there were hours of separation to be faced; for on Tuesdays Rose dined at school to take "extra Arithmetic" in the afternoon, and it would be evening before they were reunited.

"Good-bye, darling!" she whispered "You'll get your prep. done in time to talk in the garden with me before prayers, won't you?"

For the evening stroll in the little strip of garden at the back of Minerva House, Rose lived all day. Fate had done its best, as she bitterly reflected, to separate her from her beloved; for not only were they divided at school, but the boarding-house being in reality two houses joined only by a door between their respective halls, Helen must needs have been placed in the further dwelling, and even at meals their places were at separate tables. Rose was always first at the tryst on these hot summer evenings, and her heart leaped when she saw Helen at last emerge from the lower room leading into the garden on her side of the double house.

This evening Helen put her arm round her with more than usual *empressement*. There were two gardens at the back, corresponding to the original two houses, but a doorway, or rather a doorless gap, had been cut between them, and Rose preferred the little strip at the base of her own part of the house. She was drawing Helen towards it when her friend resisted.

"No. We'll stay in this garden to-night, because it's under Miss Quayle's window," she said. Helen never condescended to the puerility of "the Dragon" as a synonym for the head mistress, and Rose, in slavish imitation, had also dropped the term of opprobrium.

"But that's the very reason why the other's better!" she exclaimed.

"Not for my purpose," Helen enigmatically returned.

"What purpose?" asked Rose in surprise.

"I wish to show her that you are my friend, and that I am no more to be turned by her from my friendships than my father is likely to change his mind about examinations."

"Has she been trying to?" exclaimed Rose incoherently.

It was one of the amazing things about Helen that she could withhold interesting news which Rose herself would have been unable to keep for a moment. Here was a revelation which might have been made hours ago, and it was kept till now! Rose thrilled at the realization of Helen's self-control, though she was hurt by the thought that she *could* hold such a thing back.

"Yes," pursued Helen, apparently unmoved. "She disapproves of our friendship. She wishes me to become intimate with Mary Cartwright, because, as she won a scholarship last term, she considers her a better associate for me than you, who failed in the Junior Cambridge last year."

Rose did not see Helen's scornful smile, for her eyes were suddenly blinded by tears.

"Why don't you?" she cried angrily. "I *knew* I wasn't clever enough for you. I never pretended to be. Go and be Mary's friend. You'll like her better. She can do Algebra and Euclid, and I am only——"

Her voice was choked as she tried to wriggle away from Helen's arm.

"You are being *almost* as foolish as Miss Quayle," declared Helen in her calm voice. "And quite as unreasonable. Why are we walking under her window? Merely to show her that I consider her interference with regard to my choice of friends as impertinent. What more can I do?"

"All the same, you *ought* to have a clever friend." Rose's voice, though still choking, sounded mollified.

"I *have* one. My father would say that Miss Quayle doesn't begin to know what cleverness is. She thinks, poor thing, that it's marks and examinations and scholarships. I believe father would consider you the cleverest person in this house, Rose."

Rose flushed to the roots of her hair.

"You're laughing at me," she murmured. "I can't do anything. I'm always half-way down the class—that's the Arithmetic, you know. And—and when I hear you talk, Helen, and I think of all the books you've read, I feel like a stupid little worm beside you. Why—" She paused, overwhelmed, yet excited.

"I couldn't have written that thing you showed me yesterday," said Helen, in her grave, assured, grown-up voice. "No one here could have written it. You imagine I'm cleverer than I am, because I've been brought up with people who think and write and talk. No one talks here. I never met such people before. Father made the mistake of his life when he sent me to this place," she went on, with a superb disdain which would have been comic to grown-up ears, though Rose listened with respectful awe. "If it were not for you I should die of boredom," Helen went on. "It all seems so childish to me, these marks and rules and that absurd signing book for girls of our age. They seem to imagine we're fools."

"I suppose most of us *are*," remarked Rose, with an involuntary gleam of humour incomprehensible to Helen. The observation slipped from her almost without volition. All but the minutest fraction of her glowed with pride at being the mitigating circumstance in Helen's boredom, even while she despairingly mistrusted herself. Helen, the wonderful, the august, was somehow deceived in her, and the day would come when she must discover her mistake and experience a lofty contempt for its object.

"But, darling, does even the *college* seem childish to you?" she asked timidly. "I suppose it does. I suppose you know everything they think they're teaching you, already?"

She sighed, and Helen, like Adam, "smiled superior."

"Of course I don't. You *must* learn, Rose, not to

confuse quality of brain with instruction. There's a
great deal of instruction at the college but not much
education, which means something quite different.
And no culture at all," she added, in the manner of
Mrs. Mackenzie Gore, a somewhat precious member of
the Human Progress Society, of which Professor
Fergurson was president.

Rose gasped. New worlds were opening to her:
vistas lined with something called "culture" opened
dazzlingly before her impressed and venerating eyes.

"You see," proceeded Helen, with some candour
and a veracity of which she was unaware, "I've been
spoiled by living with really intellectual people. After
my father's house and the talk that goes on there,
everything else seems commonplace and stupid to me.
It would be the same in any school, I expect, so I shall
not trouble father with it. He's very busy just now
over some important work, and I don't want to worry
him."

"Would he take you away if you asked him?"
inquired Rose, catching her breath in apprehension.

"Of course. I'm not a baby. We discussed this
matter of school together, and though we agreed that
I should learn much more at home with my tutor and
with him, father thought I ought to know younger
people. In theory, of course, he was right. But what
are these girls to me?" She swept a scornful glance
about the garden, where linked couples strolled, chattering and laughing; and Rose felt a little stab of pity
for the foolish young things whom Helen scorned, and
a trembling fear lest in time, she too, might be weighed
in her balance and found wanting.

"However," continued Helen, "I shall stay. As
father says, and in that I agree with him, it's all

experience for me. And then I couldn't leave *you* now, darling. You're worth all the stupidity of the place, and no Quayle shall tear you from me!" She pressed Rose closer to her, and for a transient moment became and looked, just like any other despised and foolish schoolgirl of a lesser breed without the law.

An ecstatic happiness flooded Rose's heart, and the little twilit space, with its square of sun-baked grass, became a paradisaical garden enclosed, full of sweeter fragrance than could ever have arisen from the mignonette and stocks planted by the "little ones" in the beds they spasmodically tended. Her joy was enhanced by the knowledge that from her window Miss Quayle could see her strolling with the wonder of the world—who dared to defy her.

"She may kill me if she likes, but she'll never separate us!" she exclaimed, all the fervour of her being in her eyes.

"You have really beautiful eyes, Rose," said Helen critically, dropping the last and sweetest drop of honey into her already brimming cup.

The prayer-bell rang, harsh and discordant, and the girls began to flock towards the house. Many of them pointedly ignored Rose and Helen, who lingered, the last to go in. Rose caught Lulu Robinson's remark to Chrissie Field.

"Stuck-up cat! I hate her! And Rose is getting just as bad."

The words recurred to her later with an unpleasant little shock, as she lay awake, thinking of Helen and dreaming deliciously of their recent conversation. What Helen said about Lulu Robinson was of course quite true. She *was* vulgar and stupid—and all the rest of it. Rose was deeply ashamed of the partial

intimacy into which, before Helen's advent, she
had drifted with Lulu. And yet—Lulu was kind
and warm-hearted and sympathetic. Those things
counted. They counted, at least, to Rose. A stab
of compunction pierced her at the thought of how
completely she had "cut" Lulu. There was May, too;
and Chrissie Field; and Ethel Cummings. None of
them were clever, none of them were particularly interesting, yet she liked them; they had been kind
and comfortable, and it had been jolly to laugh with
them and to plot all sorts of absurd little clandestine
and innocent diversions, so futile, so amusing to the
average schoolgirl, and so enjoyed till lately by Rose
herself. Her mind was full of tumult. Surely no
one ever wanted so many and such different things
altogether, as she in her futile stupidity desired.

Helen's friendship, Helen's approval were priceless,
of course. Not for all the world would she lose one
nor forfeit the other. And yet—she liked being
popular! It was bitter to know that she was losing
her popularity. She liked also, but secretly now, all
the "silliness" which Helen loftily despised—the
giggling, the surreptitious purchase of sweets, the
hairbreadth escapes from detection and punishment,
the thrilling tales about "Frank" and "Charlie."
Rose blushed in the darkness. If only Helen knew
of these low tastes and unconfessed desires!—Helen,
with her grave, disdainful, beautiful face; Helen,
who cared only for the really important things of
life: books and "art" and intellectual conversation.
Rose gave herself up in despair. She was fundament-
ally unworthy of Helen, but the fact must be for ever
concealed.

XIV

HEAD AND HEART

A MORE stormy period than ever was ahead for the girl in regard to her relationship with Miss Quayle, who from an unprejudiced standpoint, was at the moment not unworthy of pity.

Rejoicing at the outset, in her success at acquiring as a pupil the daughter of Professor Fergurson,—that luminary of the intellectual world,—not only was she debarred from making use of her for the honour of the school, but she must find Helen obstinately attached to a child for whom she had no liking, and for whom, now that her illusions as to her mental capacity were dispelled, she also had no use.

In her annoyance she went so far as to write to Professor Fergurson on the subject, begging him not only to reconsider the vexed question of examinations, but to use his influence during the holidays to induce his "dear child, a girl of exceptional ability," to choose her friends more carefully.

To both requests the Professor returned a polite refusal. With regard to examinations, like the psalmist, his heart was fixed, and with his daughter's private concerns and predilections, as he told his correspondent, he had neither the power nor the will to interfere. He moreover added that he had perfect confidence in Helen's judgment.

Miss Quayle was baffled. Fate, constantly ironical, had hoisted her with her own petard by giving her to deal with a girl whose nurture in modern notions went a step farther than her own. To Professor Fergurson and his self-possessed daughter, Miss Quayle was already old-fashioned. Children to her, were still slaves to be modernly ordered and directed. She had not arrived, and she would never arrive at the very latest doctrine—that of non-interference and self-development for the younger generation.

Irritated and baffled by Helen, whose scrupulous if contemptuous obedience to rules gave her no opportunity for the scenes which her nature had grown to demand, her attention was more than ever concentrated upon Rose, for whom a season of real persecution set in. That Miss Quayle had persuaded herself that she acted from a sense of duty, and was sincere in her attempts to correct the girl's many faults, was no consolation to the object of her unceasing vigilance.

"Why do you play into her hands by so constantly signing that ridiculous book?" Helen one day put the question with calm reasonableness, which, joined to a slight note of disdain, cut Rose to the quick. "Surely it's better not to be late and to remember to put your things away, than to give her the chance of making these undignified fusses over which you upset yourself so unnecessarily?"

Certainly it would have been "much better," and to Helen, the soul of order, the essence of scrupulous neatness, such a course presented no difficulties. It was otherwise with Rose, whose existence was one long struggle against forgetfulness of the minor duties of life.

"Does she think I do it on purpose?" was her silent, heart-broken comment on her friend's remark.

It was a wet Sunday afternoon, and the girls, who would otherwise have been in the garden, were herded together in the dining-rooms waiting for tea. Some were reading, others talking; Miss Bird in charge to restrain undue noise.

Rose was crying hopelessly. Everything that week had gone wrong. She had begun to work again, or rather to overwork, in the feverish, excited fashion, which she brought to new enthusiasms, and in addition to the mental strain of carefully prepared exercises and unremitting attention in class, she had been "interviewed" in the study four times between Sunday and Sunday, forced to listen to the thunderous denunciations of Miss Quayle, and to endure subsequent "exile." For two successive days her schoolfellows had been forbidden to speak to her. The ban had been recently removed, and again, though unknown to Helen, another quite recent "row" had resulted in a further isolation-order from headquarters. Nerves were not allowed at Minerva House. They were never mentioned except in accents of scorn as the long ago discarded encumbrance of early Victorian womanhood. Yet, incredible paradox, Rose was suffering from this non-existent cause.

"Helen Fergurson," said Miss Bird timidly, looking up from the pages of *Good Words*, "do you know that no one is allowed to speak to Rose?" She blushed while she made the remark, necessity only, forcing her to address Helen, whose manner always made her desperately embarrassed and uncomfortable.

"No, I did not. Since when?" inquired the girl coolly.

"Since after lunch-time. I think you were out of the room when Miss Quayle came in, so you couldn't be expected to know," she added, in a flustered, apologetic tone.

"Obviously not," returned Helen. She got up at once, and leaving Rose's side, strolled over to the bookcase, from which she selected a book and began to read.

Rose continued to cry because she couldn't help it. Tears were now beyond her control, and they dropped fast behind the book which with shaking hands she held before her face as an ineffectual screen. They had been tears of sheer weakness before, but now there was bitterness as well as weakness in their flow.

"Have some chocolate, darling!" whispered Lulu Robinson, leaning over towards her. "It'll make you feel ever so much better. It's a shame! A perfectly disgusting shame! But it's lovely chocolate with pink cream." She dropped a stick of the delicacy on to Rose's lap just as Miss Bird for the second time looked up.

"Lulu Robinson, were you talking to Rose?" she inquired sharply. She had no fear of Lulu.

"Yes, I was," returned the damsel with defiance.

"Then you'll sign your name for a conduct mark. There's no excuse for *you*. You heard me speak to Helen just now, so it's direct disobedience."

"I don't care! It's a shame!" muttered Lulu as she took up the pen offered by Miss Bird, and angrily inscribed her name on the register's accusing page.

Rose, listening behind her book, was conscious of sudden tumultuous waves of emotion and half-realized thought. It was not for the first time that she had almost unconsciously, and to its disadvantage, weighed Helen's dignity against the impulsive warm-heartedness of Lulu Robinson and other kindred spirits of doubtful refinement and undoubted meagreness of intellect. Her critical spirit, never wholly submerged, was for the moment alive and clamorous, and though it was devastating, almost unbearable to detect any flaw in her idol, she found herself hurt that Helen's sense of the unworthiness of an "unseemly wrangle with a woman like Miss Bird," had not been overborne by her affection.

Rose had suffered acutely during the few past weeks from the insistence of the critical spirit. She had endured the pain of coldness from Helen on account of a certain *rapprochement* with Lulu Robinson who now slept in her room. Lulu suffered agonies from toothache, and Rose, overwhelmed with pity, had so deftly ministered to her all one night that Lulu's former rancour against her was forgotten in gratitude, and even after the extraction of the tooth Rose refused to break the bond established between them through suffering. She felt drawn to Lulu by the mere tie of humanity, and it was this which Helen failed to understand.

"It was quite right of you to do anything you could for her when she was in pain," she repeated, in answer to Rose's supplications, "but I fail to see why you should go on being intimate with her now that she's all right. She's quite unworthy of you!" This with a scornful tilt of her delicate little nose.

"But I'm *not* intimate with her," Rose protested. "I never spend a minute away from you that I can help. I only can't help feeling rather fond of Lulu. It's just as though my baby had been ill and I was thankful to have it well again," she went on desperately, finding that Helen was silent. "Oh, *Helen*, do understand!"

But Helen was obdurate and uncomprehending.
"It seems to me perfectly ridiculous," she declared,
speaking truth. "But do as you please. Don't let
me interfere with your friendships."

The icy words had cut Rose to the heart, but she
had refused to be cold to Lulu. She *could* not be cold
to a girl who had clung to her and cried, and whose
pain she had soothed. It might be ridiculous, but
there it was, and though Helen's partial estrangement
was the result, and she was desperately miserable, she
continued to be "nice" to Lulu. She felt a warm rush
of gratitude towards her now, and furtively squeezed
her hand as Lulu passed her after signing the book.

"Never mind, duckie!" whispered the buxom young
woman, taking advantage of Miss Bird's scuttle out of
the room to ring the tea-bell. "I'm going to speak
to you whenever I get the chance, and so are Joan
Milbank and Chrissie and Eva. I don't care a hang
for the old conduct mark. It's a horrid shame that
you're always in rows about nothing. Only do stop
crying. You'll be ill!"

Rose made a valiant effort to pull herself together,
and succeeded in checking her tears. Lulu's warm
partisanship was comforting, as were also the clandestine pats and hasty caresses of other girls moved to
pity and indignation by the girl's white, tear-stained
face. Miss Mortlake also was kind. She would like
to have been kinder, but Miss Quayle's personality
dominated the house, and it was a nice point whether
teachers or pupils stood in the greater terror of her
wrath. To Miss Mortlake it had ever been an article
of faith, that however uncomfortable the result of her
activities, Miss Quayle could do no wrong. Timid
criticism always died before the recollection of her

Principal's "great intellect" which must, of necessity, lead her to "the right course." To-night, for the first time, she criticized in a free spirit without fear, and with the child's worn-out face as witness against her, came to the conclusion that Miss Quayle's methods were not always wise.

These unusual reflections occurred while she was marshalling the girls for evening church.

"Rose Cottingham will walk with me," she announced, when the crocodile had formed for its journey to Divine service. As she spoke, she was painfully aware that the girl would consider herself taken into custody, and she sighed at the necessity for upholding discipline where her feeling favoured leniency.

"I'm sorry, Rose, to have to prevent you from walking with one of the girls," she began awkwardly, "but you see, you have brought all this upon yourself, haven't you?"

Rose's only reply was a jerk of the shoulders. She was tired, worn out and wretched, as only the young can be wretched, and her one desire was to escape any further lectures and admonitions. Destitute of the tact to discern this, Miss Mortlake strove gently to improve the occasion.

"If only, dear," she began, "you would pray to-night for strength to be less heedless, more mindful to keep those wise rules which Miss Quayle has laid down, I'm sure you would find——"

"Oh, *do* let me have a little peace!" Rose implored angrily, rudely even, yet with so much misery in her suddenly unchildish voice, that Miss Mortlake was startled into comprehending silence.

"Yes, dear, I won't say any more," she returned, after a pause. "I see you're—tired." She put her hand gently for a moment over the girl's little gloved hand, and though Rose turned her head abruptly away, she returned the pressure, and Miss Mortlake went into church curiously moved and happy. It was odd, but she would have given much for this child's affection. It was she, not Rose, who prayed for strength that evening, and it was vouchsafed to her in such measure that at nine o'clock, with scarcely a tremor, she found herself knocking at the sacrosanct door of Miss Quayle's study. No mortal ever learned what went on within, but to Rose's stupefaction, next morning she was engulfed in the Principal's embrace, told that she was forgiven, and in hyperbolical language bidden to go and sin no more.

She walked to school with Helen, and received official confirmation of what she knew before with regard to her friend's attitude during the period of the Principal's displeasure.

"I felt sure you would understand that I was in no fear of the conduct mark," she explained. "That is an absurdity which is neither here nor there. But I will never give a woman like Miss Bird the satisfaction of power over me, and the only way to avoid such an indignity is to give her no opportunity. You understand, dearest, don't you?"

Rose understood; but in spite of the joy of a full reconciliation with Helen, who even agreed, though without comprehension, to condone "niceness" to Lulu Robinson, her heart was still unreasonably sore. While she admired the firmness, the consistent attitude of Helen, she realized miserably that its imitation was beyond her.

Dignity and proper pride, for her, would have no meaning, she felt, if Helen ever needed help or support.

There was however little likelihood that this would ever be the case, for above the turmoil of school existence, Helen walked serene, self-sufficient, contemptuous of its trivialities, indifferent as to her status amongst the other girls. As a matter of fact she rather enjoyed her unpopularity, amused by the attitude of those who affected to dismiss her with the epithet "prig," usually associated with one or more opprobrious adjectives.

She knew that her schoolfellows did not really dismiss her. One could not dismiss Helen, though it was quite possible to dislike her, and the "prig" theory advanced to explain her, was not altogether adequate, since it did not cover the ground. She was merely an exceedingly clever girl, whose environment had been in all respects different from that of the average young person, and that the result should have an exasperating effect on the average young person was not surprising.

She interested and annoyed most of the Minervarites; she both interested and fascinated Rose.

It was not only that she could read Greek and Latin —though that in itself was a stupendous and awe-inspiring fact—it was rather the ease and readiness of her diction, the familiar allusions to books of which Rose had never heard, the introduction into familiar conversation of topics like socialism, or of something called metaphysics (a marvellous and exciting mystery imperfectly understood, as she owned, by Helen herself), which, to some extent, accounted for Rose's infatuation. But chiefly it was her delicate, elusive beauty, and her slow, curious smile which ravished the younger girl, and silenced, though it never quite killed, the critical spirit within her. Intimacy with Helen was a tremendous spur to her ambition, and with her pupil's renewed interest in work, Miss Quayle's hopes revived. Though fate decreed that Helen should be academically useless, Rose, whose alternate stupidity and brilliance were her despair, might yet justify her existence by winning scholarships.

"She says I'm to go in for the Senior because Miss Woods told her I was first in the Literature and Composition exam.!" Rose hastened to confide one morning to her friend. "Isn't it perfectly awful? I wouldn't mind if it *was* only Literature and History and those sort of things. But it's the awful Mathematics. I *can't* do Mathematics, Helen. I waste all my time over it, and it's all no good, and I shall fail in the end."

"But write and tell your grandmother to say she won't allow you to take the exam.," advised Helen.

Rose laughed at the comic notion. "Grandmamma doesn't know what the 'Senior' is," she explained. "And if she did she'd say that though it was perfect nonsense for girls, so long as I am in this new-fangled sort of school I must do what I'm told."

Helen shrugged her shoulders.

"I suppose we shall never understand one another's home circumstances. To me your grandmother seems to live in a feudal castle."

"And to me your father lives in a castle in the air," Rose returned, guiltless of irony. "But what shall I do, Helen?"

"If I were you, I should just concentrate on the subjects you're good at, and not bother about the Mathematics at all. Do as you did before. I think that was perfectly *splendid*," declared Helen musingly.

"You got all the real honour without any of the vulgarity. Let Miss Quayle rave. She's only a Philistine."

Rose smiled. She knew now what a Philistine meant, and the idea of causing it to rave, appealed to her. She began to put the suggestion at once into practice by the careful reading of *Julius Cæsar*, the play set for the "Senior" and the as careful ignoring of Algebra.

.   .   .   .

Two events before the end of the term stood out in Rose's after memory as ineffaceable; landmarks in different departments of consciousness, each in its separate fashion illuminating and instructive. Much as the two girls had talked, various as were the topics which with infinite gravity, if with some immaturity of thought, they had discussed, the question of religion had not so far arisen. The matter, sometimes looming so large in Rose's mind, at other times forgotten, suddenly, as was its wont, re-emerged one evening into troubled significance.

"Helen," she began, with a quick, childish question, "do you believe the Bible?"

"In what sense?" inquired Helen, raising her eyebrows.

"Why, as they all believe it here. As *every one* believes it. As God's Word, you know. As our religion."

"'Every one' doesn't believe it in that sense. My father doesn't. Neither do I. I'm not a Christian."

"You mean—you're an atheist?" demanded Rose breathlessly.

"There's no such thing. I'm an agnostic."

"What does that mean?"

"It means one who doesn't know, and *can't* know, anything about the existence of God."

"Then that's what I am!" exclaimed Rose, with a gasp of conviction and a surprise worthy of Monsieur Jourdain. "Only I didn't know what it was called. But, Helen, are there many people like that? Agnostics?"

"Ever so many. Most of the thinking people nowadays are agnostics," returned Helen, speaking with calm assurance for her "set."

Rose was silent, too overwhelmed for comment. It was a stupendous discovery to make—and she had made it alone, for until this moment she had never heard of agnostics, though that there were wicked men dwelling in outer darkness who called themselves atheists, and blasphemed, she was aware.

"Then agnostics only say they don't know? That's quite different from being an atheist, isn't it?"

"Of course. It's just as foolish to say there *is* no God as to say we are *sure* there's one, and to declare, as the Christians do declare, that He must be Jesus Christ. Agnostics don't deny God; they simply say that as human beings we can know nothing about Him."

"But perhaps we shall some day?" Rose asked eagerly.

Helen shrugged her shoulders, with an habitual gesture.

"That's as far as one can go. The other is mere speculation."

For a long time while they walked to and fro over the grass-plot Rose reflected silently, her head in a whirl of new thoughts.

"Does Miss Quayle know you're not a Christian?" she asked at length.

"She must know my father isn't. Everybody who
knows his work must be aware of that. She probably
thinks with her old-fashioned ideas that I'm a child,
and therefore I know nothing about it."

"Well, there are two agnostics in her school at any
rate!" Rose observed as the prayer-bell rang. "How
angry she'd be if she knew!" she whispered, laughing
in sheer childish amusement at the joke against the
unsuspecting lady, who passed them on the top of the
stairs, and stopped to remark that their hair was
untidy.

"Go downstairs, both of you, and attend to your
appearance, and do not again venture to appear before
me in a slovenly fashion," she commanded, unaware,
poor soul! that the younger generation the arrangement of whose hair she could still command, had
already summed her up as an old-fashioned Christian.
Whatever possibilities of humour the situation held
was lost equally upon both generations.

In the other unforgetable revelation, it was Miss
Quayle who played the chief rôle. The occasion was
an afternoon party at the house of a wealthy woman
whose girls were pupils at the college. Miss Quayle
was bidden to the feast, and an invitation through her,
was also extended to Rose and Helen, the only girls
among the Minervarites known to Frances and Katie
Colquhoun, the two daughters of the house.

Thus it chanced that at four o'clock one Saturday
afternoon, chaperoned by Miss Quayle, they drove
across London to Queen Anne's Gate, the scene of
festivity.

The experience was as unusual as to Rose at least
it was terrifying. She was always tongue-tied in the
presence of the Principal, whose voluminous grey silk

gown almost filled the cab, billowing on to the laps of the slim girls opposite.

During the drive, Rose was scarcely once addressed, Miss Quayle having acquired the habit of ignoring her, except for the pur oses of "rows." To Helen, whose cool, unembarrassed replies were the envy and wonder of her friend, she condescended affably. Miss Quayle's conversation with all and sundry, was always in the nature of a condescension. When she conversed, it was much as a queen might speak to some unimportant subject from whom for purposes of her own she wished to elicit information, and though with Helen, mindful of her parentage, she unbent considerably, the regal tone was never wholly abandoned, and never failed to impress Rose, even while Helen's insouciant manner in the face of it, caused her fearful and secret amusement. "How can she be so cool!" she thought. "I nearly die of fright when she speaks to me. She makes me feel so small. And it's not only me; it's every one—except Helen, who is just wonderful! I'm sure they'll all feel small this afternoon directly she comes into the room."

Once out of the cab, however, and freed from her immediate presence, she forgot Miss Quayle. The Colquhouns' house was beautiful, and all Rose's gaiety of spirit responded to the air of festivity which exhaled from the open door—a door disclosing a wide staircase thronged with laughing and chattering people. Ostensibly a young people's party, there were nevertheless plenty of elder folk present, sitting or standing in groups about the spacious rooms, one of which had been cleared for dancing. Frances and Katie ran out to meet their friends, and Rose, who loved dancing, was soon whirling over the polished floor with Katie, absolutely happy, sensuously enjoying the beauty of the banked-up roses on the mantelpieces, the glimpses of the park framed by the windows, the gay music, and unconsciously also, the spectacle of well-dressed men and women of the world as unconnected with anything academic as tropical butterflies. The whole scene was an enchanted dream to her, a delicious escape from the routine and severity of her daily life.

It was when she paused once, laughing and breathless, at the end of a dance, that through an open door she caught sight of Miss Quayle in an adjoining room, sitting alone, neglected. No one hurried forward to speak to her, and as Rose half expected, she made no imperious movement to command attention. Young and old passed her without even a glance at the august presence, enthroned in an arm-chair, towards which no courtiers subserviently pressed, and Rose checked a little gasp of amazement and some other emotion, painful, but hard to define. Some one spoke to her at the moment, putting a hand on her shoulder, and, turning, she saw her hostess.

"This is the little girl who dances so beautifully! I forget your name, dear?"

"Rose, Mother. Rose Cottingham. She's a Minervarite, you know!" explained Frances volubly in passing.

"*Rose*, then, let me introduce my son. He wants to know whether he may dance with you." She took a laughing young man by the arm, who to the girl's suffocating embarrassment made an exaggerated bow to her.

She saw a slender, very handsome boy of eighteen or nineteen, with dark reddish hair, and amber-coloured eyes, who instantly placed a bold arm round her waist.

"We must wait for the music, I suppose," he began, without releasing her. "But meanwhile what's a 'Minervarite'? It sounds alarming." Then, without waiting for Rose's reply, and still to her infinite embarrassment keeping his arm about her, he addressed his mother.

"I say, Mater, who's the old girl sitting over there all alone?" he asked.

Mrs. Colquhoun drew him aside, thus releasing Rose, upon whom she cast an uneasy glance.

"Miss Quayle," she heard her whisper.

"Not the girls' school-marm? Why ever did you ask her?"

Mrs. Colquhoun shrugged her shoulders. "Policy; but I wish I hadn't. She's on my mind. No one wants to talk to her, of course, so I must go and cope with the situation myself." She made a comic grimace.

"Well, if you *will* ask school-marms—" The young man's words were drowned in the opening bars of a new waltz, and once more capturing Rose, he forced her to dance. She did not enjoy the waltz. Her partner was too tall for her, and not only was it a strain to keep all the time on the tips of her toes, but she was consumed with shyness and troubled by a new, bewildering feeling of pity. It amazed her, but she was actually feeling sorry for Miss Quayle! For Miss Quayle, the despotic ruler who had so often struck terror into her heart. When the music ceased and with a laughing, absent-minded word or two the boy left her she was thankful. Her first glance was for Miss Quayle. Yes, she was still sitting alone, and Rose thought she looked curiously dejected and unlike her usual self. Again she felt the stab of pity,

and it was with unfeigned relief that she saw Mrs.
Colquhoun crossing the room to speak to her neglected
guest. She was glad Miss Quayle did not know she
was a "situation" to be coped with.

Through the rest of the afternoon an undercurrent
of bewildering thought ran through her mind. Miss
Quayle, the Thunderer, the Autocrat, was, then, supreme only in her own little kingdom? Outside, there
were realms in which she was only "the girls' school-
marm," and a bore! Helen's attitude towards her—
an attitude which she had thought peculiar to the
exceptional and wonderful Helen herself—probably
only expressed what the great world thought of the
principal of Quayle College This was an instance in
which a prophet's honour was in her own country and
nowhere else. It was a lesson in relative values which
made a deep and lasting impression upon the girl.

The drive home was almost a silent one. Miss
Quayle, drawing a pamphlet from the satin bag she
carried on her arm, became apparently immersed in
pages of statistics, and Rose reflected painfully that
she might be feeling sore and hurt. It was curious to
be thinking of her with something like tenderness as
an old, neglected woman. Rose wondered at herself
and inwardly hoped that Helen had not overheard
the little conversation between mother and son. She
resolved in any case not to mention the episode.
Possibly her friend hadn't noticed it, and in any case
she had an instinctive knowledge that Helen wouldn't
understand her feeling about it. She had so often
expressed her vehement dislike of Miss Quayle that
Helen would now think her quite ridiculous. "But
this is different, somehow!" Rose asserted, without
definitely defining the difference, which was that she

could abuse Miss Quayle, the aggressor and school-marm, but could take no pleasure in the humiliation of a lonely old woman. And the two were strangely one.

It was supper-time when they returned after the afternoon's unusual dissipation, and Rose was fallen upon by dozens of girls eager to know "what it was like," Helen being considered too unapproachable to question.

"You look *sweet* in your white frock, duckie!" Lulu assured her. "I hate Helen's dress. It doesn't suit her. Did you really dance with a man? Wasn't it heavenly? . . . Oh, you silly child, why didn't you have fun with him? Didn't he want to sit out with you? I do wish *I'd* had the chance!"

Helen drew her away from Lulu for a walk round the garden during the ten minutes' interval between supper and prayers.

"It was awfully nice, wasn't it?" began Rose, rather nervously. "Didn't you enjoy it?"

"Yes. Miss Quayle wasn't much of a success, though, was she?" Helen smiled quietly. "It's good for her to discover occasionally that there's a society in which she doesn't count."

"I was sorry for her," declared Rose almost defiantly, after a silence.

Helen glanced at her. "Were you? I believe you were. I know what you mean," she added meditatively, and Rose was both surprised and grateful. "You're much more human than I am," went on Helen, after a pause. "That's why the girls are fond of you and hate me. Perhaps it would be better if I cared more. But I don't. I don't particularly want them to like me. Now, you take a real interest

13

in their toothaches and their new frocks, and their
letters from their mothers and aunts. Of course it's
quite right of you, and very nice, I suppose——"

"I never thought about its being *right*—it's just
natural," protested Rose, rather bewildered.

"Yes, that's the difference between us. You're
natural. I *understand*. And you *feel*. I understand your feeling about Miss Quayle, for instance,
but I don't share it. I just look on, and am interested
and rather amused, but not in any way touched."

Rose was puzzled again. Helen's habit of intro-
spection, caught from her sophisticated home set, was
still new and confusing to her. She never consciously
analysed herself. Things happened, and she responded
to them, that was all; and she humbly realized how
crude and childish she must seem in the eyes of her
friend.

"I suppose I have the reasonable, intellectual way
of looking at life," pursued Helen, still further
dazzling her, "and you have the emotional way.
Yours is more attractive, of course—people will always like you—but it will get you into lots of
trouble," she added, with a flash of foresight rather
remarkable.

"How will it?" asked Rose, profoundly impressed.
It was news to her that she "looked at life" at all.
She was only conscious of accepting it with joy or
rage or boredom as the case might be.

"It will be a tie. It will keep you back from doing
what you might do. People will always be bothering
you," said Helen, more vaguely than usual. "You
have too much pity, Rose," she went on decisively,
after a moment, as though she had been striving to
arrange her thoughts. "And you haven't a grain of

self-confidence. You always give people credit for being much cleverer and more important than they are. Most people are very unimportant."

"But they're all—*alive*," Rose protested meekly, unable to express the matter more coherently.

"Yes, you have far too much feeling," declared Helen, apparently understanding her.

XV

THE FERGURSON HOUSEHOLD

THE next eight or nine months passed swiftly, with a lack of any exciting outward events and a marked decrease in "rows." Rose was working hard, and in proportion as Miss Quayle's renewed hopes for her intellectual achievements resulted in a certain measure of affability towards her, Miss Bird's eagerness to report her for carelessness and untidiness decreased. It was not safe to report a girl who was in favour, and Rose was therefore permitted to overwork herself in comparative peace.

Overwork in individual cases was the result of a system, on paper safeguarded by rules, in practice disregarded. Miss Quayle made a great point of her insistence on the physical health of her pupils, and admiring and satisfied parents were shown printed leaflets on which every girl recorded daily the time she expended on the preparation of lessons. "These leaflets," explained Miss Quayle, "are carefully checked each day by the form mistress, and no girl is allowed to work longer than the maximum number of hours, the time limit as you see being clearly stated above."

She spoke in good faith, and in good faith her statement was accepted by the parent of anxious temperament, while just as naturally the time-tables were systematically "cooked" by ambitious girls, who regarded them merely as a formula of no more account than the rule of silence in the bedrooms. As a matter of fact Rose worked from morning till night, with no physical exercise beyond that of the flannelled morning drill, the walk to and from the college, and the weekly dancing lesson.

Quayle College, so advanced on strictly intellectual lines, was lamentably behind the times in regard to opportunities for games. At a period when games for girls were becoming not only the fashion but a recognized need, the college remained without a square inch of playground, and no attempt was made to obviate this defect by the hiring of a field for outdoor sports. At Minerva House the strips of garden were too small even for the mild diversion of croquet.

That to any appreciable extent the girl's health did not suffer, was probably due to the preceding season of idleness, and to the fact that she was, on the whole, happy and interested. Things were going well with her. Her devotion to Helen, though less ecstatic than during the first weeks of their friendship, still satisfied her emotions without jeopardizing her popularity with other girls. Helen was now less exacting, and Rose felt the relief of being free to giggle occasionally in an atmosphere less refined and superior than that exhaled by her dearest friend, who was, nevertheless, responsible for a great deal of Rose's quick mental development and increasing maturity of mind. At this time, though with occasional lapses into childishness, she was terribly intellectual, and took herself very seriously. It was a phase which the mildly ironical attitude of her grandmother during the holidays did much to encourage.

"Leave your sister to her studies, Lucie," she would recommend. "Remember, we have a blue-stocking amongst us, who mustn't be disturbed when her brain is working," and though angry and hurt, as in her younger days she had been under her grandmother's snubs, Rose was grateful for one or two privileges denied to her as a little girl.   She could sit in her bed-room now, unchallenged, and was even permitted the use of an old bureau, which, ever since she could re-member, had stood locked in a corner by the window. In the holidays, Helen sent her parcels of books men-tioned in the course of their earnest conversations together during the term, and with thrilling eagerness Rose read *Looking Backward*, *Merrie England*, and other popular literature connected with the socialism of the period.   It was of socialism she liked best to talk with Helen.   Already the idea had seized her, char-acteristically on the emotional side, and she began to look upon every poor man or woman she met, with eager admiring interest, as the rulers in disguise of some vague but glorious future.

The holidays for Rose were almost as strenuous as the term.   She found herself an outsider in the home circle, a fish out of water whose only possibility of return to its native element was solitary reading and writing.   Lucie, as she observed with wonder, had lost all fear of her grandmother, with whom she was now on easy terms, as near affection as with Mrs. Lester could be attained.   The child was very pretty even at the gawky stage of half-grown girlhood, and the old lady, proud of her beauty, treated her with tolerant amiability.   There was, indeed, very little to scold Lucie about.   Always neat, always even-tempered, she did marvellous embroidery, spoke French fluently with a fairly good accent, was clever and capable in household ways, behaved very prettily

when she called on the neighbours with her grandmother, and, in short, fulfilled all Mrs. Lester's ideals
of perfect womanhood.

Upon Rose her grandmother still looked askance.
She had grown, she had certainly improved somewhat
in looks, and she bade fair to have a pretty, erect
figure. But she was still, in her eyes, an odd-looking,
uncomfortable girl, whose preoccupation with books
stamped her as a born "blue-stocking," and as such,
ridiculous. She was so serious, so earnest, so annoyingly ungirlish, so lacking in charm. At least, so Mrs.
Lester judged her granddaughter till a chance episode
gave her an opportunity of seeing Rose in a different
and to her, bewildering aspect.

Visitors called one day during the Christmas holidays, amongst them Major Hawley. Mrs. Lester,
giving her attention to two rather dull ladies, saw Rose
talking to the old man, who had always liked her and
was now in a genial fashion chaffing and teasing her.
The ladies professed an interest in china, and by way
of respite from boredom, Mrs. Lester led them to
her china cupboard near the corner in which Rose
and the Major were seated. While her guests were
occupied in examining its contents with ecstatic exclamations on their beauty, she listened and looked
at Rose, to whom her notice had been directed by the
Major's frequent laughter. Rose was amused, and
Mrs. Lester did not know the girl with her face lit
up, her eyes sparkling, and her tongue going at a
rate which amazed her grandmother, who felt that she
had never before heard the child talk. And she was
talking well—almost wittily. Her repartees were
quick and pointed, and her companion had to work
hard to match her nimble replies to his badinage.

Rose was going to be witty, then, if she could not be beautiful! Mrs. Lester was as surprised as she was gratified, for in the salons during the old *régime*, her constant standard, wit was always accepted as a fair exchange for beauty, and even sometimes eclipsed it. If Rose could be amusing with strangers, it was a pity she did not extend the faculty to her own home, she thought rather acidly, without the smallest realization that the flint must be there before the spark can be emitted, and that the flint offered, had been of a peculiarly unresponsive nature.

"You like Major Hawley?" she asked, when the visitors were gone.

"Yes," said Rose, rather surprised at being addressed.

"Yet he isn't at all *clever*," returned her grandmother, laying a somewhat mocking stress on the word.

"I don't know. I never thought about it. He's funny!" The sparkle had not yet died out of her eyes, and her grandmother thought she looked almost pretty.

"*I* never know what to say to him," remarked Lucie, who had been pouring out tea. "He seems to me to talk nonsense."

"I like nonsense," said Rose.

"I thought you were much too superior," observed Mrs. Lester in a tone more amiable than her words. "I thought only books and learning pleased you?"

"I like everything—when it's good," declared Rose comprehensively. . . . "I wish the Winters were here," she added with a sigh.

Mrs. Winter's now even more infrequent home-coming had never once coincided with the holidays, and it was nearly four years since Rose had seen her.

She had again this year passed the winter in Egypt, and was now in Switzerland with her husband and Geoffrey, who was in his third year at Oxford.

"They were home in June for a little while," Lucie said. "Mrs. Winter looks awfully ill, and Geoffrey's grown very ugly," she volunteered further. "He's got such enormous feet and hands, and he's so clumsy and gawky!"

"He's going to be a very fine man," remarked her grandmother, inspecting the china cupboard with critical attention. "Lucie, can I trust you to dust this china to-morrow? It needs it badly."

It was not till the following Easter that Rose paid her long-deferred visit to Helen's home. Professor Fergurson had been much abroad, and Helen had always either joined him or stayed with friends during the holidays. But now that he was once more settled in London, he sent, at his daughter's request, a formal invitation to Mrs. Lester requesting the pleasure of a visit from her granddaughter during the whole of the short holiday.

In her turn Miss Quayle received a lesson in conflicting values, when as a result of the Professor's invitation, Mrs. Lester wrote to her making stringent inquiries as to the social status of the Fergursons, of whom, to the stupefaction of the principal of Quayle College, her correspondent had never heard. She had not allowed for the claims of the "County," nor had she realized that Rose Cottingham, to her a mere country girl whose relatives were obviously not in affluence, was a person of sufficient importance in her own provenance to be protected from casual invitations from learned men of European reputation.

In the ensuing correspondence between the two ladies, there was material for comedy.

I have no doubt that he is a clever man [wrote Mrs. Lester in reply to a list of academic titles furnished in sarcastic vein by Miss Quayle], but my inquiry had no concern with that. I asked whether he and the sister who I understand keeps house for him are gentlepeople of the class with whom my granddaughter may fitly associate.

Miss Quayle's reply, though given in ignorance of Mrs. Lester's exacting requirements, presumably satisfied her, for Rose received permission to accept the Fergursons' invitation.

That Professor Fergurson was the son of a small shopkeeper in a remote Scottish village, did not transpire, Miss Quayle probably being ignorant of a fact which, with Mrs. Lester, would have made all his intellectual achievements dust in the balance of her decision against the propriety of allowing her granddaughter to stay as a guest in his house.

Rose looked forward to the visit with a mixture of delight, excitement, and trepidation.

She would not for the world have missed it, but she was desperately afraid of her own ignorance and her unworthiness to enter intellectual society.

She drove across London with Helen on the breaking-up day, to a fairly large house in one of the Kensington Squares. The door was opened by a neat parlourmaid, and an almost simultaneous opening of another door within the hall, revealed Professor Fergurson, a tall, handsome man of five and forty, whose velveteen coat and eyeglasses were the first attribute of his personality noticed by Rose.

He enfolded Helen in a grave, tender embrace, and

then turned to her companion, who was lingering shyly behind.

"This is Rose, Father," said Helen, drawing her forward.

"I'm very glad to see Rose," the Professor returned smiling as he shook hands with her. "I've heard a great deal about her."

"Here's Aunt Aggie!" Helen exclaimed without much enthusiasm, and Rose found a small, slim, mouse-like little woman at her elbow, who greeted her in a voice curiously like her brother's and Helen's. The family, Rose noticed, spoke with a certain precise, clear diction, which betrayed their Scottish blood, though Helen and her father were guiltless of the accent which in Miss Fergurson's speech rather pleased her.

"Will you come to your room?" asked the mouse-like little lady, and Rose followed her up a flight of green felt-covered stairs, while Helen lingered below with her father, whom it was obvious she adored.

The bedroom she entered, had Morris cretonnes, a Morris wallpaper, and an austere little bed in plain, dark wood. The walls were hung with coloured prints of Italian masterpieces, and there was a stone jug filled with daffodils upon the dressing-table.

To Rose who had never before seen Morris designs, the whole effect of the room was enchanting, and when later Helen took her over the house, which had recently been decorated by the then fashionable firm, she realized that to understand Helen, one must see her amongst her surroundings—in her right setting, so to speak.

When her young hostess changed her dress for tea, discarding her ordinary school frock for a Liberty gown of peacock blue with hanging sleeves, copied from one of Rossetti's pictures, Rose's admiration knew no bounds.

"I keep these dresses for home wear," she told her. "One can't introduce them amongst the Philistines at school. *You* ought to have an artistic dress, Rose, to wear at home, you know. Why don't you get one while you're here?"

"Grandmamma would have a fit!" declared Rose with a little bubble of mirth.

Professor Fergurson came in to tea, which Helen poured out at a little black table near the fireplace, which had a screen of peacock's feathers to conceal the empty grate, the weather being unusually warm for spring. Miss Fergurson sat in a chair covered with cretonne, whose design showed conventional tulips, and as soon as she had put down her cup, knitted silently while Helen and her father talked.

Rose listened, admiringly respectful of both. Professor Fergurson, she noticed, treated Helen as though she were a woman, and for all the affection in his tone, there was about his conversation with her, the touch of deference he would have accorded an acquaintance who was also an intellectual equal. They talked of his travels in France and in Germany, whither he had gone to investigate the results of certain experiments in socialism, and to study and compare different phases and schools of progressive thought on the subject. Helen glibly alluded to organizations and societies in London, and asked questions about analogous institutions in Berlin, grasping intelligently all that her father said with regard to them.

It was marvellous to Rose, who in the depths of her spirit sighed her discouragement. Never, she felt, could she hope to know what Helen knew on all these matters so mysterious and so fascinating.   Never could she "catch up" with Helen, who all her life had lived in this atmosphere of intellect and mental and physical refinement.   Even while she listened eagerly to the talk she was conscious of the spacious room, so wonderful to her in its decoration.   A green dado, divided into panels, was surmounted by a stretch of neutral-tinted wallpaper, above which ran a painted frieze of stiff sunflowers in a row.   Plates of blue china and pewter were ranged on the ledge above the dado, and the curtains at the window had a design of peacock's feathers on a green ground.   There were big grey jars, holding lilies, on various tables about the room, whose effect as a whole seemed to Rose to express the last word in austere culture.   Helen and her father she thought, dwelt in a sort of enchanted world, far removed from the sordid trivialities of ordinary existence.   Miss Fergurson was perhaps a little out of the picture.   She looked homely, almost ordinary; and as she did not talk at all, Rose wondered whether, like herself, she imperfectly understood the conversation.

Its general drift, nevertheless, was intelligible to the younger listener, who from her reading had gathered some vague notions of its subject.   How to bring about better conditions for the poor was, she understood, the practical problem which underlay all the technicalities of the discussion in progress, and as the reflection came to her, for a moment she wondered what the poor had to do with the Morris curtains, and the plates, and the sunflowers?

The idea had scarcely time to shape itself in her mind as an incongruity, before the Professor turned to her with his singularly sweet smile.

"Are you interested at all in these matters, or are

we boring you?" he asked, and Rose flushed shyly.
Instinctively she noticed that in addressing her his
tone changed. He speaks as to a child, and she thought
sadly and humbly that every one would always do that.
She would never grow up. No one would ever treat
her as they treated Helen!

"Oh, I'm *very* interested," she exclaimed. "Only
I know so little. You see, I—" She paused and
blushed again. How could she explain Miss Piddock
and school and Grandmamma—all the factors of her
obscure existence as against Helen's background of
mature enlightenment?

"But Rose writes," said Helen.

"Ah! Then we must take off our hats to the creator
—we who are merely theorists and executants," said
the Professor gravely, but with an undercurrent of
pleasantry understood by Rose.

"She *really* writes, Father!" Helen exclaimed re-
proachfully. "I mean, it's good."

"That's interesting," observed the Professor, in a
different tone. "Is it indiscreet to ask so young a
lady her age?" He smiled again delightfully.

"I'm nearly sixteen," murmured Rose, in an agony
of shyness.

"Really? She looks such a child, doesn't she, Helen,
my dear? Do you come of a writing stock? I mean,
is your father, for instance, a literary man?"

"No; he was a soldier. He died when I was a baby."

"You will let me show father some of your poems,
won't you?" begged Helen, and Rose gave her an
imploring glance.

"Oh no—please! They're only quite—quite childish and silly, you know," she declared, tripping over
her words in her shyness and trepidation.

"Perhaps you will when we get to know one another better," said the Professor. "It would interest me, and I'm more inclined to take my daughter's opinion on your work than your own. She's a good critic, though a young one. I'm always inclined to forget how young you are, Helen," he added, turning to her with a fond smile. "The reverse fault is common in most fathers."

"It would be dreadful if you were the ordinary father," said Helen, laying her cheek for a moment against his.

"Aunt Aggie thinks it would be better if I were," observed the Professor, with a laughing, rather provocative glance at the silent little woman opposite.

Helen shrugged her shoulders, and Miss Fergurson, without raising her eyes or seeming to notice her brother's remark, said suddenly: "Is there to be a meeting this month?"

"Yes. The session begins on the eighteenth. I sent out notices last week. Why?"

"I'll have to see to the refreshments."

"Yes, yes; of course," he agreed absently, and turned to Helen." I forgot to tell you that we're going to try an experiment. Cathcart is very anxious that we should get some of the more intelligent of the working-class to come to our meetings. There's, for instance, a man he talks about, a young fellow called Dering, rather a firebrand, I gather, but Cathcart says he's a wonderful speaker, and that he's well known in Poplar and Whitechapel. He promises to get him to speak here on the eighteenth, and he thinks he'll be a draw for some of the fellows we want to get at. Cathcart's engineering the thing. I promised to leave it to him."

Miss Fergurson looked up swiftly from her knitting and as swiftly looked down again.

"Is he a working-man?" asked Helen. "Dering, I mean."

"Yes—or, at least, he *was*. A factory-hand somewhere in the North, I believe. Now he's a strike leader and public speaker." The professor smiled a little. "I don't know whether he finds that a more profitable means of livelihood. Very possibly. Anyhow Cathcart seems much impressed with him. He says he's sincere and a born orator, and that if we can get him, he knows at least half a dozen men of the class we want, who would come to hear him."

"Why do you want them?" asked Miss Fergurson unexpectedly.

"Why? To get into touch with them socially. To get at their views. To break down the barriers if possible. Surely that's what we want, isn't it?" asked her brother, with a touch of impatience.

"Do you think that's possible?"

"Why not?"

"Well, don't you think they'll feel rather uncomfortable?" She gave a quick, comprehensive glance about the room.

"Why should they, Aunt Aggie?" protested Helen rather aggressively, "when they know that we're in sympathy with them? When they know, or they ought to know, that father and his friends are working for them?"

"I shouldn't care to be asked to tea at Buckingham Palace, however much the Queen was in sympathy with me," returned Aunt Aggie, with a dry smile.

"It isn't a bit the same thing!"

"It's near enough," said Miss Fergurson placidly.

"Well, as I say, Cathcart's arranging it. I'm leaving it to him," the Professor observed after a short silence.

"And he's got about as much tact as a bull in a china-shop."

"I envy him his practical acquaintance with the working-classes, at any rate. *I* haven't time for anything but the theory of socialism, alas!"

"Ye'll do better at that, Jamie," returned Miss Fergurson significantly in the intervals of counting her stitches.

The Professor smiled tolerantly as he got up. "A prophet has no honour in his own country!" he murmured. "Well, now to work." He went out, and Miss Fergurson, folding up her knitting, presently followed him from the room.

"I've no patience with Aunt Aggie when she speaks so to father!" exclaimed Helen when she and Rose were alone. "She doesn't understand any of his ideas. She's not a bit clever, as you see, and she doesn't in the least realize what a wonderful man he is. To her he's just her younger brother. That's all very well till she begins to criticize him. I think it's a splendid idea to have working-people at our meetings, don't you?"

"Splendid!" agreed Rose enthusiastically. "But what are the meetings? What do you do?"

"It's the Human Progress Society, you know. We meet at one another's houses once a month, and the discussions are always interesting. They're about socialism. I'm so glad the next At Home is at our own house, and that you'll be here for it. So far we've only had people of our own class, but I think Mr. Cathcart is *quite* wise to try to get real working-people to join us."

"So do I!" declared Rose, glowing. She remembered and reproached herself for her half-formed criticism of ten minutes ago. Working-people, then, after all, were to be invited to share in the joys of the Morris curtains, the plates, and the peacock-feathers! They were not excluded from this world of beauty and culture. She was beginning to have a better idea of what culture meant now that she had seen Helen's home and entered, even tentatively, into its atmosphere.

She shared to the full Helen's resentment against Aunt Aggie. What right had a narrow-minded old lady to set herself up against a brilliant man like the Professor? It was altogether absurd and impertinent!

XVI

DIVERGING VIEWS

THE fortnight that followed was crowded with so many strange impressions, revealed so many glimpses of fresh worlds, of new activities, new interests, that Rose's brain was on fire with excitement and constantly over-stimulated by appeals to its receptivity.

Professor Fergurson and his intimates were "in the movement." It was a movement some years antecedent to the Beardsley era, and though it definitely included art as part of its intellectual programme, it was approached in a spirit differing greatly from that in which its later devotees worshipped at the shrine. Art inseparable from the capital letter, was also inseparable from "morality." It was something to be followed gravely, seriously, in a spirit of balanced criticism, and with interest which, however fervent, was always expressed calmly, with due regard to its beneficial effect upon "the masses." The Professor entertained a good deal. There were At Homes, gatherings at tea-time, of men and women, and Sunday-night suppers for the elect, all of whom talked much, earnestly, and chiefly upon abstract subjects. Rose listened, tried to learn, and was often puzzled.

It was the conversation of the Professor himself which chiefly delighted her, and when she had overcome her first fear of him she began to dwell upon his

words as inspired utterances, to listen to the explanations he gave her on the principles of socialism, on the
importance of William Morris as artist and philosopher,
on the dawn of the new drama and all that it presaged
with awe, but with comprehension.

The Professor enjoyed talking to her.   The school-
master in him died hard—he had been a tutor in his
youth—and Rose's quick receptive mind in conjunction with her ignorance, presented interesting material.
Compared with his daughter, she was a babe intellectually, but there was a freshness about her, a sort of
ingenuous originality lacking in Helen, and this
quality amused him.

When visitors came she was silent, but the Professor
saw that she was drinking in the conversation with
an eagerness like that of physical thirst.

In the Fergurson's house there was a large room
called the Workshop, in which stood a printing-
press, a solid table for the wood-carving which Helen
affected, as well as a harpsichord and several other
curious musical instruments.   It was lighted from
above by a glass roof, and its walls were hung with
coloured prints on rollers—affairs of simple lines and
flat colours, with such titles as "Spring," "The Sower,"
"Maternity," "Charity."   Helen and her father used
the room a great deal, the Professor being an amateur
printer, and Helen having in her holidays taken up
wood-carving.   Men wearing velveteen coats and
slouch hats, and women who wore mustard-coloured or
sage-green gowns with angel sleeves, came to the Workshop in the evenings, and quoted Ruskin, and talked
of "applied art," of "founts" and "types" and the
decoration of books.   There was a great deal of conversation about the establishment of a Press by

William Morris, and from time to time specimens
of printed and decorated pages were brought by some
of the men and handed round for inspection amidst
flying criticism or exclamations of delight.   There was
also much discussion about a newly opened exhibition
called "The Arts and Crafts," to which Rose listened
with special interest, because the Professor had promised to keep an afternoon free before the end of the
holidays to take the two girls himself.

From the discussions, the comments, and the allusions she heard in the Workshop, Rose gathered that
"Art" (which she had hitherto imagined only concerned pictures), till now in a very bad way, was undergoing a great revival, and that people who made
chairs and tables could and ought to be artists, since
Ruskin said that Art was the expression of man's joy
in his work.   She thought it a very beautiful idea, and
was nevertheless uneasily conscious that she did not
like the atmosphere of the Fergursons' "Workshop,"
nor the houses of certain of the Fergursons' friends to
which Helen had taken her.   They seemed cold and
bare to her, and reminded her painfully of the sensations she derived at school from stone-grey walls and
pitch-pine dadoes and yellow desks.   There was a chill
austerity about them which affected her unpleasantly,
and she found herself recalling, with a sense of warmth
and communicated gaiety, the pink-lined curtains, the
crimson Bohemian glass, and the altogether absurd
and trivial frilly-muslin dressing-tables at Brook Hall,
where the inmates knew nothing and cared less about
Arts and Crafts.   Even the dresses of the women she
met, so much admired by Helen as "perfect in line
and so beautifully simple," did not really please her,
and though she tried hard to appreciate them, it was

the costumes in a picture which used to hang in Mrs. Winter's sitting-room which gave her real pleasure— a picture in which the ladies wore silks and satins of brilliant colours and ridiculous high-heeled shoes, and were bedecked and beflounced and as thoroughly ornate and frivolous as the spirit of Fragonard could conceive.

"I suppose I have very bad taste," she thought, with a discouraged sigh. It cheered her to remember that she really liked the Morris drawing-room and bedrooms. But that was because there was colour about them, and very probably it was not at all the proper reason for admiring them.

One evening when there was an informal party in the Workshop, Rose, who was turning the pages of a new decorated book, which, as she observed with wonder, had scattered over it, little leaves instead of full stops, listened idly to a conversation between Mrs. Cathcart and the Professor.

Mrs. Cathcart, who seemed elderly to her, was a gentle though rather dignified-looking lady, with serious eyes and a soft voice, the wife of a writer on sociology, whose views were subversive and whose voice was anything but soft. Rose heard him across the room engaged in a truculent discussion with a poet in brown velveteen, with hair that hung nearly to his shoulders.

"Of course you've seen 'The Doll's House'?" asked Mrs. Cathcart of the Professor.

"No. I've got seats for to-morrow's performance," he answered. "I'm taking Helen and her friend."

Rose saw Mrs. Cathcart's delicate eyebrows go up a little.

"Aren't they rather young?"

He smiled. "My dear friend, you know my views!"

"Yes, and I agree, of course—in a measure," she spoke rather hesitatingly. "But I don't suppose they will understand," she added, as though reassured.

"Helen will understand."

"Academically, perhaps."

"Well, that's all that matters at her age." Again the Professor's frequent smile lighted up his face.

"But is it any good?"

"Good?"

"I mean she will form a judgment which can have no value till she understands—emotionally."

"It is more judgment and less emotion that we want in women. Helen has known all the facts of sex since she was twelve years old."

"The *facts*—yes."

"Well?"

"Wait till she falls in love!"

"It may never happen. In any event she will have something better than mere emotion to guide her as in the case of most ignorant girls."

"I wonder!" murmured Mrs. Cathcart. She glanced at Helen, who across the room was talking to a young man and from time to time looking at some designs he was showing her for simple chairs. Rose followed her glance. Helen wore her peacock-blue dress, with strings of greenish, iridescent shells round her neck, and looked, as usual, gravely self-possessed and austerely pretty.

"She's remarkably mature in every way," remarked Mrs. Cathcart.

"I suppose so," said her father. "Till she went to school she lived habitually with grown-up people."

"How did you teach her 'the facts' of sex?" asked she suddenly.

"I engaged Miss Hansen to instruct her—Miss Hansen, the Swedish writer on health and sex, you know."

"Helen has a very advanced parent!" she exclaimed half smiling.

"I may be twenty years or so ahead of my time, I confess. We shall live to see a great movement on those lines if I'm not mistaken. And so much the better. Don't you agree?"

"Yes. Certainly. If the lines don't get too stereotyped, too scientific. I mean—" Involuntarily she glanced again at Helen.

"I'm afraid you don't approve of the result of advanced parenthood?" asked the Professor. He spoke genially as ever, but there was the faintest trace of hurt resentment in his tone. He adored his child.

"I think Helen is charming!" returned Mrs. Cathcart hastily. "She's the cleverest girl I ever met, and her manners are *perfect*. It's only—I'm afraid I must be hopelessly old-fashioned at heart—but a child, a real *child*, with all its ignorance and simplicity, is so attractive and—and beautiful. Helen is wonderful, of course, but—" she hesitated in her rather incoherent and flurried speech.

"She has never been a child, you mean? Well, perhaps not. I don't know anything about children, and I'm afraid they bore me. I've treated Helen as a reasonable being ever since she could talk, so perhaps, as you say, she *has* never been a child." There was not much regret in the Professor's tone, and the slight trace of resentment still informed it.

"She's a dear girl!" murmured Mrs. Cathcart, a trifle uncomfortably. "Where is her shy little friend?" she went on in some haste to divert the conversation.

"I don't know. Shall we go and look at Young's designs?"

They moved away without noticing Rose who had been too nervous to make her presence known, half-concealed as she was by the printing-press.

In bed that night, she reflected upon the conversation she had involuntarily overheard. She realized that the lady had said more than she meant to say about Helen, and she felt sorry for her, even while she shared the Professor's resentment of the implied criticism. It was absurd to count Helen a child at sixteen! She was almost grown up, and it was her very grown-upness which Rose envied and admired. . . . *"Her shy little friend!"* The phrase rankled, though she suffered it with resignation. She ought to be grown up, too—she was only a few months younger than Helen—but while Helen was everywhere and by every one treated as a woman, she, Rose, was looked upon as a baby and ignored. It was just and natural, of course. Helen was so clever and talked so well, and was so self-possessed amongst all these wonderful people who struck awe into her own heart by their achievements and conversation. Rose sighed, and presently cried a little about her babyishness and incompetence before she forgot both, in anticipation of to-morrow's treat. The theatre meant glamour to her, and mystery, and an ecstasy of delight. She had only just heard of Ibsen, who Helen told her, was a wonderful modern playwright about whom people quarrelled. This was the first time a play of his had been acted in England, she said, and the newspapers were full of it,

and most of them gave very silly criticisms, according
to the opinion of Mr. Millward the poet, and of Mr.
Young the designer. Helen, however, knew nothing
about "The Doll's House," which from its title Rose
imagined to be a sort of fairy-tale. Anyhow, and
whatever its nature, it was heavenly to be going to the
theatre, and her excitement in the prospect kept her
awake for an hour or two. But before she slept, her
thoughts had turned again to Mrs. Cathcart's talk
with the Professor and her allusions to "sex." It was
a word which hitherto she had scarcely heard mentioned at all; certainly never by a woman to a man,
and at the time she had experienced a curious little
shock of half-shamed surprise. But here at the Fergursons' house, men and women alike apparently
talked about anything and everything, and her reason
approved, even though her first instinct had been a
shocked one. Helen then, had been taught "that sort
of thing" by a clever woman? She remembered that
though she and Helen had never talked about sex, she
had always been aware that Helen knew, but was not
interested in the subject. She thought of her own
initiation into mysteries, and blushed in the darkness.
If only she had been told in the way her friend was
told, she thought, perhaps she wouldn't have the
"horrid mind" of which at intervals, when the subject
of sex recurred to her, she was desperately ashamed.
Helen seemed to ignore certain matters with which she
herself was still occasionally preoccupied, and this
was only one more proof of Helen's immense superi-
ority. For the twentieth time she resolved never to
think of "that" any more, but to live as Helen did
for books and pictures and talking, and—the things
of the mind. Yes, that was it, the things of the

mind, she repeated to herself drowsily before she fell
asleep.

It was hard to restrain her excitement the next
evening when she found herself in the front row of the
dress circle before the curtain lifted. Helen, though
she cared for a variety of interests, was never excited.
But then, as Rose reflected, the theatre was no novel
experience to her. She watched her now, admiring her
fair, clear-cut little face as she leaned over the velvet
edge of the circle and scanned the house, discovering
an acquaintance here and there; now and again mentioning the name of some well-known writer or painter
or critic whose face she recognized in the stalls. She
was keenly interested without doubt, and anxious to
see the play, but Rose knew that she was not trembling
with excitement like a child at her first pantomime,
and just for a moment she felt sorry that Helen was
missing her own tumultuous emotions. The Professor
glanced at her once or twice with his sweet, tolerant,
slightly amused smile, and she felt at the same time
grateful and abashed. She knew that he considered
her very young, and remembering that children bored
him, she made a great effort to ask questions in a calm,
detached voice, and to present only that amount of
intelligent inquiry which should establish her in his
eyes as a person at least as grown up as Helen. There
was a continuous murmur of conversation in the house,
which was filled with an audience curiously mixed in
character. Some of the women, Rose noticed, were
very fashionable, while others were dressed either in
the limp "æsthetic" gowns to which she had lately
grown accustomed, or as nearly as possible like men,
with stiff shirt-fronts and dark coats of manly cut.

There were men here and there with long hair, and women whose hair was cut short. Everybody seemed to be talking. Then suddenly the curtain went up and silence fell.

As the evening proceeded, Rose grew more and more puzzled, and her sensations became increasingly chaotic. She had hitherto seen none but Shakespeare's plays, and the new naturalistic type of acting seemed very wonderful to her, even though it was sometimes difficult to hear, when Nora turned her back and talked into the porcelain stove. She was enthralled by the story and by the acting, and at the same time her æsthetic sense was offended by the drab ugliness of the Helmers' room, and by Nora's dowdy dress, and the slovenly garb of the men. All this depressed her just as the Fergursons' Workshop and the classrooms at school, depressed her, inducing a well-known feeling, which she described to herself as "staleness." The diction of the play appealed to her always too ready sense of the ludicrous, and she giggled irrepressibly when Helmer inquired whether "his lark was twittering there" and if "it was the squirrel skipping about." She loathed Helmer with vehemence, and shuddered when Nora kissed him. How could she kiss a man with that smug face and horrid necktie! But then, Nora was a little silly, and Rose despised her for her lying evasions over the "macaroons." "Why didn't she eat them and tell her husband not to interfere?" she thought. "The idea of marrying a man who interferes over stupid little things like that!" It was not till the net began to close around Nora and she began to understand the carefully worked-up situation created by the dramatist out of the slave-woman's upbringing and the conditions of her married life, that Rose began to have sympathy with her and comprehension of her words and deeds. She followed the play then, with tense excitement and passionate pity for Nora, till the last five minutes of the dialogue between husband and wife, and the now famous banging door, brought her the shock of a violent revulsion of feeling.

On the way home in the cab, forgetting to be shy in her eagerness, she almost quarrelled with Helen, who upheld Nora's "duty to herself."

"It was *awful* to leave the children!" Rose declared. "Horribly selfish! Just to save her own soul."

"But she thought she wasn't fit to bring them up."

"That's nonsense!" returned Rose sharply. "People don't 'think' when they have children. They *feel*. And what was to prevent her from learning in her own home to bring them up properly?"

"With that man?" inquired Helen calmly. "He'd begin calling her a squirrel again by the end of the week."

"If he did, she could have bitten him!"

"And spent the rest of her life in quarrelling? Her duty was to herself. She was quite right to want to make herself a better human being."

"She would *never* make herself that, by deserting her children. She would only be a horrid, cold, stuck-up —prig."

"You always put feeling before reason."

"It *does* come before it," said Rose hotly.

"What do you think of it, Father?" asked Helen, with the tactful intention of avoiding a wrangle.

The Professor had been silent, leaning back in the darkness of the four-wheeler.

"Of the play or of the discussion?"

"Well, of both, if you like," said Helen, laughing.

"I think they're both interesting; but the discussion interests me most."

"Why?" asked Helen, while Rose felt suddenly abashed to think of her own recent volubility.

"Because it represents two opposing views that will be held by women in the near future, and it's rather amusing to hear them expressed by the very young 'younger generation.'" The light from a street lamp flashing into the cab for a moment showed Rose that he was smiling.

"But you like the play, Father?" asked Helen. "You think it's good?"

"Better than good; very important as propaganda," returned the Professor characteristically. "It has great ethical value. I prophesy that it will have more influence in furthering the Woman's Movement than anything that has yet been written on the subject."

"What is the 'Woman's Movement'?" asked Rose.

"You're in it now," he told her. "Miss Quayle's school is part of it. Girton is part of it. So are Art Schools and Ibsen and games for girls. It's the movement in which you women are going to find yourselves, in which you are discovering, as Nora says, that before all else you are human beings with a right to live as you choose."

"I'm sure I shall never find myself," she answered disconsolately. "I'm all in a muddle."

That the muddle had increased considerably since the beginning of her visit was not surprising. Discussions in the Fergursons' household never ceased, and the points they raised were bewildering and novel to Rose's unsophisticated mind.

While she brushed her hair before plaiting it for the night, she remembered that to-morrow was the

evening At Home, when Socialist workmen might be
expected, as well as a great deal of fluent and allusive
talk, difficult to follow. And the day afterwards
school began! Rose dropped her brush in the shock of
the realization that in a comparatively few hours she
would again be ordered about by Miss Bird, and have
to sign her name for leaving a pencil on the table.
This after a fortnight's grown-up life concerned with
the things that mattered; like socialism and Ibsen
and Arts and Crafts and Liberty frocks and Morris
tiles! It was utterly ridiculous.

Excitement induced by "The Doll's House" kept
her long awake. The play seemed to have brought
the question of marriage very close, and she gravely
considered it. It might be awful to be married. She
found herself engaged upon a dramatic dialogue, which
on her side began with, "Once for all, I do not intend
to be called a squirrel. I am a human being just as
much as you are!" Whereupon a shadowy husband
who bore a subtle and perfectly disgusting likeness to
Torvald replied: "My dear, you are my wife, and I
expect you to obey me."

The remark, though it was certainly her own,
lashed Rose into a fury, and she turned and twisted
in bed, her heart beating with indignation, too perturbed to compose a suitable and dignified retort.

"But then, of course, I *needn't* marry. Perhaps I
shall never even be asked to marry any one," she reflected when her anger had died down. It was a solution certainly, but it left her with a feeling of rather
annoyed dissatisfaction.

XVII

FIRE AND THE UNINFLAMMABLE

WHEN Rose went into the drawing-room next evening after dinner, she found it arranged as for an informal meeting, with chairs placed irregularly, but all facing a table on which there was a decanter of water and a tumbler. She and Helen had arranged the flowers during the afternoon, and lilies in Japanese pots and daffodils in bowls were disposed about the room. A maid came in with the coffee, and Professor Fergurson, who was in morning dress, stood leaning against the mantelpiece when Helen passed him his cup.

"What's Mr. Dering going to speak about, Father?" she asked.

"I don't know," he returned rather absently. "I'm afraid he'll be late. Cathcart sent round a note just now to say he was busy with the dock strike, but that he'd come on as soon as possible. We shall have to trust to music and conversation till he appears."

"Did you tell every one it wasn't evening dress?"

"No, I just left the matter. Cathcart never dresses, and one or two of the others won't either." Rose noticed a certain nervousness in his manner which apparently escaped Helen, who was moving about the room altering the position of the flowers.

"It *will* be fun to have real working people, won't it?" she exclaimed, more girlishly than usual, as she lighted the candles on the piano.

The Professor did not reply, and Rose suddenly remembered Miss Fergurson's remarks on the day of her own arrival at the house, and wondered whether he too, recalled them. Miss Fergurson herself entered the room at the moment and placidly settled herself in one of the arm-chairs. In spite of Helen's rather contemptuous indifference to her aunt, Rose had grown to have a sneaking affection for Miss Fergurson, who though she never conversed and rarely even spoke, somehow interested her and piqued her curiosity. Helen said she wasn't clever, but Rose thought she had very clever eyes, and she appreciated her dry smile. She had a feeling too, that Miss Fergurson liked her in return, and Rose was generally grateful to people who liked her.

The door-bell rang, guests began to arrive, and before long the room was fairly full of people, some of whom Rose had met before and others who were strangers. Helen introduced her to many of them. She moved about the room easily and gracefully like an accomplished hostess, with her pretty smile and her ready words, and Rose saw that she was the centre of attraction to men and women, many of whom had known her from her babyhood and looked upon her as a rare and wonderful little person, destined to great things. There was a sort of cult for Helen amongst the Professor's friends, and by now Rose completely understood the aloofness and the disdain implied rather than expressed in the girl's attitude at Minerva House.

"How does the school experiment work, dear child?" asked a lady who wore a straight gown of art serge embroidered with marigolds, and was, as Rose had been told, a bookbinder of great skill and renown.

15

"Much as I expected," replied Helen with her clear little laugh. "Only I couldn't persuade father I was right. I'm staying on for another term at my own wish, though, for one or two reasons, but chiefly because of Rose. This is Rose, my only friend at Minerva House. But she's quite worth all I've endured there." She put her arm round Rose's shoulder and drew her forward towards Mrs. Molesy, who held her hand with fervour, and gazed at her in an intense fashion which Rose found most embarrassing. Helen always knew how to respond to people who looked at her like that, and she herself had encountered the manner so often of late, that she felt annoyed at her own inability even yet to cope with it.

"I am so intensely interested in this scheme of bringing real working people to our meetings," she said, in her low, deep voice.

"Yes, I wish some of them would come," answered Rose, looking about the room, which so far was filled with the silks and art serges of the women, and the black cloth or velveteen coats of men who were obviously not "real working people."

"Here's Mr. Cathcart!" exclaimed Helen, as a loud voice was heard on the staircase.

A moment later he entered with two men whom he had the air of almost driving before him. They were artisans of the respectable class, tidily though clumsily dressed. One of them wore a red tie, and both moved awkwardly and looked profoundly uncomfortable.

"Here are two of my friends, Fergurson!" shouted Mr. Cathcart, whom Rose remembered as the noisy, blustering husband of the lady who had almost ad-

versely criticized Helen, but whom she was nevertheless inclined to like.

The Professor came forward with his flashing smile
and shook hands in turn with the newcomers.

"Mr. Robinson. Mr. Maltby. Professor Fergurson," said Cathcart, while every one else in the room
furtively looked, and while affecting to continue their
conversation, listened with interest. Rose suddenly
felt profoundly sorry for the two young men, who were
obviously awkward, abashed, and as she also noticed
—surprised. She wondered for a moment whether
they had known they were coming to a private house,
and then forgot her surmise as the Professor spoke.

"It is kind of you to come to our little gathering,"
he began, in his gentle voice. "We are all looking
forward to meeting Mr. Dering, who I'm afraid will be
late."

"Busy with the dock strike," muttered one of the
men, shuffling his feet.

"So I hear. That is most important, of course, but
I hope he won't be detained too long. I want to
introduce you to Mrs. Fletcher, er—Mr. Robinson,
I think? Oh! Mr. Maltby? I'm sorry." Rose
watched the Professor steering the man with the red
tie across the room towards a lady wrapped in a lace
shawl. She rose with rather flurried impressiveness,
while Mr. Cathcart, seizing the reluctant Robinson
by the arm, cheerily pushed him in the direction of
Mrs. Molesy, who assumed the air of bracing herself
for the greatness thrust upon her.

The two guests precariously disposed of for the
moment, Cathcart hastened to draw the Professor
aside, and Rose, who was standing near the door by
which they stopped, heard the hurried conversation.

"Look here," said Mr. Cathcart in as near an undertone as he could compass, "I'd better hover about in the hall. Your maid found an opportunity to tell me that one fellow bolted as soon as she opened the door. If I'm there, I can seize them and prevent that. Shy, you know. Won't come upstairs!"

"Did you tell them it was a drawing-room meeting?" asked the Professor in a low voice.

"No, I shouldn't have got any of 'em if I had. That's no good. We've got to *compel* them to come in, you know. They'll soon get used to it." He chuckled.

"Oh, well, it can't be helped now, but—er—I'm sorry," said the Professor, knitting his eyebrows. "And what about the other man—Dering? Does he understand——"

"Oh, I just said it was a meeting. Purposely left it rather vague, you know. But Dering will come because I've helped him a bit, and he's a good fellow, though a trifle wild and inclined to run amuck. Thought I'd just tell you why I was disappearing. I'll bring 'em in. Don't you worry."

The Professor turned away, looking scarcely inclined to obey his friend's counsel, and Rose's latent aversion to Mr. Cathcart flared into secret anger.

"No wonder Miss Fergurson called him a bull in a china-shop!" she thought. "It isn't fair! It's horrid to the poor men!" She looked across at Mr. Robinson, who sat with his hands hanging between his knees, while Mrs. Molesy, with an intense and rigid expression on her face, strove to engage him in conversation. The other man she could not see, hidden as he was by skirts and pots of flowers, but she guessed him to be equally miserable. Some one went to the piano, and while an Impromptu of Chopin was in progress, Mr.

Cathcart ushered two or three fresh unhappy individuals into the lighted, flower-filled, crowded room. They sat on the edges of their chairs, their eyes on the floor, except when they furtively raised them to glance about miserably as though seeking to escape. Rose felt they would have given worlds to bolt to the door, and her heart began to beat desperately in sympathy with their plight. She could not bear to look at them, and in seeking to avoid them, her gaze wandered to Miss Fergurson, who had kept her place in the arm-chair near the fireplace. She saw her eyes travelling about the room, and in them she read the mixed emotions of pity and amusement. When the music ceased, the little lady got up and went over to one of the newcomers, a red-haired, hatchet-faced man, who during the Impromptu had been staring stolidly before him.

"I'm sure you must be a Scotsman?" she began. "I'm a Scotswoman, and I don't think I can be wrong about a fellow-countryman."

"Ma name's Macpherson," he returned with a slow smile, "so that settles it, A'm thinking."

Miss Fergurson laughed, and when Rose, who had turned away in response to a signal from Helen glanced again in his direction, she saw him talking without a trace of self-consciousness to his hostess.

"It'll be perfectly *awful* if the other man doesn't come soon," Helen whispered. "Whatever are we to do with them? No one can make them talk, and every one's being so horribly polite to them."

Rose agreed, for amusement had mingled with her pity at sight of the solicitude of the ladies, who speaking in their gentlest voices, seemed to be treating the men as invalids, of whom they were nevertheless more than a little afraid.

There was a little stir at the door, and Cathcart presently bustled in and caught the arm of the Professor.

"Here's Dering at last!" he exclaimed exultantly. "Awfully good of him, for he's been speaking more or less all day. He's coming upstairs now."

Rose turned eagerly towards the door, and as Professor Fergurson hurried forward, she caught a glimpse of the young man as he paused a moment irresolutely on the threshold of the room.

She saw a tall, very slim figure, and a curious, dark-skinned, clean-shaven face, which as she put it to herself, "didn't look English." This impression grew more pronounced while she watched him exchanging a few words with the Professor, and noticed the play of his hands, which he used like a foreigner, making with them quick and expressive gestures.

The news of his arrival had spread; every one turned expectantly to the door, and when the Professor announced that Mr. Dering would very kindly say a few words at once, there was a general feeling of relief from tension. People began to move towards the seats arranged in front of the table, and as though with one consent, for mutual support, and in spite of smiling invitations to come closer, the "working men" crowded together along a row of chairs at the back of the room. Dering was still talking to Cathcart near the door. Rose could not hear what he said, but, watching his face, she knew he was displeased, and when Mr. Cathcart turned away with a slight shrug of the shoulders, she hoped rather vindictively that he had been made to feel himself the bull in the china-shop which, in her opinion, in more senses than one he resembled.

"Of course he hates talking here," she thought. "He must feel that he's being made a show of. *I* should hate it!"

The young man walked up to the table. He walked easily, gracefully even, and as he stood facing his politely attentive audience, several of the women noticed that his shabby suit of blue serge hung well upon him, and doubtless because his figure was good, had none of the uncouth effect produced by the clothes of the other workmen.

"I didn't expect to speak in a drawing-room to-night," he began moodily. "There's bin some sort of mistake. Perhaps it was my fault. I've bin too busy to attend properly to letters and so forth. I've bin where there's trouble, and it seems—strange to talk about it here." His eyes swept the room before he looked down at the table, and was for a moment silent. Then, with a half-deprecatory, half-defiant movement of his hands, he threw back his head.

There was a slight subdued murmur of applause before he launched into a vivid, dramatic description of the great dockers' strike then in progress. He spoke with a North Country burr, not unpleasant, and though his sentences were often ungrammatical, they were well built. There was a sense of structure about them, and he spoke with a fluency, a dramatic fervour rare in an Englishman.

Rose sat spellbound, all her generous instincts aflame and tortured as he talked of the homes he had seen that day; of the men's dogged fortitude, the women's patience and loyalty even in the face of their children's cold and hunger. It was an emotional, one-sided speech, in which the rights of the men alone were insisted upon, and the employers were attacked with scathing virulence as monsters willingly, relentlessly crushing the people. But the speaker was tremendously, overwhelmingly in earnest, and Rose thrilled with indignation as he scarified the capitalists and denounced a system under which honest men starved.

There was magnetism about the man, some compelling influence which radiated from his personality and made him show like a flame in a dull room. Once in a momentary arrest of the torrent of words, Rose glanced at his audience; at the intelligent, cultured, over-civilized faces upraised to his. Though she did not know what it was in them that irritated and dissatisfied her, she had a vague feeling that they were only half-alive, that no one in the room was alive except this slight young man with the dark, vivid face above the carelessly knotted red tie. She could not see the other workmen, but she wondered whether they were stirred, excited as she was? They must be, she thought, for they alone realized to the full the lives of the poor. She was glad now that they had come. They were avenged for all the embarrassment they had suffered by the knowledge that *they* were the important people after all! They, the makers, the producers, upon whom the whole social fabric rested.

This was the substance of her racing, chaotic thoughts, divined only, not reduced to shape or deliberately expressed in words; and when Dering stopped abruptly, she started as though violently roused from an exciting, tremendous dream.

"That's all I've got to say," he concluded, relapsing into his former moodiness.

He moved brusquely away from the table, and

there was a clapping of hands and an immediate murmur of conversation and discussion, interested, but quiet and restrained, as Professor Fergurson went forward to shake hands with the speaker, who was already making for the door.

Two or three ladies tentatively followed him, and for a moment he was detained and surrounded. Rose noticed that all the workmen had risen and one behind the other were furtively edging towards the entrance.

"But you will come downstairs and have something to eat and drink?" Rose heard the Professor saying. "We are all going. Agnes, my dear, I suppose there are sandwiches and so forth in the dining-room?" He looked from Dering to the other men.

"I must go at once if you'll excuse me," said Dering decidedly, but with no ungraciousness. "I have a good deal of work to get through still; and it's late."

"We're coming along too, Dering!" put in the Scotsman in a whisper indicative of eagerness to get out. "No, thank you kindly, ma'am. We'd best be getting along." The half-dozen men tramped with alacrity downstairs, and when Rose and Helen presently followed towards the dining-room, they saw the Professor shaking hands with them all at the hall door.

In the dining-room people stood in groups with glasses of lemonade or claret-cup, and talked animatedly.

"Quite an orator!" "Wonderful fluency!" Rose heard disjointed remarks and comments on the departed guest as she went about passing plates of sandwiches and cakes.

"He doesn't look English!" said Mrs. Molesy, addressing Cathcart. "Thank you, dear!"—to Rose.

"One of these adorable little chocolate biscuits, I
think."

"His mother was an Italian," returned Cathcart
leaning his elbow on the mantelpiece. "She died at
his birth, I understand, and he worked as a child
in some factory or other in the north."

"Ah! that accounts for the dramatic sense, of
course," pursued Mrs. Molesy, on her deepest note.
"The Latin race——"

Rose passed on with her plate of sandwiches to a
group of people near the window, who, to her amazement, had forsaken Dering as a topic and were discussing exhibits in the Arts and Crafts Exhibition.

"It hasn't the right simplicity of line," she heard
Mr. Young explaining to a girl in a green velveteen
dress, with a fillet of shells round her hair. "What
one should aim at in decoration is to preserve——"

Rose turned away with a shock of indignation. They
had forgotten already about the poor women and the
starving children! It was ridiculous, futile, to be
talking about furniture when there were such things
in the world as those they had heard about to-night.
How Mr. Dering would despise them! How *she*
despised them! . . . By degrees the room emptied.
Ladies went upstairs and returned wrapped in cloaks
of sage-green silk or coats trimmed with oriental
embroidery, and their husbands joined them in the hall.
There were leave-takings and cheerful chatter about
wood-carving classes and picture exhibitions, and
arrangements to meet on certain days next week; and
embraces for Helen, whom a lady, with the intense
manner which seemed fashionable, declared "more
than ever like a Burne-Jones picture," and finally only
one or two people were left talking in the dining-room.

Mr. Young and Helen were discussing Greek art near the fireplace, and Cathcart was waiting for his wife, who had gone upstairs with Miss Fergurson.

"No, I'm afraid it won't do, Cathcart," the Professor was saying. "The men were uncomfortable, as surely you must have noticed. And so were we for that matter," he added, with his bland smile.

"Just a little put out at first. That's only natural," protested Mr. Cathcart, drinking off the remains of a whisky-and-soda. "They'd get used to it if only we would persevere. Now, don't shake your head like that, there's a good fellow!" he urged, with his loud laugh. "Anyhow, Dering was a success. What d'you think of him?"

"He's got much to learn," returned the Professor judicially. "Intemperate, of course, and unbalanced. He's young. But if he'll only keep cool, and study the questions he talks about more thoroughly, and avoid getting his head turned, he ought to make a fine leader. He has quite a remarkable gift of speech."

"He has, hasn't he? A difficult chap to manage. Fiery, you know. Intemperate, as you say. Always inclined to violence. But he'll calm down. We all do with age, don't we?"

"You're an exception, at any rate," asserted the Professor in his tolerant voice. "There are apt to be wigs on the green when you start an argument."

"Oh, my bark's worse than my bite," declared Cathcart jovially. "Come, Alice, my dear, are you ready?"

Mrs. Cathcart, who had entered, was taking leave of Miss Fergurson. She kissed Helen as she passed her, and coming across the room to Rose, held her hand for a moment in both her own.

"Good-bye, my dear," she said kindly. "I hear

you are going back to school to-morrow. You were interested in what Mr. Dering said?" she asked suddenly, looking down at the girl.

Rose could not for the moment speak. She felt rather stunned and bewildered by the many and rapidly alternating emotions of the evening. Besides, "interested" was not the word, and she didn't know how to explain.

"I saw you were. Don't be—" she paused. "You know, you're a very emotional little thing!" she substituted for whatever it was she had been going to say. She touched her lightly on the cheek, and then, as though moved by a sudden impulse, kissed her. "Don't take things too hardly," she added in a low voice, as her husband, who had been standing with the others out of earshot, turned to call her impatiently.

When they were gone, Rose moved slowly towards the end of the room where Helen and her father and Miss Fergurson were gathered round the fire.

"You were right, Aggie," said the Professor, laying his hand on his sister's shoulder. "It was a mistake. That sort of thing doesn't work. I was as sorry for the poor fellows as I was sad for ourselves. It's desperate that with the best will in the world one can do nothing. One can only help a little at a distance. A very little," he added, with a discouraged sigh.

"Poor laddies!" murmured Miss Fergurson, looking into the fire. "Nice laddies!" and Rose, who had been feeling bitterly resentful of the Professor's measured criticism of Dering, felt a sudden rush of affection for both of them. They, too, were "nice" people.

She went upstairs feeling that life was altogether too bewildering and big for her, and too complicated.

There was a fire in her bedroom, for the weather had changed within the last few days; it had grown intensely cold, with a bitter wind that cut like a razor-blade. Her room was warm, and looked charmingly pretty as she opened the door, and with a sigh of physical satisfaction knelt down on the hearthrug and put out her hands towards the glowing mass of coal. Then all at once she remembered with a shock of dismayed self-reproach, the children, the women who were even now shivering and hungry. The picture Dering had evoked was vividly, hideously present in her mind, when there was a knock at the door, followed by the entrance of Helen.

She was in a white dressing-gown, and that and her short, fluffy hair gave her a childlike appearance unusual to her.

"Your fire is much better than mine," she exclaimed. "Do let me get warm! Mine isn't burning properly."

She sat down in front of it on the floor, while Rose, jumping up, went to the dressing-table and began brushing her hair.

"You are very quiet to-night," Helen complained, looking across at her. "Is it the depressing thought of school to-morrow, or didn't you enjoy the party?"

Rose came back to the fire, brush in hand.

"I'm thinking of what that man said," she answered slowly.

"Yes. . . . Did you notice what a beautiful figure he had?"

"No," said Rose.

"Didn't you? He was like a Greek statue. What a pity it is most men are so ugly. I was looking round to-night and thinking what bad figures they had. It's rather splendid to see a man like Mr. Dering!"

She gazed thoughtfully into the fire, and Rose looked at her, amazed and disconcerted. For the last hour and more she had been longing for the talk in the bedroom which always closed the day. Helen at least, she thought, would be thrilled and absorbed by the ideas presented by Mr. Dering, even if the others had failed to respond passionately to his speech. And now, instead of discussing it, Helen was talking about his figure! Rose felt overwhelmed.

"I wasn't thinking about *him*, but about what he said!" she broke out at last vehemently. "Surely you were, too? Isn't it awful that things should be like that? And then for Mr. Cathcart to say he was violent, as though he blamed him for it. I was furious! Why shouldn't he be violent? We ought all to be violent when men and women and children are starving because of the capitalists! It's awful just to sit here by a fire and do nothing."

"Violence isn't any good," returned Helen absently. Her eyes had strayed to a photograph of a Hermes above the mantelpiece, and she reluctantly withdrew them to look at Rose. "That's why the Human Progress Society was formed," she went on, with slightly more interest. "To further socialism by peaceful means—on intellectual lines, you know."

"How *can* any one be peaceful when such things are happening?" asked Rose, her eyes blazing. "If the poor people all joined together, and those who agree with them, were to help them to make a revolution, it could be stopped."

"Things wouldn't be any better if they happened like that."

"Why not?" demanded Rose breathlessly.

"Because—" Helen yawned a little. "I'm so sleepy," she said apologetically. "You must ask father, Rose. There's such a lot to explain, and I don't know enough about it. But things aren't as simple as you think."

"But weren't you—what did you feel when that man was speaking?" asked Rose after quite a long pause. It seemed incredible that Helen should not have been more moved. Her own thoughts raced chaotically, and she was all on fire to know just what Helen was feeling.

"I think he's a wonderful speaker," she answered readily. "Mr. Cathcart says he'll come to the front and be very valuable in time. He heard him at the Trafalgar Square meeting two years ago, when there was a riot, you know, and he's not lost sight of him since. He thinks he'll make a name."

Rose was silent. That was all, then. This cool appraisement of a "performance"! It was as though the man had been playing something,—a sonata or a fugue upon the piano, she thought incoherently. In Helen she detected the same attitude of which without being able to define it, she was conscious as characteristic of the Fergurson "set."

Later, when Helen had gone, she strove to put it into words, and succeeded in fashioning for herself some expression of what that attitude conveyed to her. Imperfectly defined, the substance of her criticism was that her new acquaintances were "onlookers." "They're not very alive," she thought. "They 'think' this and that, and they're 'of opinion' that so and so would be advantageous, and they're 'inter-

ested' in things they call 'movements,' but I don't
believe they feel much!''

After her reply to Rose's question, Helen had put
out both hands lazily for her friend to pull her up from
the hearthrug.

"We *must* go to bed!" she declared, yawning again
like a sleepy little cat. "School to-morrow! Isn't
it vile?" She spoke and looked more like a child
to-night than she had ever done, and it was odd that
this should happen just when Rose felt more grown
up than usual.

"You do look so pretty!" exclaimed Rose, for a
moment diverted from her puzzling thoughts by a glow
of admiration. "You ought always to wear white.
It suits you beautifully."

"Does it?" Helen went up to the dressing-table and
looked at herself in the glass. "I think it does. I
shall have a white evening-dress for my first dance. I
should like these next two years to pass quickly, Rose,
shouldn't you? Every now and then I feel I should
love to go to dances and meet—all sorts of nice men."

"But you meet them now!" said Rose, rather
surprised.

"Oh yes. But that's not what I mean. They're
mostly old, you know. I don't mean that sort of man
either; I mean young men who ride and dance and
have nice figures and dress properly."

"You are funny!" murmured Rose, bewildered.
She had never heard Helen talk like this before. "I
thought you didn't care a bit for dances and—and—
well, the sort of things ordinary girls like."

"Don't you have moods?" asked Helen impatiently.
She took up Rose's comb and fluffed up her yellow
hair a little. "I've got a frivolous mood to-night. I

should like—oh! I don't know what I want!" she exclaimed rather wildly, lifting her arms above her head and letting them fall heavily against her sides. "But it's like that!" Suddenly she burst out laughing at Rose's puzzled face. "Good-night, darling; you are so funny and serious!" she declared. She threw her arms round her, and held her so tight that Rose gave a little scream of pain.

"What a tiny thing you are! It's like squeezing a child," said Helen, releasing her and holding her at arm's length.

"You'll be quite pretty when you grow up, Rose," she went on, regarding her critically. "At least, not pretty, perhaps, but *attractive*. It will depend how you do your hair and on your mood. It was silly of me to ask if you ever had any moods, because you're the moodiest creature I ever met! When you have the blues you're quite ugly, you know. And when you're out of them you're sometimes quite pretty. So do always be cheerful."

She turned at the door to smile at her, and Rose thought she looked lovely and—excited somehow. It was the excited look which made her so pretty, but she could not think what there was to be excited about, and Helen's behaviour puzzled her. It puzzled Helen, too, who for hours could not sleep for a strange new restlessness which possessed her and made her toss and turn in her bed half the night.

Rose also did not sleep, though the moment Helen had gone, her thoughts fled from her friend and turned again to the speech about the dockers. Again indignation and burning pity seized her. Surely what Helen said wasn't true. Something *could* be done if only people had the courage to do it! She would like to lead

16

the mob against the capitalists, and her imagination
leaped to a dramatic picture of herself with a red flag
storming some height surmounted by rank upon rank
of stony figures, to whom she hurled defiance. It was
a splendid dream, and it occupied her till a clock struck
two, when suddenly she again remembered Helen.

It was so funny of her to talk about Dering's
figure! Rose had been truthful in saying she had not
noticed it. It was the man's eyes she remembered,
for the reason that they showed her what he was feeling. Rose always looked at people's eyes because they
told her things, but as yet, beyond the fact that he was
tall or short she knew nothing about any man's
appearance, and never at all considered the question
of his looks. A pretty woman, on the other hand,
invariably excited her admiration just as flowers or
graceful trees excited it, while men, so far as outward
appearance went, were to her uninteresting-looking
creatures who wore ugly clothes. She had not connected them with "figures" at all. It was funny of
Helen! . . . She was growing drowsy when some
words she had heard during the evening slipped into
her mind: *" You know, you're a very emotional little
thing!"* She wondered why Mrs. Cathcart had
thought so, and finally drifted into sleep with the dull
realization that school began to-morrow. To-morrow?
It was already to-morrow.

XVIII

THE LAST TERM

ROSE entered upon the next term with a mind full of grief and apprehension. Helen was to leave at the end of it, and also it was the term of the Senior Cambridge.

She could not now imagine herself at Minerva House without Helen. True, she was on good terms with many of the other girls; true she was popular. But her liking for the majority of her schoolfellows was only on the surface, and to lose Helen was to lose the one real friend she had made. She dared not think of her coming bereavement. Yet her mind was full of it as they drove across London together the following afternoon, and "the Cambridge" which would have otherwise engrossed her attention, sank into insignificance before the impending infinitely more terrible occurrence.

"But there's all the term," Helen reminded her when she began to bewail it. Helen had regained her customary calmness and there was nothing remaining now in her manner of the previous night's "funniness."

"Yes, but it will get nearer and nearer and spoil everything!" said Rose miserably. "And then there's that awful exam., and I shall have to cram and there'll be so little time to be together."

"You'll come and stay with me again in the summer. Anyhow don't let's think of it before it comes," Helen urged philosophically. "All sorts of things may happen."

The rather hazy prophecy was a few hours later fulfilled in a fashion which took away Rose's breath. Some hint of its nature might have reached her in Miss Quayle's manner when just before prayers, she entered the dining-room and shook hands with each girl in turn. But in the interest of other greetings, and excited questionings and answers, she did not sufficiently remark the touch of irritated annoyance in the perfunctory words of welcome with which the Principal addressed her. It was only when the last post brought a letter from her grandmother that in startling fashion the bolt dropped from the blue.

She had read only a few lines of the sheet before her when with a smothered exclamation she let it fall into her lap.

"Helen!" she exclaimed. "I'm to leave this term! Grandmamma says she's written to Miss Quayle." She took up the letter again and hurriedly skimmed through the remaining half-page.

Mrs. Lester wrote briefly that an exceptional opportunity having occurred for Lucie to go to France in the summer, she proposed to avail herself of the chance to send her there. Meanwhile Rose must leave school, where Mrs. Lester considered she had remained "quite long enough to learn all that was good for her," and in future give all her attention to the study of French with Mademoiselle La Touche, who was to stay on with Rose, instead of Lucie as a pupil.

Whatever else they may have taught you at your advanced school, it certainly isn't French [she wrote], for you couldn't speak two words of the language the last time you were at home. We must see what Mademoiselle La Touche can do before you too go abroad to perfect your languages, which in my humble opinion will be of considerably more value to you than Euclid. I have written to Miss Quayle, and have already received a communication from her to the effect that you were to be "sent in" for the Senior Cambridge—whatever that may mean— next term. She seems to think that a good and sufficient reason for me to reconsider my notice. I have of course written to tell her that it will not be convenient to me to alter my plans, and the matter is therefore closed. I hope you have had a pleasant visit. Who is Ibsen? You seem to think I ought to know. I can assure you I don't. But then, I do not profess to move with the times. Nevertheless I trust you enjoyed the play to which in your last letter you told me you were going. *The Doll's House* sounds rather childish. Perhaps your friend the Professor thinks grown-up plays unsuited to your age. He was right to be on the safe side, though at sixteen I was taken to see the dramas of Racine. I hear that Mrs. Winter is again very seriously ill, so I'm afraid we shall not see the family at Brook Hall yet awhile. It is a sad trial for her husband and that fine boy of hers. I always pity the husband of a delicate woman. . . .

Rose looked up at Helen mutely when she had hastily scanned the letter, forgetting to be amused by, scarcely indeed noticing, the reference to "A Doll's House." She was overwhelmed by the suddenness of this announcement. It seemed to her that she had been all her life at Minerva House, as though she could not think further than its walls, and the walls of the college.

"Are you glad?" asked Helen.

"I don't know," she returned, speaking slowly as though stunned. "It would be awful to come back without you, but—I don't know what it will be like at home, without Lucie even. With only Grandmamma and Mademoiselle."

She *did* know what it would be like, or rather a **faint** foreshadowing of it already began to oppress her.

But Helen was optimistic. "At any rate, you will be your own mistress. You won't be in leading strings. You won't hear *that* sort of thing, for instance," she declared. Her lip curled scornfully as Miss Bird passed through the room, calling in her irritating voice for Gladys Courie, who had left her pencil-box about, to go at once and sign her name.

It was true; but, on the other hand, she would not hear the gay voices of the girls nor any irrepressible, cheerful giggling, nor meet young eyes and youthful smiles; and some realization of this began to weave a grey veil over the future.

"Well, I shan't have to cram now for the Cambridge. We shall have more time together, that's one good thing," she said with a satisfaction that was only half-real. In the depths of her heart, though she was very doubtful about passing it, she was disappointed about "the Cambridge." It would be awful to fail, but it was depressing after a good deal of work not to be given a chance of passing.

The prayer-bell rang, and Miss Quayle, who had returned to her study after her formal greeting to the girls, entered, prayer books in hand, and took her place at the head of the table. That she was in an irritable mood was apparent from the way in which she turned over the leaves of the Bible in search of the chapter for the evening, and the girls nudged one another furtively under the shelter of the table.

Betty Ayrton, a delicate, pale-faced child, who to-day would have been undergoing the open-air treatment, began to cough. Miss Quayle looked at her sharply once or twice, without pausing in her reading, but when the coughing, augmented by nervousness, continued, she let the open Bible fall on to the table with a crash, and addressed the offender.

"Elizabeth Ayrton, if you haven't sufficient self-control to avoid disturbing the whole room in that fashion, you'd better get up and go away!"

The child struggled for a moment with the racking cough, and then, with scarlet cheeks and tears in her eyes, left her seat and ran out of the room.

"Betty can't help coughing. She coughs all night long!" cried Rose suddenly, burning with indignation and too angry to care for the consequences of her interference.

There was a fearful pause, during which one or two of the girls turned pale. What was to be the result of this amazing, unheard-of audacity?

"You may go into my study, Rose Cottingham, and wait there for me," said Miss Quayle at last, with flashing eyes and convulsive movements of her hands.

Rose waited for her at the trysting-place in a tumult of emotion.

"I'm *glad* I'm going to leave! She's a wicked, cruel woman! I hate her! Pouncing on a poor child who's ill, before the whole school like that!" she muttered to herself jerkily as she raged about the room. "And now she'll come and rave at me for an hour, I suppose!"

To her surprise, to her stupefaction, indeed, Miss Quayle entered more quietly than was her wont. Her wrath seemed subdued, and at first she actually made no allusion to the interruption of prayers.

"No doubt you are aware that your grandmother intends to remove you at the end of the term?" she began.

"Yes," returned Rose shortly.

"Now, my dear child—sit down. Can you not persuade her to allow you to stay at any rate till after the examination which as you know, falls early next term? You have been working very well, Rose. I am pleased with the reports of your form-mistress, and it is a thousand pities that you should not be given a chance to do honour to the school before you leave it. I repeat, can you not influence your grandmother?"

"No," repeated Rose sullenly. "Grandmamma doesn't think the exam's at all important, and if she's made up her mind that I shall leave, nothing will alter her."

Miss Quayle was silent for a moment. "If you know that to be the case, there's no more to be said," she allowed unwillingly. "I admit her letter to me gave me little hope. Now, my dear child," she went on briskly, "what are you going to do when you leave? Are you going to waste your time idling at home, or are you going to use those gifts of mind which God has given you, for the example and glory of womanhood? You ought to go to Girton, Rose Cottingham. You are a girl of brains and character, and if you will only bend your will to the mastery of subjects you dislike——"

"Grandmamma would never let me go to Girton."

"It's your duty to overcome her objections!" returned Miss Quayle, thumping upon the table with her clenched fist. "Will, strong, determined will, can do anything. *I* have fought through opposition and prejudice, and difficulties of all sorts in my time, and I know that all that is required in women is the *will* to succeed. Now my dear Rose Cottingham, you are in many ways a talented girl. I have just been shown

by the editor of the School Magazine a little article of
yours which she proposes to print. It gives promise
of great things. You may become a writer, even a
great writer, Rose Cottingham; but in the meantime
your mind needs the training which only a University
education can give it. My dear child, Girton is the
place for you——"

Rose was dimly aware of the continuance of a long
address, in which a sketch of herself was given with a
mind fortified and rendered clear and logical by the
training of Girton, emerging upon a startled world as
a marvellous writer, an exponent of all that was "good
and fine and noble in womanhood." "You might be
the brightest jewel in the crown of Quayle College,
my dear Rose," was the peroration, "if only you would
first go to Girton and then bend your gifts reverently
to the service of Woman's Progress!"

She heard the last words, however, and was not
greatly affected by them nor attracted by the prospect
they invited, even though the flattery they implied
was very sweet. The fact, the one fact singing in her
mind, was that her little story was going to be printed!
That, and that alone, seemed the summit of her wildest
dreams, and her heart was beating fast with pride and
ecstasy. She had forgotten Betty Ayrton till, after
the suffocating embrace which ended the address, Miss
Quayle said suddenly—

"I forgive your remark at prayer-time to-night,
because I understand that it sprang from mistaken
kindness, and was not at least intentionally impertinent. My dear child, do you not yet understand that
what I wish to inculcate in young people is self-control?
In the past, women have been lacking in that quality,
and it must be conspicuous in the new womanhood.

It is not *necessary* to cough. It is not *necessary* to faint, nor to have hysterics, nor to indulge in any of those weaknesses which used to be considered 'pretty' in a woman!" She laid an accent of ineffable scorn upon the adjective.

"But I think Betty is really ill," Rose demurred much more mildly than half an hour ago she would have spoken. "I often hear her coughing in the night. She sleeps in the next room to mine."

"That a doctor will decide to-morrow. Meanwhile, my dear child, please call her Elizabeth, and not *Betty*. I thought you knew that I object to nicknames? A woman should bear the name by which she was baptized. *Elizabeth* Ayrton must see a doctor, and if her cough is really beyond her own control, which I doubt, her parents must remove her. And now, my dear child, good-night. Think over all I have said, and make Girton the goal you must and *can* reach by a patient effort of will. You owe it to the school. Remember that the glory must be to the school!"

Rose went slowly upstairs. She understood why one or two of the more studious girls "adored" Miss Quayle. She was an adept at a flattery which gained rather than lost in value by the violence of the condemnation with which it was generally mingled. She had flattered Rose, who was the more susceptible to flattery because its effect so soon wore off, neutralized by her fundamental lack of self-confidence. Praise to her was like champagne, stimulating but evanescent, and as one of the more discriminating teachers at the college remarked, "She could swallow bucketfuls of it without its going to her head." It was a little in her head to-night, however, and it caused her to take a more lenient, and possibly a juster, view of

Miss Quayle's attack upon poor little Betty, whom as she passed her room, she heard still coughing distressfully.

"It's all very well, of course, to want girls not to be silly and affected, and not to imagine they're ill when there's nothing the matter with them—and I suppose that's what she thinks she's aiming at. But she's got no imagination, and she fits everything into her own theories. That's what it is. No imagination! Any one can see that Betty oughtn't to be here at all." Her indignation to some extent revived, but was certainly not so violent as it had been before the interview in the study. She went to sleep with the words "possibly a *great* writer" ringing pleasantly in her ears, aware nevertheless that all the savour of the phrase would in a day or two have escaped, and she would have come to the conclusion that her writing was "nonsense." She regretted that she had not yielded to Professor Fergurson's wish to read her literary efforts, but shyness and a dread of his criticism had kept her firm in her refusal. She was sorry now. It was Helen who in spite of her protests, had taken her "fishing-boat thing" to Miss Solly, the editor of the school magazine. And Miss Solly had really accepted it! That, at least, was something substantial. It was a fact; it would not evaporate as did so many of her visions in the cold light of morning.

Before Rose had been back a week, the insistent, crowded life of school made her visit to the Fergursons seem like a dream—a vivid dream which recurred to her at odd moments and startled her when she remembered that it had been reality. One thing alone stood out an actual, naked fact, and that was the dockers' strike. She was eager for tidings of it, but no news-

paper was ever seen by the girls of Minerva House,
and she was forced to daily questioning of Miss Mortlake, who was known occasionally to glance at a copy
of the *Morning Post* before the servants took it out of
Miss Quayle's study for use in the kitchen.   Miss
Mortlake had little time for newspapers, but stirred by
Rose's interest, she managed to read the *Morning
Post's* summary of events every day, and was finally
able to tell her that "a settlement had been reached."

"That means that the men have won, doesn't it?"
asked Rose joyfully.   "I suppose you're a socialist,
Miss Mortlake?"

"I know very little about it, dear.   I wish I had
more time to study these questions."   She sighed, and
Rose suddenly realized that Miss Mortlake was a sort
of slave, and perhaps quite as much to be pitied as the
dockers themselves, "except that she has enough to
eat!" she added to herself.

"If socialism is trying to help unhappy people, I'm
a socialist," continued Miss Mortlake, with a melancholy smile.   "There are so many unhappy people
in the world."

The little dialogue took place outside the study
door one morning just as the crocodile was due to
start on its daily walk to the college.   Before Rose
could pursue the conversation, Miss Quayle dashed
into the hall.

"Surely it's time to go, Miss Mortlake?" she exclaimed in her usual tone of only half-suppressed fury.
She glanced at the clock with an accusing face.

"That's five minutes fast, Miss Quayle," began the
teacher meekly.   "I was just——"

"Now, my dear Miss Mortlake, don't argue!"
interrupted the Principal in a lower key intended to

be audible only to her listener, but failing in that intention. "I have given orders about punctuality, and I expect those orders—" Her voice was drowned in the clamour of the bell, which she herself seized from the hall-table and rang violently to the consternation of the girls in the cloakroom, half of whom were not ready. Rose, having put on her hat early, on purpose to have a moment with Miss Mortlake before starting, was so to speak, saved by the skin of her teeth.

"*It's five minutes too soon, Miss Mortlake!*" "*Oh, what a shame!*" "*We aren't ready! How can we possibly—*" Rose heard the clamour as she ran downstairs after Miss Mortlake, who with a flush on her cheek, was trying to hurry off the indignant and protesting girls.

"It must be *awful* to be Miss Mortlake!" she thought as she joined Helen for the walk to the college. Looking back at the procession starting from the side gate, she saw that Miss Mortlake was walking with a new girl who had found no partner, and she recalled her own first day at school and wondered whether the new girl felt as miserable as she herself had felt then.

"It's dreadful that there are so many unhappy people in the world, isn't it?" she remarked suddenly to Helen as they swung down the road.

"What makes you think of it just now?"

"Something Miss Mortlake said—and that new child walking with her, and the dockers, and all the poor people who are always struggling—and Miss Mortlake herself," said Rose comprehensively.

"Why Miss Mortlake?"

"Don't you think she is unhappy? You ought to have heard the way Miss Quayle spoke to her just now!"

"She's used to it. You always think people are as unhappy as *you* would be in their circumstances."

"Why shouldn't they be?"

"Because most people don't feel much. I don't suppose Miss Mortlake does. She's just *dull*."

"Well, I can't imagine anything much worse than that, even if she is. Perhaps she didn't *start* dull. The dulness has come because she's gone on so many years without any happiness. That's the worst thing of all!"

"People have different sorts of happiness that you know nothing about," Helen assured her. "I'm sure Miss Mortlake's religion makes her happy, for instance."

"And that's all she has!"

"Well, I daresay it's enough—when you're her age," said Helen, with the superb, unconscious cruelty of youth.

"But there was all the time before she came to be that age. She told me the other day she's been here fifteen years. Just imagine! She's got all grey and old just doing this every day—every day for fifteen years!" Rose shuddered.

"Yes, it's rather awful, of course. But all the same, she hasn't been so unhappy as *you* would have been, I'm sure. And you never would have done it! You would have broken away somehow. People who want things very much get them somehow, I'm sure. I expect Miss Mortlake didn't want anything very much."

Rose was silent. Helen was always so reasonable, and she nearly always recognized, if not at the moment, then later, the truth of what she said. It was true, and she knew it, that she would never have been, could never be, a Miss Mortlake, but she felt very sorry for the people who hadn't the courage to "break away." It must often be difficult—almost impossible—if one wasn't very clever, and if one had no money. And without being very clever people might want things badly, she reflected. "What am I going to do at home, for instance?" she thought, with a sudden, panic realization of her own circumstances. "Grandmamma will expect me to stay there, and if she won't give me the money to go away—and of course she won't—what am I to do?"

"*Now* what are you thinking about that makes you look frightened?" asked Helen, after a glance at her friend's face.

Rose tried to explain. "But it's no use explaining Grandmamma to you," she concluded hopelessly. "You have always done what you liked, and your father is quite different. He thinks you *ought* to do what you like. But Grandmamma thinks there's only one thing for girls to do. To get married."

"Well, get married, and then you can do what you please."

"But there's no one to marry at Glencove."

"You'll come up to London, of course, and marry some nice, clever man, and have a *salon* like the French people long ago. And all the clever people will come to it, because you'll be a great writer by that time and every one will want to know you!"

Rose brightened at this rosy prospect. It sounded quite incredible, but it was a splendid idea, and splendid of Helen to have thought of it.

"Anyhow, that couldn't happen for lots of years," she demurred, "and all that time I shall be at home, while you're at Girton."

"Perhaps I shan't go to Girton."

Rose turned to her in surprise. "I thought you wanted to!"

"I *did*, but I'm not so keen on it now, somehow. It will depend upon how much I like going to parties and dances. I shall try that first."

"You've changed, Helen," said Rose suddenly. She was thinking of Helen's "funniness" again in conjunction with this new talk about dances.

"No. How? Why shouldn't I like dances?" asked Helen rather hurriedly. "You know how I love dancing. And so do you," she added. "We can both dance well, thank goodness!" Helen and Rose were the show pupils at the weekly dancing-class held in the winter in the "cally"-room, and taught by a voluble old Frenchwoman, never tired of praising the grace of the two girls, who were always partners. Rose looked forward to the lesson from week to week. On the dancing evening she was always completely happy.

"Oh yes, I know. But you used to be so down on the Robinsons for always talking about their parties."

"The sort of parties *they* go to!" returned Helen, with her head in the air.

"Oh, well, they think they're lovely! . . . I mean, I thought you cared too much about books and learning and clever talk and all that, to think that dances were worth giving up Girton for."

"Well, perhaps I shan't. I can do both."

Rose sighed. It was magnificent to be Helen, who had only to choose what she would or would not do.

There was a pause, in which she tried not to think of "studying French" with Mademoiselle La Touche.

"Have you ever read any of Swinburne?" asked

Helen suddenly, while Rose was listening mechanically to snatches of talk from the couples before and behind her. The question fell oddly between their exclamations and remarks: *"Perfectly awful!"* *"So she said I was to take a conduct mark, and I said—"* *"I tell you she'll get the History prize——"*

"No," she replied, pulling herself together. "He's a poet, isn't he?"

"I found *Poems and Ballads* in father's study two or three days before the end of the holidays, and I read some of it. I wish I could have brought it back," Helen went on, rather dreamily. "But it would have been confiscated, of course."

"Why?"

"Not proper!" said Helen, with a mocking inflexion in her voice.

"Isn't it?"

Helen shrugged her shoulders. "From Miss Quayle's point of view, I suppose not. But it's beautiful. I'll lend it to you in the holidays."

"What sort of poems? What are they about?"

"Oh—love," said Helen, as they went up the steps of the college.

The term fled with inconceivable rapidity, and left Rose with a sense of grasping continually at something which eluded her. The visit to the Fergusons had given a tremendous stimulus to a nature which, without extraneous aids, was of the slow developing order, and for the first time she began to be dimly conscious of the complexity of things—above all, of the complexity of human beings.

Her intuitions, as a child keen and true, had for a time been overlaid by the more or less stultifying

17

routine of school, but now they re-emerged and were backed by conscious thought. She began to view even the teachers with different eyes. Formerly she had never thought of them except in relation to herself and to "school," of which they had seemed component parts, existing only as machines for the accomplishment of certain ends. Now she often watched them, and wondered "what they were really like inside."

Once, that term, when Miss Stuart, her present form-mistress, was dictating some notes to the class, she paused. Rose, who had finished the sentence and looked up expectant of the next words, found her gazing out of the window, with a preoccupied expression which stirred her curiosity. Miss Stuart was rather young and rather pretty, with bunches of dark curls drawn back from a white forehead, and a round face in which were set deep blue eyes. She had evidently forgotten the waiting class, and the girls began to giggle and exchange glances. A slight outburst of mirth from the back row, finally recalled their teacher's wandering attention. She blushed to her white forehead, and hurriedly taking up the book, continued her dictation. Rose wondered of what she had been thinking. That absent, far-away gaze had made her realize that Miss Stuart had a home, friends, joys, troubles, perhaps—a whole life, in fact, of which she knew nothing. That the Miss Stuart out of Quayle College might be a very different person from the rather cold, rather detached, very formal little lady she appeared to her pupils, seemed to her now not impossible.

"People are so 'mixed up'!" she said to Helen. "It's so worrying, because one never knows all the things that make them what they are. I wonder what sort of life Miss Bird has had, and what she does in the holidays?"

"I don't care a bit what Miss Bird does in the holidays," returned Helen coldly. "She's an underbred, insignificant woman, beneath one's notice."

"She is. I mean, she's a little toad," agreed Rose, with fervour. "But I don't think she's beneath notice. I've come to the conclusion that no one's beneath notice. People are so interesting!"

"I don't find many people here interesting."

"Not what they say, but what they *are*—I mean what has made them like that. Sometimes I feel I should like to pick every one to pieces to see what's going on in their heads and how it came there. But I dare say I shouldn't know any better if I *did*," she added reflectively, "because when I try to take myself to pieces I'm just as muddled as ever about myself even."

.   .   .   .

"Show me what you're writing," said Helen. It was Saturday afternoon, too hot for a walk, and most of the girls were lounging in the garden, reading or doing needlework. Helen and Rose were in the rickety little summer-house, which Rose liked because of the rustling noise of the poplar-tree outside, which always reminded her of the sound of the sea.

"Oh no!" said Rose, hastily covering the sheets she had written with both hands. "It's all nonsense. I can't do it properly. It's in my head, but it won't come out."

"You say that about everything you do," complained Helen; "and you'll never do anything if you take that sort of attitude. Why on earth haven't you more self-confidence?" She had asked the question

a hundred times before, and a hundred times Rose had
given up the puzzle.

But she was happy that summer.   It was warm, and
she loved the heat and the scents of the poor tiny
London garden.   She loved the long twilight, in which
she strolled on the dried-up grass-plot with Helen,
or sometimes with other friends, for she reached the
height of her popularity that last term, and nearly all
the girls bewailed her impending loss.   Rose felt fond
of all of them.   Free from the strain of an examination,
she worked only moderately hard, and had time to
breathe and feel and think.

One painful occurrence, however, made a deep
impression, and marred the peace of her last few weeks
at Minerva House.   Betty Ayrton had left during
the first week of the term.   The doctor had given an
unfavourable report, and the child was taken away
into the country by her mother.   Ten weeks later a
little girl who had been Betty's chief friend received
a heart-broken letter from Mrs. Ayrton with the
news that Betty was dead.

Miss Mortlake read prayers that morning, for Miss
Quayle did not appear till breakfast-time; and when
she came, she entered the room quietly, and going up
to the child who had received the letter, and was
crying, she bent over and kissed her.

"I'm sure you will all be grieved to hear that poor
little Elizabeth Ayrton died two days ago," she said,
addressing the room in a low, moved voice.   "She was
a good, gentle little girl, and we shall—" she paused
abruptly, apparently unable to trust her voice.   "Perhaps some of you would like to send a few flowers to
her mother," she added when she had gone to her
place at the end of the table.   She sat down, and the

girls, who had been looking at their plates in an embarrassed and uncomfortable fashion began to talk in low voices amongst themselves.

Rose was silent, her heart beating painfully. She was conscious first of a rush of pity for Miss Quayle, who must be thinking of what had practically been her last words to Betty. Perhaps she was wondering how many of the girls remembered them. It must be *awful* for her, she thought; and suddenly her mind went back to a day long ago, when in a fit of temper she had said she wished Lucie would die. Lucie developed measles next day, and Rose still remembered the black, awful horror of her remorse when she thought God might be going to take her at her word. Suppose Miss Quayle was feeling anything like that! If so, it was Miss Quayle she pitied rather than Betty. She recalled the child's pitiful, frightened little face when she ran from the room after being reprimanded for coughing, and as it rose vividly before her, tears choked her. It was awful that a child who was going to die should have been frightened. She was a timid little thing, Rose remembered, who always started and trembled when Miss Quayle came into the room. How unspeakably dreadful it must be to know that some one had been afraid of you and was now dead.

Her pity for Miss Quayle was so acute and painful that it was with intense though shocked relief that she heard her the same evening, in a towering rage, fulminating against Cissie Crofts and May Woodford for daring to go out in the damp garden in their indoor shoes!

"I needn't have bothered," she told herself, with contempt for her own soft-heartedness. "She felt it for a moment, and now she's forgotten. I'm glad she has, because I don't like her, and I don't *want* to be sorry for her. And now I needn't. I wonder whether most people are like that? Perhaps it's silly to waste time on other people's feelings. Helen thinks so, I know. I wish I could help doing it." She was glad she had said nothing to Helen about the passionate unnecessary pity she had carried about in her heart all day, and of which she now felt ashamed. In her schoolgirl language she told herself that she had been "sold."

As the term drew to an end she became obsessed by the realization of the "last" of all the common, every-day experiences of which she had so often wearied. There was the last Sunday, with the walk through roads bordered by stucco houses to the grey stone, ordinary-looking church, where, so far as Rose was concerned, the Reverend Butts enunciated the last of his platitudes. Then the long afternoon devoted to sweets, the simulated reading of Sunday stories, and the frequent writing of her name in birthday-books for girls, who were going to write to her every week all their lives and would never, never forget her! The word "shame," the hackneyed word of all work at Minerva House, was on every lip. It was a shame she was going! "Oh, what a horrid shame!" "Oh, Rose, what a shame it is this is the last Sunday!" "Oh, Rose darling, it will be *awful* without you! It's a shame!" . . . She went to bed with the word ringing in her ears.

Then came the last flannel-clad "cally" before breakfast on the last day; the last walk down to the college with Helen; and the last morning's school,

which, unlike an ordinary school day, was largely devoted to the reading out of class lists and places in
form, and the tidying of lockers and books. Her form-
mistress, Miss Stuart, shook hands with her while the
other girls were filing out after the last bell had rung.

"Good-bye, Rose. I hear you are leaving," she
said, in her unemotional voice. "I hope you will do
well. If you are going in for any of the higher examinations later on you must work at your Mathematics,
you know." She hurried away in response to another
insistent bell which called her to see the girls out of the
cloakrooms, and Rose glanced round the now deserted
classroom, with its yellow Swedish desks, its distempered walls, and the bleak windows wide open, framing
squares of intense blue sky.

In passing along the gallery outside she looked down
into the big Hall, at the rows of shiny seats, at the
platform and the organ, and at the large, framed black
tablets on either side of it, on which in gilt letters were
inscribed the names of the winners of scholarships and
of special honours for the school. Her name was not
there. It would never now be there, and she experienced a dreary sense of failure as a schoolgirl. There
was a dreary pain altogether at her heart, made up of
many undefined emotions. She had always hated the
atmosphere of the college, even though custom had
reduced her first violent antipathy to a vague distaste
for the hygienic ugliness of her scholastic surrounding.
She liked it no better now, but she was wretched to
leave it. A door was closed, never to be reopened, and
behind it lay so much that "counted." Excitements,
triumphs, despairs, idleness, feverish striving, fun,
laughter, silly but delightful giggling, trifling hopes—
as trifling fears. Rose vaguely thought of them all,

and they were all vaguely precious now that she was leaving them behind. A teacher hurrying along the gallery, scolded her sharply for loitering, and she rushed downstairs, forcing back her tears.

Minerva House was a whirl of packing, of laughter, of sentimental gush and endearment, of lamentation mingled with rejoicing for the coming summer holidays.

The afternoon passed like a worrying dream, and at dusk she and Helen strolled for the last time up and down the grass-plot at the back of the house, whose lighted windows showed figures passing and repassing. A babel of gay, chattering voices rose and fell upon the summer air. Rose was crying silently, and Helen's eyes were wet.

"I can't help knowing exactly what it will be like," said Rose, in a choking voice. "Day after day, with no one to speak to. I mean, no one who understands. It will be *awful!*"

"You'll find a way out," Helen assured her. "I know you'll find a way out. And there's always me, you must remember, and our house. Father is so fond of you. You must come often."

"If Grandmamma will let me," murmured Rose.

Miss Quayle's address to her in the study after prayers, was a little lacking in cordiality.

"You ought to have done better in class," she said. "For a girl of your ability to be only twelfth out of twenty-five, is not creditable. It's the old tale of the Mathematics, over which you have been incurably obstinate. But leaving that aside, let me adjure you, my dear girl, not to waste your time at home. We may yet see you at Girton, winning honours which will reflect glory on the college."

Rose refrained from again insisting on the baseless-
ness of this vision. She was tired and depressed, and
needed no reminder that she ought to have done better.
On the whole, she had done her best, and things
"hadn't come off." It was the Mathematics, of
course, but she felt that there would always be *something* against the achievement of complete success.
She was up against her limitations again, dimly realizing them as she had done since her childhood.

The cab that was to take her to Paddington was
early at the door next morning. She had taken leave
of Helen alone in the empty "cally"-room downstairs,
and she came up white and tearless, scarcely noticing
the kisses showered upon her by the group of girls in
the hall. Miss Quayle sailed from the study, scatter-
ing them, and embraced her, though with less fervour
than when she subsequently enfolded in her arms
Mary Cartwright, the winner of the Goldsmiths'
Scholarship, who was also leaving.

Rose had been a disappointing girl, and the possible
chance of amends through the Senior Cambridge having failed, there was a coldness about Miss Quayle's
farewell. Rose caught a glimpse of her as the cab
drove off, swaying angrily towards a retreating girl.
Then the Hall door closed upon the stout, awe-
inspiring little figure which had stood for so much in
the past few years.

Pushing down the ramshackle window of the four-
wheeler, she looked for the last time at Minerva House,
with sensations which worried her because she could
not define them. She had been unhappy there, and
also happy; but that did not seem to matter. What
mattered now was that it was all over. The door had
closed.

Miss Mortlake, who had been told off to see her to the station, wondered, as she sat beside her in the cab, of what she was thinking. She was sorry Rose was going. She had always liked but never understood her. This last term the girl had been charming to her, and there were few girls at Minerva House of whom that could be said. Miss Mortlake, who was going to a Home of Rest for Governesses at Broadstairs, that afternoon, sighed, and wondered how long she could afford to stay there. The summer holidays always made a great hole in the term's salary, and she had no cool dresses, and scarcely knew how to breathe in the winter coat she was still wearing at the end of July.

Though she pulled herself together and took a cheerful farewell of Rose after she had seen her into the train, the girl saw the smile die out of her eyes almost before the carriage had glided past the spot where she stood waving on the platform. Another human being had passed out of her life, of whose unofficial existence she knew nothing, and Rose felt that this was desperately sad.

XIX

THE HUNGER OF THE HEART

FOR a time the holidays had their charm. Rose could not realize that they were "holidays" no longer, that Glencove had, so to say, become permanent, and through the sunny days of August she revelled in the beauty of sea and country. The Manor House was unchanged, except that it had grown interiorly a little shabbier—the carpets more faded, the chintzes dimmer. But she found no fault in this respect with her home, which, consciously now, as always it unconsciously had done, pleased her by its air of dignified repose.

Then came the preparations for Lucie's departure. She was to go to Tours, where her grandmother's convent days had been passed, and Mrs. Lester, whose mistrust of schools had not diminished, congratulated herself upon having found a family *très convenable* into which the girl was to be received. Mesdemoiselles Leblanc, the daughters of an old schoolfellow of her own, were coming to England in September, and Lucie would return with them. Lucie was enraptured at the prospect of going to France, and for a month her clothes were the absorbing topic of the household. A dressmaker worked in the house all day copying things which came from London, and Rose's dawning delight in dress was awakened by the sight of silks and chiffons and fine underwear. She was amazed at Lucie's skill in dressmaking as well as in the trim-

267

ming of hats, and felt keenly her own incompetence in this and every other practical respect. Mrs. Lester herself took Lucie to London to meet her future hostesses, and it was only when she returned next day that Rose began to feel the weight of the dulness to come. Lucie might not be interesting, but she was young, pretty, sweet-tempered, easy to get on with, and Rose often felt for her a renewal of the tender, protective emotion she had experienced when they were both children and Lucie had been frightened in the night. Now there would be no one but Grandmamma, and of course Mademoiselle La Touche, who was to return from her holiday in a day or two.

Lucie had loved Mademoiselle La Touche, whose nature, very much like her own, was "bright," capable in all material ways, contented with trifles, demanding little of life, never profoundly moved either by grief or joy.

In due course she arrived, and reminded Rose of a dark canary whose continual aimless hopping and chirping irritated her beyond endurance—a little, black-haired, vivacious woman who chattered incessantly and never said anything that mattered.

Mademoiselle La Touche had now been four years an inmate of the Manor House, and by this time had fallen into the ways of the household as one of the family, never so happy as when she could do the marketing, wash china, and clean plate with Mrs. Lester, arrange the flowers, and generally attend to all the domestic side of life, in which alone she was interested. Mrs. Lester viewed her with the paradoxical approving contempt which she accorded to all women who fulfilled her theoretical notion of the feminine mission. She despised equally, the women with

intellect and the women with none. If they had
brains, they were useless as women, and therefore
ridiculous; if they had none, they were contemptible
in themselves, and though in theory she held the
latter state preferable, she concealed a very real disdain for their inconsequence and lack of reasoning
power. She spoke of Mademoiselle La Touche as
"a true woman," and flattered herself that the irony
lurking in the description was always carefully concealed. On the surface indeed, she agreed admirably
with the little lady, whose pretty, easy manner appealed to her as graceful and becoming in her sex.

Life gradually settled down at the Manor House
with outward monotony, even though for Rose it held
something like frenzied despair. Passionately alive,
she was a prisoner, cut off from every mental stimulus, doomed to pass her days between two women,
neither of them young, one mentally atrophied, the
other possessing no mind at all. And she beat upon
her bars in vain, since neither woman realized that
the prison existed.

Mrs. Lester had long ceased to desire anything
fervently, to hope anything that was unreasonable,
or to experience active emotions of any kind. She
read very little except the daily paper. Her interest
in politics was her one remaining link with the world
of thought, and that link expressed itself now in
bitter, sarcastic comment on the trend of the times,
on all modern institutions, ideas, and tendencies.
She had reached the stage in intellectual decadence
when every new idea is necessarily a bad one, or at
best futile and ridiculous, a sign of the ultimate dog-
ship towards which the country was declining. That
her granddaughter was of an age and temperament

to welcome new ideas, that it was, in fact, inevitable that she should do so since she represented the younger generation, never occurred to her. In her eyes Rose was a wrong-headed little fool, to be mocked at for holding "views" of any kind.

Again and again Rose determined never to give her grandmother an opportunity of "ragging" her. She thought of how Helen in her circumstances would act, and strove in vain to emulate her coolness and reticence.

"Helen could live in this house and never let Grandmamma know what she was thinking or feeling," she thought despairingly. "Why can't I?" It was obvious that she could not.

Incurably careless, she left books about which she had sworn to keep under lock and key. She rose like a silly little fish at every purposely sneering remark of Mrs. Lester's directed against "the lower classes," or the aspirations of "the New Woman," and acrimonious wrangles, ending on Rose's side in a fit of exhausting temper, were the unvarying results.

There was a streak of cruelty in Mrs. Lester, a vent possibly for the restrained bitterness of so much of her life, and for all her underlying sense of failure, which found exercise in the half-playful, half-vindictive harrying of her granddaughter.

"You to claim so much for women, when you can't stand criticism and you can't stand chaff!" she exclaimed one day seeing Rose on the verge of tears. "How do you suppose men would get on if they cried every time their ideas were attacked?"

"It isn't criticism and it isn't chaff!" retorted Rose with justice. "If you argued, I should like it, and you would get the best of it because you know more than I do. And if you teased I shouldn't mind; I've been teased at school. But you don't; you only sneer and say beastly things."

"You can go up to your room and stay there," was Mrs. Lester's only reply. "I am no more disposed to take impertinence from you at seventeen than I was when you were seven." And Rose rushed up to her room in a state of indignant revolt at injustice, and in a temper as violent as any she had experienced at the age last mentioned by her grandmother.

Mademoiselle La Touche she found even more exasperating in her futility, than her grandmother in her narrowness and irony. Forced to spend many hours a day with Mademoiselle to acquire the language for the sake of which she had been led into domestic captivity, Rose was bored till she could have screamed aloud by the little woman's ceaseless inane chatter about nothing.

"*Mon Dieu, quel beau temps!*" she would begin as they started on their daily walk. "It is strange how the sunshine makes happy. Have you not noticed that, Rose *chérie?* On a dull day one is *triste*, on a sunny day one is full of gaiety. How is that? Can you explain, my little Rose? Ah, see! There goes Madame 'Arrington, driving in her carriage. What a hat! Where do you think she bought it, my Rose?   Blue! I—I detest blue. Which do you prefer, my little Rose, blue or pink? You do not answer. Why? Is it that you are sad? But why are you sad, my child?"

"Because I'm bored to death."

"*Mon Dieu!* but that I cannot understand! Your sister, the dear Lucie, was never bored. You are young. The young should be gay. Why are you not gay?

Lucie was always gay, like a little bird. And always occupied. From morning till night she was occupied, and always happy. She fed the birds, the dog, the cat. She played on the piano. She sang. She made her frocks, but with a touch! Like a Parisienne. She did not read much, *la petite paresseuse.*" Mademoiselle laughed indulgently. "But why, then? She is young, she is beautiful, and that is enough for a young girl. Why should she spoil her so pretty eyes with books? Learned books are for men. The young girl should be gay and seek to please. You study too much, Rose *chérie.* You might be a boy. Look at me! 1 never cared to read dull books to improve my mind, and I am gay, but gay! Everything pleases me." Mademoiselle burst into a little song composed chiefly of "tra-la-la," and flicked her fingers playfully before Rose's sombre face.

In her own mind Rose was more or less consciously translating the little Frenchwoman's chatter into canary language.

"Hop, hop, hop! Chirp, chirp! What lovely groundsel! Sugar? *Quel bonheur!* Peck! Peck! Now I will sing!" and a strain of earsplitting trills and shakes immediately followed.

"I envy you!" she said one day with sudden vehemence.

"But, yes; I have the contented mind," sang Mademoiselle complacently.

Certain it was that Rose had not. The boredom from which even as a child, she had suffered acutely enough in her home, was intensified a hundredfold now that she stood on the brink of womanhood, with mind and body alike eager for life, for change, for movement. A born traveller, she saw herself stranded on a desert island, where she stood stretching out imploring hands in vain, scanning the horizon for the white flutter of a sail. Letters were her one means of communication with the active, breathing, outside world, where things happened and people were alive and doing. She wrote them feverishly, and lived for the two posts a day, which haply might bring her tidings of that outer world. But her correspondence with half a dozen girls still at Minerva House soon dwindled and died. They were busy, careless, forgetful, and Rose had become a memory.

Helen alone was faithful, and without her frequent letters and the books and papers she sent, Rose thought she would have died. As it was, her correspondence with her gave her as much pain as pleasure for the fierce jealousy it roused.

Helen was enjoying life to the full. She was seventeen and a half now, and she had begun to go to dances, chaperoned by a Mrs. Tregold, the most worldly of the somewhat strenuous set of women by which the Fergurson household was surrounded. Her letters held mention of white satin and tulle, and a pearl necklace, a birthday gift from her father. They also dwelt upon the "perfect" waltzes she had enjoyed with a certain Claude Coulson, who was intellectual, and talked as well as he danced. These, and similar passages in the letters, Rose devoured with greedy interest and envy, mingled with astonishment; scarcely recognizing in this strange talk about young men, frocks, and hinted compliments, the Helen she knew. To assure herself that it was indeed her friend who wrote, she had to recall the midnight conversation in her bedroom at the Fergursons on the occasion of the Human Progress meeting, and one or two of Helen's

18

unexpected remarks during the last term at school. It was strange, and Rose puzzled over it. Helen's new world of frocks, flirtation, and fashion, was a glamorous vision of an existence not only unattainable, but unthinkable as a state in which she herself might live and move. Helen had passed beyond her into an enchanted land, whose denizens were required to possess mysterious qualities to which she herself might never attain. She tried to fix her mind upon the "serious" passages in Helen's letters—the passages in which books and lectures were discussed, and accounts of drawing-room meetings bestowed in the vein to which she was accustomed from Helen, the vein through which she regained touch with her friend.

Rose had recently been promoted to a small dress allowance, and she made inroads upon this for a subscription to a London library, and by the purchase now and again of a coveted book mentioned by Helen or reviewed in the *Morning Post*, the only paper she ever saw. She tried to plan out a course of reading, writing, and study, designed to fill every hour of the day not occupied by French lessons, meals, and walks, and for a week or two at a time she achieved comparative content. Then would come a letter from Helen with fresh accounts of ballrooms shining with lights and flowers, of a ritual known as "sitting out" with thrilling young men, of hints as to engrossing dialogues during this *solitude à deux;* with news of plays, of the most recent "movements" in art and the conduct of life in general and particular, and Rose would relapse into misery that was passionate and vehement, or hopeless and apathetic according to the mood with which the arrival of the letter coincided. Helen had grown tired of repeating invitations which

Mrs. Lester never allowed her granddaughter to accept. To Rose, Mrs. Lester assigned as an all-sufficient reason, the cost of the journey and the expense of a London visit, never mentioning the fact that she had plans for her entrance into society which had no relation to the Fergursons, who from the little she had troubled to gather about them, appeared to her people of a nondescript class and of negligible importance.

"Say that I do not wish your French studies interrupted," was her unvarying formula for the letter of refusal in which Rose, raging, and cruelly disappointed, was more than once forced to close against herself the gates of paradise.

In such a crisis as this Mademoiselle proved, if not a comfort, at all events a safety-valve for the girl's bitter complaints. That Rose should desire parties, pretty frocks, and the society of young men, was perfectly comprehensible to the little Frenchwoman.

"But wait, *chérie!* Be patient a little longer!" she counselled. "When Lucie returns next autumn your grandmother will surely send you both to London before long, to make your *début* into society."

"Grandmamma never says so," returned Rose sulkily. Useless to explain to Mademoiselle that "society" was only part of what she longed for day and night. It was a full life she craved, the companionship of interesting people, the mid-stream, in exchange for a stagnating backwater of existence.

"Madame your grandmother is reticent. But reticent!" exclaimed Mademoiselle, raising her hands and eyes to heaven. "She speaks not, but that does not mean that she has no plans for your future. How can that be? A *parti* must be found for both of you, and most naturally you will go to London, there to seek for husbands."

"Disgusting!" cried Rose, with her nose in the air.

"How so? Be reasonable, my little Rose. You would not enjoy to be an old maid like me?" Mademoiselle laughed cheerfully. "Alas! I had no *dot*, so I am still *Mademoiselle*. But here in England it is different. Men marry girls because they are pretty, and they fall in love with them. It is an illusion—generally. But you English love illusions. And it is convenient. *Mon Dieu*, convenient. For at least you marry!"

Rose looked at her scornfully. "French people are funny!" she remarked enigmatically, so far as Mademoiselle's comprehension carried her. "But after all, you're like Grandmamma," she added. "She thinks marriage to *any one* is better than no marriage at all."

"*Mais oui! Certainement*," said Mademoiselle, as though stating a self-evident fact.

Rose opened her lips to argue, and then closed them again with an impatient shrug of the shoulders. What was the use?

"Well, I'm not pretty, so even that chance isn't for me!" she declared ironically.

"You're not pretty, ma petite, but you could make yourself *chic*," returned Mademoiselle, regarding her with a critical eye. "You are a type more French than English. Madame has said there is French blood in your family, and in you one perceives it. Come, I will make you a frock, my Rose, in which you shall look charming! But you must laugh. You must be gay. The eyes bright. The movements quick. Not always frowning and despondent as you are now. It makes one melancholy only to regard you."

There was undoubted truth in the assertion. Rose
in those days was anything but a pleasant companion.
Self-absorbed, discontented to the innermost fibre
of her being, usually silent and morose, to outward
view at least, she was an unattractive, sullen-looking
girl, and the visitors who came to the Manor House,
people upon whom with her grandmother she was
occasionally forced to call, disliked her intensely,
mourned for Lucie, and more or less openly com-
miserated Mrs. Lester upon her change of companion.

It was only in the company of Major Hawley that
her manner completely changed. By no means intellectual, the old man possessed an amusing turn of
speech to which Rose instantly responded, and in his
society she became attractive, *piquante*, and, as Mrs.
Lester secretly admitted, almost pretty.

"Why, if I may venture to ask, can't you find as
much to say elsewhere, as you do at Greenways?" she
inquired sarcastically once when they were driving
home after lunching with the Major. "At Lady
Driver's the other day and at the Totfields' on Saturday you sat dumb, looking as heavy as. lead and as
gauche as a sulky child of ten. If you can be pleasant
at one place, why not at another?"

"Because it's no good trying to talk to those
people!" returned Rose vivaciously. "If I say anything for fun, they stare at me as though I were mad,
and how can any one talk even seriously to people like
Lady Driver and Mrs. Totfield? They never talk at
all. They say: 'I do hope it will be fine for the
cricket match. I hear that the Red House is let.
Do you happen to know who's taken Mr. Harben's
shooting?' And when you've said yes or no—that's
all. They chatter about nothing at all, in jerks, and it

doesn't matter whether you answer or whether you don't. But the Major always says something funny, and that makes me say something which *he* thinks funny, and so we keep it up—like battledore and shuttlecock. He doesn't *talk* either, but he knows how to play. No one else here can either talk *or* play! And I *love* playing!"

But for the animation induced by her recent visit, Rose would not have tried to explain herself. As it was, Mrs. Lester, with a sidelong glance at her flushed cheeks and bright eyes, understood very well what she meant, though her rejoinder was merely, "You are altogether too superior for ordinary society,"—a remark which succeeded in bringing the sullen look once more into the girl's face. Years of contemptuous acquiescence in the banalities of her surroundings, had not completely obscured Mrs. Lester's own appreciation of wit, but it was characteristic of her to feel irritation rather than sympathy with the young creature who also recognised its existence and craved for the atmosphere in which it flourished. It was so troublesome of Rose to want what it was difficult to obtain! She had always been troublesome. Why couldn't she be the pretty, ordinary, brainless girl of whom Lucie was a pleasant example? Lucie would marry automatically; but as she realized with apprehension, there would be nothing automatic where Rose was concerned.

The months dragged on and brought only increasing unhappiness and increasing though impotent revolt against the sterile monotony of her days. Her birthday passed. She was now in her eighteenth year, a woman, and as she told herself with bitterness, a slave—a slave in the power of her grandmother,

who as guardian of the supplies, could order her life
and keep her in the prison of home with never a congenial companion, with no hope, no prospects! Over
and over again she recalled a conversation with Helen
during the last term of school. "*You would never have
been like Miss Mortlake,*" Helen had said. "*You
would have broken away somehow. People who want
things very much always get them.*" The words had a
confident ring, but they amounted to little, she
thought. Heaven knew she wanted "things" desperately. Yet without money how were they to be
attained? She exhausted herself in devising plans
which later reflection showed her to be futile. Without money one was helpless, hopeless, lost.

Latterly, too, a fresh misery had begun to be
added to dulness and lack of mental stimulus. · Rose
could not think what possessed her, nor what was
this new, unbearable restlessness which took the form
of an aching longing for something—something? . . .
She could not express it, but it meant all that mattered in the world, all that was absolutely unattainable.
For her birthday Helen had sent her Swinburne's *Poems
and Ballads*, and this new insupportable wretchedness
dated from her first eager skimming of the poems.
They were, as she discovered, remembering at the same
time Helen's description, "all about love," and their
immediate effect was to kindle a flame in her hitherto
quiescent imagination with regard to the passion.
Here was a realm till now ignored by her, a world in
which "wild kisses" and wilder embraces seemed the
sole occupation of its denizens; a world of thrilling
experiences, of unimaginable joys. Always sensitive
to words, she lingered over the languorous, beautiful
cadences of the poems, and in the daily constitutional,

walked to the music of "Dolores" or the "Hymn to Proserpine," while Mademoiselle chattered of hats and the coming Paris fashions. Hearing from Mademoiselle that French novels were improper and by no means *convenable* for the *jeune fille*, she put on the library list the names of all those she found mentioned or alluded to in the *Morning Post*, hiding them carefully amongst her clothes when they arrived and reading them at night in bed. In this way she came across some of the stories of Maupassant, as well as *Madame Bovary* and *La Fille Elisa*. She read with curiosity, imperfect understanding, and a sense of guilt similar to that with which as a little girl she had listened to the recitals of Millie Cripps. She hated the books, even while they filled her with interested bewilderment. Rose was as yet untouched by any feeling for realism, and too immature to recognize power in a writer. The brutal treatment of "love" shocked and puzzled her. These novels dealt with the same theme as that she had found treated in the *Poems and Ballads*, yet where was the glamour, the mystery which in Swinburne's poems of the passion of love so excited and disturbed her? Here, stripped of all romance, it was ugly, sordid, horrible! Where was the truth? What did it all mean? What was it like to love and be loved? Rose felt she would have given her soul to know this. Did Helen know? she wondered. She recalled the forms and features of several young men who had called at the Fergursons' during her visit, and could not picture any of them inspiring the overwhelming feelings which permeated the poems of Swinburne. Except perhaps—and sometimes for a moment she saw him as he must then have appeared to Helen—the man who spoke at the drawing-room meeting? Helen had talked of Greek gods in connection with him. She wished she had not been so childish then! She wished she had looked at him, instead of merely listening to what he said. As it was, she had only a blurred vision of a dark figure with easy movements and eyes that seemed somehow alight.

Day by day Rose grew more restless, more insupportably listless and wretched. She no longer tried to read anything but novels, and those in secret; she never now wrote anything at all. The school magazine containing her little essay had appeared the term after she left. It was sent to her, and though at the time she had experienced a delicious thrill of pride at seeing her work in print, its effects had long since passed away. She looked at it now with cold, indifferent eyes. She seemed to have no ambition left.

After her French lessons and reading with Mademoiselle she wandered aimlessly from the house to the garden, from the garden to the house. She sat for hours at her bedroom window staring at the sea, weaving impossible romances in which she was the heroine wildly adored and passionately embraced by some shadowy demi-god. She had nothing to do— nothing that she was forced to do. Accepting with a shrug of the shoulders and an occasional sarcasm, her granddaughter's hopeless incompetence in domestic matters, Mrs. Lester never either sought or demanded her help. She herself was always busy in the house, Mademoiselle was at hand, only too ready to give assistance, the staff of servants was sufficient for the small family, and Rose's interference would, in her grandmother's own phrase, have been "more bother than it was worth." Mrs. Lester was, moreover, insensibly growing tired; more lax, less disposed to do her duty by a girl who constantly and constitutionally annoyed her. Increasingly Rose was left alone, practically ignored by her grandmother.

It was Mademoiselle who pointed out that the girl was looking ill, with dark circles round her eyes and an increasing pallor.

"Of course she looks ill," was Mrs. Lester's rejoinder. "A girl with no feminine instincts, no love for the proper avocations of woman to keep her cheerful and occupied, is certain to look ill. But I wash my hands of Rose. I have no patience with her!"

"But she is fond of dress," declared Mademoiselle, clinging to the thread which to her bound Rose to ordinary womanhood. "That is so remarkable. And she has taste for it, too. She knews what suits her."

"Yet she can't put a stitch towards it herself," returned Mrs. Lester scornfully. "A more useless, unattractive, hopeless girl I never met!"

"The poor little Rose!" sighed Mademoiselle. "It is a little more gaiety she needs perhaps?" she ventured tentatively. A kind-hearted little creature, despite her shallowness, she was sorry for Rose.

"She can't have it yet. I intend to wait till Lucie is old enough to come out before I make a move for Rose." She paused abruptly as though annoyed with herself for having allowed even so much to escape her, Mademoiselle's inquisitive glance not lost upon her. The two women were in the pantry washing a delicate old dessert service which Mrs. Lester never entrusted to a servant, and for a moment she went on rinsing plates and passing them to her companion to be dried.

"Besides,—gaiety for Rose!" she added contemptuously. "Does she look as though she would enjoy it? She never takes advantage of any social pleasures here. Only yesterday she refused to go to the Totfields', where there are two girls of her own age."

"She says these young ladies bore her. She has nothing to say to them."

"Stuff and nonsense! Why can't she chatter the usual rubbish that contents young people? The Totfields are nice, wholesome, lively girls, with no brains to make them ridiculous, fortunately for themselves and their mothers!"

"*Hélas!* It is just that which infuriates my lady. She who is *femme savante* with all her learned books!"

"I made the greatest mistake of my life in sending her to a new-fangled school," Mrs. Lester admitted after a silence. "If I had my way, girls should be taught to read and write and handed over to an appropriate husband at seventeen! And I'm not even sure about the reading and writing," she added, with a grim smile. "They'd do all that's required of them just as well, possibly better, without it."

The same night when Rose went up to bed at ten o'clock, she first lighted, then blew out the candles on her dressing-table and knelt at the open window with her elbows on the sill.

The evening had passed as for a year had dragged all the other evenings of her monotonous days. She had strolled out into the garden after dinner, only to be recalled some twenty minutes later by her grandmother, who inquired what on earth she was doing out there in the dark. She bade her come into the drawing-room at once and occupy herself like a reasonable being. Mrs. Lester and Mademoiselle were playing bézique, as every evening they played it together at a little table illumined by shaded candles, and from the shelter of the book she was not reading Rose allowed her eyes to wander about the room, which, with all its shabbiness concealed by the subdued, mellow light looked charmingly mellow, restful, and dignified. The French windows were open to the garden, where the outlines of motionless trees hung massed against the sky. Not a sound broke the stillness of the late yet warm summer night. Within the pool of light thrown by the candles, sat the two women absorbed in their game. Mrs. Lester's severe, beautiful profile, clear-cut against the surrounding gloom, and the smooth dark head of Mademoiselle downbent over the cards. From time to time little chirps of wonder or triumph broke from her, or Mrs. Lester would let fall a murmured word. Then silence again, while a flood of almost unbearable restlessness and revolt gathered in Rose's heart. How could they, she wondered, sit there night after night, content to play an idiotic game of cards? Content with this silence, this stagnation, this illimitable, crushing boredom of existence, while somewhere outside, the life that was pulsating in her own young blood was surely to be met with response—was surely satisfied and used? She saw long, dreary years stretching out into the future—years like this past year, in which she frenziedly beat her wings in vain against the bars of a hateful existence, with nothing to do, nothing to hope for, no one to speak to. Till she also accepted her fate, benumbed, apathetic, drained of vitality.

Suddenly a panic seized her, and, without waiting to say good-night she slipped unobserved from her corner of the sofa and ran upstairs to her bedroom. She knelt long at the window, striving to beat down the rising hysteria which frightened her. She wanted to scream, to send out wild shrieks into the dark, sweet-scented night. She felt they would have been screams for help—for help either to fulfil, or to be saved from, the passion that was sapping her life. From a girl intellectually restless indeed, but practically untroubled by sex, Rose had passed rapidly into an acute stage of the malady, and, unknown to herself, was in grave peril of that mental disorder threatening girls with insufficient interests and occupations, aggravated by imperfect comprehension of what is the force against which they either struggle or in propitious circumstances, yield.

"What is the matter with me? What do I want? I don't know, but I *must* find out. I must have it!" Vaguely, incoherently, questions and exclamations started up for a moment in her mind, which all the while was busy weaving a romance in which some one met her and loved her, and told her that to him she was beautiful. Even while she spun this fairy-tale she was conscious of its futility, its ludicrous remoteness from her life.

"Because I'm *myself*, and not beautiful! I'm ugly, in spite of what Mademoiselle says about dress and all that!"

All at once she sprang up, lighted all the candles in her room, and began to tear off the high-necked gown she was wearing. Mademoiselle had made her one that was cut a little low, and she snatched it from the peg in her wardrobe and with hands that trembled with eagerness, put it on, leaving the top hooks undone that she might push it down lower over her shoulders. Lucie had sent her for her birthday a hair ornament of cut steel in the shape of a star, and this she fastened into her hair, so recently put up that it was still unmanageable and inclined to escape from the hairpins and tumble untidily about her neck. Holding a candle in each hand above her head, she stood before the long glass in her wardrobe and surveyed herself with breathless anxiety, scarcely knowing whether to be pleased or despairing at the reflection the glass returned to her.

Certainly she looked very different from her normal self, the self over which she habitually despaired. The dress, of a soft yet vivid red, suited her, and her neck, though thin, rose startlingly white from the crimson sheath of the gown. But her face was white, too, almost as white as her throat, and remembering the clear, vivid pink in Lucie's cheeks, Rose could have cried in bitterness of spirit. Still, her eyes looked big and starry in the whiteness, and the sparkling ornament in her hair was becoming to its soft dark masses, even though it neither curled nor waved, but was merely silky and limp and very thick.

For a while she stared at herself irresolutely, then with another breath-taking impulse she unfastened not only the dress, but all her other clothes, throwing these hastily from her on to the bed. In a moment she stood, a slim, white figure, erect in the midst of the crimson circle made by the dress which had fallen round her feet. Then, indeed, she was beautiful, and she knew it. Her body, at least, was beautiful—even in its immaturity; straight and slender as a tall lily, and almost as white and fine in texture. She smiled triumphantly. If some one could see her now! Some one who had perhaps thought her plain. Surely then she might be loved. Lovers, she supposed, must see

the women they loved—like this? Of course! There
was Swinburne's poetry, and——

The door creaked, and though she had locked it,
Rose started in a guilty panic of shame and rushed to
the chair on which her nightgown lay folded. Slipping it on in frantic haste, she threw herself on her bed
and buried her hot face in the pillow. It was awful, it
was wicked and horrible to feel like this! She was sure
she must be different from all other girls. *They*, all
had pure minds, they never had evil thoughts, they
knew nothing of this terrible gnawing restlessness
which tormented her, because they were good and
modest and innocent. She thought with envy of
Ethel and Maisie Totfield, with their placid faces,
which in her arrogance she had often compared to
fair sheep. She wished now that she had a face and a
mind like theirs. (They were so much alike that she
could only think of them as possessing one face and one
mind between them.) She recalled some of her
schoolfellows—cheerful, jolly girls of whom it was
impossible to suspect such evil as lurked in her own
mind. There was Millie Cripps certainly—but she
was different, disgusting,—like a pig! In spite of her
self-abasement Rose refused to link herself morally
with Millie Cripps. She thought of Helen, whose very
name conjured up all there was of refinement and
delicacy. Helen, with her face clear-cut as a cameo,
her graceful movements, her whole fastidious personality! And yet in some perverse fashion it was
Helen who seemed nearer to her in her shame and self-
abhorrence than any of the simple, innocent girls of
whom she had previously been thinking. It was
Helen who had sent her the *Poems and Ballads*. It
was Helen who had admired the Greek statues of

youths to which she had compared the figure of that young man—what was his name?—who had spoken about the dockers' strike.

Yes, but if Helen cared at all for "those hings" she cared more for art and books and learning—for intellectual pursuits, in short. And she, Rose, had lost all interest in them. It was awful, but she could read nothing now but poetry and "horrid" novels; she could not study; she could not write. Everything was flat, stale, and unprofitable, and there was no escape, nothing to be done. Life would drag on so, for ever and ever, till her hair turned grey, and always there would be this sickening, gnawing restlessness, this unbearable, unsatisfied longing—for what? For something wonderful, something transcending human experience, both of body and soul. Even while she beat frantically against the present conditions of her life, she knew intuitively that were circumstances ever so favourable, she would never attain it, never enter into that country of heart's desire, the faint vision of which mocked and eluded her—would for ever mock and elude her.

Meanwhile actual present life was an insupportable, hopeless misery. Filled with impotent rage against it, against all her circumstances, against herself, Rose bit and shook her pillow like some fierce animal, trapped and ready to tear to pieces its prison. Then, exhausted and realizing with shame her childishness, she broke into a passion of crying which still further drained her strength. Creeping out of bed presently, weak and unsteady, she put out the candles, and as soon as her head again touched the pillow, fell mercifully asleep.

XX

WITH THE GOD OF STARS AND FLOWERS

FROM a dangerous state of mind and body Rose was saved for the time by a shock which first shattered, then roused her.

"Mrs. Winter has come home," Mrs. Lester said one morning at breakfast-time a few days later. She looked up gravely from the letter she was reading and glanced across at Rose, whose face was alight with interest and pleasure. "She wants to see you," she added. "You'd better drive over this afternoon."

"Oh, how *splendid!*" Rose exclaimed with a ring of her old childish excitement in her voice. "Does she write herself? Is she going to stay at home now?"

"Her husband writes. Yes, she's come back to stay. Geoffrey is there, too. I'm afraid she's very ill."

Rose scarcely noticed the last words.

"Why, I haven't seen Mrs. Winter since I first went to school!" she exclaimed. "Nor Geoffrey. I wonder what they will be like? I wonder if they'll know me. What time shall I go?"

"If you get there about five it will do. You won't stay long, so you'd better keep the carriage. Mrs. Winter is an invalid, remember."

Rose pictured a graceful figure lying on a sofa. As a child she remembered her lying very often on a couch in a pretty, loose gown, and it was so she thought of her now. All day her mind was joyfully full of her childhood's friend, and the heavy cloud of depression lifted. Now that Mrs. Winter was at home everything would be different. There would be some one to talk to, some one to understand, and in fancy she saw herself almost every day at Brook Hall, for now that she was grown up, her grandmother could scarcely put obstacles in the way of her visits as in earlier years had been the case.

All the morning Rose wandered about the garden thinking of the old days and the old joys. There was Geoffrey, too! It would be amusing to see him again, though she thought only casually of Geoffrey and still more casually of Mr. Winter. It was Geoffrey's mother she was going to see, and she found her heart beating delightfully with excitement. Quite early in the afternoon she went upstairs to dress and took nearly an hour in the process. She wanted so much to look nice. She hoped against hope that Mrs. Winter wouldn't think her frightfully plain, and in her anxiety, she put on and took off again every dress in her not too well stocked wardrobe. Finally, she decided on a simple white frock made by Mademoiselle, and therefore well cut, and the least ordinary of her country-made hats. The hat troubled her a good deal. It was not "chic," and she agreed with Mademoiselle that she ought always to wear Paris hats. Still, when she had tucked a bunch of roses into her waist-belt, she surveyed her reflection in the glass without too much displeasure, and resigned herself to wait impatiently for the coming of the carriage.

On the drive, when she neared Brook Hall, her excitement grew at the sight of familiar landmarks, and when the carriage turned in at the gates, she looked

eagerly towards the porch, half expecting to see Mrs.
Winter waving from the top step.

It was, however, Geoffrey who opened the hall door—
or rather a big, broad-shouldered young man so like
yet so different from the freckle-faced boy she remembered, that she laughed as she sprang from the
low step of the carriage and rather shyly put out her
hand.

Geoffrey took it, and gave her a quick glance which
travelled from her head to her feet, but he did not
smile, and Rose suddenly caught her breath at the
sight of his grave face. Geoffrey looked old—quite
old, like a grown-up man, and she incoherently wondered why.

"Come in. She's very ill, but I think she can see
you for a few minutes," he said in a low voice. He
looked at her again. "You've grown, of course, Rose,
but you haven't altered much," he added, in a lighter
tone.

Rose was following him upstairs, and was too bewildered, as he made the remark, to answer him. A moment later he was knocking softly at the bedroom door.

A nurse in white cap and apron opened it, nodded
without speaking, and stood aside for Rose to enter.
Hesitating, and as though in a dream, she stepped
into the semi-darkness of a room shaded from the
afternoon sun by matting blinds. A faint smell of
drugs pervaded the air, and though she knew it only
by name, Rose thought of chloroform, and while her
eyes wandered to the bed she wondered why Mrs.
Winter used such stuff.

In the bed lay some one she did not know, and with
an uncertain, bewildered movement she was turning to
run away when she saw an attempt at a smile contort

the ghastly face on the pillow. Awful, incredible as it might be, it *was* Mrs. Winter. She even beckoned feebly, and horror-struck and aghast though she was, Rose found her unwilling feet drawing her slowly but inexorably towards the bed.

The sunken eyes gazed into hers, and a thin hand was moved slowly across the sheet towards her. Rose took it, hesitated, and then bent and kissed it, raising herself quickly after her lips had touched the bony knuckles. Not for the whole world could she bring herself to kiss that terrible yellow mask, which she had a grotesque notion must have been put on to hide the real face of Mrs. Winter. She tried to speak, but her tongue clove to the roof of her mouth, and it was the dying woman who spoke.

"Little Rose!" she whispered. "Grown up! But it's the same dear little face. I'm glad. I didn't want it —to change. . . . Don't cry, dear. . . . You didn't know—perhaps—that I—was so ill?" The words came with terrible painful gasps between them, and Rose could only shake her head, while her tears fell thick on the hand she held. "They should—have told you. Dear little Rose!" There was a pause, and then, suddenly, sharply, a stifled cry which made the girl's blood run cold. The nurse came hurrying in, and gently pushed her from the bedside.

"She's going to have an attack. Go now. She won't be able to see you again," she whispered hurriedly, and Rose fled. Outside the open door, in spite of her longing to escape, she paused irresolutely, for a weak whimpering filled the silence, and then low moaning and half-uttered exclamations; disjointed words, of which she caught the incessant cry, "*Oh, God! Oh, God! Take me! Take——*"

Rose covered her ears with both hands and rushed down the thickly carpeted stairs, on which her footsteps made no noise. She was close to Geoffrey who was waiting in the hall, before he saw her, and she put out her hands blindly before her, as though groping for a way of escape.

Geoffrey took them, startled by her terror-stricken face.

"Rose! You didn't know she was so ill? Your grandmother ought to have told you! It has been a shock. Perhaps you oughtn't to have seen her, but she wanted it so much, and she seemed better yesterday——"

Without heeding his hurried words she stumbled across the hall to the open door, still holding his hands, and Geoffrey helped her into the carriage. . . .

At nine o'clock the same evening he walked over to the Manor House to bring the news that all was over. His mother was dead.

Rose was in her bedroom, but her grandmother sent Mademoiselle upstairs with the message, and the girl, who had been pacing up and down the room, dry-eyed and frantic, burst into such tears of relief and thankfulness as she had never known.

Hours later, when the rest of the household was in bed, she sat on the window-seat in her bedroom and felt the soft air fanning her swollen eyelids. Though autumn was approaching, the night was warm, and so still that she could hear the murmur and pulsing of the sea far below on the rocks at the foot of the cliff. That sea, she remembered, had drowned her mother and her father, hurrying them out of life while they were young and keen and eager to live. Everywhere there lurked a terrible, impassive, relentless cruelty.

The fringe of her thought touched this afternoon's experience, and recoiled in horror. She dare not let her mind dwell on it, and in her frenzied seeking for other ideas, there slid into her mind a remembrance of something she had once read—something about all humanity being "under sentence of death." To recall it intensified her horror of life's realities.

She glanced about the room with wide, frightened eyes.

On the bed, just as she had flung them off, lay her hat, the white dress, the bunch of roses which with so much pleasure she had put on to impress—whom? what? That terrible, shrunken, yellow caricature of the gracious woman she once knew. Dying even then. And so horribly—so horribly! And she, Rose, might die like that. In awful pain. In unspeakable terror. It might come at any moment, this blow from a pitiless, unseen enemy. And then the grave and darkness and corruption and unnamed, unthinkable horrors!

A panic familiar to her in her childhood and unknown till this moment since then, swept through her being, and again she felt her forehead damp, her hands and feet icy cold, and her heart thumping in her breast. She covered her mouth with both hands to force back a scream, and scrambling from the window-seat, began to run from side to side of the room like one possessed. She had felt like this, she remembered, one day in the garden at Brook Hall—how many years ago? The garden, with the sunshine on the grass, and the flickering shadows in the little arbour, rose vividly to her mind, and then at the same instant, in fancy she saw Mrs. Winter coming towards her across the grass, a tall, fair, infinitely soothing presence. She sat beside her and took her hands, and just as a child she had been

calmed, so now her morbid, frenzied imagination
ceased to work.   She stopped her insane pacing of the
room, and dropped limply into the corner of the window-seat.   Somehow, in a flash, she had recovered her
friend in her old beautiful likeness, serene, comforting,
and assured.   She could almost hear her voice reading
the "Hymn of St. Francis to the Sun"—

Praised be Thou, O Lord, by our sister the Death of the body.

The words and the voice were mingled with the
murmur and pulsing of the sea, and Rose's eyes filled
with healing, grateful tears.   Oh yes! praise Him for
that merciful death of the body.   All the horror was
over now at least, and she would never, she told herself, think of Mrs. Winter as anything but young and
gracious and lovely!   That was the real woman, and
she must for ever keep her so in remembrance.

With her consoling memories, all the fundamental
sanity of Rose's mind welled up in a tide to wash away
unhealthy thoughts and morbid images.   All was well
with her friend.   If she was sleeping, she slept in peace.
If she woke—and again Rose heard the simple words
she had used to a child—it would be "to live with God,
Who made the sun and the stars and the flowers. . . .
And that would be more beautiful even than to go on
living in this lovely world."   It was that blessed
existence she hoped for her friend.   But at least she
was asleep.   That was comfort enough.

As she sat looking into the darkness of the trees,
Rose was conscious of great physical exhaustion, but
of a clearness of mind such as she had never experienced.
Her brain seemed to work without her volition, and
suddenly, in the midst of the happier thoughts about

her friend, there rose unbidden, in some inexplicable, ready-made fashion, a plan for her own escape from the life she was leading.

She could qualify herself as a teacher in some big school. She could work secretly for all the necessary examinations, and when the time came, if no other way presented itself, she could borrow the money from Helen, and without asking leave, go up to London to pass them. Once qualified, she would find a post, and if she could support herself without her grandmother's help, and if she resolutely refused to return home, her freedom was assured!

Rose started up and clasped her hands in ecstasy as the plan presented itself with sudden, swift clearness and precision. Why, in spite of all her previous desperate reflection, had the idea never occurred to her before? It was strange that it had come just now when she imagined that her brain was so distracted, so far from being occupied by her own concerns. Rose had as yet heard nothing of the subconscious mind and its mysterious workings, and the newly risen plan, in reality the result of long, seemingly useless groping, seemed to her little short of a miracle, which in some obscure way she connected with Mrs. Winter. *She* might have suggested it. One of the many things about which she had meant to consult the delicate but keenly living woman she had pictured, was this very question of escape. It seemed as though her friend had answered it. At any rate, the fancy still further lightened Rose's heart, and for the first time in many weeks she slept all night peacefully as a baby, untroubled by the dreams which lately almost every night had tormented her rest.

CHAPTER XXI

THE WAY OF ESCAPE

M RS. LESTER looked up rather anxiously when Rose came in to breakfast next morning.

She had been startled and alarmed by the girl's appearance when she returned from Brook Hall, and she blamed herself for allowing her to pay the visit without at least telling her that Mrs. Winter was dying. Mrs. Lester had an unconquerable aversion to illness or the talk of it, and she had never even mentioned to Rose the nature of Mrs. Winter's malady. At the first sight of her granddaughter's face she admitted to herself that she had been wrong. The girl had evidently received a shock, and it was her constant dazed repetition of "*If only she would die! If only she would die!*" that caused her to deal gently with her, and to send Mademoiselle hurrying upstairs when Geoffrey came, to announce that her prayer was answered. With relief she noticed that though pale and silent, the girl was calm, and after a few words had passed between them about the plans of father and son, the Winters' bereavement was not again mentioned.

"They are going away for a month or two after the funeral," her grandmother told her. "Very wisely, I think. And then they will return and settle down altogether at the Hall. Geoffrey has been studying farming and land cultivation abroad, at intervals, for the past two years, I understand, and intends to work the estate himself. He's a fine boy. I'm afraid he will feel his poor mother's death acutely. He was a devoted son."

Rose listened in silence. She could not speak to her grandmother of Mrs. Winter, with whom, she felt, Mrs. Lester had never been in sympathy.

In a few days, thanks to Helen's quick response to her letter, she had received all the information she wanted about the Higher Local Examination for Women, as well as the books necessary for study. She began to work, and work was her salvation. With a plan before her, with the sense of striving towards a definite end, hope revived. Absorbed by fresh interests, her mind no longer tortured her, and the terrible restlessness, the morbid obsession which had made existence a burden, gradually passed away. Once more, as at intervals in her schoolgirl days, she was possessed to the exclusion of all other thoughts by the passion for work. Finding that the prescribed course for the examination could be spread over three years, she made up her mind to take it in one, undaunted by the hours of study which such a determination involved. To procure the key which should unlock the gates of her prison-house and lead her out to freedom, was her one desire. Eagerly as she had been looking forward to Lucie's return, it was almost a relief when her grandmother decided to yield to the girl's wish to stay on at Tours till Christmas. Lucie would be a hindrance now, and without her she might count upon three months of that undisturbed quiet which hitherto she had abhorred. The days no longer dragged by, purposeless and maddening in their monotony. Every hour was filled, and it was with difficulty that Mademoiselle could drag her away from her books even for the daily walk.

"But what is it she does now?" she inquired of Mrs. Lester, having failed to gain any satisfactory explanation from Rose herself. And Mrs. Lester merely shrugged her shoulders.

"Another bee in her bonnet," she remarked, leaving Mademoiselle, who did not understand the idiom, more mystified than ever.

About the beginning of November the Winters returned, and Rose, who two months previously, would have welcomed any break in the stagnation of her life, heard the news with something like impatience. Geoffrey, she supposed, would come "bothering," occasionally at least, and she felt she could not suffer the slightest interruption to her work, which, as she had planned it, loomed in gigantic proportions before her.

If only it had been Mrs. Winter who was coming home! The examination then might have taken care of itself, and she would have thought only of the joy of recovering her friend. Rose had gone back to her childhood's memories of Mrs. Winter. The horrible impression of her last sight of her (owing doubtless to the fortunate accident of her death coinciding with the new plan for freedom), was happily almost effaced from her mind. It was the smiling, gracious presence of years ago which now presented itself whenever she recalled her. The mention of Geoffrey's name, however, inevitably reminded her of the surprise she had felt in seeing a man in place of the gawky boy who had stood to her for Geoffrey, and on the day her grandmother announced that she had asked the Winters to lunch, Rose left her writing-table ten minutes earlier to put on a more becoming dress than the morning one she was wearing. The sound of voices in the drawing-room warned her as she crossed the hall that the visitors had arrived, and suddenly shy, it cost her an effort to open the door.

Mrs. Lester sat erect and stately in the high-backed chair she preferred, talking to the two men, who rose as the girl entered. The movement increased her embarrassment. Neither of them would have stirred in the old days, when as a little girl she ran in or out of a room; and the change in their manner, slight circumstance though it was, caused her to realize, with a curious pang of regret for the past, that she was "quite grown up."

She glanced at the elder Mr. Winter as she shook hands, and noticed that his hair was nearly white. He looked almost an old man, she thought, with painful surprise. It was so strange to find that people grew old! Geoffrey came forward, smiling, but a trifle embarrassed also, and again Rose had to readjust her ideas and her memories. At least he had lost the strained, grave look which had so startled her at their last meeting, and it was easier now to recognize in him the old boyish Geoffrey.

"Bless me, how these little girls grow up!" exclaimed his father. "I shouldn't have known her!"

"She's not grown very tall," remarked Mrs. Lester, with that faint undercurrent of disapproval in her voice to which Rose was accustomed. "Lucie is a head taller."

"She's quite tall enough," put in Geoffrey. "And *I* don't think she's altered a bit."

Rose was not over-pleased. She would like to have altered very much. She thought Geoffrey tactless, and the reflection, joined to shyness from which she could not recover, made her very silent during lunch.

Mrs. Lester, with the touch of formality never absent from her manner, kept the conversation going; and whenever she could put in a word, Mademoiselle chattered to Geoffrey, who listened politely, offered a remark or two at intervals, and constantly glanced across the table at Rose's down-bent head. Once when she raised it, he suddenly smiled at her, and his smile was so like his mother's that her eyes filled with tears. She wished the Winters hadn't come. Geoffrey's presence recalled the terrible experience she hoped to have forgotten.

"Come into the garden," he said to her, under cover of the general move after the meal. "Rose is going to take me round the garden, if you don't mind, Mrs. Lester," he said, turning to her.

"By all means," she returned graciously. "It's a little too chilly for me. You and I will go to the drawing-room, Mr. Winter." She led the way, and Geoffrey and Rose meanwhile escaped by one of the long windows in the dining-room.

For a moment they walked across the grass in silence. It was a fair autumn day, with a sky of pale blue and a mild sun bringing out the gold in the tree-tops not yet stripped of leaves. At the end of the avenue in front of them, stretched the sea, calm and milky blue, a reflection of the sky.

"It's nice to be back here," said Geoffrey at last, looking about him. "Do you remember old Ginger-cat, Rose? She had a poor time chasing us about, didn't she? But you and I managed to enjoy ourselves!" He grinned broadly, as in old days.

"It was nicer at your place," returned Rose. "I used to love going to Brook Hall and being with——" She paused.

"Mother was so fond of you!" said Geoffrey after a moment, and Rose's heart leaped in gratitude that he should speak of her. Though she had dreaded the mention of her name at lunch-time, she had felt resentful that it was not spoken. It seemed as though the dead woman were neglected, forgotten.

He paused after the words, and presently in a lower, hurried voice went on: "I wish you hadn't seen her, Rose. That day, you know. It was a mistake. But poor darling, she didn't know how she had altered, and when she came home her first thought was for you, so we didn't like——"

Rose put out her hand swiftly, as if to ward off further words.

"Don't!" she exclaimed incoherently. "If she wanted to see me I'm glad I went. But I never think of her—so. I *won't* think of her like that!" she added defiantly.

"No—don't," assented Geoffrey, still softly. He drew a long breath. "If only you knew how thankful I am she's gone! I mean——"

"I know what you mean," interrupted Rose quickly. "Don't say it."

She spoke in the old peremptory, childish way, and Geoffrey smiled.

"*You haven't* altered a bit!" he declared again.

She frowned. "I wish you wouldn't keep on saying that," she exclaimed crossly. "It isn't good news. I was a hideous little girl."

"Hideous? No! I remember I thought you very ugly, but——"

"Then it's awfully rude of you to keep on about it now!" she interrupted, flushing, the tears in her eyes.

With the slow movement Rose remembered as

characteristic of him as a boy, he turned his head and looked at her in surprise. "I was thinking what a young fool I was," he said simply.

Rose gave him a swift questioning glance. She longed for him to say more, but he kept silence, and she was forced to be content with the oblique flattery implied in the remark. They had reached the gate opening upon the downward path to the sea, and Geoffrey leaned his arms upon the topmost rail and gazed straight ahead.

"What are you going to do?" asked Rose abruptly. Her transitory shyness had passed away, and Geoffrey was to her once more the old Geoffrey of easy, rather indifferent comradeship.

"Do?" He turned slowly, put his back against the gate, and looked at her.

"Yes. I mean, are you going to stay in this dull hole for ever?"

"Why yes, of course. I've come home on purpose to work the place. I've been studying land culture and all that sort of thing, you know."

"And you'll like it?" asked Rose jerkily, after a pause.

"Yes. Why not? I hate being away. Don't *you* like it here?"

"*Like* it?" She gave a little laugh and was silent. Geoffrey was exasperating in his bland lack of comprehension.

"You don't?"

"I hate and loathe it!" she returned, in an odd, choked voice. "I'm working every minute to get away. I ought to be working now."

"But why?" demanded Geoffrey, in a genuinely puzzled voice.

Rose stamped her foot. "You haven't any imagination, have you? It's all very well for you to be happy here. Brook Hall is *yours*. You can do what you please. You're a man. That's the whole difference."

Geoffrey smiled slowly. "You used to say something like that when you were a little kid—'You're a boy, it's all very fine for you.'"

"Well, things haven't altered," said Rose acrimoniously. "I'm still a girl, worse luck! *You* used to say," she went on in a gentler voice—"after I'd explained it to you a great deal—that it must be pretty horrid to be a girl. It's still pretty horrid. No, that's silly. It's—it's *damnable!*"

She spoke so vehemently that her face went a shade whiter, and Geoffrey's puzzled look changed to one of pity.

"I suppose you *do* have a rotten time," he conceded. "Why doesn't Grandma let you go up to town for a week or two and get some fun? It's a shame!"

"You don't understand!" Rose returned impatiently. "What's the good of going up to London for a fortnight and then coming back to *this* again? It's a different *life* I want. A whole life—not a little holiday to keep me quiet. You're going to have a life—a career. Something to do all the rest of your days. It isn't what *I* should choose; but you've chosen it, so it's all right. But I have nothing of that sort to look forward to. No career. No life. No money. I'm a prisoner in Grandmamma's house. Just that and nothing else. And there's no one to speak to in my prison. No one. Not a soul. Oh, it's been too awful for words! But of course I can't expect you to understand. You're not a girl."

She put her hand on the gate to steady its trembling, and Geoffrey's hand involuntarily crept towards it. He withdrew it shyly, however, before she noticed the movement, and for a moment neither of them spoke.

"But you said something about working," began Geoffrey at last. "What for? What did you mean?"

"You'll swear not to tell any one if I tell you?" asked Rose doubtfully.

"Of course not."

She unfolded her plan, and the young man whistled softly.

"Grandma will be furious. And you'll hate teaching, Rose."

"It will be better than this, anyhow."

"When does the blessed exam. come off?"

"Oh, not for nearly a year, and *then*, I expect I shall fail!" she replied despondently. "I can't do Arithmetic, you know. I'm a perfect fool at it, and if you fail in that, you don't get your certificate."

"Look here, I'm pretty good at figures," said Geoffrey, brightening. "I'll help you if you like. I mean—would you let me?" he added diffidently.

"Oh, Geoff! Would you? How splendid! Only I should be ashamed for you to know what a duffer I am. And besides, you'll be busy."

"I could come over every day for an hour, easily," he assured her. "Only what about Grandma? Won't the old lady guess there's something up when she sees us both swotting?"

"No. I'll tell her you're teaching me something, and she'll think it's Latin or Greek. She's put me down in her own mind once for all as a blue-stocking, so she'll just shrug her shoulders and think no more

20

about it. She despises me, of course, but, thank goodness, she lets me alone."

The last words were bitter, and, glancing at the girl's face again, Geoffrey faintly realized that to live at the Manor House in the atmosphere which surrounded Rose, might possibly be "too awful for words."

"To-morrow at eleven? Will that do?" he asked. "I'll ride over."

"Beautifully, and I'll try to get my multiplication table quite perfect by then!" She laughed for the first time, as she had laughed as a child. "There's Mr. Winter! He's looking for you. We shall have to go in. It *is* good of you, Geoff!"

CHAPTER XXII

CUPID AND THE LESSON BOOK

AT eleven o'clock next morning Geoffrey encountered Mrs. Lester as he passed through the hall on his way to the old schoolroom.

"Rose told you I was coming?" he asked, blushing furiously, to his own great annoyance.

"Oh yes. You're going to act the pedagogue, I understand," returned the old lady, tempering the note of sarcasm in her voice by a smile which she reserved exclusively for the superior sex. "I hope you'll find Rose a tractable pupil. She's in the schoolroom, I believe." She passed on and upstairs, holding her full skirts in both hands, and as she went, cast an admiring glance at the back and shoulders of the finely built young man. He looked well in riding-breeches, she thought, and she smiled again complacently as she watched him turn the handle of the schoolroom door.

If what since yesterday she had hoped came about, it would be almost too good to be true! That Rose, the difficult Rose of whom she despaired, should be as easily disposed of seemed a stroke of luck which was almost providential. Yet, if her shrewd old eyes had not deceived her, there was no mistaking the import of those glances which yesterday the boy had cast in Rose's direction, and she recalled with satisfaction, if with the same wonder as of old, that Geoffrey had always been fond of the child. Evidently he was one of the faithful sort! It was clever of him to have found so readily an excuse for meeting the girl every day. In her granddaughter's interests she was content to waive the claims of strict propriety, for the breach of which, indeed, Rose's childish intimacy with the boy gave some sanction, and she breathed a fervent prayer that he would bring his courting to a satisfactory conclusion before the return of Lucie, whose superior attractions might wreck the whole scheme now so neatly developing.

Meanwhile, all unconscious of projects for her future, Rose was thoroughly enjoying her first lesson in Arithmetic, and as frequent bursts of laughter from the schoolroom indicated, she was not taking it too seriously. Nevertheless, as the girl soon discovered, Geoffrey was a good teacher—patient, clear, and comically anxious to betray no surprise at his pupil's phenomenal stupidity with regard to figures.

Secretly he rejoiced at the circumstance. Rumours of Rose's "cleverness" had reached him, and he had been afraid of discovering in her a learned and superior young woman. It was an immense relief to find that the simplest arithmetical problems floored her completely, and her constant laughing appeals for help, considerably flattered his vanity.

"There now, I'm sure you've done enough for to-day," he urged at the end of an hour. "Let's go into the garden for a bit."

"Good gracious, no," returned Rose with decision. "I'm going to read French history now for ages, and then German till lunch-time. Thanks awfully, Geoffrey, but please go!"

The boy looked disconcerted. "Oh, I say, you needn't swot like that, you know. Come out and look at Bob a minute. He's my new hunter. Really stunning! I say, Rose, wouldn't you like to learn to ride?" he went on, fired with a brilliant idea. "There's the mare. She's as gentle as a lamb, and I could bring her over——"

Rose had clasped her hands in ecstasy, with a gesture so familiar to him that he almost expected to see her long dress shrink into a pinafore and her hair come tumbling about her shoulders. It had been one of the dreams of her life to ride!

"Oh, Geoff!" she exclaimed under her breath. "Would you *really?*" Delight had brought the colour to her cheeks, but with one of her incredibly swift changes of expression she shook her head. "I mustn't. I can't spare the time. I must work."

"But you can't work all day," urged Geoffrey. "Look here. Only for an hour every morning! You could take it instead of going out for a walk. It's much better exercise. Oh do, Rose! It will be such sport."

"Yes, I might do it that way," she conceded, her face brilliant again. "But remember, *only* an hour. I daren't take longer. If I fail in this exam., I shall go mad!"

"You won't fail," declared Geoffrey, with an assurance he was far from feeling, "and I'll bring the mare round to-morrow."

"Yes; but now you must go," she commanded.

The riding lessons began, Mademoiselle, and even Mrs. Lester, evincing considerable alacrity in arranging a suitable skirt and jacket for the purpose. A few days later Mrs. Lester disinterred an old riding-habit of her own which she had worn as a girl, and under Mademoiselle's skilful manipulations it was made

to fit quite creditably. Once more, and to an even
greater extent, Geoffrey experienced the joy of a
teacher and the flattery of feminine dependence, for
Rose was physically timid, and it was weeks before
the riding lessons so eagerly desired, became anything
but a terror to her. Only pride and Geoffrey's encouragement and patience made her persevere in
what even when she had mastered the first difficulties,
remained always for her a somewhat fearful joy.
Time passed, and Mrs. Lester grew impatient. Lucie
would be home in a fortnight, and she saw no change
in Rose's demeanour, though to Mademoiselle's voluble comments on the girl's improved appearance she
yielded a grudging assent.

Exercise, companionship, work, and hope for the
future had done wonders for Rose. Her always
colourless skin was clear and healthy, her eyes now
were often bright with laughter, and she carried her
slight, very graceful little body well enough to win
the approbation of her grandmother, who was usually
scathing in her denunciation of "this age of slouch."

Geoffrey nevertheless evidently had not spoken,
and Mademoiselle, to whom the atmosphere of an
impending declaration was deliriously exciting, lived
between the hope and fear which to some extent she
was permitted to share with her employer.

"It is that Rose gives him no encouragement," she
wailed. "She is to him as a sister. *Mon Dieu!*
How can a young girl be so little *coquette?*"

"English girls, I'm thankful to say, are too pure-
minded to be forward," returned Mrs. Lester, drawing herself up. "It is for the man to make the
advances."

Mademoiselle swallowed the snub as best she might,

and Mrs. Lester rather disingenuously reflected that there were "ways of managing these things" not incompatible with virgin modesty, as Rose, in spite of her youth, might have discovered. Meanwhile it was tiresome of Geoffrey not to come to her assistance.

Geoffrey, if she had known it, was only too ready to put an end to his own as well as to Mrs. Lester's suspense; but as Mademoiselle suggested, he was waiting, and waiting in vain for some sign from Rose to give him courage. He feared desperately to risk the loss of his daily companionship with the girl. As it was, this was never extended beyond the two hours to which she had agreed, and any attempt on his part to lure her into the garden or to prolong the morning's ride was met with instant opposition. Nothing would induce Rose to curtail her hours of study, and he could not fail to recognize that in her eyes the Higher Local Examination was of infinitely more importance than the society of Geoffrey Winter. She was gay, friendly, on perfectly easy and nonchalant terms with him, treating him, in fact, very much as she had done as a child, except that as he never teased her now, she did not quarrel with him. All the signs were discouraging for a lover, and Geoffrey grew daily more restless and unhappy as it daily became more difficult to preserve the rôle of simple friendship.

He brooded incessantly upon the situation and rehearsed innumerable speeches which should lead conversation gently into the channel he desired. But face to face with Rose, her unconsciousness daunted him, and he always took refuge in the brother-like desultory remarks she expected.

It seemed to Geoffrey as he lay in bed and thought of her that he had always loved Rose, even though he

had practically forgotten her during his school and
college days. From the moment he caught sight of
her standing up in the carriage on the day of his
mother's death, he realized that it had always been
Rose, and he recalled with a shock of amazed comprehension his emotion, when as an awkward schoolboy
he wanted to kiss the "ugly little kid" who had been
sent to bed on her birthday.

It was the same little face he remembered, very
subtly changed perhaps, but now he did not think it
ugly. It gave him the queer notion that some little
woodland creature had been transformed by enchant-
ment to a humanity which in the soft, blunt features,
the soft, white skin, and the soft, velvety eyes, changing
so often, but at first sight shy, unmistakably suggested
forest origin. He did not definitely put this fancy into
words—Geoffrey was not overwhelmingly imaginative
—but obscurely it was there, and the girl's pliant
figure and her quick, darting movements, increased his
vague sense of her likeness to "some jolly little beast."
It pleased him to remember how fond his mother had
been of Rose, and how the child had loved her. Perhaps that would help him if ever he could find courage
to ask her to marry him? He wished he were more
worthy of her! One or two episodes in his comparatively blameless career troubled him greatly as he
lay awake for a not inconsiderable time each night.
There was a certain red-haired girl at Oxford;—and
another, a flaxen-haired lady, with whom he had
once spent an embarrassing week-end on the river.
. . . He regretted these deviations from the path
of virtue. Their memory was hateful to him now
that he was experiencing for the first time an emotion
which made him shy and humble and at the same time

filled him with exaltation—"the sort of feeling some
chaps get when they go to church, I suppose!" he
reflected before banging his pillow into a shape con-
ducive to slumber, long delayed.

Rose meanwhile slept peacefully. She never
thought of Geoffrey unless he happened to be there.
Certainly she was very glad he had come home. He
was really of great help with the Arithmetic, she had
begun to enjoy her rides, and it was rather nice to
have some one at hand who always noticed a new
frock, or even a new ribbon, and said it was "jolly"
or "looked stunning." She liked Geoffrey. She
had always liked him, but she found him, as she had
always found him, as limited as his vocabulary.
He could not talk, even about himself, and despite
her utmost endeavour to gain some idea of his life at
college or the year he had spent abroad, she was
enlightened only to the extent conveyed by phrases
such as: "Oh, Oxford was first-rate," or "All those
places abroad are pretty deadly, you know."

She liked him best when he spoke of his mother, for
then his inarticulateness seemed pathetic, and his face
told her all that the halting words failed to express.

On the other hand, he apparently loved to hear *her*
talk, and it was immensely gratifying to have an
interested and respectful listener. He had grown
very polite, she thought, very fearful of offending,
and she often laughed to think of the teasing schoolboy from whom this punctilious young gentleman was
descended.

A week before Christmas, Lucie arrived, so altered,
so "grown up" that Rose was lost in astonishment.
She was prettier than ever now, and with her hair

done fashionably on the top of her head, with her French dresses, and her general air of elegance, she looked considerably older and more developed than her elder sister.

Mrs. Lester was secretly divided between gratification and fear. Lucie was going to be a beauty. But Rose's future was still unsettled, and she now trembled for it and watched with anxiety Geoffrey's first meeting with the girl. He came in, as usual, the morning after her arrival, shook hands as with a maiden aunt of advanced years, and turned immediately to Rose.

"Let's have the ride first and the lesson afterwards, shall we?" he suggested. "It's going to rain presently."

Rose ran upstairs to put on her habit, and when Lucie had watched the couple canter away together, she turned to her grandmother in surprise.

"How awfully good-looking Geoffrey has grown!" she exclaimed. "And he used to be such an ugly boy. You were quite right about him, Grandmamma. Does he take Rose out every day?"

"Yes, and I'm very glad he should. Rose sits over her books as much as ever, and before Geoffrey came home she was looking quite frightful. No complexion. Always dull and moping. It was quite unpleasant to see her about."

"Well, she looks very nice now," Lucie said. "Her dresses suit her. Mademoiselle makes them, she says. I wonder if Geoffrey likes them?"

Mrs. Lester did not reply. A possible and unforeseen danger loomed suddenly on the horizon, and before a week had passed, it took definite form.

In Lucie, Mademoiselle had no need to deplore a

lack of coquetry.   It was now the imperviousness of
young Englishmen which moved her to wonder and
contempt, and she privately enjoyed Mrs. Lester's
discomfiture in the face of her younger granddaughter's
efforts to attract the notice of her sister's swain.
That these were incessant and flagrant, she had better
opportunities of observing than those afforded to Mrs.
Lester, for Lucie was not destitute of a prudent dis-
cretion when her grandmother was anywhere in the
vicinity of her manœuvres.   Under the very eyes of
Rose they could be effected with impunity.   Rose,
unseeing, indifferent if she *had* seen, more than ever
absorbed in her self-imposed task.

The inevitable hour arrived, however, when Mademoiselle shared with Mrs. Lester her knowledge of
Lucie's reprehensible forwardness.

The Winters and Major Hawley were the guests
invited for Christmas Day, and Lucie having insisted
upon decorating the house with evergreens, Geoffrey
was pressed into the service.

"You *must* stay.   Oh, Geoffrey, *please* stay!" she
begged on the morning of Christmas Eve, coming into
the schoolroom when after the Arithmetic lesson, Rose
was preparing to work.   "I've got all this ivy to put
up in the hall, and I can't reach.   You might stay
and help me, Geoff!"

"All right," returned Geoffrey carelessly.   "Won't
you come too, Rose?"   He lingered wistfully at the
schoolroom door, and Lucie answered for her sister.

"Oh, you won't get Rose to move!" she cried gaily.
"She'll be sitting over these old books all the rest
of the morning.   Come along, Geoff!"   She playfully
seized his arm and dragged him into the hall, where a
heap of ivy, holly, and mistletoe had been piled, leaving

Rose to wonder why Lucie troubled to make such a fuss about Geoff, with whom she had never got on particularly well.

Only that morning during their ride she had taxed him with not being "nice" to Lucie. "She's grown up now, so you oughtn't to treat her as you did when she was a little girl and you wanted her out of the way," she said.

"Awfully sorry," answered Geoffrey; "but I'm afraid I do."

"Why? It's silly of you!" was Rose's impatient reply, and Geoffrey grasped at but missed his opportunity in a sudden maddening gust of shyness.

"Oh, I don't know," he stammered evasively. "You know I never cared much for her even when she was a kid. And now she's got affected and Frenchified I can't stand her at any price."

"Well, she's awfully pretty," declared Rose, "and I think it's horrid of you. I've scarcely seen anything of her since she came home," she went on meditatively. "She and Mademoiselle fell into one another's arms the moment she arrived, and they've been talking together in Lucie's room ever since. I can't think what they find to say. Anyhow, I'm thankful, for I'm left in peace. . . . Oh, Geoff! *do* say you think I'll pass? I can't stand any more of this. I really can't. I *must* get away!" And for the twentieth time with a heavy heart the undeclared lover gave her the assurance she coveted.

Rose heard with impatience Lucie's constant laugh and chatter in the hall outside, mingled with Geoffrey's monosyllabic replies. She wished they would go away. They disturbed her study of the irregular German verbs, and it was a relief when the sound of their voices presently grew fainter. She supposed they were now decorating the dining-room.

Geoffrey, as a matter of fact, was doing all the work of hanging the chandelier with trails of ivy, while Lucie, leaning against the table, watched him with eyes that were undecided and troubled. Suddenly she picked up a branch of mistletoe lying at her feet, and, breaking off two pearled twigs, stuck them on either side of the velvet band which parted her blond curls. She gazed at herself in an opposite glass, then at Geoffrey with a provocative little smile.

"That's rather nice, I think, don't you?"

"Yes," said Geoffrey readily. He was looking at her attentively now. Rose had said she was pretty, and for that reason he considered her for the first time without reference to the rather insipid child he remembered. Yes. Certainly she was pretty, he allowed, though "not his style."

Lucie was quick to notice his fixed regard, and she smiled with bewitching tremulousness.

"Geoff, how silly you are! I'm *under* the mistletoe, don't you see? Why don't you come and kiss me?"

Her voice held all the seduction with which a woman twice her years might have charged its meaning, but Geoffrey's furious blush was occasioned rather by the sight of Mrs. Lester in the doorway than by its appeal to his senses. He addressed the elder lady hurriedly. "We've finished this now, Mrs. Lester. You'll want me out of the way. I'll be off."

He shook hands with her, and waving to Lucie, beat a hasty retreat.

Mrs. Lester waited till she heard the hall door bang before turning to her crimson granddaughter.

"I'm ashamed of you," she said icily. "Apart

from the immodesty of your behaviour, I am surprised at your lack of pride in making advances to a young man who so obviously ignores you."

To her consternation, Lucie broke suddenly into stormy tears.

"He wouldn't if it were not for Rose!" she sobbed. "And Rose doesn't care a bit. Not a bit! She's like a great baby. And you've let him come here every day and fall in love with her before I came home. It isn't fair! It's a shame!" She had dashed upstairs before her grandmother could recover from the shock of words and demeanour so staggering in their audacity that she almost dropped the tray of glasses she was carrying. Mrs. Lester sat down to think. Life with two young women on the premises, was growing more complicated than she desired, and it seemed as though the docile Lucie might be as troublesome in her own way as in another fashion Rose had proved. She decided for the moment to ignore the incident, and at lunch-time was relieved to find Lucie apparently normal, and Rose as unconscious as ever.

Christmas Day in its earlier stages passed quietly. The Winters and the Major arrived just before the seven o'clock dinner, and any awkwardness in the meeting of Lucie and young Winter was avoided by the little excitement attendant on the exchange of presents. Geoffrey had brought gifts for every one, but in meeting Rose a moment before dinner in the hall, he had slipped into her hand an extra little packet.

"Don't open it now!" he whispered.

Rose nodded, smiled, and ran to leave it on the schoolroom table. The fact that he should have brought her an extra present was not surprising. She had always been his chief friend. But it was nice of him, she thought, not to give it to her in Lucie's presence.

She was wearing the crimson frock, in colour like a damask rose, made for her by Mademoiselle, and in putting it on that evening no memory recurred to her of another occasion when it had been hastily discarded. That phase of terrible unrest and suffering being over, was for the time completely wiped out of her consciousness, and with her mind full of the French history she had just been reading, she dressed as unconcernedly as a child.

During dinner she developed one of her occasional fits of witty gaiety, which never failed to surprise and, to some extent, gratify her grandmother. Major Hawley, as usual, was chiefly responsible for her vivacity, but Mrs. Lester, a gracious hostess when she pleased, and specially anxious to-day that Rose should appear to advantage, seconded his efforts and played up to the girl in a manner which excited and exhilarated her. Laughter rang, and in the midst of her enjoyment of her own success Rose was glad because she did not want the Winters to have "a miserable evening." Mrs. Winter would have been glad that they laughed; glad that she, Rose, could amuse them. Her eyes dancing, her changeful face alight with mirth, Rose looked that evening more attractive than Lucie, whose glance travelled often from her sister to Geoffrey. His absorption in the sight of Rose was evident to every one at the table except the girl herself. Unsuspecting, radiant, and excited, she was thinking no more of Geoffrey than of his father, or the old Major. It was the company generally she was intent on amusing, herself deriving infinite pleasure in the process.

Later on, when the young people with Mademoiselle had gone to the drawing-room, Mr. Winter looked across at his hostess and smiled. Without speaking, he raised his glass of champagne, and with answering smiles Mrs. Lester and Major Hawley followed his example.

The rest of the evening passed gaily, though Lucie slipped away unnoticed before the Winter's carriage was announced, and it was Rose who, when farewells were being exchanged, ran out to look for her.

Geoffrey followed her into the hall.

"Never mind Lucie. Come and look at your other present," he said, pushing open the door of the school-room, in which a lamp was burning faintly on a side table.

Rose began to unwrap her parcel, while he stood watching her, waiting for the look he expected when she should open the little box it contained.

"Oh, Geoffrey!" The words were whispered gently in surprised delight. She held in her hand a well-known locket, and saw that it contained a miniature of Mrs. Winter—the adored Mrs. Winter of early memories.

"Oh, Geoffrey!" she exclaimed again. "She used to wear this always. Only it had a picture of *you* in it then. Oh! I'd rather have it than anything in the world."

She raised her eager face and regarded him grate-fully. In a second Geoffrey's arms were round her. He held her so close that she could not move, and bending over her, kissed her hair, her eyes, and finally almost with violence pressed his lips against hers.

Rose struggled furiously. He loosed his arms and they stood facing one another, both breathing quickly,

Rose with anger, Geoffrey with mingled passion and fear for the consequences of his mad impulse.

"What on earth are you doing?" asked Rose at last incoherently. "You must have gone mad!"

"I have," whispered the boy. "Oh, Rose, I'm so sorry! I didn't mean to offend you. . . . But suddenly I couldn't help it. I love you so much . . . and I've waited such a long time!"

Rose gazed at him blankly. His face was working and his lips trembled. She almost thought he was going to cry, and an incoherent, uncomprehending pity began to stir beneath her resentment.

"But what do you mean?" she stammered. "*Love* me? Why, I've known you all my life! You can't want—" she paused, speechless.

"I want you to marry me," pleaded the boy, snatching at the hands which, quick as thought, she hid behind her back.

The drawing-room door opened, and as the hum of voices became audible, Rose darted away from him into the hall, where she began to talk volubly to Major Hawley, who was putting on his overcoat. Her voice, joined to the bird-like chatter of Mademoiselle, covered Geoffrey's silence, and directly she heard the roll of wheels on the drive and a hasty good-night to her grandmother had been uttered, she was free to rush upstairs.

The window-blinds had not been drawn, and her bedroom was full of soft, greenish light from an almost full moon.

Rose hastened to close the door, and leaning against it, she stood for some minutes motionless, trying to recover from her overwhelming surprise and bewilderment.

Geoffrey! It was too absurd. It was even—rather
horrid. He was a sort of brother. Not really, of
course. Still, he had always seemed like a brother.
And he had kissed her! She drew the back of her
hand hastily across her lips with a movement that
was almost disgust, and then suddenly remembered
how she had longed to be kissed by a man. Well,
Geoffrey was a man, she supposed. He was twenty-
two, at any rate. But then he was just—Geoffrey!

She began to undress in the semi-darkness, so perturbed and absent-minded that she forgot to light the
candles till she wanted to brush and plait her hair.
Then, for the first time, she saw herself in the glass,
and smiled contentedly to find she looked really rather
pretty. Geoffrey must have thought so too, and that
was gratifying, even though the annoying, disappointing fact remained that it was "only Geoffrey."

Much later, when she had been in bed some time,
she recalled his face, his trembling lips, and with a
curious shock at the possibility, wondered whether he
was experiencing any of the "awful feelings" she
herself remembered enduring some time ago. If so,
these feelings were all about *her*—Rose! Yet when
she had been so tormented it was all about nothing at
all. About no one at least. And now that a man had
really made love to her, really kissed her, she felt
nothing. It was absurd. It was also frightfully
annoying, but she supposed it would always be like
that. Perhaps there was nothing in "love" but
imagination? Rose inclined to this opinion, and sighed.
Real life was very disappointing. She had received an
offer of marriage, she had been kissed; a man had told
her he loved her. All her dreams in fact, had come
true, and had ended in a disenchantment as great as

one which had followed a fairly recent actual dream, in which, after hearing with delight of her own approaching marriage, she was introduced to the "bridegroom" who, approaching her through a mist, stood revealed at last as Maisie, the younger of the two sheeplike Totfield girls.   Geoffrey as a husband was almost as grotesquely disappointing, and Rose sighed again impatiently as she grew sleepy.   It was a great bother, and she wondered if Geoffrey came to-morrow how he would behave.   She had not answered his question, but of course, he must know there was no need to answer anything so preposterous, and she supposed he would go on with the Arithmetic and the riding lessons as usual.   To-morrow she must begin her regular work again, for there had already been too many interruptions.   In the midst of this reflection she fell asleep.

Lucie, meanwhile, in the arms of Mademoiselle, was sobbingly protesting that Geoffrey was, and would remain, the only love of her life, and that as her heart was broken she had better return at once to Tours and enter a convent.

CHAPTER XXIII

HOPES DISAPPOINTED

ROSE woke next morning to a sense of importance.
That she had received an offer of marriage was
an incontrovertible fact, even though it was "only
Geoffrey" who sought her hand. In the morning
sunlight she felt amused, a little flattered, but in no
way disposed to take seriously Geoffrey's professions
of devotion. She would like to have confided in Lucie,
but Lucie would certainly tell Mademoiselle, and it
wouldn't be fair on Geoffrey, she felt, to make his
momentary "silliness" a source of amusement to the
household. She never for an instant doubted that
their old friendly relationship would be reinstated,
and that in a few days, if not before, Geoffrey would
himself be laughing at the nonsense he had talked.

It was in the mood of an unawakened schoolgirl
that she ran downstairs to breakfast, and the mood
was as genuine an expression of one phase of the complex personality known as Rose Cottingham as that
which a few months previously had left her a weeping
and tormented victim of unsatisfied desire.

"Where is Lucie?" she asked, when Mrs. Lester had
poured out the coffee.

"*La pauvre petite!* She is a little suffering," replied
Mademoiselle with a glance at Rose, from which despite herself, she could not exclude the curiosity that
was devouring her.

"She complains of a headache," explained Mrs.

Lester, "so I thought she might as well have her breakfast in bed.   Don't disturb her, Rose, when you go
upstairs.   She may be asleep."

"I wondered why she went up to bed so early last
night—" Rose was beginning, when the parlour-maid
entered with a note.

"Mr. Geoffrey has just ridden over and left this for
Miss Rose," she announced, offering the letter-tray.

Mademoiselle choked a little over her coffee, and
Mrs. Lester, having finished breakfast, got up from the
table, and with a question to the maid on some household matter, left the room.

Rose was annoyed.   Geoffrey was a fool not to come
in as usual, and the fact that Mademoiselle made no
comment on the circumstance made her uneasy with
the sense of being watched.

As soon as she could escape from the table, she went
as usual to the schoolroom, and with some impatience
opened the letter, raising her eyebrows wonderingly
at its length.

She began to read, and as she read her expression
changed.   It was a long, rambling, rather incoherent
epistle, but there was no doubting its sincerity.   The
boy poured out his heart to her; begged and implored
her to listen and be kind.

. . . *Do, do* write to me at once, darling Rose, and say "yes,"
for unless you say it, I can't see you again.   I can't bear it
any more, and I shall go away again for a long time.   But you
will say "yes," won't you?   Think how it would have pleased
mother——

Rose put down the badly written blotted sheet and
looked about her in blank wonder and despair.   It was
a real thing, then?   No "silliness" on Geoffrey's part,

to be soon forgotten. The realization stunned her and filled her with compunction and pity. Poor Geoffrey! She dreaded to make him unhappy, and there was no way out of it, for in spite of his letter the idea of Geoffrey as a husband, seemed no whit less preposterous than it had hitherto appeared to her.

I have known you all my life, and I know now that I have loved you all my life. . . .

She read the sentence once more and marvelled. It was just this long acquaintance which to *her* put Geoffrey as a lover out of the question.

"Well, I must be quick and get it over," she thought at last with a long sigh, as she took up her pen to begin her difficult reply.

It took hours to compose, but congratulating herself upon its explicitness, she managed to run out and post the letter just before lunch-time. On her return she found Lucie at the table, pale, silent, her face stained with recent tears, and when, on her wondering inquiry, her sister began to weep afresh, she looked in amazement from her grandmother to Mademoiselle. Neither of them offered an explanation. Mrs. Lester began to talk on indifferent matters, and when the uncomfortable meal was at an end, Lucie rose hurriedly and made her escape.

Rose was about to follow when Mrs. Lester called her back.

"Sit down, my dear," she said, when Mademoiselle had gone out and closed the door, and Rose was amazed afresh at the cordiality of her tone. She looked inquiringly at her grandmother.

"I conclude," pursued Mrs. Lester, folding her

table-napkin with precision, "that Geoffrey Winter
has proposed to you?"

"Yes," said Rose, flushing, and startled into an
admission. "How did you know?"

Mrs. Lester smiled.

"My dear girl, because *you* are a little ostrich you
mustn't imagine the rest of the world follows suit."

Rose was silent. "*The rest of the world!*" Then
every one had noticed? Every one had been talkng?
It seemed incredible.

"Well, when is your future husband going to implore
my blessing?" asked Mrs. Lester, still amiably smiling.

"My—? You expected me to—to say 'yes'?"
Rose inquired in a dazed tone.

"You have done so, of course?" demanded Mrs.
Lester, looking up sharply.

"Marry *Geoffrey?*" She laughed a little. "Why,
it would be too absurd! I've just written to say 'no.'
What else could I do?"

"And why, may I ask?" Mrs. Lester forced herself
to speak calmly.

"Why? But I don't understand you! How could
I possibly be in love with Geoffrey? He's like a brother. He's always been like that. You said I was
an ostrich. But how could I be anything else? I
never *thought* of such a thing. He was just Geoffrey!"

Mrs. Lester checked an impulse to box the girl's
ears. The proceeding would have relieved exasperated feelings which prudence warned her, for the
moment, at any rate, to conceal. Much was at stake.
It would be unwise to rouse opposition if reasoning
might prevail.

She regarded her granddaughter therefore, with a
tolerant smile that was truly heroic.

"I quite understand that the idea seems strange to you," she began. "But after all, my dear, it is a very natural one; and the fact that you and Geoffrey have known one another all your lives, as you say, is all the more satisfactory. It proves that his is no light fancy, and——"

"I can't help what he feels. *I'm* not in love with him," interrupted Rose hurriedly, with an uncomfortable blush. It was hateful to have to mention the word "love" to Grandmamma.

Mrs. Lester, silently invoked the shade of Job, and with outward calm continued:

"Allow me in the first place to point out to you," she said, "that at your age, and very rightly, you know nothing about the 'love' you so glibly mention. That will certainly follow marriage in the right and proper course. It would be strange indeed if it did not," she added rather more quickly, "with such a husband as Geoffrey Winter. You do not, I presume, complain of his personal appearance? One might go far before meeting a better-looking young man; and you can have no fear as to his character. A fine, handsome, exemplary young fellow! On what conceivable grounds do you refuse him?"

Grandmother and granddaughter furtively glanced at one another and looked away, both conscious of insincerity. Mrs. Lester knowing that love did not "certainly follow marriage," even though that might be its theoretical right and proper course, and Rose uncomfortably aware that her grandmother considered her an innocent child, when there was Swinburne . . . and Bel-Ami—and—all sorts of things! She was however, obliged to speak, and confusion made her voice as obstinate as her feeling.

"I simply don't care for him—like that," she said with decision.

"Am I to understand then, that you definitely refuse his offer?" Mrs. Lester's eyes began to flash.

"I *have*. I told you so."

Her grandmother walked to the window, looked out a moment, and wheeled round again.

"Now listen to me, Rose," she began, still preserving a forced calm, "and let us talk reasonably, leaving all this nonsense out of the question. You have received an offer of marriage from a man who in the future will be worth five or six thousand a year, and who even now can offer you a beautiful home and all the advantages of an excellent social position. If you expect to do better, I fear you will be disappointed. At your majority you will come into an income of less than a hundred a year, and even at my death this pittance will scarcely be augmented. As you know, I have as much as I can do even now to make both ends meet, and the property is rapidly deteriorating. In the sense cf the word you have no money—and you are not beautiful. It is quite true that you are responsible for neither circumstance, but that in no way alters the position. These are the plain facts. Surely in the face of them, you will not be mad enough to throw away a chance so providentially offered you at the very outset of your career?"

She spoke peremptorily now, and, with one hand resting on the uncleared luncheon-table, stood waiting for a reply.

It was amazement and nothing else that she saw written on the girl's face.

"I didn't know I had any money at all!" stammered Rose.

"You *have* none—in the sense of the word. A possible ninety pounds a year——"

"But it's a lot! Enough to live on!"

"It depends upon what you call 'living.' However, that is not the point. We are not discussing a question of pocket-money. It is the important matter of your future that is to be decided."

Mrs. Lester was possessed by uneasy fear. She wished she had not mentioned the infinitesimal income. Yet it was inconceivable that the girl would be fool enough to consider it a substitute for matrimony.

"Grandmamma, I've decided it. I couldn't *possibly* marry Geoffrey. The very idea makes me laugh. It's absurd! As though any one would take Geoffrey seriously! I mean any one who has eaten sticky sweets out of his pocket and fought with him over dolls and toys. It's ridiculous, and if you don't understand what I mean, ask Lucie. She was practically brought up with him too, and if he went and proposed to her, I'm sure she would feel just as I do about it."

"You are a perfect fool!" retorted Mrs. Lester, with so much conviction and acrimony that Rose started, accustomed as she was to adverse criticism from her grandmother. "For a week and more," pursued the old lady, regaining an icy tone of contemptuous derision, "under your very nose your sister has been making love to Geoffrey Winter, and even now, presumably in the arms of Mademoiselle, who has no more sense than the rest of her sex, she is spoiling her complexion and crying her eyes out for the sake of the young gentleman you despise!"

Rose went suddenly white.

"*Lucie?*" she whispered, and paused, stunned and bewildered. "Is *that* what's the matter with her, then?

You mean she's—in love with Geoffrey? . . . Oh,
then, why doesn't he—" She checked herself, looking miserably at her grandmother, who shrugged her
shoulders.

"You see it's a pretty kettle of fish," she remarked,
relapsing into homely metaphor, "and the solution of
the difficulty would be for you to accept him without further ado."

"No!" said Rose. "I wouldn't, anyhow. Not for
all the world! I don't want to. I should hate it. And
now that Lucie—Oh, why doesn't he care for her? Perhaps he will now he knows I shall never marry him?"

She looked imploringly at her grandmother, like a
child yearning to be reassured, but Mrs. Lester's
inimical expression gave her no comfort. She merely
shrugged her shoulders with a gesture of impatience.

"You talk like a baby! Is it likely that the young
man will accept Lucie instead of you? Like an infant
contentedly picking up one toy when another one has
been taken away from him? . . . My dear Rose,
you are a born fool. You always were, and I'm afraid
you always will be. However, if you won't take advice
there's nothing further to be said, and you must be
left to suffer for your folly. Kindly ring the bell for
this table to be cleared."

Mrs. Lester swept from the room, and Rose mechanically moved towards the bell.

When the maid appeared in answer to its summons,
she as mechanically opened one of the French windows
and went out into the garden. A fine rain was falling,
but she did not notice it as she walked in a sort of
dream along the damp paths leading towards the edge
of the cliff. Two threads of thought were interwoven
in her whirling brain: Lucie was in love with Geoffrey

—and unhappy; and, incredible thought—she, and presumably Lucie also, had money of their own!

When the second reflection was uppermost, she was conscious of anger. Why had her grandmother not told her of this before? But it was so like her to be secretive! Rose knew that but for the special circumstances, the disclosure would not have been made till she was actually twenty-one. Even now there were more than two years to wait before she could call herself independent. . . . Still, what a difference the knowledge would have made during the past eighteen months of hopelessness! . . . Such half-formed thoughts flitted across her mind in the intervals of miserable speculation about Lucie. How incredible, how *awful* it was that Lucie should be in love and unhappy, when she herself was so absolutely indifferent to the object of Lucie's affections!

With a sudden longing to see her sister, she turned and ran breathlessly towards the house and upstairs to Lucie's room, before the door of which with sudden timidity she paused.

Lucie as love's victim had become an important person, and it seemed sacrilege to disturb her grief. Nevertheless, after a moment's hesitation she knocked gently, and when a muffled voice replied "Come in," shyly opened the door.

Lucie was sitting in an arm-chair by the window, eating chocolates out of a pink-and-gold paper bag, and a particularly large sweet of an adhesive nature, rather than emotion, accounted for the husky quality of the voice which had struck trepidation into Rose's soul.

"What do you want?" asked Lucie crossly and with difficulty, as her sister stood hesitating on the threshold.

"She wants a little talk, *chérie!*" cooed Mademoiselle soothingly as she rose, brushing crumbs of chocolate from her own mouth. "*Voilà!* It is but natural. I will go and leave the little sisters together." She kissed Lucie with pitying fervour, threw a glance of mingled sorrow, congratulation, and admonition at Rose, and as she passed her, raised her eyes to heaven and sadly shook her head.

"What an ass she is!" exclaimed Rose irritably, when the door closed upon her. It was not in the least what she had meant to say, but Mademoiselle's sentimental attitude, joined to the chocolates and Lucie's cross tone, had a disconcerting effect upon her own emotions.

"Why is she an ass? You always think yourself so clever," was Lucie's not too conciliatory reply.

A sharp retort was on Rose's tongue when she noticed with a pang that if Lucie's lips were chocolate stained, her eyelids were still reddened, and her heart melted within her.

"Lucie! . . . I came to tell you that—that of course I'm not going to marry Geoff," she began, sitting down on the edge of the bed.

Lucie turned round swiftly. "He *did* propose to you last night, then?" There was a sharp note of jealousy in her voice. "I was sure he would. And I was sure you'd say *no*," she added, looking inimically at her sister.

There was a little pause. "I'm so sorry that you— because, you see, I don't. It seems so absurd to me! I never was so surprised— But anyhow, Lucie, as I'm not going to, perhaps he'll— I mean he would be an idiot not to!" stammered Rose, with fine lucidity.

"Why don't you like him?" inquired her sister after a pause.

"I *do* like him, in a way. But to *marry!* Why, it would be too silly! I mean—" She checked herself, remembering Lucie's unaccountable passion and the necessity of treating it with respect.

"It's not silly at all!" declared Lucie, her eyes swimming. "It's so like you to keep me from getting what I want and not to want it yourself."

Rose felt the injustice of the reproach, but Lucie's miserable face filled her with pity.

"He'll fall in love with you. I'm *sure* he will!" she declared. "Don't cry, Lucie!" She put her arms round the girl, who moved pettishly from her embrace. "You see," she went on, still striving desperately after comfort, "you're pretty and I'm not, and men only really care about prettiness, so directly he finds——"

Again she checked herself, remembering with consternation Geoffrey's threat of a prolonged absence. Hastily she decided to say nothing about this to Lucie. He might not go after all.

"It's all very well," sobbed Lucie, "but you've made him in love with *you*, and I'm so miserable—so dreadfully miserable! I shall never get over it. I shall never, *never* care for any one else all my life!"

Yielding now to Rose's heart-broken caresses and revelling in the luxury of a fresh sympathizer, Lucie sobbed anew, pausing now and again to listen half hopefully to her sister's eager assurances that Geoffrey must and should respond to her love for him.

There were renewed tears the following day when Geoffrey failed to appear and the confession had been wrung from Rose that he might have gone away.

During the afternoon the elder Mr. Winter called,

and was received in secret conference by Mrs. Lester in the drawing-room. He brought the news, later disclosed by her, that Geoffrey had decided to return to France to finish the course of horticultural study interrupted by his mother's last illness, and that he would probably be away six months at least.

The ensuing week was a period of torture to Rose. At the death-blow to the hopes she had secretly entertained, Lucie gave herself up to unrestrained grief, and in spite of her grandmother's silent annoyance, of Rose's distracted appeals, and of Mademoiselle's petting, cried from morning till night so successfully that she began to look ill enough to regard her own reflection in the glass with melancholy satisfaction.

In the meantime Rose's position in the household so far as her grandmother's attitude was concerned, was that of a criminal to be coldly ignored, and the girl alternately raged and wept in secret at the general misery caused by Geoffrey's untimely avowal. He had begged her to keep the miniature of his mother, and she often looked long at it, yearning in vain for her friend. *She* would have understood! Even to further her son's happiness, Rose felt, she would never have urged her to be false to the instinct which put Geoffrey as a husband out of the question.

When eight or ten wretched days, during which Rose tried unsuccessfully to work, had dragged away, Mrs. Lester came one morning to the schoolroom, and, with a sarcastic apology for intrusion upon "important study," sat down and intimated that she wished for a conversation with her granddaughter. Rose pushed her history note books wearily aside and prepared to listen.

"I have decided," said Mrs. Lester, without preamble, "to send you and Lucie to London for a few months." Then, as Rose uttered a sharp, dismayed exclamation, she raised her hand peremptorily.

"Kindly allow me to speak. I will listen to your comments afterwards. . . . I had intended to send you almost at once to Tours, keeping Lucie at home during that time and deferring your entrance into society till next year, when you would both have gone to your cousin Gertrude's house for the season. However, as things are, I think it advisable to send you now,—instead of later. I have written to your cousin, and she very kindly offers to chaperon you both and is ready to receive you immediately."

"But, Grandmamma,—" interrupted Rose wildly.

"Please wait a moment till I have finished. You see the condition into which your sister has worked herself. If this goes on, the girl will be seriously ill, and as I wish her to recover herself before the season begins, she must have change of scene and mental distraction at once. You shall not lose your year abroad. Directly an opportunity offers—possibly next autumn—you shall go. Meanwhile you will both be presented this season. Lucie is young, it is true, but she looks much older than her years, and she is certainly precocious." Mrs. Lester gave an expressive little sniff of mingled amusement and annoyance, and calmly continued her discourse. "After all, she will be nearly eighteen and you in your nineteenth year before the end of the summer, so, though I would rather have waited——"

"But why can't she go alone?" broke out Rose irrepressibly. "Why need I go with her? I *can't* go just now, Grandmamma. It's quite impossible!"

"You will go together or not at all," returned Mrs.

Lester decisively. "For one thing I shall not allow your younger sister to come out before you, and for another I do not intend to go through all the fuss and bother of presentation two succeeding years. And why, may I ask, is it impossible for you to go to town? I don't flatter myself that it's any affection for your home? If so, you have successfully disguised your emotion."

"I have something to do. I can't leave my work. I simply *can't*," returned Rose, too feverishly anxious to resent her grandmother's more than usually disagreeable tone of sarcasm.

"Your serious studies? Any one would think you were preparing for an important career in life."

"I am!" exclaimed Rose desperately. "I didn't want to let any one know. Oh! it's *hateful* to be worried like this. . . . But now, I suppose, I must tell you. I'm working for an examination in the summer. I've been working three months. If I go away, all that will be wasted. . . . *Why* can't Lucie go alone? She'll get on much better without me, and——"

Mrs. Lester got up. "You will go together next week or not at all," she repeated. "I can't force you out of the house, since in spite of your behaviour, in years, at any rate, you are not a child. But if you persist in your ridiculous refusal, you will have the satisfaction of knowing that you deprive Lucie of her London season and of all the advantage which a change just now would mean to her. I leave it to you to decide. But please let me know before the six o'clock post, for I must write one way or the other to your cousin."

The last words were uttered at the door, and when it shut, Rose jumped up and furiously sweeping books and papers from the table, threw them into a

22

cupboard and herself into the shabby schoolroom arm-chair. Indignation, anger, hesitancy, and bitter disappointment were some of the emotions which caused her to clench her hands till she hurt herself, and to drive her in a frenzy to and fro, from the chair to the window, in her agitated pacing of the room.

To be at one moment treated as a child and the next appealed to as a woman, roused as it had always done, her sense of injustice. "I intend you to do this or that." "I propose to send you here or there." Rose mentally repeated the phrases with increasing anger. It had always been so. She was always disposed of, with never a word beforehand of consultation or respect for her wishes or for her plans, which were held in light contempt. And now after all her work if she went to London she would miss the examination, upon which her hopes were built.

Rose rushed suddenly from the room to look for Lucie, and found her in the morning-room, crouching over the fire.

"Has Grandmamma said anything to you?" she began breathlessly.

"Yes. She says we're to go to Cousin Gertrude's next week. I suppose you're excited about it. *I* don't care whether we go or not. It's all the same to me," replied Lucie in a dejected voice. Rose noticed, however, that she was putting fresh ruffles into the sleeves of her best dress.

"Oh, Lucie! Then you won't mind if we don't?" she gasped, sitting down beside her on the fender stool, "Grandmamma says I'm to decide it, and——"

"You haven't said you won't go?" asked Lucie sharply, dropping the lace frills.

"But you've just said you didn't care, and I have

a special reason for not going. If you'll swear not to
tell, I'll explain to you!" urged Rose eagerly. "You
will swear though, won't you?"

Lucie nodded impatiently. She was beginning to
speak, but, giving her no time, Rose rushed into an
explanation of her plans and hopes for the future.

"And I've been slaving for three months, you see,"
she concluded, "and it will be all no good if I'm to go
off to Cousin Gertrude's, where there won't be a
moment to work. You do understand, don't you,
Lucie?"

For answer Lucie began to cry. "You want to keep
me here, where everything reminds me of—of—*him*,
just for a stupid old exam.?" she sobbed. "It's too
selfish of you! And it's absurd, too. How *can* you
be a teacher? You'd hate it, and besides, Grandmamma would never let you. And I was longing to
get away. Simply longing. I'm awake all night long,
and I'm awfully unhappy, and you don't care a bit!"

"But, Lucie, you said you didn't mind one way or
another," repeated Rose, harassed and torn by conflicting considerations.

"You might *know* that a change would be something! But you don't care. You have no feeling.
You sent poor Geoffrey away and kept him from me,
and now——"

Rose sprang up and rushed away to her own bedroom. Half an hour later, she sought her grandmother with the brusque intimation that she was ready
to go to London with Lucie, and Mrs. Lester complacently went to her writing-table to conclude arrangements with her niece, Lady Gertrude Cummings.
She was aware of the trump card she had played in
pointing out to Rose that her refusal would mean

disappointment to her sister, and the girl's decision was no surprise to her.

Rose has many faults, but she is not selfish [she wrote]. You may find her difficult, but though I consider her plain and usually unattractive, certain men (as events have proved) fortunately do not share my opinion, so there may be hope for her after all. When she pleases she can be quite amusing, but I trust you have one or two young men in your circle clever enough to come up to her ladyship's standard? Otherwise she and they will fare badly. Lucie, though she is not looking her best just now (owing to a ridiculous little love affair which she will forget in a fortnight), is in my opinion remarkably pretty. She is like her poor mother. Rose unluckily, as the nurses say, "favours" her father's side of the family, and the Cottinghams always had more brains than beauty. It is for that reason I am annoyed with the girl for her refusal of young Winter's offer. His father called upon me the other day and said the boy has taken his disappointment desperately to heart, and has insisted upon going away, apparently convinced that Rose's determination is final. He (the father) is also disappointed, chiefly I think because his wife had a sort of infatuation for Rose, and being a newly made widower he is in that acute but ephemeral stage of sentimentality natural to men in the circumstances of bereavement. I am not without hope that should young Winter remain faithful, Rose will come to her senses. At present she is a mere child in regard to men, and as ignorant as a baby of all that side of life. Lucie is infinitely more precocious, and I fancy there will be no difficulty about the arrangement of her future. . . .

Rose cried herself to sleep that night, thinking alternately of her lost chances and of Lucie, who had come to her room before going to bed, to embrace and thank her.

"It's quite true that nothing will ever make any difference to me," she had plaintively declared. "I never forget him for one second. But oh, Rose, it will be such a relief to get away, and perhaps the change of air will at least make me sleep!"

The pathetic words rang in her ears, and at moments made her decision seem absolutely necessary and inevitable. At other moments she wavered. Rose was unfortunately endowed with a highly critical as well as with a highly emotional faculty, and the two were in never-ending conflict. When Lucie's pale, wretched little face rose before her, stirring her pity to unbearable poignancy, a vision of chocolates in a pink-and-gold bag concurrently presented itself with an accompanying cynical reflection. This was immediately repressed as unfair, since because she could not imagine *herself* enjoying chocolates in the midst of grief, there was no reason why the confection should not afford solace to Lucie, who might be differently constituted. And Lucie undoubtedly looked ill, so she *must* be unhappy! Still, the chocolates rankled, and just before she fell asleep some words spoken by Helen—long ago, it seemed—darted suddenly into her mind.

"You have too much feeling, Rose. . . . It will stand in your way. . . ."

Well, this perhaps was a case in point, and what if she had sacrificed herself unnecessarily? The thought of Helen was the one bright ray in her cloud-filled sky. In London, at any rate, she would see her friend, and her last waking reflection was concerned with the irony she had discovered to be latent in the very fact of existence. With what overwhelming delight three months ago would she have looked forward to this very visit to town, which now by the turn of circumstances bade fair to wreck all her hopes of ultimate freedom.

CHAPTER XXIV

A SOCIAL FAILURE

LADY GERTRUDE CUMMINGS, the not inconsolable widow of the late Lord John Cummings, a man of undoubtedly distinguished birth but doubtful temper, lived in a somewhat imposing house in a highly imposing square near Hyde Park. She was a childless widow of five and forty, stout but well dressed, conventional but shrewd; altogether a woman of her world—a world that was entirely materialistic, from which imagination was not so much excluded as never-imagined.

She received the two girls with kindly hospitality. Lady Gertrude was often at a loss for an occupation, and the thought of chaperoning her two little cousins through the coming season rather amused her than otherwise. It seemed likely to provide some change in her monotonous life of assured comfort and lack of interest in anything but ladylike gossip and match-making, directed on mercenary rather than upon amorous lines. Metaphorically at first, and actually not much later, she and Lucie fell into one another's arms, while Rose puzzled and disconcerted her as being totally unlike all she expected, or had ever experienced, of girlhood.

There was indeed some excuse for her first unfavourable impression, for Rose, unhappy and discontented, was by no means a pleasant inmate of any household. Added to her disappointment about the examina-

342

tion, she had suffered a blow almost as crushing, by the discovery that Helen was not in London. On the eve of her departure from home she had received a letter from her friend with the news that the Professor was ill, and the doctors having ordered him to Switzerland for several months, she must as a matter of course go with him.

It seems too cruel [she wrote] that just when we might have met, this should have happened. But of course father's health is the first consideration, and I am very troubled about him. I had so much to say to you, and I was counting the days till you came. But in spite of my delight I should have scolded you for giving in to your sister! It's like you, Rose, to sacrifice all your plans for some extravagant feeling of pity which most likely is entirely wasted. I won't say anything more about it just now, when we are both unhappy and worried, and I shall leave the other matter also—you know what I mean—till we can talk, instead of writing about it. To have had an offer of marriage makes you seem very grown-up. How did you feel when he asked you? I am rather jealous of you. But the men in our set don't marry, I find. In some ways I'm getting rather tired of them. . . . Do you remember the man who lectured here when you stayed with us? (What a long time ago it seems!) I meant to tell you in my last letter that he is standing for Parliament as a Labour leader, and great things are expected of him. Father is most interested in his career. Dearest Rose, I am so sorry and disappointed about everything, but I mustn't write any more, for I'm in the midst of packing. We start early to-morrow.

Rose read the letter in the train with the conviction that fate had done its worst. She sank into gloomy silence, while from habit Lucie wept. Her tears had received fresh impetus from the parting with Mademoiselle, who as soon as another field of activity could be discovered for "a gentlewoman of cheerful disposition and pure French accent," was leaving the Manor House.

Long before London was reached, however, Lucie's
tears were dry, and by the time she and Rose stepped
into their cousin's brougham at Paddington, she was
radiant, while Rose, endeavouring to be polite, could
scarcely summon a smile.

"I haven't seen you since you were almost babies,"
said Lady Gertrude, with a glance that implied comparison, from the younger to the elder sister; "but I
remember this hair!" She touched Lucie's fair locks
flatteringly. "And those blue eyes! *You're* not looking very well, my dear," she added, turning to Rose.

"It's Lucie who hasn't been well," declared Rose
maliciously. Her sister's cheerfulness exasperated her,
and she was prepared for and insensible to, the deep
sigh which followed her remark.

"Oh well, a little gaiety will soon put that right,"
their cousin comfortably assured her.

It did. By the end of a week Lucie was blithe,
cheerful, and sweet-tempered enough to justify the
popular ideal of the fresh young English girl, and
Rose, listening to her laughter and her incessant chatter, so like the bird-like chirping of Mademoiselle, experienced an irritation which, though she felt it to be
unreasonable, was none the less acute. She wanted
Lucie to be "cured." It was, of course, for that
reason she had consented to the London visit. Yet
she had a shrewd suspicion that the cure would have
been effected, though possibly a week or two later, at
home.

Meanwhile, though youth asserted itself, and she
enjoyed the shopping, the drives in the park, and
above all, the theatres, she was bored in her cousin's
house, whose very aspect displeased her as greatly as
it delighted her sister. Lucie loved the fat satin cush-

ions in the drawing-room, tied with expensive bows of
pink ribbon, the thick, soft carpets, the luxury of her
expensively furnished bedroom, the general air of
opulence which the house exhaled.

To Rose the undistinguished costliness of everything was as oppressive as the undistinguished mental
atmosphere of Lady Gertrude and her friends, who
"chatted" instead of talked and never uttered a word
which, to her at any rate, was of the smallest interest
or could possibly provoke a smile.   They belonged, in
short, to that huge crowd of the dull, the rich, and the
correct which London continues to produce in vast
numbers and twenty years ago was particularly successful in causing to flourish.

Lucie accepted gladly the environment, and was
petted and flattered by the ladies, who in her presence
archly warned Lady Gertrude that she would have her
work cut out to chaperon "a young beauty" through
the coming season.   They spoke of her as "a sweet
girl, so unassuming and natural and affectionate,"
while Rose was secretly branded with the term "ec-
centric."   There were those who were afraid she
possessed "modern ideas," and they deplored her
plainness, while grudgingly admitting that her taste
in dress was better than her sister's, and that she
was probably quite aware that her figure was good.

In spite of all the trivial occupations of the day,
time hung heavy on Rose's hands, at any rate till the
real business of preparing for the season began, and
as the only books in Lady Gertrude's house were
"sweetly pretty" novels, she took to reading the newspapers carefully and trying to understand the subject
vaguely designated as "politics."

One morning after breakfast, while Lucie and her

cousin were gossiping at the fire, she interrupted a discussion on the probable cost of a certain Mrs. Colwyn's furs, by an exclamation which caused Lucie to look round.

"It's only about an awfully exciting speech by John Dering," she explained, half-apologetically.

"Whoever is John Dering?" asked Lucie, without interest.

"I told you about him, but I expect you've forgotten. The Socialist who spoke at the Fergursons' when I stayed with them. He's a Labour leader."

"My dear, you've surely not met any of those awful socialists?" demanded Lady Gertrude, in a tone half-shocked, half-derisory.

"My friends the Fergursons are socialists," said Rose, shortly.

"But I thought socialists were all of the lower classes? Surely Aunt Rose never allowed you to stay with people of that sort?"

"John Dering is one of the lower classes, as you call them," returned Rose, still more shortly. "Professor Fergurson is a gentleman."

"And you mean to say that he allowed this John What's-his-name to hold forth at his house? Dear, dear! What is the world coming to?" exclaimed Lady Gertrude, with lazy disapproval.

"It's getting altered, thank goodness," returned Rose with rising temper. "Some day, perhaps, it won't be so deadly dull as it is now."

She made her escape from the room, and Lady Gertrude turned to Lucie.

"What a strange girl Rose is!" she remarked. "She takes interest in things so unsuitable for women. Politics and socialism, and all that. She's such a funny mixture, dear, isn't she? I declare I'm surprised to find she likes clothes, and knows how to choose them too. I should have thought with her learned tastes she wouldn't have cared a bit how she looked."

"Oh, Rose is as funny as she can be!" said Lucie, shrugging her shoulders. "Just imagine, she didn't want to come to London just because of some silly old exam. she took it into her head to try to pass. I had an awful bother to persuade her. And then refusing Geoffrey Winter, too, when any other girl would have jumped at the chance. Oh, Cousin Gertrude, I can't *tell* you how handsome he is! And such a *dear* boy!" Lucie, who for a month had never thought of Geoffrey, heaved a deep sigh, and was gratified to find her eyes filling with a return of half-forgotten tears.

"Now, now, darling!" expostulated her cousin, shaking a reproving finger. "No more repining over that rather dense young gentleman! Only wait till the gaieties really begin, and you will have all the young men at your feet. I predict a really brilliant marriage for you, my dear. You'll be glad enough then that you didn't doom yourself to a country existence, where you would be wasted."

Lucie not unwillingly dried her eyes and began to take a keen interest in the details of a new frock, the designs for which soon littered the breakfast-table. . . .

Before long both girls were absorbed in the whirling toils and pleasures of the season, and not a little surprised at the amount of money at their disposal. Expenditure, indeed, was controlled by Lady Gertrude, but there was no stint in the supplies, and Rose occasionally reflected that her grandmother must have "saved up" a good deal for the extravagances of their first season. Even then she was far from realizing what of planning, contriving, and sacrifice this "saving up" represented, and with the carelessness of youth, she and Lucie accepted with glee the novelty of possessing in three months more frocks and frills and elegances than had ever fallen to their lot in twice that number of years.

That the Cottingham girls were well turned out was universally admitted, and at her presentation at Court in due course, Lucie took rank as one of the new youthful beauties of the season. Rose grew accustomed to seeing her surrounded by men at dances, at race-meetings, and garden-parties. With a curious medley of emotions, in which pride, admiration, and wistful envy were mingled, she wondered how her sister managed to get on so well with people who to her were as savourless as, in her own metaphor, "boiled mutton with no caper sauce."

"How do you do it, Lucie?" she asked one night, or rather, early one morning, when they had returned from a ball at a neighbouring house. She had gone into Lucie's room to have her dress unlaced, and after the process she sat down on the bed and watched her sister brushing out her fleece of hair, which, in the gaslight, sparkled like gold thread.

Certainly Lucie was very pretty, but there were other girls, quite plain girls, who also seemed to get on with their partners and to find interest and amusement in talking to them. How was it that she alone failed? So far as the actual dancing was concerned, Rose had not lack of attention, for she danced well; better, in fact, than Lucie, and she danced with delight. It was the "between times" that baffled her, when she found a young man, perfect as a companion in a waltz, as a conversationalist in a secluded corner, absolutely impossible.

"What do you talk about? When I look at you, you always seem to be chattering nineteen to the dozen. What do you find to say?"

"Oh, I don't know," returned Lucie. "What *do* people talk about?"

"Nothing," declared Rose tersely.

"Well, I like talking about nothing. I'm not clever like you, and I'm glad. Men don't like clever women. Besides, it's not all *talking!*" Lucie significantly dimpled and smiled at herself in the glass.

"I'm *not* clever!" declared Rose impatiently, stamping her foot, "but I can't see anything that could amuse a codfish in conversation with a young man who says, 'How many dances have you been to this season? I suppose you've been to the Academy? Have you seen "The Mikado"?' And then when you say you *have* been to the Academy, or seen 'The Mikado,' and you try to talk about them, he says, 'Oh yes! an awful lot of pictures—what?' and that's all, till your next partner begins, 'Been to many dances this season—what?' and the idiocy goes on all over again!"

Rose's mimicry of young Dallow and his like, was perfect, and Lucie laughed.

"Yes, they begin like that," she allowed, "but then comes the flirtation."

"What do you call flirtation?" asked Rose. "The sort of boring stuff Charlie Graham tried on with me this evening, I suppose: . . . 'Oh, I say, you *might* give me that flower you've got in your hair. It's a rose, isn't it? And *your* name's Rose, isn't it?

Funny thing—what? Anyhow, it'll always remind me of you, don't yer know!' . . . And then when I asked him how he managed if girls' names didn't happen to correspond with the names of the flowers in their hair, he stared at me like a cross baby and said he supposed I was laughing at him, and I was 'much too deep' for him. Then he immediately took me back to Cousin Gertrude, and bowed like a penny wooden toy, and never asked me for another dance!"

"Oh, of course, if you don't like flirtation!" exclaimed Lucie, smiling again at herself in the glass. "And that's only the beginning of it," she murmured.

"If that's flirtation, I don't!" declared Rose emphatically, ignoring the last words. "I can imagine it being very amusing, though," she went on after a moment. "A sort of game of wits. I believe I could write a good verbal flirtation," she added meditatively.

Lucie turned round and regarded her sister with critical attention.

"Of course you don't get on with young men! You talk in a way they don't understand. What was that you said just now—'*verbal flirtation*' or something? Half of them wouldn't know what you meant, and anyhow, they'd think you were giving yourself airs. *I* don't, because you always *have* talked like that. At any rate, since you went to Minerva House."

Rose opened her eyes wide in genuine astonishment.

"I didn't know I talked differently from other people!" she exclaimed. "Certainly most of the men we meet don't talk at all, so one can't judge."

Lucie began to plait her hair, humming under her breath the refrain of the "Myosotis" waltz, and Rose gave a long sigh.

"I shall never get on in society!" she said, in a dis-

couraged tone. "It's nothing but a waste of time and
money for me to be here."

"It's three o'clock!" returned Lucie, as the chimes
from a neighbouring church clock cut into the silence.
She yawned. "Good-night. I'm sure you could
get on better if you tried," she added rather patro-
nizingly. "You dance so well, and you have a very
good figure. That dress suits you too. Wear it at
the Churchills' party next week."

Rose heard six o'clock strike before she slept. She
felt sore, not a little depressed, and altogether "out
of it," as she dejectedly told herself. If this was
"society" she certainly did not suit it, and if not, where
did she belong? Not, as she now shrewdly suspected,
to the Fergurson circle of arid intellectuals. Recalling them, she feared they would now bore her almost
if not quite as much as the Charlie Grahams of her
present acquaintance, or the county people of the
type she met at home, a type of which Geoffrey Winter
—poor Geoffrey!—was the best example.

And yet, paradoxically, she had every wish to be
popular with all of them. To be as successful as Lucie
everywhere appeared. Rose sighed as she thought
of her sister's beauty, even though she had never
been and was not now, jealous of Lucie. Accustomed
all her life to hearing Lucie admired, she regarded
her good looks as a family asset, and was proud of
them. At Minerva House she had always boasted
that her little sister was prettier than any girl in the
school, and now when she entered a ballroom it was a
matter of congratulation to her that Lucie compared
favourably with any of the beauties of the season.
. . . It was only that prettiness was such an easy
passport to favour!

Just before she slept, when the sunshine was streaming through the blinds, it occurred to her that she might go and call upon Miss Ferguson, who during the absence of her brother and her niece, remained to keep house at home. The idea pleased her. She had liked "Aunt Aggie," and at any rate it would be a change from the sort of life she was beginning to detest.

Lady Gertrude drove her to the Fergursons' door next day, promising to call for her at five, after a visit to a dressmaker, and Rose, who had learned from the parlour-maid that Miss Fergurson was at home, was ushered into the well-remembered sitting-room, where the mouse-like lady sat knitting as though for three or four years she had not moved.

She got up with a soft exclamation of pleasure when Rose entered, and looked her up and down with kindly eyes.

"The lassie has grown up!" she observed, ringing for tea.

Rose sat down by the little old lady, feeling happy and at home; and for the first ten minutes the talk was only of Helen and the Professor, whose health still gave cause for anxiety.

"And your news, my dear?" asked Aunt Aggie presently. "I hear you're in the midst of all the gaiety."

"I suppose so. It's not very gay for me," returned Rose. In two minutes, half-humorously, half-dolefully, she was pouring out to Miss Fergurson the history of her social failure.

The old lady looked at her a moment over her spectacles without speaking, when she paused on a hopeless gesture.

"Did ye ever try talking to these laddies about themselves?" she inquired at length.

"No," said Rose, astonished. "I never get to know them well enough."

"My dear, ye cannot know a man too little to begin on *that* subject!" replied Miss Fergurson, her eyes twinkling.

Rose laughed. "I'll try it," she promised.

"Do, lassie. Ye'll find it works like magic, and they'll say ye're a true woman. As, indeed, ye will be!" she added. "And ye'll get some interest and amusement out of it for yourself, my dear, pending the time when you meet the people that really suit you."

"Shall I ever?" asked Rose. "I know it sounds awfully 'superior'!" she added hastily. "And I don't mean that a bit, because no doubt it's my fault. But all my life there have only been two people I've *really* got on with—a grown-up friend who died, and Helen. And now you!" she added, with the smile that made her charming.

"And Helen only suits one side of you," asserted Miss Fergurson in her quiet voice as she counted her stitches.

Rose started, realizing for the first time, with a feeling like disloyalty, that this might be true.

"I'm not denying that you're a difficult lassie," the old lady went on, with her queer humorous smile, and no further allusion to her previous remark. "But ye'll find yourself in time, never fear. Have you seen this photograph of Helen?" she added after a moment.

"No," exclaimed Rose, all eagerness. "It's a new one. Oh, she *does* look different!"

She gazed with wonder at the picture of Helen in a

23

fashionable ball-dress, and glanced half-inquiringly
from the photograph to Helen's aunt.

"Yes, she's altered in many ways—as I thought she
would," was Miss Ferguson's placid rejoinder to the
unexpressed question in Rose's eyes.   If she had been
going to say more, the words were interrupted by the
entrance of a visitor, in whom Rose immediately
recognized Mrs. Cathcart, the wife of the burly loud-
voiced man once compared by Miss Fergurson to a
bull in a china-shop.

After one puzzled glance, and before her hostess
could speak, the lady put out her hand to Rose with a
pleased smile.

"You are Rose!   I forget your other name, but you
were Helen's little friend.   I expect you've forgotten
me?"

"No.   The last time I saw you, was after John
Dering spoke here, nearly four years ago," replied
Rose.   "And you said good-bye to me."

"You hear?   *John Dering!*" repeated Mrs. Cathcart, turning to Miss Furgurson.   "Every one
says 'John Dering' now.   It's almost a household
word.   Yet that evening, most of us were asking his
name!   I suppose you've been to hear him speak, my
dear?   I haven't forgotten how thrilled you were at
the meeting here."   She smiled kindly, and Rose
thought she must remember the parting words they
had exchanged on that occasion.

"No," she said.   "I'm staying with my cousin,
and—there's not much time."

"Rose is doing the London season," observed Miss
Fergurson, passing her new guest a cup of tea.

Mrs. Cathcart looked interested.   "And enjoying it hugely, no doubt?" she observed.

"Oh yes," agreed Rose hurriedly. "But I should like to hear John Dering speak," she added.

"He's addressing some working-people at Hoxton next week. I wonder if you could spare an evening to go with me?"

"Oh, I should love it!" Rose exclaimed excitedly. "I don't believe we're doing anything next Friday. And if we are, I'll try to get out of it."

"It's a tribute to John Dering that a young lady in her first season should be willing to give up a party for him!" declared Mrs. Cathcart, laughing. "How these young people grow up and grow frivolous. Don't they, Miss Fergurson? Helen, too. I never should have thought that Helen would care much for gaiety. But she's insatiable!"

"I haven't seen her for ages. Not since we left school," Rose said, "and in her photograph she looks —different."

"She *has* altered. She's prettier—no, that's not the word—more beautiful than she was. But she's not quite the old Helen?" She turned again to Miss Fergurson, who had resumed her knitting.

"On the contrary, it *is* the old Helen. The very oldest Helen of all. I've known her since she was a baby, remember." Her quiet smile vehemently stirred Rose's curiosity, but she waited for Mrs. Cathcart to speak.

"And Helen as I knew her, from twelve to sixteen, or thereabout—?" she began.

"A phase. Girls are impressionable."

There was a pause. "She is a devoted daughter," said Mrs. Carthcart.

"Yes. She would make sacrifices for her father."

Miss Fergurson's even tone conveyed nothing but

just what her words implied, and just as the conversation turned upon the Professor's health, the maid entered to say the carriage was waiting for Miss Cottingham.

"May I come again?" Rose asked of her hostess. "And may I write to you about next Friday?" she added, addressing Mrs. Cathcart, who searched in her handbag and found a card.

The two women watched her as she ran down the steps and got into the victoria, a slight, peculiarly girlish figure in spite of a certain air of distinction which already made her something of a personality. She looked a slip of a thing, white-clad and frail, beside the portly lady in black silk and waving plumes who almost filled the carriage. As it drove away, Miss Fergurson turned to her guest.

"Can ye imagine Rose getting on with what that woman represents?" she asked in her demure voice.

"The child interests me," said Mrs. Cathcart. "She ought to get on *somewhere*. Even as a schoolgirl one felt there was something about her—some power. A personality, but whether a successful one, I don't know. Probably not."

"It will depend upon the setting," Miss Fergurson replied.

"My dear, next Friday is out of the question," Lady Gertrude was saying to Rose. "Why, it's the night of the Churchills' dance! Besides, I don't know anything about your friend's friend. In any case you can't go on Friday."

Protest was unavailing, and Rose was obliged to send a note to Mrs. Cathcart begging her if possible to suggest another evening when John Dering would again be speaking.

During the days that intervened between her visit to Miss Fergurson and the Churchill's dance, she thought constantly of Helen, and of Miss Fergurson's enigmatic remarks.

Which was the real Helen? she wondered. The graceful, fashionable woman of the world as shown in the photograph, or the intellectual, rather disdainful girl she remembered? Or was there a "real" Helen at all? If people were very complex—and Helen was certainly that—there might perhaps be no fixed personality, but merely a succession of phases? Rose sighed. The idea of Helen as a "succession of phases" saddened and troubled her. At the moment she felt as firm and consistent as a granite rock— "*herself*," whatever happened; entirely forgetting the many phases through which in a few months she herself had passed—phases each differing from her momentary present self, as completely as they differed from one another.

CHAPTER XXV

FINDING HER WORLD

IT was in her most pessimistic and rebellious mood that Rose dressed for the Churchills' dance the following Friday. She resented for one thing her enforced absence from John Dering's meeting, and moreover, a chance reference to a notebook had reminded her that this was the opening day of the examination she had missed.

"What will Mademoiselle wear?" inquired Lady Gertrude's maid, who had been sent to help the girls, and finding Lucie unable to decide between two equally becoming frocks, had come with the patience of despair to Rose's room.

"I don't care in the least," said Rose, who was listlessly doing her hair.

The matter thus simplified, Marie swiftly fastened her into the dress she herself preferred as most becoming to her favourite of the two young *demoiselles;* and with scarcely a look at the glass, Rose went downstairs to wait for Lucie and her cousin.

Marie had an eye for effect. Nothing could have suited Rose better than the brilliant colouring of the Paris dress she had selected.

Unaware that she was looking her best, a fact which ordinarily would have elated her, Rose sat by the open window in the twilight and gave herelf up to bitter reflections, which the entrance of Lucie and a simultaneous turning up of lights did nothing to dispel.

Lucie all smiles, a really lovely white and gold vision! Lucie obviously without a care in the world. This, she reflected, was the heart-broken young woman for whom she had sacrificed her ambitions and condemned herself to months of boredom. She anathematized herself as a fool.

"Don't be so lively, Rose! You let your spirits run away with you!" exclaimed Lucie once, during the drive through squares and streets where in the summer dusk the lights began to glitter.

Lady Gertrude laughed consumedly. She considered Lucie very amusing and could not understand Rose's superior reputation as a wit.

"Why, you absurd child, Rose looks as though she were going to a funeral!" she declared.

"I am," said Rose, thinking of her buried hopes.

"What on *earth* do you mean? Here we are!" exclaimed Lucie in the same breath, as the carriage stopped before a lighted entrance. "We've never been to the Churchills' before, have we? I do hope the floor will be good."

It was, and as Rose stepped upon its polished surface and heard the first strains of a waltz, her mood unconsciously changed. She looked about her curiously as she and Lucie followed Lady Gertrude towards their hostess, and a first glance made her suspect that here was a rather different set of people from the vacuous crowd to which of late she had grown resigned. The people looked interesting, she decided, and some of the men, at any rate, were not of the species that nightly thronged the stalls at a musical comedy.

"It's quite an informal little party, as you see," Mrs. Churchill was assuring Lady Gertrude. "But sometimes they're the most fun, aren't they? And we have some good dancers." She was a young and beautiful woman of a type unfamiliar to Rose, who looked at her with interest, and the thrill of a sudden new sensation. She was like an orchid, she thought; a splendid white orchid with scarlet leaves, beautiful but uncanny with her colourless skin, her flaming hair, and her eyes obviously darkened under the lower lids. She was dressed fantastically too, in floating gauze of dim purple girdled with gold, and she spoke in a languid, thick, but rather sweet voice, laying her hand at the same moment with a familiar movement on the arm of a young man who was waiting to address her.

"Here is one of them." She murmured an introduction which included the two girls, and drifted away.

"I hope you can give me a dance?" Rose caught the same languid ring in the voice of the man who held out his hand for her card, as that she had noticed in the voice of her hostess, and as she glanced up at him a vague, puzzling memory stirred. She saw a strikingly good-looking young man of three or four and twenty, with a graceful figure, and a face which struck her as being rather cultivatedly effeminate;—clean-shaven, fair as a girl's. He had a thick crop of smooth, carefully arranged dark auburn hair, and large, clear eyes the colour of amber. The hands which held her card were delicate, long-fingered, and white, and he moved them in a curious, studied way which amused yet fascinated her.

"I've taken this one," he said. "Let us give the room an exhibition of our skill while the night is yet young, and the floor empty."

His smile, at once gay, audacious, and nonchalant, again fascinated Rose before he swept her towards the middle of the shining floor.   They danced in silence; Rose, who was fastidious, having no fault to find with a perfect partner, and while the room slid round her in a delicious haze of light and colour, a memory darted into her brain.   She had danced with this man before, but then her toes had scarcely touched the ground, and she had been thankful to escape from his embarrassing presence.   "I've grown," she thought, with an inward chuckle. "Both ways, I suppose, because now I don't want to escape."

"You dance so beautifully that I should like to know your name," the young man observed when the music ceased and he was leading her towards an inner room.

"For future reference?" inquired Rose demurely, replying to a humorous note in his remark which saved it from impertinence.

"Certainly.   I will make a note of it against every other waltz you will give me."

"Then there's a chance that you won't forget it again, though you've heard it before."

"Never!" he protested. "You have hitherto concealed yourself from me in the most barbarous manner."

"I have danced with you before," replied Rose with a teasing laugh, "and your name is Colquhoun— *Jack* Colquhoun," she added rather shyly.

"If you gathered that from Mrs. Churchill's method of introduction you're even more of a witch than you look.   And as to having danced with you before, firmly I repeat, *never!* The one thing I don't make a point of forgetting in life is a perfect experience!"

"Then I must have improved in my dancing."

"*Do* tell me," he urged, relapsing into a tone of absurd childlike entreaty. "First your name."

"Rose Cottingham, and I danced with you when I was fourteen, at your mother's house, and I was so shy that I wished I'd never been born."

"I remember! I remember!" he agreed vivaciously, with a sudden abandonment of the languid manner. "I'd been watching you, and there was a portentous old woman present with a double chin who looked like a public building."

"The 'school-marm,'" quoted Rose. "My school-marm, Miss Quayle. How are your sisters? Frances and Katie?"

"Both at the Slade, both talking Art, both considering themselves very much in the 'movement.'" He smiled tolerantly, and moved his hands with the affected but rather charming gesture she had previously remarked.

"What movement?" asked Rose innocently. And then, in reply to his expression of mock horror and amaze, she added, blushing, "I suppose I'm very silly, but I live in the country, you see."

"Forgive me," said Colquhoun blandly, "but I can't believe it."

"Why not?"

"Because you look a *mondaine*, and a *mondaine* of the newest type. You *must* know that you're exactly like a Beardsley? You do know it, don't you?" Again his tone became childlike.

"If I knew what a Beardsley was, I might tell you."

Colquhoun clasped his hands together. "It's a genuine case, I believe," he murmured. "You really don't know that London has become a nest, if not of singing birds, of budding geniuses?"

"No," said Rose, laughing. "Are you one?"

"Certainly. I lie in bed till twelve, attend Mrs. Churchill's tea-parties all the afternoon, meet her again in the evening, and talk French literature till two in the morning in the midst of another conste la- tion. What further proof do you require?"

"Mrs. Churchill is lovely—in a curious way," said Rose, watching her hostess as she crossed the ballroom with an attendant string of young men.

"It's the new way. We're all doing it."

"But what *are* you doing?" she demanded insist- ently, disregarding the weary mockery of his tone. "Besides talking 'art jargon' and French literature, I mean? Do tell me! I live in a place where no one knows anything, and no one cares to know, and though I'm up for the season, my cousin isn't in this sort of set." She waved her hand vaguely. "We're here by mistake. Just by chance, and I *feel* the difference, and it interests me so much. *Do* tell me about it!"

She looked at him with the eager, questioning eyes of a child who will not be gainsaid nor put off by fool- ing, and the young man laughed, as one laughs and obeys the insistence of a child.

"Well, we really seem to be waking up to the fact that we can do something in art, and we *have* some good men, you know—writers, and black and white artists, and so on. Men who will make some sort of name. And we're all very young and very conceited and cocksure, which is just as it should be. And we talk a lot of rot with some sense in it, and we're all nicely affected and precious, with pretty women like Mrs. Churchill and two or three others to spoil us and make centres for mutual admiration and everlasting talk. But something may come of it. There are all sorts of new ideas in the air. Have you seen Beardsley's poster, for instance?"

Rose shook her head. "Poster? Do you mean a street advertisement?"

"Yes. Instead of the beastly things that have been done so far, you understand. There are other men working that vein, too. And have you heard of *The Puce Quarterly?* Well, you *will*. It's just going to be started, with a whole crowd of new people—contributors."

"Are any of them here?" asked Rose eagerly.

"Yes, I'm one. There's another—that clean-shaven little man over there with the exquisite clothes. Julius Bertram. He's quite brilliant; I'd like to introduce him to you."

"I should be afraid of him."

"I can't pretend as I ought, that he would be afraid of *you*, because Julius has the assurance of an iced cucumber, but as he's also got the manners of a sucking dove, you needn't be alarmed."

"And *you* write too?" Rose looked at him with awed respect.

"Oh, yes. Just attempts at a new form, you know, but it's rather amusing," he returned airily. "I'm supposed to be a barrister between whiles, but that's by the world forgetting and by me forgot. . . . I want you to look at Harwood Dix, because he's the man who's out to *épater les bourgeois*. We all try the game, more or less, but he makes them rage more furiously than the rest of us."

"He doesn't look as though he could *dance*," said Rose dubiously, looking with interest at the loose-jointed, pale, sandy-haired man her companion indicated. "And he isn't in evening dress!"

"Harwood Dix dancing, and in evening dress, would be a spectacle for the gods. I expect he's just come away from a Fabian meeting to report himself to Mrs. Churchill, who likes to imagine she drags him at her chariot wheels. He'll be off in ten minutes. Here comes Julius! I want you to know him."

Rose found herself responding to a courtly bow from a cherubic-faced, bland youth with a single eyeglass suspended from a piece of black ribbon, who a moment later was making hieroglyphics upon the programme she tendered him. At the moment Mrs. Churchill came up to dispose of two or three more of the train of men constantly in attendance upon her.

The evening, beginning well for Rose, developed into what she delightedly recognized as a real success. These men interested and amused her. New as to her was their way of talking, she liked their occasional witty levity, and quickly accepted the paradox as it was cultivated and cherished amongst them. With a little practice, she thought, she too could "talk like that." With Julius Bertram and Jack Colquhoun expecially she could even now hold her own in conversation, and in her turn amuse them. The new atmosphere in which she found herself, pleased, excited her, and stirred her curiosity. It was as though she had exchanged flat beer in pewter mugs, for champagne served in sparkling, slender glasses, and that there was something besides the foam and froth on the surface of the goblets, she was dimly aware. Beneath the affectations, the rather studied levity, and the straining after effect evinced by these people, she realized a keenness, an enthusiasm, a real love for the art whose varied aspects they glibly discussed in terms often to her unintelligible.

This night, in contrast to others which had so often dragged, fled like the fairy-tale ball night of Cinderella, and when wrapped in her white cloak she stood at the carriage door, she was amazed to find it already dawn.

Jack Colquhoun had followed her out on to the awning-shaded pavement.

"We must meet again; much and often!" he declared. "My mother would like to call, I'm sure. We must arrange something. I'll send you the book with the Beardsley frontispiece to-morrow, and you must compare it with your own reflection in the glass. *Au revoir!*" He was still holding her hand when Lady Gertrude, followed by Lucie, came down the steps.

"Who is that young man?" asked her cousin, settling into the carriage with a rustle of draperies and a prolonged yawn. "You've been dancing with him rather too much, my dear."

Rose, bright-eyed and eager, plunged into an explanation concerning their former meeting, and was interrupted by Lucie.

"Do be quiet and let me go to sleep!" she urged querulously. "I should like to have come away *hours* ago. It was the dullest dance I've ever been to. I didn't like anybody!"

"*'What's all the world to me? Robin's not there!'*" quoted Lady Gertrude, in arch allusion to a promising flirtation with Lucie as heroine. Upon which circumstance she was building great hopes for the future of the younger Miss Cottingham.

"*Dull?*" echoed Rose. "Why, I enjoyed it awfully. I should like it all over again!"

She gave a little excited laugh, and Lucie, tired and listless, looked with annoyance at her sister's bright eyes and radiant face.

"You always get on with people who think themselves clever," she remarked. "I thought it was a *horrid* set, didn't you, Cousin Gertrude? I hate that Mrs. Churchill! Affected, made-up thing! And all the men were affected and stupid, too."

"Stupid? That's the last thing you could say of them," retorted Rose hotly.

"It's what *I* call stupid, anyhow. Don't you, Cousin Gertrude?"

"I don't like the tone of the house," replied Lady Gertrude in her best oracular manner. "Mrs. Churchill's acquaintance is one I shall make a point of dropping. I understand that she goes in for Bohemian society. I'm sorry now that I took you girls there."

"And I'm very glad," declared Rose. "If that's Bohemian society I like it better than the kind we're supposed to mix with. At least one isn't bored."

"Speak for yourself!" retorted Lucie, yawning. "You're always in opposition."

The quarrel was interrupted by their arrival at their own door, and Rose ran into the house and upstairs, without again speaking to her cousin or to Lucie.

She forgot them, indeed, in satisfaction caused by her own appearance when she threw off her cloak before the glass, for her eyes were so big and bright that they startled her into the belief that she looked really pretty. Anyhow, for the first time this season she had been a success, a real success, —and moreover, she had found the sort of people she wanted.

"I knew they must exist somewhere!" she told herself exultingly, as she wrestled with the lacing at the back of her dress. "And I must find out all about the things and people they discuss, and read the books, and see the pictures. I wonder whether I shall like the frontispiece he talks about? ("He" standing for Jack Colquhoun.) I do hope he won't forget to send it!" was her characteristically diffident afterthought.

She fell asleep at last in the carefully darkened room, and a throng of confused memories haunted her dreams, in which were spoken names that seemed significant: Oscar Wilde, Beardsley, Arthur Symons, Max—someone. She could not remember all of them. They were names to which belonged vague shapes which eluded her, shapes evoked by allusions, and scraps of description all hazy and incoherent, floating, as it were, on the tide of new impressions which flooded her half-conscious mind. Marie with her breakfast-tray roused her about half-past ten, and she sat up in bed feeling happy and excited.

The sunshine which poured into the room when the maid drew the curtains, seemed in every sense of the word to usher in a new day; a day of new interests and utterly new sensations.

.　　.　　.　　.　　.　　.　　.

These fair promises were unfulfilled. It was the last week of the season, and though throughout the week Rose watched for every post for the expected book from Jack Colquhoun, it did not come, and she was left to make bitter reflections on the perfidy of man and her own lack of power to make any real impression on any one—except Geoffrey. Of him she thought with quite irrational impatience. She supposed he had "got over it." Anyhow, she didn't care. Geoffrey had passed out of her life like a dull, uncomfortable dream.

Lucie and Cousin Gertrude were busied from morning till night with preparations for a country house visit, in which Rose had no concern since she had declined the invitation more or less perfunctorily extended to herself.

Letters of grave import had lately passed between Lady Gertrude and Mrs. Lester, and Lucie's visit to the Hamiltons' shooting-box in Scotland, with her cousin as chaperon, had been carefully arranged with a view to bringing a titled young gentleman "to the point."

It will be a *splendid* match for her! [wrote Cousin Gertrude exultingly]; and it's almost a sure thing if they are thrown together, as they will be in a house party. I have made all inquiries, and the other girls don't count. Cissie Hamilton is as keen on it as I am, so the thing is as good as settled. Cissie has asked Rose, of course, but she doesn't seem to care about going, and as she doesn't get on very well with the Hamiltons, she is wise to refuse. She has written to tell them she's going to France for a year. This, of course, after the receipt of your letter offering to send her there at once if she pleased. I confess I don't understand Rose. She only makes friends with people that Lucie and I don't like. Of course they are people we *know*, but not the most *desirable* of our acquaintances. She is engaged to go out to-night with a Mrs. Cathcart, a friend of those Fergursons with whom she stayed as a schoolgirl, and as there seems no valid reason against it (I have satisfied myself that Mrs. Cathcart is a fit associate) I have given my consent. But there's no doubt about it, Rose is a strange girl! . . . I cannot tell you how pretty Lucie is looking just now. Wherever she goes she creates a sensation, and if my young Lord Robert doesn't make use of his opportunities during the next month, he's a greater fool than he seems. Anyhow, with three of us to manage it, he ought not to escape. . . .

On the evening that Lady Gertrude posted her letter, Rose was driven to St. John's Wood in time for an early dinner with Mrs. Cathcart before a meeting which John Dering was to address at a hall in Camden

24

Town.   Between her first enthusiastic acceptance of Mrs. Cathcart's suggestion and the night of its realization, Rose's ardour had cooled, and only a sense of politeness forced her to keep an engagement which though made with considerable trouble on both sides, had now to her at least become something of a bore.

Throughout the drive to Mrs. Cathcart's modest little house near the Swiss Cottage station, her mind was full of the glimpse she had obtained of an enchanted world in which she longed to enter.   It was as though through a chink in a door, she had seen streams of sparkling light, and had heard the sound of laughter and of dancing feet.   Even though the door had been shut in her face, she was disinclined to enter another which would disclose rows of dull grey working-folk, and in their midst a strenuous preacher.   She did not want to listen to John Dering.   It was laughter and gay talk she wanted to hear; it was Jack Colquhoun and Julius Bertram and Mrs. Churchill, with her strange white face and flaming hair and graceful, indolent movements, she wanted to watch and admire.

And instead, she was going to sit through a speech to working-men, and a few days later be shut up in a dull, foreign town in the company of two old ladies with whom she would have the privilege of talking French from morning till night!   Rose chafed and raged at the prospect, to which the alternative was a return to the Manor House and a repetition of deadly monotonous days and months already endured.

How was it that she could capture and hold fast nothing, not even a fraction of the gaiety, the interest, the excitement of life?   Nothing, nothing of life except fleeting glimpses to be withdrawn, came her way.

Jack Colquhoun had never written, and the hope she had entertained of having made an impression, proved itself by that fact, the imbecile dream of a hopelessly unattractive girl! She felt sore, humiliated, and almost too irritable to reply to the coachman's question as to the hour at which he should be in attendance after the meeting. Mrs. Cathcart's welcome indeed shamed her into a semblance of graciousness, but it was secretly in the same black mood that after a journey by omnibus, she took her place in the lecture-room.

Here was all the dulness she had expected, and in her present state of mind would have been disappointed not to have recognized—the rows of dingy people, the murky light, the sound of Cockney voices, the fidgeting, shuffling, and coughing of a drab-coloured crowd in a heated, malodorous atmosphere.

Rose set her teeth and trembled with impatience, while she wondered if she dared to feign illness as a means of escape. . . . And then a cheer which startled her into self-forgetfulness, broke from the crowded house, a cheer of real enthusiasm. No perfunctory shout, but the cheer of welcome from people who are stirred, admiring, grateful. Men sprang from their seats, waving hats and caps, women fluttered handkerchiefs, and Rose found her heart beating with the communicated excitement of a great highly strung crowd.

When the tumult subsided, when men and woman at last had resumed their seats, a silence as impressive as the cheering, fell with dramatic suddenness, and for the first time Rose was able to see the man who had caused both demonstrations. She recognized him at once, though he had broadened, grown bigger in every

way, she thought, and there was little trace in him
now of the boyishness she remembered. Dimly she
felt that the change was a moral rather than a physical one, for Dering was still slight and graceful rather
than powerful in figure, and he was handsomer than
ever. It was not so much that he had changed physically as that he had evidently "found himself," had
established, at least over the audiences he was accustomed to address, a spiritual ascendancy.

He began to speak, and Rose listened, breathless.
Again, as at a former time when she had listened, a
great industrial crisis had arisen, and working-men
were once more waging a bitter struggle against the
employer. Once more, as when almost a child, she
was carried away, swept off her feet, hypnotized by the
power of oratory. The low, growling murmurs of
assent from the crowd, the sharp, ringing cheers which
punctuated the pauses in his speech, seemed to her
like the thunder and lightning in some furious, terrifying, exciting storm. Only when the final shouting
and cries of "*Dering! Dering!*" had subsided, and
through a struggling mass of excited people she and
Mrs. Cathcart had pushed their way out of the
hall, did Rose draw a deep breath of relief from
tension.

She was so pale that from time to time her companion glanced at her anxiously. They had turned
into a side street to look for the brougham which Lady
Gertrude had insisted upon sending for Rose.

"Well? You were interested?" she asked super-
fluously, when the coachman had caught sight of them
and was drawing up to the kerb.

"Oh!" exclaimed Rose on a long sigh. "I was—I
don't know. I must think!" she added incoherently,

hurrying into the carriage as though for shelter. It was only when Rogers was shutting the door that she remembered in her confusion to ask if she might drive her companion home, an offer which Mrs. Cathcart with a smiling shake of the head refused.

"I can get an omnibus just round the corner," Rose heard her say, and was glad a second later to lose sight of her. She wanted to be alone; she thought she wanted to think (though in reality it was to *feel*), and she was thankful to discover on her return to Chatworth Square that her cousin and Lucie, taking advantage of an "off" night, had gone to bed.

Till the dawn light began to steal from behind the curtains she lay awake, now staring rigidly into the darkness, now tossing and turning in her comfortable bed, too excited to rest.

Once more as when she was a child, she had been stirred to the depths by a man's flaming words. To-night, contrasting them with other words she had recently heard, echoes from a world of which a few hours previously she would have given her soul to be a citizen, she told herself that these were as mere sounding brass and tinkling cymbals. The world in which John Dering walked proudly like a king, the world in which he fought for suffering men and women, freed them from bondage, and made them shout like the sons of God for joy, was the true kingdom—the kingdom to which henceforward she would belong! It was in this exalted mood that she slept at last, waking late to a grey day of rain, and a sense of flatness and depression.

Gaieties were over for the season, and there remained nothing but packing and preparations for the departure of the household—Lucie and Cousin Gertrude for the Highlands, and Rose, under the escort of Mademoiselle Leblanc, for Tours.

Mademoiselle Aimée Leblanc was paying her annual visit to London, and it had been arranged that Rose should meet her and leave for France before her cousin's house was finally closed for the summer.

CHAPTER XXVI

THE time in France, entered upon in a spirit of dull resignation, proved one of the happiest in her life.

Almost at once Rose was taken to the hearts of Mesdemoiselles Aimée and Clothilde Leblanc, two gentle, aristocratic spinsters whose little old house in the heart of the old city, was a miracle of dainty cleanliness and well-ordered repose.

It was with trepidation that the sisters had agreed to take into their quiet household a young girl fresh from the excitements of the London season, and Rose's content seemed to them little short of miraculous. It would have still more amazed them had they known how very little of the London season she had really enjoyed, and how gratefully she responded to the peace which breathed from their quiet lives, a peace which for her held no disappointments, no humiliating sense of failure.

She was not only content, she was actively happy in an atmosphere of love and approval hitherto unknown to her, and the endearing epithets showered upon her by the maiden ladies would have caused Mrs. Lester to laugh sardonically—she who had known a different Rose!

She was their "little sunshine," *l'oiseau qui chante*, their "white rose with the golden heart." They exhausted themselves in the manufacture of

375

fanciful similes; waxed lyrical over her perfections.
And Rose laughed and amused them with her light-
hearted raillery, and flattered them by her enthusiastic
response to their affection.   In their eyes not only
could she do no wrong, but all that pertained to her intellectually as well as morally, savoured of perfection.
They held up their hands in amazement and delight
at the purity of her French accent, the correct-
ness of her speech in their own tongue, and would take
no heed of Rose's tribute to the excellence of the
teaching of her former governess, Mademoiselle La
Touche.

"*Mais non!   Mais non!*" they exclaimed in concert.
"The little Lucie had the same teacher, and her accent
was bad—terrible.   And she was careless, *mon Dieu,*
but careless!   She had not your intelligence.   She
is destitute of your brains.   It is not only we, but
the professors, who bear testimony to the intelligence
of Mademoiselle!"

Rose, in short, was thoroughly spoilt by the good
sisters, who lavished upon her all their frustrated
maternal emotion.   And the experience of being de-
monstratively loved and admired was good for her.   It
restored her self-confidence; it seemed to put her right
with the world.

Life became very simple, very pleasant to Rose in
that quaint, peaceful house, and she grew to love the
daily routine which left her plenty of free time for
occupations unconnected with her study of French.
After the hours spent in attending lectures at the
Institut, and in reading with Mademoiselle Aimée,—
the *femme savante* of the sisters, she was her own
mistress, and her thoughts turned at first to the idea of
taking up her interrupted work for the examination

now a year distant. She tried, but failed, partly because she had not the right books for the course, partly because of a restlessness, a craving to do something else—a something as yet so undefined that its insistence worried and perplexed her. It was during this period of comparative idleness that Mademoiselle Aimée became confidential on the subject of *la petite Lucie*. She and her sister, she avowed, had, of course, been fond of the little Lucie. Was she not young and pretty and in short charming? But *enfin! la petite* had given a great cause for anxiety. There were young men! But always young men. One could not keep them away, and the little Lucie had encouraged them beyond all the bounds of what was *convenable* in the *jeune fille*. She had also been clandestine in her behaviour. There was, for example, the young student, Georges Martinet, to whom she had secretly written, and with whom she had made appointments that escaped the vigilance of Mesdemoiselles Aimée and Clothilde. It was for him, for his sake, that the little Lucie had affected so great a longing for improvement in the French language as to induce her honoured grandmother to consent to her sojourn in Tours till Christmas of last year. Figure to yourself!

"And we," continued the scandalized lady, "we were innocent of the true cause, till the mother of the young gentleman called upon us, and with fury denounced the behaviour of *cette jeune fille!* Then, what tears, what supplications! The heart of Lucie was broken. For a fortnight she cried day and night, and we lacked the determination to be stern as she deserved, and gave her the promise she desired not to acquaint Madame *la grandmère*. It was weak, but

what would you? We feared an illness. However"—
Mademoiselle Aimée shrugged her shouders—"in
a week from then she was gay once more, *riante*, she
had forgotten! I tell you this in confidence, naturally, *chérie*, and never must it reach to Madame *la
grandmère*. But I fear for the child. Yes, I fear!"
Mademoiselle hesitated, and dropped her voice to a
whisper. "Lucie has not the heart pure," she sorrow-
fully asserted. "She is not by nature chaste as a
young girl should be chaste and innocent. It is a hard
thing to say, but alas, I fear it is true. . . . Now you,
my Rose, you are different. One sees it in those
clear eyes, that occupy themselves only in regarding
the intellectual, the spiritual. You are pure. You
are innocent. Pray to God, my child, that He may
keep you in that holy state!"

Rose blushed as memories crowded upon her—
memories of thoughts and emotions, a hint of
which would make Mademoiselle Aimée shrink
from her with incredulous horror. But even while
she blushed she remembered these thoughts, these
emotions with amazement. How could she ever
have experienced them? They seemed now so remote,
so impossible, to her present mood of calm indifference
to the passionate side of life.

When she was alone she reflected, with a sort of
bitter amusement, upon the confidences of Mademoiselle Aimée. Previously then, only a few weeks in fact,
before her desperate love for Geoffrey, Lucie's heart
had been broken—and healed. She had forgotten
Geoffrey as she had forgotten the student, in less
than a month, and now every day Rose was expecting
to hear of her engagement to young Lord Robert
Glenkirk.

It was a mad world. Rose, who was half-heartedly examining the syllabus for the Higher Local, pushed that and her books away from her with an impatient gesture. She had no heart to begin again work that ought already to be over and bearing its fruit. And this result would have been achieved if only she had not been such a fool—such a silly, sentimental fool!

Gradually as the summer days went on, the unformulated craving that worried her, took shape and resolved itself into a desire to write. It was long since she had tried any creative work, and at first she fumbled, playing with the sort of fantastic ideas which had pleased her as a child, and were now, when it came to their shaping, thin and unsatisfactory.

She spoiled much paper, and groped blindly for what she wanted, till one day light broke, and she found she wanted to write something "real."

Unknown to herself, she was now considerably better fitted for the task than a few months earlier would have been the case. She had done a great deal of thinking lately, and unconsciously she had to some extent reviewed her life, seen it, so to speak, objectively and from the more or less impartial standpoint of an observer. When, for instance, she thought of her visit to London, it was in some curious way another girl who had gone to dances and been bored, amused, or critical; another girl who had listened to and been stirred by John Dering's speech, and fascinated by the conversation of Jack Colquhoun and Julius Bertram. It was only when her thoughts turned to another and very frequent subject for meditation—that of the money presently to come to her—that she became Rose Cottingham, perplexed, chaotic, uncertain how to deal with new conditions of existence. That

difficulty, however, lay outside the realm of her retro-
spection, and it was the past about which she felt
impelled to write.

At the top of the house there was a roof-garden, a
tiny but charming place, tiled, arched over with a bower
of morning glories, and bordered by flowering oleanders
in big grey pots.   Here, with a view between pink
and white blossoms of fantastic roofs and chimneys,
and the green country beyond, Rose began her novel,
for her own pleasure, and because she must.

Profoundly difficult at first, her interest grew when
she found she could imagine a character whose outward circumstances were utterly unlike her own, but
whose thoughts and emotions were hers, or at any rate
had been hers.   And as she wrote she saw herself
more and more dispassionately, objectively, as though
she were contemplating some other person whose
life nevertheless she understood with an intimate
knowledge.

She was very happy, very busy during those summer days in her little study amongst the chimney-pots,
and when winter came, in her own bedroom, where
for her benefit the stove was always kept lighted.
It was almost spring before she realized that winter
had gone, and by the first days of spring the story was
finished.

The day on which she wrote the last word, fortunately brought a letter from Helen, and this to some
extent mitigated the sensation of blankness which
to her own surprise enveloped her mind and heart now
that she emerged perforce from a world in which all
unconsciously she had been living with greater actu-
ality than in the world bounded by Tours.

Helen had returned from Switzerland, but only for a

few months. Before long, she wrote, she must return to Davos with her father, whose illness was now definitely ascribed to lung trouble. She begged to see "the story," to which some time previously Rose had alluded, and because in her pity for Helen she could not bear to deny her anything, Rose, though unwillingly, sent her the manuscript. Now that it was finished she felt desperately shy about her work, and regretted that she had taken even Helen into her confidence.

From home there were also letters, enclosing cuttings from society papers fixing for June the date of Lucie's marriage. The engagement had been made public during the previous autumn.

. . . You will therefore return the first week in June [wrote Mrs. Lester, in her usual peremptory strain]. Though this cuts off nearly two months from your year in France, if half I gather from the somewhat gushing letters of Mesdemoiselles Leblanc is true, you seem to have little more to learn so far as the French language is concerned! I congratulate you upon the impression you seem to have made, and trust that it corresponds to fact. . . .

Rose threw down the letter with the old remembered rush of anger and impatience. It brought the life at the Manor House very near, and she had been so happy, so peaceful, of late. If only she were already twenty-one! Her French visit had been indeed in every way a happy experience, a time of emotional rest, during which she had tasted the sweetness of affection unmixed with sarcasm and adverse criticism. Under its influence she herself had sweetened, mellowed, and grown riper; content had taken the place of dissatisfaction and bitterness of spirit. The past year, little as she knew it, was moreover a halting place from which, passion and restlessness for the moment submerged, she had paused to look back on her childhood and her early girlhood. The next step on the journey would be towards maturity.

XXVII

ACCEPTED

SHE had sent her manuscript to Helen early in March, and beyond a postcard acknowledging its arrival, for nearly a month she heard no more from her friend. As time went on without bringing a letter, Rose's apprehension grew, and with it her shamefaced regret for having sent the novel. Helen, of course, in her own phrase, considered it "poor stuff," and was diffident about writing. It was, no doubt, "poor stuff"! The longer she thought of it the more the glamour which at first had clung to its memory, faded and left the inept little book stranded in the light of a very common, uninspiring day. Every time she remembered it, Rose became hot with shame, and when at last she saw a letter in Helen's handwriting on her plate at breakfast one morning she grew hot and cold together. A rather bulky envelope addressed to her lay also on the table, but it was Helen's letter that she seized. After the first frightened glance the colour suddenly flamed into her face, and with a shout of triumph like a schoolboy's she sprang up, waving the open sheets round her head.

"*Ma petite*, what have you? What is it? Why are you thus excited?" babbled Mademoiselle Aimée and Mademoiselle Clothilde, thoroughly startled and alarmed.

For answer Rose rushed from one to another, embracing them in turn.

"My book!" she stammered. "My book! Helen took it to a publisher, and he likes it, and it's coming out soon—quite soon—as soon as I've signed this!" She fluttered a blue document before the mazed eyes of the spinsters, and once more embraced them rapturously. "Oh, but let me look once more!" she added, on a note of frightened anxiety. "I may have read it wrong. But anyhow, here's the agreement and a letter from the publisher."

It took fully half an hour to explain to the little French ladies that the writing about which Rose had always been vague and they incurious, was a book, a *roman* which had been accepted by a publisher *très célèbre*; and only when their kisses had been showered and their tears of excitement dried, was Rose able to rush upstairs to the roof-garden to re-read her correspondence and endeavour to calm her own mind.

Helen's letter was enthusiastic:—

. . . I got the book typed (your writing is *awful*, dearest) before I showed it to father, who read it, and to my delight said, "That's the real thing, that's vital stuff!" He took it himself at once to Bartlett, who kept it only three weeks (fancy that for a publisher!), and then asked father to come and see him. Bartlett is writing to you himself, and you will probably get the contract with this letter. Father has gone through the contract and thinks it pretty fair for a first book, so you may sign it without feeling you're being done exactly, though of course it isn't half what you ought to have! And as you will see, Bartlett wants to get the book out at once. He thinks it *might* sell just because it's so original, and you'll be getting the proofs almost directly. Oh, Rose! I can't tell you how glad I am, and how proud. It's what I always foretold, isn't it? Aunt Aggie is awfully pleased too, but of course she doesn't understand as father and I do how really good the book is. . . .

In the midst of her elation and gratitude, Rose remembered that Helen had never appreciated Aunt

Aggie, and she pictured suddenly the quiet smile with which Miss Fergurson would accept the imputation of a good heart and lack of intellect. It was curious that Helen, who was so clever, should in some ways be so little discerning. But Helen was a darling! A real darling! About that there was no mistake.

The sky was bluer than it had ever been in the world before, the crocuses on the roof-garden were blossoms in Paradise, and all the earth was fair as she sat down to reply with trembling hands to a very cordial and appreciative letter from a well-known publisher, and to sign a contract that she did not in the least understand.

By the middle of April proofs were coming in thick and fast, forwarded in batches, the frequency of which taxed all her powers to deal with them before the next set arrived, and Rose never forgot the frightened thrill with which she saw for the first time her own words in print. They conveyed to her a sense of unreality, a profound conviction that she had never written them, so different, so alarming they looked set down in cold type, robbed of their familiar appearance in her own untidy handwriting. She was seized with panic and obsessed by the beginner's instinct to re-write her novel on the proof-sheets. A politely expressed intimation from headquarters that her corrections were "very heavy" pulled her up short in her headlong attempt at demolition and re-building, and, the customary reaction setting in, she was now afraid to alter a word or to replace a stop.

With inexpressible relief, yet trembling with apprehension, she posted the last pages of the most carefully and worst corrected proofs on record, and forced

25

herself to realize that May had come and in three
weeks' time she would be at home.

As yet, shyness, an immense reluctance to confess
authorship to her grandmother, had kept her silent on
the point in her letters to Mrs. Lester and to Lucie,
and when a fortnight before her return a newspaper
cutting fell out of the letter she was opening, she
caught her breath in dismay.

. . . What*ever* does this mean? [inquired her sister, eloquent
with the aid of enormous exclamation stops and heavy flourish-
ings.] You will see it says you have written a book which is
shortly to appear, and that you're the sister of the beautiful Miss
Cottingham (ahem!) whose approaching marriage with Lord
Robert Glenkirk, etc. . . . Have they gone mad, or have you?
I don't mean gone mad, but have you *really* written a book?
Grandmamma looked as if she didn't know what to say or how
to take it when she read the paper which Major Hawley brought
round. Of course in her young days ladies didn't write books—
or at least not often. But Major Hawley got quite angry with
her, and said she ought to be proud of you, and he'd always
known you would make a name for yourself. And Grandmamma
said in her dry way that she'd wait and see what sort of name it
was before she got proud. Oh, Rose, I do *hope* you haven't said
anything in it to upset her! You know how old-fashioned she is
in her ideas, and she thinks you have "modern notions." . . .
Of course you know I am to be married from Cousin Gertrude's?

Rose smiled, with a return to her old cynical
bitterness.

"*L'école pour grandmères!*" she murmured.
"Lucie could probably give her more practical instruction than she'll find in my book. Lucky for
Grandmamma—and Lucie—that she doesn't know
that!"

She tried to steel herself to indifference against her
grandmother's opinion by recalling the stupendous

fact that she was an author now, and authors must be
independent of grandmotherly verdicts; but in her
heart she dreaded unspeakably the arrival of the book
at the Manor House.

Thank goodness, every one would be too occupied
with Lucie's wedding to pay much attention to the
appearance of a mere novel! It was thus, in lofty and
would-be-careless fashion, that Rose mentally alluded
to what in reality was the supreme fact in the universe.

Then—the days vanished with such inconceivable
rapidity that she could scarcely believe it was there
—the morning of the parting came.

Mademoiselle Aimée and Mademoiselle Clothilde
stood on the doorstep of their house, watching Rose
mutely as with the aid of a loquacious *cocher* she
arranged her small luggage on the seat of the carriage
that was to take her to the station. They could not
trust themselves to go to the station. They did not
offer to help with the luggage. They had forgotten
everything, were oblivious to everything but the one
heart-breaking fact that the child they loved was going
out of their lives for ever. They stood there, dressed
exactly alike in dark-flowered delaine and black frilled
aprons, rigid, with tear-stained faces, forgetting as she
was driven away to respond to Rose's waving hand,
forgetting everything except that they were ageing
women who had no right to mothers' hearts, no ties to
bind them to fresh young life, nothing vital between
them and death. They went in and closed the door,
and almost before it shut, Rose's last look through a
blur of tears was directed, not to them but towards the
little roof-garden where she had written her novel.

Lucie was to be married from Lady Gertrude's
house, and, accompanied by a travelling companion

arranged for by Mrs. Lester, a lady's-maid whom she
duly met at the station, Rose travelled straight
through to London.

The maid (destined for Lucie in her forthcoming
character as Lady Robert Glenkirk), though French,
was unvivacious and to Rose's relief, untalkative, so
that she was free to dream a great deal on the journey.
The dream, full of mingled hopes and fears, was exciting, and, thanks to the egoism of youth, not materially
dimmed by memories and regrets. She loved the
gentle spinsters, of course. But one couldn't live in
Tours all one's life—and her book was coming out!
That reflection even now made her start and set the
blood tingling in her veins.

She found, as she expected, the Chatsworth Square
house in the state of tumult inseparable from an
approaching wedding. Lucie, gay, laughing, more
lovely than ever, rushed from dressmaker to milliner.
There were Rose's own dresses waiting to be tried on;
there were constant visits from "Robin," a good-
looking, good-tempered, but otherwise undistinguished
youth; there were stacks of presents, hundreds of
notes going in and out of the house from morning till
night. In the midst of the confusion, partly to her
relief but somewhat to her chagrin, Rose's book was
scarcely mentioned. Mrs. Lester, who did not arrive
till the evening before the wedding day, made no
allusion to it, but contented herself by remarking that
Rose looked well, and that her new way of doing her
hair was "some improvement."

The wedding passed in what seemed to Rose as one
of the ten bridesmaids, a suffocating mist, made up of
sweet scents, white tulle, white satin, and showers
of rice, through which she saw, as in a dream, an

unfamiliar, beautiful Lucie, self-possessed, slightly affected. But at times this vision, oddly enough gave place to a little girl in a white nightgown, with tumbled curls, calling in a frightened voice for protection from the dark. Whenever this child appeared Rose felt a lump in her throat, by which she was untroubled when the satin-clad young woman filled the scene; and it was this unfamiliar woman, in a fashionable travelling-dress, who drove away at last, smiling and complacent, leaving her sister unmoved.

XXVIII

FAME AND AN INVITATION

SCARCELY a week after the wedding, when Rose
and her grandmother had returned to the Manor
House and life had resumed its normal course, Rose's
book came out. She had spent the week in expectant
terror, which the sight of a packet on the hall table
one morning heightened to panic point. Fortunately,
she was the first down to breakfast, and could rush
with it to her room and hide the "advance copy" in a
drawer before her grandmother appeared in the dining-
room. That day passed in abject misery. She read
the book from cover to cover, and was in despair, so
lifeless, so feeble did her own work, which she already
knew almost by heart, now appear to her.

She was near hating Helen for her officiousness in
allowing the manuscript to fall into the hands of a
publisher so uncritical, so puerile in his tastes as
Bartlett had proved himself by his idiotic readiness
to accept it. Many times during the dragging hours
she wished the earth would open and swallow her
before there were any notices in the papers—or before
she learned from their silence, the contempt in which
the brilliant critics on their staff regarded her rush to
a spot where angels fear to tread. After an almost
sleepless night, she went down to breakfast next
morning to find Mrs. Lester reading the paper by the
window, and, with a shiver of horror, a large packet on
her own chair, with the publisher's name compro-
misingly printed across it.

Mrs. Lester turned and looked her granddaughter up and down a moment, before her lips relaxed into a smile that was partly satirical, partly gratified.

"It seems that I have entertained a genius unawares," she remarked, and tapping the paper, handed it to Rose, who grew white and then scarlet before she allowed her startled eyes to sink to the indicated column. It was headed, "A Remarkable Novel."

It was a whole column, and while her eyes saw words and phrases of eulogy, her mind saw those very words turned suddenly, magically, into expressions of scathing contempt. Yet they did not change! The laudatory words were really there. When she looked up, dazed, only just beginning to feel the incoming rush of a tide of joy, her grandmother was examining the bulky parcel on the chair.

"Is this the masterpiece? If size is the criterion, it deserves the title. My dear, you must have been writing day and night for a year!"

"They send you six copies," stammered Rose.

"Then will you present me with one?" She picked up a knife from the table, and by holding it out, gave Rose a smiling invitation to cut the string of the parcel.

"I haven't read a novel for years," she remarked, looking critically at the green binding of the book, which bore on its cover a small design in gold, admirably drawn, "and now my granddaughter forces me to resume a youthful habit. It's inconsiderate, to say the least of it!"

She was smiling quite kindly now, and Rose made an effort to return the smile, though she had an intense longing to snatch the book from her hands. She felt like a mother whose plain but much-loved child is suddenly sent for to be inspected by a critical relative ready to pour secret if not open ridicule upon the defenceless infant. If only her grandmother would not read the novel!

The desire, futile as she knew it to be, drove her out of the house so that she might at least be spared the sight of its perusal. Once out of doors, however, she forgot everything except her joy, the intense, surprised joy which made her tread on air as she rushed down to the shore, where she stood watching the waves breaking on the pebbles. The sunshine fell upon her like a benediction. The soft wind ruffled her hair and touched her cheeks.

There were other criticisms to come, of course, and they might, probably would be, bad; yet nothing could unsay what had already been said. That would remain a delight for ever, in spite of subsequent verdicts, however unfavourable.

But they were not unfavourable. A press-cutting agency obsequiously offering its services by the next post, Mrs. Lester, greatly to Rose's surprise, at once sent off the guinea which paid for numberless packets of "cuttings." By the end of the week the old schoolroom was littered with precious literary matter, every line of which, in her inexperience, Rose took seriously, with alternate elation or depression of spirits. She was more often elated than depressed, for the book was on the whole, wonderfully well reviewed. Appearing to-day, it would have attracted very little attention, but Rose was fortunate in the hour of her literary début. It was the hour of the apotheosis of youth, her publisher was the fashionable middleman between the cult of the moment and its receptive public, and the novel was nothing if not youthful. Despite crudity, lack of proportion, and hasty generalization, that fact gave it charm. It was sincere; it told part, if not the whole, truth; above all, it was fresh— utterly unsophisticated. And as the new cult, the "new movement" was many-sided, the book gained the approbation even of those young gentlemen who revelled in a reputation for exotic tastes and perverted instincts. Its very callowness appealed to people fresh from the perusal of a brilliant essay on the "mereness" of a half-grown actress who captivated audiences by her lack of "make-up" and her curt, childish nod in response to applause. In Rose's artless story such critics professed to find a piquant stimulus to jaded nerves, and they reiterated praises of its simplicity, its fidelity to life, its value as "a human document." That it was nothing of the sort Rose in the depths of her soul knew perfectly well. The young girl she had drawn, though up to a certain point true to life, was true to that point and no farther. There were omissions, suppressions; there were reticences which her creator neither dared nor wished to overpass. To be more 'exact, it was her shyness which dictated to Rose this policy of reticence, of suppression and omission even while the spirit of truth that was in her clamoured for avowal. Yet how to make avowals which would seem to make her heroine shameful? How could she be on the whole a "nice girl" and yet sometimes a prey to infamous thoughts and desires? And yet, with her intimate knowledge of the young woman in question, Rose was quite sure that she *was* on the whole a "nice girl," in spite of many unstated things for which she blushed for her— *really* blushed—so well she knew the workings of her mind and emotions.

In writing about her she had puzzled long over this difficulty, and had finally taken refuge in the hazy surmise that perhaps she oughtn't to judge from her own experience of herself, sadly admitting that she was probably exceptional—not really "a nice girl." This, in spite of the deductions drawn by Mademoiselle Aimée from her "clear eyes" and intellectual expression. These merely showed how people might be deceived! And yet. . . . "Anyhow, one can't do it, and I should *hate* to do it, so there's an end of it," had been her final decision.

Unabashed, therefore, though something of a fraud, her heroine presented her clear eyes to a world which apparently accepted her in good faith. That her psychology was only true up to the approximate age of fifteen, did not matter. Even when they knew better, critics applauded the "faithful and fearless delineation of the mind and heart of a young girl," and Rose winced when she thought of what they might have said if she had been *really* "fearless."

In addition to the excitement of reviews, the post brought letters which deliciously flattered her. Helen had, of course, written at once from Switzerland, and every day came fresh congratulations from people whose very existence she had almost forgotten, as well as from some of whose existence she had never heard. These strangers who wrote to express admiration and to ask for information on points which she had never considered, were the most interesting of all her correspondents. She religiously answered their letters, feeling important, and at the same time inclined to laugh because she was being taken so seriously.

One letter rather touched her. It was from Geoffrey, the first he had written since she had parted

from him nearly a year and a half ago. He was home
again now, but he made no suggestion of coming to
see her, and in the midst of his congratulations there
was a wistful note, as who should say, "You are
farther than ever away from me now."   Rose privately
agreed with him, but she felt transiently sorry for
Geoffrey, and hoped he would marry some one quite
soon and be very happy.

In the general atmosphere of praise and adulation,
her grandmother's lack of enthusiasm did not much
affect her. Innocent as, from the modern standpoint,
was the novel of the moment, its ideas, its tendencies,
were those of the rising generation, and as such,
repugnant to all Mrs. Lester's prejudices. Privately,
she had been bored by a book which seemed to her flat,
unexciting, and dull to the last degree. It was not her
idea of a novel, this description of an uneventful life,
and this everlasting prying into people's minds. A
novel, if one must waste one's time over such a thing,
should deal with hairbreadth adventure and, above
all, with romance; and evidently Rose had no idea
of romance. She confided these sentiments to Major
Hawley one day when he had ridden over to the Manor
House, full of real enthusiasm, to congratulate the girl
whom he had now left in the garden, picking flowers
for the dinner-table.

"My dear madam, it's the new way of writing,"
he assured her. "It's all the vogue, that sort of thing,
and the little girl's damned clever to have picked it
up, considering she's never been in literary society.
Can't think how she did it, the little baggage! It's in
the air, I suppose. The young things drink it in without knowing it."

"Well," returned Mrs. Lester, with a shrug of the

shoulders, "you read modern novels, so no doubt you know more about it than I do, but I can't think why any one should make a fuss about a story at all. I've waded through no end of stuff in which these newspaper-men take the thing as seriously as though it mattered. I thought a novel was a light thing for amusement when one hadn't anything better to read. To hear these men talk you'd think a novel was as important as a work on politics or history!"

"So it may be! So it may be!" declared the Major. "I'll tell you what it is," he broke out irascibly, "you've never appreciated that granddaughter of yours. I'm willing to wager that you think ten times more of Lucie for marrying a title, than of Rose for writing a book which has already made her some sort of name?"

"I do," returned Mrs. Lester, with provoking calm. "Though I'm glad of Rose's success, even if I don't understand it," she added, with some cordiality.

"There's the postman!" cried Rose. She came running from the garden through the drawing-room, her hands full of flowers, which she dropped unceremoniously on to a chair. In a moment she was back again, laughing, with a pile of letters. All her former half-defiant constraint in her grandmother's presence had vanished with her happiness, and the Major saw Mrs. Lester watching her. There was a gleam of tolerant amusement in the old lady's eyes which softened the usually rigid face.

The girl had opened an envelope, and after a puzzled glance at the letter it contained, turned to the signature, the sight of which sent a rush of colour into her cheeks.

"Why, it's from Jack Colquhoun!" she cried exultantly, and without premeditation.

"And who is Jack Colquhoun?" asked Mrs. Lester,
in an amiably teasing voice.

"Oh! A man—a very nice man I met last year
in London—who never wrote—" She went on talking absently, while her eyes eagerly travelled over
the neat, clear handwriting before her. As she read
her face grew more and more radiant.

"He likes my book, and he says his mother has
written to me!" she exclaimed jubilantly. "This must
be the letter." She snatched up another from the pile
and opened it with trembling hands. "Oh, Grandmamma! She wants me to go and stay with her!"
she broke out, stumbling over the words in her excitement. "They're awfully nice people. I went to
school with her daughters Katie and Frances, and
I've been to her house with Miss Quayle. . . .
She says so many people want to meet me, and I
ought to be in London just now. I don't know why
they should want to meet me. But read it—do read
it!"

She thrust the letter into her grandmother's hand,
and as the old lady adjusted her spectacles, stood
watching her impatiently, her own eyes blazing,
forgetting the presence of the Major, forgetting everything in her excited suspense.

"Well, you'd better go," said Mrs. Lester quietly,
after a careful perusal of the letter. "They must be
the Ross-shire Colquhouns, I think," she added. "If
so, I remember them. Bertie Colquhoun married a
Miss Stewart. She signs herself 'Stewart Colquhoun,'
I see," Mrs. Lester went on. "It's just as well to
turn the expenses of a wedding to account."

"Oh, how *splendid!* How perfectly splendid!" murmured Rose, under her breath. She swept her letters together and rushed out into the garden like a child who must shout and sing, or die.

The Major laughed.

"Don't you envy that?" he asked. "She's young and she's happy for once in her life, if she's never happy again. I was always fond of little Rose," he added inconsequently.

"I hope to goodness she'll get married," observed Mrs. Lester, looking after the girl with a quizzical smile.

"It won't be Geoffrey *now*."

"I'm afraid not."

"My dear lady, he'd never do for her," returned the old man irritably. "Do you see a young literary lioness the wife of a country squire like Geoffrey Winter?"

"No. I'm afraid I see her what in your modern jargon is called, I believe, 'a bachelor girl,' and for which the plain English is 'an old maid'!"

"And you can't imagine a worse fate?"

"No," returned Mrs. Lester, with a decisive snap of the lips.

The Major decided to laugh.

"You're an uncompromising retrogressionist," he declared, rising.

"If that's a woman who hasn't lost her common sense, I agree!" returned Mrs. Lester, exercising her woman's privilege of the last word.

"Well, give my love to Rose, and tell her not to get her head turned," said the Major. "I don't think she will, though," he added at the door. "She's not conceited."

Rose stood in the garden and leaned over the gate that led to the sea. It lay beneath her, blue, calm, illimitable, and she laughed for sheer joy. The reaction from the despair of a week ago to the glittering prospect of to-day was almost too overwhelming. The gates leading to the enchanted land had opened as though by magic before her, and she was about to enter her kingdom. All the glamour of youth was about her; the birds sang for her, the roses bloomed, trees spread their shade for her delight, and for her pleasure the sea was of a jewel-like blue. She was profoundly, ecstatically grateful to be alive. . . . And Jack Colquhoun liked her book!

Whatever of joy or of sorrow the coming years might bring, the remembrance of this one perfect hour would be with her forever.